EMILY

The Curiosity Club of St Foy
Book 2

M. K. Jones

EMILY AND STAR
The Curiosity Club of St Foy - Book 2

© 2023 Mary Kathryn Jones

This is a work of fiction, any similarity to persons living or dead is entirely co-incidental. Places and historical details have been modified for dramatic purposes.

The author asserts the moral right to be identified as the author of this work. All rights reserved. This book is protected under the copyright laws of the United Kingdom. Any reproduction or other unauthorised use of the material or artwork herein is prohibited without the express written permission of the Publisher.

First Paperback Edition, 2023 – published by M. K. Jones
Cover by Alison Morgan, Alicat Design

Category: Crime & Mystery

ISBN: 978-1-7392284-4-6

Published by M. K. Jones

Chapter 1

Bette Jones was enjoying her party, or at least, that's what it looked like to Belle Harrington, who could recognise the difference between real and feigned enjoyment. Bette's husband Bert, knowing Bette didn't like to be surrounded by crowds, had managed to keep the group of well-wishers to under thirty – all of them people that Bette liked, or at least could put up with for a couple of hours. They filled the sizeable farmhouse kitchen with chatter, laughter and congratulations to Bette.

The members of the Curiosity Club were there: Belle Harrington, Posy Simmonds, who had closed her café for the afternoon, Rose Teague, accompanied by her husband Harry, the local vicar, and Mavis Tregoss now Penhaligon. Mavis had reverted to her maiden name following her divorce from Andrew Tregoss, her abusive husband who was no longer seen on the streets of St Foy.

The remainder of the group were close family – Bette's children, her mother Edna and sister Charlie with husband – and a few friends.

The Club's honorary member – when he was in the country – Dan Walker, having just arrived home, had joined them.

Belle watched the little groups that formed, with interest. It was clear from the moment Bette's sister Charlie arrived, that there was no love lost between them but, as Bert explained in a low voice to the club members, it would have been more trouble than it was worth to leave her out. He'd been hoping she would just hand over a card and present, greet her mother and sister, then leave. No such luck.

Snacks, drinks and present and card giving completed, Bert gave out a theatrical cough. 'Time for the main event.' Bert's cakes were well known to anyone who visited Posy's café. He had become an expert and superbly creative baker – a diversification from farming, to help the family income.

Silent anticipation followed, as he removed the top of a box sitting in the centre of the table. The cake didn't disappoint. In one layer, it was a work of perfection, covered in piped roses in pink, dark at the bottom, fading into shades of violet – Bette's favourite colour – to the lightest touch of violet at the top and surface, then topped off by a ring of fresh strawberries.

Bette beamed. 'Beautiful, my darlin'. Best one yet.'

There were half a dozen candles surrounding the strawberries, which Bert lit, as the group sang 'Happy Birthday To You'; Bette trying to smile.

'Blow them out then, and make your wish, mum,' said Ben, the youngest of Bette and Bert's four children, home from University with a huge pile of washing.

She did so and Bert handed her a knife. Chatter began again, as Bette stood at the table, cutting and handing out slices. The chatter halted at a loud banging on the kitchen door, as all heads turned to see who was turning up.

'Someone's late to the party,' Posy remarked.

'Don't know who,' Bert replied. 'I didn't invite anyone else.'

'At least it can't be Pearl Hawkesworth Fox trying to invite herself, yet again,' Mavis whispered to Belle Harrington. The Hawkesworth Foxes, the bane of their lives for eighteen months, had disappeared suddenly, three months earlier, leaving a partly furnished home and a great deal of speculation.

Before Belle could reply, Bert reached the door and flung it open. The group looked over to see who had arrived.

For a second there was anticipatory silence. Then, all hell broke loose. Charlie screamed in the back of the room, and other family members gasped, as a woman who looked to be in her mid to late twenties, dressed in a kaftan style coat, with badly plaited long blond hair and a familiar looking face, stepped into the kitchen.

A young man, who had been quietly chatting to Bert, ran forward, pushing people out of the way. Belle thought he was going to hug the woman, but instead aimed a flying punch, which the woman dodged. Bert grabbed his arms and held him back. Belle looked at Bette, whose face had drained of colour.

'We thought you were dead,' she whispered to the woman.

'Clearly not,' the woman replied in a voice dripping with sarcasm. 'Hello, Aunty Bette, Uncle Bert, Aunty Charlie, Grandma, and my darling brother, little Georgie. I thought some of you might be pleased to see me.'

Bette stepped forward. 'Of course we're pleased to see you, Emily, we're thrilled, of course we are. It's just… the shock, you know.' She went to give the girl a hug, but Emily shook her off.

Georgie pulled himself clear of Bert. 'I'm calling the police, you murdering bitch.'

'Stop, Georgie,' Bert said, taking the shaking man by the arm and lowering him down into a chair. He turned to the woman. 'You have a lot of explaining to do, my dear. But please, sit down. It's Bette's birthday.'

The rest of the group had crowded together behind the chair in which Bette's mother, Edna Morris, was sitting, grinning.

'I'd rather not. But, Aunty Bette can help me, can't you,' she said, looking down to pick at her nails, but taking a quick appraising glance up at the crowd.

Bette, who had sunk into a chair, stood up and put her hands on the table to steady her shaking legs. 'Everyone, this is my niece, Emily. Emily Duggan. Three years ago, when she was doing her PhD, based up at the University, she disappeared after the murder of her best friend, a fellow student called Star Bright. Our family has come to believe Emily was dead, too.'

'But here I am,' the woman replied. 'And I didn't kill anyone.'

Chapter 2

'Everyone except family, I would be grateful if you would leave,' Bette said, her voice restrained but firm, brooking no argument.

No-one argued. In silence they found coats, bags and anything else they'd brought and exited via the kitchen door.

'Well, that was a turn up for the books. Any idea what…' Belle shushed Margaret Noble, who had been invited to the party as a member of Belle and Bette's book club.

'No, Margaret, and I'm not going to speculate. It's family business. It sounds very serious and we should keep our opinions to ourselves until we know more.' She spoke knowing that Margaret had no ability to keep anything to herself, and that as soon as she reached St Foy, the town would know within an hour that a murderer was lurking at Bette's farm.

'Back to the café,' Posy whispered to Belle, Mavis and Rose.

**

Ensconced in their usual table at the back of the café, with the "closed" sign on the door and accompanied by Harry Teague, Mavis began. 'I know something of the history, as I think does Harry.'

He nodded. 'I remember it well, but you tell it, Mavis. I'll join in if I think there's more to say.'

'I heard this from Andrew, who had contacts in the local police. Emily was a student up at the University of St Piran, you know, the campus on the outskirts of Bodmin. It had been a college upgraded to University status and its reputation is very good, now. There were seven of them, living out in a residence called Cheshire Hall, about a mile from the campus. Everyone round here knew it as "Bedlam Heights".

'Is that the place you can just see from the road, on the moor, standing alone, with dead trees at the front? Looks like a Victorian asylum?' Belle asked.

'Yes, that's the place. Bleak, gothic-like. It looks terminally ill. I never understood how the University thought it was suitable accommodation for students. They did it up a bit, decorated the bedrooms, and so on. But it was still a bleak, depressing place.

'Anyway, I remember there were seven of them living there in that first term of the academic year, four girls and three boys. Emily and Star were particular friends. That's why it was all so strange, what happened.'

'What did happen, Mavis?' Posy asked.

'I don't know all of the details. It was the end of term. Bette was taking Emily into town to do some last minute Christmas shopping. When Bette went back for her, she wasn't there. She waited an hour or so, then, well, you know Bette, she was angry and went home, expecting to find Emily already there. But she wasn't. Emily's mum, Rita, eventually called the police. They didn't take it seriously, 'course not. Young student, Christmas, parties, you can imagine. I know Bette and Rita didn't sleep that night, nor did Georgie.

'By the next day, the police began to take it more seriously. They went to the digs. All but one of the students had packed up and left for the holidays. Star had gone. No-one had seen Emily since she left to do her shopping.

'You can imagine what that Christmas was like. An appeal was put out on the radio and the social media, but there was no sign of her. Then, it just sort of faded from public interest.

'After the New Year, five of the six others came back, but not Star. After a couple of days, one of the students told the University Star hadn't come back. They tried to contact her, but it turned out her address wasn't real.

'It was about a week before they found her. A man walking on the moor noticed something odd in a tree.' Mavis stopped, swallowed and took a long gulp from the glass of water Posy had put in front of her. Her voice sank to a whisper. 'Her body had been put onto a low, flat branch of the tree, naked, but part covered with a blanket. Some bits of her was half eaten away, by birds mainly. Some said it was like a pagan ritual. It was disgusting. I don't know much more about what happened to her after that. I didn't want to know. She was just twenty-three years old. The police concentrated on the student group and concluded quickly – too quickly in my opinion – something had happened between Star and Emily, that had resulted in Emily killing Star. They never really looked at anyone else. Emily wasn't ever seen again. That was three years ago – until today.' She stopped, slowly shaking her head. 'I can't believe it. How could she just walk in like that?'

'I remember that case. "The girl in the Tree", the papers called it. It was quite a sensation at the time. Front page of the tabloids for a couple of days, then slowly faded away,' Belle said. 'I think it said they were looking for another student, who had disappeared.'

'It was chaos around here,' Mavis said. 'You couldn't move for reporters and cameras, and television people, knocking on your door day and night, pushing their way in. Margaret had a great time, being interviewed, giving her opinions on everything and everyone.'

'Oh,' Belle said. 'I'm sorry now I invited her into the book group. You should have told me.'

Mavis shrugged. 'She didn't say anything bad about Bette's family. She just liked being in front of the cameras.'

'Is there any more you know, Harry?' Posy asked.

'Not much,' Harry Teague replied. 'After the autopsy we buried her in the church grounds. She didn't have any family. No-one came to claim her, despite the publicity. Her identity couldn't be verified. The details she had given the University were all false.'

'That's very odd,' Belle mused, 'in these internet days. We're only talking a few years ago.'

'I agree,' Harry said. 'But Star had no internet presence, nothing at all. I heard she claimed to dislike it as intrusive and boring. My suspicion was she was hiding from something or someone. I do know that the police tried everything, but nothing came up, not through fingerprints, such as they were able to get, or DNA. In charge of the investigation was Inspector Susan Lewis. She'll hear pretty quickly that Emily is back. The family was convinced that Emily was innocent. And honestly, there was no proof that she was involved in any way, but with her missing, she was an easy target, guilty until proved innocent.'

'So why did Georgie attack her, Harry?' Rose asked. 'That was odd, too. His sister had been missing, presumed dead and his reaction on seeing her was to attack her.'

'I can't answer that,' he said. 'We should wait until one of you hears from Bette. I'm sure she'll be in touch, as soon as she can.' He checked his watch. 'I must go. See you later, love.' Rose nodded, as he gave her long hair a gentle stroke.

'Do we think Bette will get in touch today?' Belle asked. 'The shock they've all suffered is huge. They'll have so many questions for her.'

'And so will the police, if Georgie carries out his threat and calls them,' Posy said. 'I'm OK to have you all stay here, if you want to.'

Before anyone could answer, Rose's phone rang. 'Bette,' she said, and answered the call. She listened for a couple of minutes.

'Well?' Posy asked.

'The policewoman, Susan Lewis, is now a Chief Inspector and she's on her way to the farm. She's going to take a statement from Emily. The girl, or I should say woman, has given the family a brief summary, about most of which Bette is sceptical. But there's something she urgently needs to get off her chest before the police arrive and she wanted to check we were all here. I told her we were and she should come on down. She'll be here in five minutes.'

'Is she in a fit state to drive?' Belle asked.

Rose shrugged. 'Nothing I could say was going to make any difference. Whatever it is she needs to say, she's determined to say it to us, not the family, or at least tell us before the family finds out.'

'Then we wait,' Belle said.

Chapter 3

They waited in silence, sitting at the Curiosity table at the back of the café, Belle with her ubiquitous notebook, writing down many questions. She might not be able to ask them all, not until Bette was ready, but she could record them all until that time came – if it came.

Bette arrived ten minutes later. She had changed out of her party dress, back into her old combat trousers and hoodie over t-shirt; her regular and more comfortable wear for farm and friends.

Posy put her usual large latte in front of her and Bette nodded thanks. Bette's eyes were fixed on the coffee cup. She hadn't yet looked at any of them. When she did look up, she saw sympathy, compassion and empathy, and she burst into tears. Rose produced a bunch of tissues, with which Bette wiped her already red eyes and blew her nose. 'I don't know where to start,' she said. 'For the first time in a very long time, I don't know how to speak. Not like me, is it?'

'Don't put yourself under pressure,' Belle said gently. 'If you can't, you can't. It will come out, in its own way and time, but if that's not now, so be it.' She put a hand on Bette's and gave it a soft squeeze.

Bette shook her head. 'Thanks, but it has to come out. The police are on their way and this time, I'll have to tell the truth.' The tears began again.

'How about you start with some background,' Belle suggested. 'I know very little about your family. I've only met Bert and Georgie before today. Would that help?'

'Yes, you'll need to know to understand. Mavis knows some of this already. I'm one of three sisters. I'm the eldest, then Lana, Charlie as you know her, then Rita. Rita is – was – George and Emily's mother. She had George before she married Ronald Duggan. We all got on well enough, but we were never proper friends. Emily used to have the occasional spat with her mum when she was a teenager, but nothing out of the ordinary, as far as I knew.' She turned to Belle. 'You've met Georgie. He's a bit slow, but he's a good lad. Emily was the clever one. Not just clever; brilliant. First at everything, right through school. Always the best results. She easily managed her place at University, to study economics. She could have gone to a top University in London, she was offered a place, but she didn't want to go so far away from home. St Piran's was developing a great reputation and it seemed ideal.'

'What was she like, your Emily?' Belle asked. 'As a personality, I mean.'

'As a little girl she was nice enough. She had friends, but her friendships never lasted as she changed schools. She went on to new people. And the same at University. I was surprised when she chose to live at the Heights for her PhD. She didn't know any of the other six who lived there. She and Star became friends, but knowing Emily, I doubt it was a strong friendship.'

'What kind of girl was Star?' Belle asked.

Bette paused for a moment and drank more of her coffee. 'I only met her a few times. She was beautiful to look at. I mean, Emily is pretty, but Star outshone her and everyone else. She was medium height, about five feet six-ish, she had waist length black hair and green eyes, huge eyes, that shone when she looked at you. A lovely figure. You could see the boys all gawping at her, Georgie included.'

'Is that why he tried to punch Emily?'

Bette nodded. 'He was obsessed with Star, even though he and his wife Mandy had been together for years. He thought Star felt the same about him. She didn't, although she was always kind to him. He believes that Emily killed Star, but I think it was just his grief talking.'

Bette's voice took on a sharper tone. 'Yes, Star was nice enough to Georgie, but you could see that she really didn't care much for any of them. She was friends with Emily but she didn't really care, deeply care, about anyone. She was always guarded, holding something back, that was my impression.'

'Did you like Emily?' Belle asked.

'That's an interesting question, why are you asking?'

'For a reason I think you've just answered,' Belle smiled. 'You prefer Georgie.'

'Yes, I love Georgie. There's nothing hidden about him. What you see is what you get. There was always something about Emily. She was lovely to everyone when she was little, a real crowd pleaser but, she changed. As she grew older and cleverer, she kept away from us. She thought she was above her family, embarrassed by us, especially Georgie. Used to call him a stupid retard. In the end, we all kept away from her.

'Anyway, it was the worst time of our lives for the family – not for me and Bert, we had lost Marcie a few years before, nothing was worse than that – but the rest of the family was in a state when she didn't return after the shopping trip.' Bette laughed. It was a hollow laugh, a laugh of disgust, of horror.

'What really happened, Bette?' Rose asked.

Bette drew in a deep breath. 'She didn't go shopping. She'd been to see me the week before the end of term. She was pregnant and she wanted rid of it. I asked her why she didn't talk to her mother. She laughed. She knew Rita well enough to know she'd never be allowed to forget it. It would be held over her and against her forever. Rita wanted the perfect family. She was ashamed of Georgie, but Emily was the family star, so Rita ignored Emily's sarcasm and nasty behaviour, in public at least. Always boasting about her brilliant daughter, was Rita. When Emily got into trouble, she knew she couldn't go to Rita. I suppose she saw me as a soft touch. She came to me, asked me to help her. And I did. She'd found a clinic and booked the appointment. I took her to the first meeting. She didn't change her mind, so I took her, on the appointed day. I dropped her off at the end of the street and she walked away. She turned once to look at me, waved, then walked around the corner. I never saw her again.'

Rose went to speak but Bette stopped her. 'Let me finish. When she wasn't there when I went to pick her up, I waited for an hour. I was annoyed at first, then scared. Perhaps something had gone wrong. I parked the car and went to the clinic. I explained that I was her aunt and was due to pick her up. That's when the bombshell landed. She hadn't gone there, never kept the appointment. I went back to the student digs at the Heights. None of the students was there. I went to Rita's but Emily wasn't there either. I said she hadn't come back to meet me after her shopping trip. I guess Mavis has told you the rest.'

'And you've heard nothing, for the past three years?' Belle asked.

'Not a word. I thought she had chickened out, taken herself off somewhere to have the baby and she'd come back afterwards, make some excuse about a breakdown, or something.'

'And when she didn't come back?'

'Bert and I tried to find her. I mean, everyone else was looking, but they weren't looking for a pregnant girl. In the end, we thought she might have had complications with the birth, or something, and died, without anyone knowing who she was. It happens.

'Then I found out something else, by accident. She told me after the positive pregnancy test, the sort you buy over the counter, she had been to see her GP who had confirmed the test. After a couple of months I went to see the GP, told him of my suspicions, poured out my soul about what I'd done for her and I thought that something terrible had happened and Emily had died in childbirth. He looked at me strangely, and told me she'd never been to see him. He probably shouldn't have told me, but him and me grew up together. He knew I wouldn't tell anyone he had told me. Another lie.'

'And you never have, until now,' Rose said, her hand on Bette's arm.

'I was taken for a fool and it was all my fault.'

Her body began to shake. Posy walked up from where she had been standing behind her counter and enveloped Bette in a tight hug. 'It was not your fault.'

'Bette, in your heart, what do *you* want to do? Never mind Emily. What would feel the best course of action for you? Have you talked it over with Bert yet?' Belle asked.

'Not yet.'

'Then my suggestion is that you go back and talk to him. You said he knew about what happened. This must be torturing him too.'

Bette stood up, clattering the chair backwards. 'I should have done that first. Thank you, all of you. I was so confused, I just ran away. Bert'll be waiting for me. I'll go now.'

She walked out of the café without looking back.

'Won't Bert be angry with her for walking out?' Posy asked.

'No,' Rose replied. 'He'll know where she's gone and that she'll be back. Those two are joined at the hip, and the soul.'

'Well, I don't know about the rest of you, but I'd like some time alone,' Belle said. 'There's going to be a lot more to come and Bette will need our support and, I think, our help.'

'Will Emily be arrested, do you think?' Mavis asked.

'Probably,' Posy replied. 'She was a person of interest in the death of Star Bright and the police weren't looking for anyone else. She'll certainly be formally questioned.'

'Are you opening up tomorrow, Posy?' Rose asked.

'No point. I was planning to cut down my days and hours. Midday to four, up to Christmas Eve. Then I'll be closed until after the New Year.'

'Can we still meet here? Mavis asked. 'Bette will need somewhere to go to get away from the family.'

'Of course,' Posy replied. 'Look, it's dark already. I'll be locking up now. Unless there's anything else, or Bette needs us again, I suggest we meet back again in the morning, around ten.' She began to close down the coffee machine that filled the back counter.

Belle pulled on her overcoat, wrapped her scarf around her face, ready for the cold wind off the estuary and left them to it.

She took the longer route back to her cottage, along the deserted High Street, around and up past the church, and down again into the back streets. It was truly her cottage now. The owners, who had rented it out to her for a year, had accepted her offer and sold it to her at the end of her second six-month rental. She had found a builder to carry out an extension to the back of the cottage to give her a bigger kitchen, with double doors that opened onto the garden, where she had installed a patio with a removable roof. It was a double height extension, allowing her also to replace the outdated bathroom. The cottage was now everything she wanted. Except, still, a lingering doubt that this was her final place to settle.

As she walked, Belle thought about her decision to finally reveal to the club her reason for coming to St Foy, to find the boy "Johnnie", that her now deceased mother Gillian, had convinced her she had killed when, at the age of ten, she had deliberately pushed him off the rocks at Cash Cove. Gillian had admitted on her deathbed, two years before, that it wasn't true, that the boy had slipped, but had kept Belle enslaved and guilty in the belief she was a wanted criminal. That was, until Belle got away to University, met her husband Sam and together they had discovered no report of a death of a boy at the time Belle, Gillian and Belle's father were on holiday. But having lived with the lie all of her life up to this point, she now wanted and thought she was ready to handle the truth. She had come to St Foy after Gillian's death and her own breakdown, rented the cottage and begun tentative enquiries. So far, only Rose and Harry Teague knew the truth. Harry had urged her to ask the women of the so-called Curiosity Club for help, but she had held back.

And now, having decided, at last, that she would tell them, the events of today had put her own concerns into the background. Only Bette's problems mattered now.

Chapter 4

It was one of those foggy December evenings when the brume was low enough to swirl around your head, reach out in front and close behind your back, blocking out all sound, which Belle found unnerving. As she had entered through her old, wooden front door, locked and bolted it behind her and walked around switching on lights in the living room and kitchen, her shoulders relaxed and her breathing slowed.

Once she had closed the blinds and curtains, she took off her shoes and coat and lit the log burner. In her bedroom she took off her party dress and put on old jeans and a sweater and unclasped her wild auburn curls. She had wondered about having them cut off, at last. Sam had loved her hair, which she had kept as it had been since her teenage years but since his death, and now in her fifties she wondered if it was time. A glance in the mirror told her she still had a good figure, nothing drooping, yet. No sign of middle age flab or rounded shoulders. That was probably due to the walking and swimming she had indulged in daily since coming to the seaside town. At a little over five feet six, she still cut a reasonable figure. But the hair? Maybe in the Spring. New year, new look. She went back downstairs. As the flames began to spit and crackle and to take off up the chimney, she made herself a mug of tea and sat in front of the now roaring fire, notebook in hand.

For the first five minutes she thought nothing, sipping tea and letting thoughts swirl around. She had already recorded immediate questions, but these were about Emily's re-appearance, to retain the detail of the event as it had happened, not about what might have led her to return so suddenly and, for her family, so catastrophically. This tale began well into the past, the long-forgotten past, of both Emily and Star. There had been a few small clues in the sub text, as Bette spoke about her niece, which gave Belle to understand that, like all families, the Morrises had had their share of complications and problems as the three sisters grew up. Were they different from, or worse than, any other family going through the ups and downs of life, growing up, marrying, having children, bringing up teenagers, etc, etc? She needed more information, if she was to be of help to Bette. She needed the truth without rose tinted glasses or happy filters.

As for the second character in this scenario, Star Bright, she was sure this was not the girl's real name. So, who was she? Where had she come from? What had been her past? How much did Emily know about any or all of these questions?

A brief knock at the door was one that she recognised; she smiled and went to admit Mavis. As Mavis sat, Belle could see her hands working themselves together, then apart, fingers stretching and curling.

'That was a shocker, wasn't it, Mave?'

'Never in my life expected anything like it. I couldn't just sit at home, I had to talk to someone.'

'I'm glad you've come to me. Have you heard from Bette?'

'Not exactly. She texted to say the policewoman was already there when she reached home. And the family were all still there. I don't know if they've taken Emily away or not.'

'I expect they'll question her at the farmhouse, then, if they decide to arrest her, she'll be taken to the station. She'll need a solicitor. Would you like a drink, Mave? Tea, coffee?'

'Whisky, if you've got one, please.'

'Of course. Ice?'

Mavis shook her head. Belle got up to pour the drink. Mavis downed the contents of the glass in one go.

Belle waited a few moments, then said, 'There's not much we can do to help Bette, right now. We'll have to wait to see what the police do. From what you and Bette and Harry said, the police at the time didn't have any other suspects for Star's death. Do you think there was anything that made them assume Emily was the guilty one, not one of the other students, apart from her disappearing?'

'I heard there had been an argument between Emily and Star, but I don't know what it was about, or whether it was anything important, but more than just a couple of girl students having a spat. Margaret told me. She was one of the cleaners, up at the Heights.'

'Something else that occurred to me,' Belle said. 'Bette once told me that Georgie and his wife had been childhood sweethearts. If he had such a crush on Star, what happened to his relationship with Mandy?'

'It did split them apart for a while and Mandy was upset and angry with Star, but after Star died she forgave him and they got back together again. They were already married and had a son. Mandy's a lovely girl and he's lucky she forgave him.'

'Mandy wanted to make sure of him,' Belle replied.

Mavis grinned. 'I suppose she did. But they have a happy marriage, as far as I know. This won't help, though, will it, Emily coming back and everything being brought up again.'

'No-one is going to come out of this well,' Belle said. 'Poor Bette least of all, once the rest of the family find out she lied back then and has been lying ever since. Three years is a long time to hold onto a lie.'

'I would never have thought her capable,' Mavis replied. 'For me, it's the worst part of it all. I've always thought of Bette as such an open, honest person.'

'She is,' Belle said firmly. 'But, let's face it, Mavis, we all have our secrets.'

Mavis blushed. 'Yes, we do.'

'I didn't mean to be insulting, Mave…'

'I know,' Mavis interrupted. 'You know about me, and what I kept hidden for years. That's why I won't judge Bette. Still, there's a lot more to come.' She paused for a moment, opened her mouth, bit her lips, rocked a few times back and forward, then stood. 'Right, I'll leave you to it. I just needed a quick chat.'

'Any time, Mave. You know you're always welcome here. Mavis, is there something else on your mind?'

'Mavis hesitated for a moment, then shook her head. 'Not yet.'

Belle let Mavis out and watched her walk up the road, rocking and bending slightly to her left, favouring her arthritic hip. Mavis was well over sixty, although she never told anyone her actual age. Slightly built, with pepper and salt hair falling in a bob to the sides of her thin cheeks, she appeared frail and dithery. Belle knew that was the outside. Inside Mavis was a strong woman, strong enough to have challenged and left her abusive husband, growing stronger as she grew older.

There was no further news from Bette during the evening. Belle's list of questions increased to two pages. Nor did anyone else contact her. They were all probably at home, thinking about what to do, not knowing, waiting. Belle had a suspicion that Mavis had something she wanted to tell her, but had changed her mind. Whatever it was, Mavis would talk, when she was ready.

**

The following morning at ten, they were gathered around the Curiosity table at Posy's café. Bette hadn't joined them yet, and no-one had heard from her. Margaret Noble had telephoned Mavis earlier to ask if there was any news, but was told *no*. Mavis asked if the news had spread about Emily's return and Margaret replied that most of the town knew already.

'She was thrilled to fill me in,' Mavis said, sighing.

'Is it worth giving Bette a call, or a text, to see if she'll be joining us?' Belle asked.

'Can't do any harm,' Posy replied, taking out her phone and sending her fingers flying over the keys. 'There. I've said we're here, if she wants to come down, or just let us know how she's doing, if that's not possible. I've said we're here for her, if and when she needs us.'

The reply pinged within seconds.

'She's on her way,' Posy replied. 'She has a lot to tell us and she's going to need help. A lot of help.'

Bette arrived a few minutes later.

'Were you texting from your car? I hope you weren't,' Posy said.

Bette ignored her. 'Susan Lewis, that's Chief Inspector Lewis, has arrested Emily, on suspicion of the murder of Star Bright. She won't tell us anything else. Bert found a solicitor. a local man, Simon Davies. He has a good reputation. He's with her now and he'll come to the farm when he's done.'

'What about you, Bette? How did it go when you got back to the farm last night?' Rose asked.

Bette gave a short hack of laughter. 'I thought Charlie might have gone, but she was still there, weeping away. One minute saying how relieved she was Emily wasn't dead, the next berating Georgie, then moaning about what people will think. Bert eventually managed to persuade her to go home, told her she could come back in the morning. She arrived at eight, shoved her long nose through the door, like a dog with the scent of a rabbit.'

Rose patted her on the back. 'She's family. How are the others?'

'Bert sent the kids away, all except Ben. Term's already finished for him.'

Bette tried to pick up her coffee cup, but her hands were shaking so badly she spilt the coffee on the table. Belle put her hands over Bette's on either side of the cup and lowered it to the saucer.

'If you like, I can feed it to you with a spoon,' she murmured.

Bette gave a shout of laughter. 'That's why I need you lot.' She picked up the cup, steadily now as Posy wiped away the spillage, and sighed. 'I don't know where to start.'

'Start with what you believe,' Belle asked. 'And why you believe it. Did Emily kill Star?'

'That's the problem,' Bette replied, looking around the table. 'I can't say either yes or no.'

'Do you want to know the truth, Bette?'

'Absolutely, I do, Belle. But I can't speak for the rest of the family. You saw the split down the middle. Georgie believes she did. Charlie and the rest believe she didn't.'

'Do you think any of them has knowledge behind those beliefs?'

'Yes.'

'Then the place to start is with what you know – not believe – but actually know. No matter how painful that might be.'

Bette nodded slowly. 'What I know, is that Georgie was involved.'

Rose gasped. 'But he's such a good man. How could that be?'

'Anything else?' Belle intervened. 'Before you go into detail?'

'I have an idea of Star's real name, her first name, that is, was possibly Anastasia. I heard Emily call her that, just the once, sarcastically. I thought it was a joke between them, but now, I remember Star glared at her and changed the subject.'

'That's something for us to work with,' Belle replied. 'Anything else?'

Posy gave Bette a hug. 'You know you can trust us, Bette. What's said at this table stays at this table, until you want it otherwise.'

Bette nodded. 'Okay.' She shrugged out of Posy's embrace. 'But it will all have to come out now, won't it?'

'It's probably best it does,' Belle said. 'Why don't you go back and speak to Emily, about the pregnancy thing, if the police let her go, or go to see her at the station, tell her you're going to tell the family and the police the truth, the full story?'

'I did that before Chief Inspector Lewis took her away, last night.'

'And?'

'She told me she'd never forgive me if I told anyone. She wants to tell the whole story first, because it's her story to tell, not mine. I don't know what to do.'

She began to cry.

'Then let's hope she has told it, in full, and truthfully, at least to the police, because she'll have to explain why she lied and why she disappeared. It will increase their suspicion of her. So, unless she has an unbreakable alibi for when Star died, I think they'll keep her, possibly charge her,' Belle murmured, more to herself than to the group. She turned to Bette. 'Bette, was there a definitive date for Star's death, and how did the police know it was murder, not an accident?'

'It was before Christmas. Margaret went there to clean when they had all gone. She said Star's room had been cleared, you know, like she had packed to go away for the holiday.'

'So she had somewhere to go?' Rose asked.

'Good point, Rose. Did she tell anyone where she was going?' Posy asked Bette.

'Sorry, Posy. We never got that much detail. It felt like we were all under suspicion. I don't know exactly when she died, but I can pin it down to within a couple of days'.

'You said you believe Georgie had something to do with it,' Belle said. 'Can you tell us anything about why you think that?'

Bette nodded. 'I'm going to tell you something now that no-one else knows, and I hope we can get through this without anyone else knowing. I want a promise from all of you that you'll keep this secret. Rose, this will be hardest for you, because of Harry, so if you want to leave now, you can. Take a minute all of you. It's got to be your choice.'

As she spoke each of them sat upright, Rose's eyes widening. 'If I don't tell Harry and it comes out that I knew and kept it from him…' she broke off.

Bette put a hand over hers. 'Then go now. Anyone else?'

No-one spoke.

'Fine. Then you're all breaking the law with me. Rose, off you go.'

'I'm staying,' Rose whispered. 'Heaven help me, but we're a special band of friends and it won't work if you all know something I don't. How about this. If whatever it is comes out, which I believe it will, because the truth always does in the end, and Harry asks me if I knew, I will tell him I did, and bear the consequences. This is my decision.'

'And if he says or does anything against you, I will personally throttle him,' Posy said. 'We're about to become secret keepers, and Harry will need to understand that.'

They all turned to Bette.

'Right, the reason I know that Georgie was involved was, well, I knew something was wrong, seriously wrong, so I challenged him, and he told me. You know what he does for a living, his gardening, his love of the countryside.'

'Of course,' Belle muttered.

'He went to the Heights on Christmas Eve, when Emily had been missing for almost a week. He had already asked Star to spend Christmas with his family, because she had told him she had nowhere to go and would be spending Christmas alone with a turkey sandwich.'

'As I'm planning to do,' Posy said.

Bette scowled at her.

'Sorry, carry on.'

'He told her he would come to fetch her on Christmas Eve. She had refused, but he went anyway. She wasn't there.

He searched everywhere, inside and out, but couldn't find her. He thought she might have had an accident.' Her voice lowered. 'Emily once told me that no-one ever went upstairs to the attic at the Heights. Georgie said he had a "feeling". There was some rustling and shushing sounds. The stairs squeaked, the door rattled, he thought he heard moaning and his idea about an accident was right. He was scared rotten, but he went up anyway. There was an odd smell. He found her… wrapped up in an old carpet. He lost it, wept, cried out for help, but there was no-one else there. He sat with her for a while. She was not long dead, he thought as there didn't seem to be any stiffness or decay. But she was cold and blue. There was nothing he could do for her. He didn't know what to do. He was terrified that if he called the police he would be blamed. You all know Georgie. He's not the quickest thinker any time and this time he didn't think at all. He picked up her body and took her out onto the moor, where he laid her out on the branch of a tree, as if she was sleeping. Then he covered her with a blanket from the back of his van,' she smiled weakly, 'so she wouldn't be too cold.'

Silence followed for a minute or so.

'When did he tell you, Bette?' Belle asked.

'When she was found, in January. He told me it was the "old way", whatever that meant.'

'There are stories of an old pagan custom,' Posy said. 'But they buried their dead inside a hollowed-out tree trunk.'

'He thought he was honouring her, in his own strange, stupid way,' Bette said.

'He probably destroyed invaluable police evidence,' Mavis said, speaking for the first time.

'Yes,' Bette replied with a sob in her voice. 'He still doesn't understand that.'

Mavis went on, not unkindly, but with a firm voice, for her. 'Bette, you must encourage Georgie to speak to the police, to come clean. They're going to need to know what he can remember. He'll be scared, but he should be able to have an appropriate adult with him.'

'Mavis is right,' Belle said. 'Better it comes from him, than Chief Inspector Lewis finding out, which will not go well for him.'

'You've kept that from the police,' Mavis said. 'That was wrong, Bette.'

Bette nodded. 'Yes. I'd best get back now.' She stood up, but her legs gave way and she fell back into the chair, put her arms on the table, and covered her face with her hands. 'Why did she come back?' she said. 'We'd all got over it, moved on. Come to terms with it. Forgotten, almost.'

'Just one thing more,' Belle said. 'You told us Star had left the Heights for Christmas; toiletries, clothes gone, et cetera. But she'd told Georgie she had nowhere to go. Someone had packed up her stuff and made it look like she'd gone for a Christmas break. Could it have been Emily?'

'I… it could have been, maybe. The police should be asking her,' Bette stammered.

As she spoke there was a sharp knock at the door.

Posy jumped up and marched to the door. 'If that's Margaret, I'm going to give her an earful; she's the one who's set the gossips…' She didn't get any further. As she opened the door she stood aside, and Dan Walker entered.

He walked up to Bette and put his hands on her shoulders.

'Brace yourselves, ladies. The circus is about to hit town. Someone has informed the press about Emily. And that's probably the good news.'

'What could be worse?' Posy demanded.

'I just had a phone call. The leading inquisitionist is none other than Peter Day, dashing here as we speak, scenting blood in the lovely waters of St Foy.'

Rose looked up at him in disgust. 'So not only do we have this chaos, but we're going to have to contend with Britain's most disgusting, so-called investigative reporter, who will dig into every bin, question everyone with an opinion, and there's going to be plenty of those.'

'Don't forget, he's on TV now as well. There'll be cameras, too.' He glanced around the table. 'Belle, are you OK?'

Belle had sat back into the farthest corner of the room. 'Fine thanks, just thinking about what this will do to Bette's family.'

This was true, but she was also thinking about how far Peter Day might go. If he found out about the Curiosity Club, could his interest be sparked sufficiently to investigate each of them? She wouldn't put it past the man. He would do anything for a story.

She banged her hand on the table and the murmuring ceased. 'This is a dangerous man, for all of us. I would prefer that he doesn't find out about the Curiosity Club, although that's unlikely if he gets anywhere near Margaret. If he can't get what he wants on Emily and Star, he could turn his gaze outwards, to people close to the family. I don't know about the rest of you, but I do not want this man prying into my life.'

Posy gasped, shook her head. Rose began to tremble.

Only Mavis seemed unphased. 'I agree,' she said. 'We'll have to go underground.' She turned to Bette. 'Go on home, Bette, but please keep us informed. We need a plan. Posy, lock the door. Dan, I assume you're with us on this?'

'Of course,' he replied, looking puzzled. 'But I'm thinking there are things I don't know?'

Bette stood and put on her coat. 'Tell him, everything. Then we'll arrange to meet again, later, when I'll know more.'

'Sounds like I came home just at the right time,' Dan Walker replied. 'Let the planning begin.'

Chapter 5

Dan Walker strolled home, ruminating on what he had heard. He lived in a first floor flat above a mariner's retail store, on the edge of the estuary. It had a balcony leading from the living room out over the water. It wasn't much of a day to sit outside, but perhaps the fresh breeze and the rippling waters below would shake some ideas into his head about what to do and how he could contribute. His main thought, which he hadn't yet shared, was how Peter Day had assembled a crew and arrived so quickly in St Foy. He had been there first thing in the morning on the day after Emily's return. This meant he might even have been there the previous evening, soon after Emily's arrival. Someone had tipped him off. Who? And Why?

He had known Bette and her family all his life, and considered Bert and Bette to be amongst his closest friends. That their lives could hold such secrets worried him not at all. He also knew both Bette's sisters, and their mother. Now, there was a woman with a secret, one that Peter Day shouldn't be allowed anywhere near. If he could help at all, it would be in steering that charlatan of a reporter away from the wider family. He smiled. Peter Day had secrets too. Dan knew a few, but he also knew where to find more. If blackmail became necessary, so be it. He'd have to make some phone calls.

**

After dinner Mavis sat alone in her cottage in front of a blazing fire, but didn't feel its warmth. Maybe the time had come to tell. But was it the right time? Was it even something worth telling? She closed her eyes and cast her mind back to that day, three years before.

She had been into the city, to do some pre-Christmas shopping, gifts for Andrew's colleagues, staff and friends. The lazy git gave generously at Christmas. They were delighted, of course, never guessing that the choosing had been down to Mavis. She had attended every dinner at the golf club, every event he organised for the staff throughout the year, had listened carefully to their stories, learned their likes and dislikes, had chosen well and wisely, for which the colleagues, staff and friends thanked Andrew with a heartfelt expression of gratitude, having no idea that Mavis was involved, and been happy to take the praise. She smiled. They'd have quite a shock coming this festive season.

But, never mind that. Back to her problem. She had been in the lanes, searching the smaller, out of the way shops for a trinket for a particular colleague of Andrew's, when she saw them through the window of a café. At first she had assumed it was just a student thing, a quick pre-Christmas meet-up; they were both laughing. She had paused for a moment, and was about to go on her way, when Emily leaned over and kissed him. It was a long, lingering kiss, until they both pulled away.

She had hurried away down the street, quite sure they hadn't seen her. She had never mentioned it to anyone, not even after Emily had disappeared. Was it important? She wanted to say 'no', but the better demon inside her told her that it was significant, somehow. She should say something. But to whom? And what good would it do, now, three years later? But now she knew it was after Emily was supposed to have been at the clinic, when she was supposed to be missing.

As night drew in, Mavis pulled the curtains tight shut and put more logs on the fire, but didn't put any lights on, just sat and thought, for several hours.

**

It was agreed Rose could tell Harry what she knew, provided he would also be a secret keeper. Harry had agreed, provided he wasn't asked to retain any information that could help a police investigation. Rose assured him that Bette was going to convince Georgie to speak about what he had done. Nothing further had emerged that would be vital to an enquiry.

'Harry, do you remember when we met?'

He looked up from his newspaper. 'How could I forget? That great cloud of golden hair flying around the beautiful girl, dancing by herself around the maypole, her long skirt floating out as she looked up to the sky and laughed and laughed.' He reached across and took her hand. 'I loved you instantly. I still catch my breath every time I see you.'

'That was fifteen years ago. I've changed. I'm running to fat.'

'Imagination. There's no pickings on you at all. And, more importantly, not on the inside. You're still the happiest, most honest, loving person I know.'

'My hair is losing its colour.'

'I shall love you when you are old and grey and wrinkled. As I will be, and I hope you will love me, if I'm still around, in another fifteen years.'

When I'm sixty-four, she hummed. 'You'll be almost eighty.'

'And retired, hopefully.' He paused. 'Rose, No-one is going to go burrowing into your past. People love you and respect you. You are not your past. If they do, well, what will be will be.'

After their discussion, they sat together reading, but no pages were turned. Rose knew that if her past emerged, it would be embarrassing for them both, but, hopefully, nothing the church would deem relevant to Harry's job and career. However, the same couldn't be said for certain members of his congregation. She crossed her fingers as she gazed at the words on which she was unable to focus and sent up a silent prayer to the universe to protect them both.

**

Posy Clements locked the door of her café and made a sudden decision. It was going to stay locked, until the outcome of Emily's return was resolved. She didn't want Peter Day and his crew deciding to pop in for a quick coffee. She knew the man was famous for his memory and he was bound to recognise her. It may have been twenty years ago, but that wouldn't matter to him. She had had her notorious fifteen minutes of fame and he was just the man to resurrect it.

The Club could still meet in the café of course, if they chose, but she'd let them in the back way. Tomorrow, she would begin the shut-down, but tonight she would start by lowering the blinds. A number of the smaller businesses had already closed, so it wouldn't look unusual, except to local people who knew she had planned to remain open for a few days yet, but she could pass that off easily enough, tell them there were so few people around it would cost more than she could make to stay open. And, she deserved a break, didn't she? It had been a busy summer, the busiest for many years and she had been run off her feet. That should be good enough.

She turned the "open" sign in the window to "closed", adding "until January".

She paused for a moment, hands on the window, closing her eyes and clenching her teeth. Then, with a deep breath, went up to her rooms on the first floor. She had a few calls to make, to ensure certain friends didn't decide to make a sudden visit.

**

Peter Day settled himself into an armchair in the living room of his suite in St Foy's only five star hotel. He had put up the crew in pleasant accommodation elsewhere. They couldn't complain. He had already communicated with his contact in the police station in St Loos, where he knew Emily Duggan had been taken. So far, nothing had emerged, at least nothing the well-greased palm had been able to feed him. Not that he needed it. He had other, far better, closer sources.

He poured himself a post-dinner brandy – a Hors d' Age ordered in especially for him – and picked up the thick file from the table next to him. This was going to be his best story yet. Little did the good folk of St Foy know what was about to hit them.

Chapter 6

By seven the next morning, Belle was in planning mode. She considered planning to be one of her better and more useful skills. Not just action lists: contingencies, alternatives, 'people of interest', timelines, all to be included. And this time, she needed to add diversionary tactics. The first of these would be the suspension of the book club, Bette being the excuse. They couldn't hold a meeting without all members being present; that had been agreed from the start. She would propose it as a temporary measure, until Bette felt able to join them again. That should take care of Margaret's gossiping.

Someone had once said to Belle, that when she looked in a mirror they wouldn't be surprised if she could see her own back. She had laughed and replied that it was useful to know who was standing there with a knife. Well, knives would be out. Her experience in her former role as a Human Resources specialist dealing with 'employee relations' – a job description that occasionally included dealing with the most difficult, offensive, devious employees and removing them – had given her this ability: to observe their behaviour and think as they did. Was that a bad demon or a good demon? She wasn't sure, but it gave her one hell of an advantage, especially when she came face-to-face with Peter Day, as she was certain she would, soon.

She was going to propose to the Curiosity Club that they carry out their own investigation without the knowledge of the police, but not withholding any information they found, that could be crucial to Emily's return and Star's murder.

Also included in the plan was how to deal with Peter Day. That was trickier, and a dilemma. She didn't want to meet him until it was absolutely necessary, but until she met him, took a good appraising look at him and had a conversation with him, she wouldn't be able to fathom his actual agenda. She didn't for a moment believe this was just another story for him. The pieces he had done so far on television – just short ones – all hinted at something big to come. Her gut was telling her he was intimately related to this story. But how?

She hadn't seen or heard from Bette for over twenty-four hours. The solicitor should have provided some feedback to the family by now. This had given her some time to stand back from the Curiosity Club and think about Emily. Really think about Emily. Although she had only had a few minutes in her company, Belle had noticed a couple of things.

First, was Emily's apparent coolness with the trauma she had created. She would have known that coming back the way she did would cause uproar, yet the young woman seemed… what, unagitated, even by Georgie's attack? Amused, almost? Which told Belle that this return had not been done on the spur of the moment, nor out of any longing to see her family again. It had been planned and orchestrated. She must have known that Bette's party was in full swing, and judged the best time to make an entrance. Co-incidence? Not a chance.

Second, she hadn't been phased when Georgie said he was going to call the police. She must have expected that someone would, Belle supposed.

Third, Emily's statement that she hadn't killed anyone was spoken firmly and without any hesitation or gesture. She had appeared coldly certain of her own innocence in the death of Star Bright. Whether that had changed after everyone except the family left, she didn't know. Only Bette could tell her.

She thought for a moment about calling Bette, but decided against. She shouldn't do it without telling the others first.

She sat back, notebook open on her knees, thinking about where to start, when someone hammered on the kitchen door. Only the Curiosity Club knew the code to open the reinforced back gate that led into her garden. Bert Jones had installed it the previous year, after the act of vandalism that destroyed much of the planting.

She hurried to the door. Bette and Bert were standing there, pressed up against the door, against the hammering rain. She ushered them into the kitchen, took soaking raincoats and boots, led them through to the living room and sat them in front of the fire, where they both sat, staring at the flames.

'We had to get out of there,' Bette said after a few minutes. She was grasping Bert's hand so tightly his fingers had turned white, but he didn't try to disengage her. 'Charlie and Trevor have invited themselves over again. And that stinking reporter called us both last night, wants to hear our side of the story,' Bette hissed. 'Bert told him to stay off our property.'

Bert nodded. 'I told him not to come near us, any of us. I'm worried he'll try to find the kids. Ben's at home. He knows to say nothing and I've told the others to beware Peter

Day might call.' He gently pulled his hand from Bette's and ran it through his wet hair.

'Is there any news of Emily?' Belle asked.

'Not much,' Bette replied. 'She's still at the station. The solicitor called late last night. They're going to question her this morning.' Bette hadn't looked away from the fire, but now she turned to Belle. 'He told us that Emily has an alibi.'

After a few seconds pause, Belle said, 'And you don't believe her.'

Bette shook her head. 'Not right now. I mean, if she had one, why did she stay away for so long, behave in a way that made us think she was dead?'

'I thought she might have been abducted,' Bert said. 'By the same person who killed Star. You know, like those terrible stories you hear from America, of women kept prisoner in a dungeon.' His voice tailed off.

'What else, Bert?'

He smiled for the first time. 'Bette's always told me you can see right through people and back again. I don't know if Emily is guilty or not. But I don't trust that policewoman, Susan Lewis. She's lazy. She's notorious for wanting a quick solution, whatever the cost. She'll want to wrap this up quickly, and quietly. I'm thinking she'll only look at Emily, not go back to what happened when that girl Star died. I want justice.'

'Who for?'

'For both of them, whatever that means and whatever it takes. This may end up hurting our family something terrible, but if that's the cost, so be it. Bette and I are agreed on that.' He paused, then said, 'I want to see you and the others take this on, find out what really happened. Please.'

'That's what I was planning to propose to you.'

'I thought you might,' Bette said. 'When can we start to plan?'

'I already have,' Belle replied. 'But. And there's a huge 'but', you're right about the consequences. Emily may be totally exonerated. Or not. Once we start, there's no going back. For me, that's the meaning of justice.'

'We agree,' Bert replied. 'Where will you start?'

'With information. Lots of information. About everyone in your family who had any interaction with Emily, and with Star. And the truth. No fudging. Opinions will be fine, but the whole story must be told.'

Bette nodded.

'Good. My first idea is to put a hold on the book club. I don't trust Margaret Noble.'

'She loves gossip, I agree, but I don't think there's any harm in her,' Bette said. 'But, whatever you think best. Don't think I could read anything at the moment anyway.'

'I'll say we're putting it on hold until after the New Year.'

Bette sat up. 'Right. Let's get going. Meeting at the café?'

'I'll check with Posy. We'll have to go in the back way and—'

Bert's phone rang. He listened for a few moments, then turned to Bette, with a puzzled expression. 'That was the solicitor. They're going to interview someone who can confirm Emily's alibi. If it holds up, they'll let her go, for the time being. He wants to meet us at the farm.'

'Where's she going to go?' Belle asked. 'It's only five days to Christmas, including today.'

'She'll have to come to us, I suppose,' Bette replied. 'Although,' she turned to Bert, 'Rita's house is empty.'

'Could you let her stay there, alone?' he asked. 'On Christmas Day, love?'

'Up to her,' Bette replied. 'It's empty because of her. Georgie wanted to sell it when his mother my sister Rita died but he couldn't because of Emily. Because the probate couldn't be resolved.'

'Don't decide yet,' Belle said. 'Let the day play out. Why don't you go back to meet the solicitor?'

Bette stood up. 'You're a good friend, Belle Harrington,' she said, giving her a quick hug. Belle couldn't remember being hugged by Bette in the time she had known her. She had never thought of Bette as the touchy-feely kind of person. Circumstances changed people.

'I'll call you later,' she replied with a smile to each of them, and let them out the back door.

Chapter 7

The day became progressively colder and by lunchtime the rain had moved through sleet to snow. Belle had not expected snow on the south coast of Cornwall. She presumed it would melt as quickly as it had fleetingly arrived. However, as the temperature plummeted below zero it became cold enough not to melt on impact, nor did it stop. She went down into the cellar and dug out her snow boots. As she pulled them on she remembered the last time she had worn them.

It had been a skiing holiday in Austria with Sam and Jamie, just before Jamie had gone off to University. Sam and Jamie were great skiers, Belle not so much. She kept to the lower slopes, whilst her husband and son progressed further up the mountain, each time racing each other down. There was a great deal of laughter that evening, as they sat around the open fire in the lodge in the resort of Seefeld, drinking gluhwein and schnapps, before eating wiener schnitzel and… what had that dessert been? She couldn't remember. She did remember it had snowed heavily that evening, too. She and Sam had stood out on their balcony, watching the floodlit evening skiers and tobogganers. That must have been almost ten years ago. She pulled on the boots with an unnecessarily strong tug and shook the memories away.

Down at the seafront there were couples and families out walking, taking in the unusual sight. For many of the children of St Foy, this was the first time they would have seen such a heavy snowfall. The Christmas tree in the square had snow dripping from its branches. Children were skidding and sliding through the streets. Christmas lights were already on in the main street. It was a sight to gladden the heart, except, she guessed, not for Bette's family right now.

'Oh, Belle, there you are!' Aggie Lewis had been standing at the back of the Christmas tree and beckoned Belle over. 'What time are we meeting up tonight? I don't expect Bette will be able to attend, will she?'

'Actually, Aggie, I'm cancelling the book club meeting. We did agree at the start that it had to be when we could all make it, you do remember?'

'I'd forgotten that.' Aggie looked downcast. 'Of course, we can't meet without Bette. How is she?'

'I've no idea,' Belle replied. 'I haven't heard anything from her, and I'm not expecting to.'

Aggie pulled her scarf further up, covering her mouth. 'Lovely isn't it? Makes the town look so pretty.'

'Yes, it does. I've just come out to take a quick look myself. I'm off home now. Too cold for me. If I don't see you before, have a good Christmas, Aggie.'

'You too, Belle.'

Belle turned away and started up the hill towards her cottage. Before she turned the corner away from the square she took a quick look back. Aggie was talking to someone else, shaking her head. The someone was Margaret Noble, who was responding with wide arm gestures and a pointed finger.

**

At five o'clock, five figures dressed in overcoats with hoods and scarves slipped down the dimly lit alley way, battling against the onslaught of snow, and into the back storeroom of Posy's café. The main lights in the café were out, the corner table lit by candles. As Posy made drinks, the discussion began.

'Bette, what news of Emily?'

Bette looked down into her cup. 'She came back about an hour ago. They've let her go, for the time being. Whoever provided the alibi has been interviewed. We don't know what he, or she, said, but it was enough.'

'So, she's not in the clear?' Belle asked.

'Not entirely, but the solicitor says the police will have trouble making a charge of murder stick, or any kind of charge. Emily swears the last time she saw Star was when they had a huge row the weekend before she disappeared.'

'She's spoken to you, then? And the family?' Rose said.

'Yes, to me but not to the family. She's keeping to the pregnancy story, but said at the last minute couldn't go through with the termination. She says she was confused, upset, overwhelmed. She got on a bus and just kept going, for twenty-four hours. She ended up in Scotland. She's been there ever since, on a commune.' She looked up at the faces dancing in the candlelight. 'I don't believe it. Emily wouldn't last five minutes on a commune. She always had expensive tastes. She liked nice clothes and long manicured nails.'

'Are you going to tell her?' Mavis asked.

'No, don't, please,' Belle interrupted as all eyes turned to her. 'Something is very much off about this. Bette, you and Bert asked if we could do some investigation. I said yes, but I want to be sure, right now, that we all agree.'

Every head nodded.

'Good. I thought so. I've started, on what little we have. I want to know more about Star, who she was, where she came from. So, just before I came out I called my friend Maggie in

Wales, who helped us out with information last year. I'll explain later, Dan. I've given her the name Anastasia and the year we think Star was born. She'll take a look, but says not to expect anything before Christmas.'

'Talking about Christmas and turkey sandwiches,' Rose said. 'I want no argument about this. Bette, you'll have enough on your plate with the family. Belle, you, Mavis, Posy and Dan are coming to have lunch with me and Harry. It'll be late-ish, around three, after he's finished the morning services and before the evening ones.'

Mavis went to speak, shaking her head.

'No, Mavis. I'm insisting on this. Don't argue with me. It's not an imposition. I've already spoken to Harry and he thinks it's a marvellous idea.' She turned to Bette. 'If you can join us on Christmas Eve, that would be lovely. There's a carol service at seven. After that we'll go back to the vicarage for mince pies, and whatever. Just us. No-one else invited. But, of course it's up to you.'

'Thank you Rose, it's a lovely gesture,' Mavis replied.

'I can't be there, sorry, but thank you for the offer. I have family in London,' Dan Walker said. 'I have some news. I'm not sure how relevant it is, but I thought you'd want to hear it.'

'Of course,' Belle replied. 'Let's have it.'

'Up at St Foy Manor, now the Grand Hotel, tomorrow lunchtime there's going to be a book launch. It's by one of our leading local celebs, Professor Sir Joseph Knight.'

'I know him,' Belle said. 'Isn't he the one on TV who's called on to pronounce on world economic events. He's very imposing.'

'And handsome,' Rose added. 'And knowledgeable, of course.'

'Bette, something to say?'

'Yes. Sir Joseph Knight, Dr Joe Knight, as he was then, was Emily's personal tutor during her degree and was supervising her PhD. He came to see us a few weeks after she disappeared. He was distraught.'

'Why distraught?' Belle asked.

'He said the work she had done on her PhD was the finest he'd ever come across and she was going to be a leading figure in world economics, one day. He asked what he could do to help. We told him nothing, really, just hope.'

'Have you seen him since?'

'He called a few times, to ask if there was any news. But eventually he stopped calling.'

'What did you think of him?' Belle asked.

Bette shrugged. 'Nice man, sympathetic, kind, I think. I don't really remember much more.'

'Is it a public launch, Dan?'

'I believe so. He'll be selling and signing books, of course. Likely to be national TV there. He's a big name, now. Shall we go?'

'I think we should,' Belle replied. 'Might as well check him out. Anyone else coming? No, OK.'

'Tomorrow at twelve, then, Belle.'

'What about Georgie?' Mavis asked.

'I haven't had chance to speak to him,' Bette replied. 'He looks dreadful, like he hasn't slept in days. I'm going to try to get him on his own later.'

Belle put a hand on Bette's arm. 'I hope for his sake you can persuade him. Last thing, I have a plan that I'd like to put to you all now, if you have time.'

'You'll have to make it quick,' Rose replied. 'I really do have to get back to the church.'

'It's easy enough. Homework. Each of you was here at the time of Start's death and Emily's disappearance. I want to know everything about every character involved. What you know about them, what you thought about them. All of the other students, any other tutors, like the Professor, any other friends, family, police, anyone who could have been involved with both Emily and Star. Plus, anything you know about where they are now and what they're doing. Write it all down, and do it as soon as you can. Can you all come to my place tomorrow, same time, five o'clock?

They all nodded.

'Anything else, anyone? No. OK. Dan, we'll meet in the hotel carpark ten minutes before the launch. Let's take a look at Professor Knight and see who else turns up.'

Chapter 8

The carpark of the St Foy Grand Hotel dominated the hillside of St Foy, commanding a magnificent view of the estuary. Belle had been surprised to learn that the hotel was actually built as a hotel in the late 1890s, as opposed to the typical journey made by this type of building in England, starting out as the family home of some long forgotten Victorian business mogul. It would have eventually been given up as too expensive to maintain and left to tread the downward path to a private nursing home, a business centre, or some failed enterprise and ending up a second-class hotel, impressive on the outside, inside riddled with damp, out-of-date decor and noisy plumbing.

The St Foy Grand had been built as a luxury hotel for the Victorian elite and had remained both expensive and exclusive. She hadn't visited before, but could tell from the luxury vehicles in the carpark that this was going to be a delicious experience. The parking area was lined on either side by rows of exquisitely decorated Christmas trees, subtle but charming. A doorman in full livery stood at the entrance, welcoming arrivals.

She had been admiring the view of the snow-covered hills on the opposite side of the estuary when Dan's taxi arrived. They took one look at each other and laughed out loud. Their previous meetings had been casual, the dress code "comfortable".

'We look like a couple of stuffed shirts,' Belle whispered as they walked to the entrance. Although she was relaxed in most places, she had felt sufficiently intimidated today to make an effort, with one of her few remaining expensive dress and jacket combos, with heeled shoes, make up, hair coiffured and hands and neck bejewelled. Dan wore a three piece suit, and black leather shoes.

'Horribly uncomfortable,' he whispered back as he tucked her arm in his, 'but, we must look the part when mixing with this shower of…'

Before he could say what Belle knew was going to send her into a fit of giggles, a concierge directed them to the Monarch Room. They gave each other a quick eyebrow raise and walked through the double doors to their left. As they entered the room, people acknowledged Dan and he waved back.

'I'm going to work the room for a few minutes, pick out the ones I think will be brimming with curiosity.'

As he disappeared into a group of people, warmly shaking hands with each of them, Belle took a closer look at the room. It was decorated in the heavy, fussy Victorian style, and was already full, with a dais and lectern at one end, at the foot of which sat a row of TV cameras and photographers. On a large screen dominating the back wall was a full length picture of Joseph Knight and his book.

'Interesting title,' Belle said as Dan re-appeared next to her, catching two glasses of champagne from a passing waiter. 'He's pushed the boat out hasn't he,' she said, taking a sip and wincing. 'Or not,' as she put the glass down.

'Oh, I'll drink anything,' Dan replied with a grin. 'The great and the good have all turned out, I see. That man over there?' he pointed to a large man, balding, with a florid red face and a prominent gut. 'That's Martin Riley, the Chief Constable. The woman next to him, the one who looks rather rat-like, that's his wife, Josie. She likes to be seen at events. She's top dog amongst the "County" women. They're talking to Sir Michael Davey; he owns one of the more popular visitor places, Herringbone House.'

'I visited it in the summer,' Belle said. 'Beautiful medieval manor.'

He glanced up at the banner adorning the back wall. 'Interesting title. "The Monster is Coming: Economics for the Twenty Third Century". That illustration is reminiscent of a drawing of Grendel I saw as a child. Put me off Beowulf for life.'

'Maybe he should have used the dragon. I read it for "A" level. A greedy, bloodsucking monster, I remember. Who do you think he's referring to?'

'We're about to find out.'

The conversations around the room died away, as the man himself appeared and walked up onto the dais. He was alone but didn't need anyone to support or bolster him. Belle felt a shiver run down her back. This was an outstandingly attractive man. Not classically handsome, but tall and slender with strong shoulders, a longish face with high cheekbones and a wide, full mouth. His hair was a mix of iron grey and white, carefully cut to accentuate his high brow. His eyes – she couldn't tell the colour – were large and deep set. The word that came to mind to describe this man was – beautiful.

Dan watched her with a smile. 'He has that effect on men as well as women,' he whispered, as she blushed. 'Wait until he starts speaking.'

Joseph Knight began his introduction with thanks for attendance and a few witty remarks about the weather. His voice was mesmerising, hypnotic. He talked about world economics and Belle had never found the subject so interesting. She was totally drawn in, and applauded enthusiastically.

He stepped back and smiled as the cameras flashed and the reporters rushed forward. But he held them off.

'I'm here to meet these good people and sign books. And I am pleased to announce that all profits from today will go to charity. I'll answer press questions when the signing is done.' More applause, as people moved forward to take a book and line up at a table where Joseph Knight went to sit.

'I see another group I'd like to talk to, when he's done,' Dan said, 'locals who're good gossip fuel and… good Lord!'

'What?' Belle asked.

'Over there, in the corner, watching him. That's Emily Duggan.'

Belle turned her head to the side. Today, Emily didn't look like the wild child who had invaded Bette's birthday party and been released from police custody less than twenty-four hours before. The Bohemian look was gone. She was wearing a plain black dress that clung to her slender figure. Her blonde hair, which appeared to have been knitted onto her head when she stood in Bette's kitchen, was now hanging long and sleek, almost down to her waist. She had put on makeup and painted her nails. She looked stunning. And quite at ease. She saw Belle and Dan looking at her and walked over to them. Several people in the room turned to look at her as she walked; the women uncertain, the men admiring.

'I saw you at Aunty Bette's party,' she said in a low voice, smiling at Belle and Dan. 'You must be Belle. Uncle Dan, of course I know you. I'm so pleased you're here.' Her voice was low and melodious. 'I wanted to meet the Professor. It's been so long, but now I'm here I'm not sure this is the right environment.'

Glancing around, Belle could see whispers racing and, inevitably they reached the group of press men and women waiting in the corner. A couple of them shrugged, but one made a beeline for her.

'That's Peter Day, heading this way,' Dan said as the reporter walked forcefully across the room. 'Brace yourselves. Emily, can you face him or do you want to leave?'

'Too late,' Belle said.

'Miss Duggan,' Day said, as he walked up to her. 'Surprised to see you here.'

'Why?'

'Would you like to make a statement? The public would love to hear your side of the story; the death of Star Bright, the disappearance of a brilliant student, your sudden re-appearance after three years. It's quite a story. Of course, if you'd like to give me an exclusive interview, I could…'

'Mr Day, you are an obnoxious slug,' Emily said quietly. 'I have nothing to say to you, or to any of your vile compatriots.'

'Come on, Emily, I'm willing to pay you,' Peter Day leered, moving in closer and peering down her cleavage. 'A couple of sexy photos, maybe?'

'If you don't leave me alone right now, this champagne will be decorating your shirt.'

'Time to go,' Dan said briskly, taking Emily by the arm.

Her concentration having been on Emily and Day, Belle hadn't noticed that Joseph Knight had interrupted his book signing and was heading in their direction.

'Excuse me. You're taking the attention away from my book signing,' he said, with a grin. The smile turned to a puzzled look, then to amazement. 'Emily? It is you?' He took a step backwards, appraising her. 'Emily? I heard you were back! It is you! How are you, my dear?' He moved in, gave her a quick hug, then stood back, smiling.

She nodded, staring at him. The thought flashed through Belle's head that you could have cut the atmosphere between them with a blunt knife. Knight took another step forward, but Emily retreated. He regained control, the smile reappearing. 'Well, it's just, what can I say, it's wonderful to see you again.' He pulled out a business card and pushed it at her. 'We must talk. And I should give you a copy of the book.' He turned his head, flicked it towards the book pile and one of his attendants rushed forward with a copy. 'Now, if you'll excuse me, I must get back to the signing. Dr Walker, good to see you too.' He seemed to notice Belle for the first time, gave her an interested, admiring smile, then turned abruptly and went back to his seat.

'We should go,' Dan said. 'Emily, you need to get out of here, before the entire press group barricades the door. You've already attracted the attention of the glitterati.' He nodded at Belle, who stood at Emily's other side, and they marched her out of the room, keenly observed by the Chief Constable's group as they passed by. Josie Riley leaned back, as if moving away from a bad smell.

'I have my car,' Belle said as they took their coats and walked towards the carpark. 'Who are you staying with, Emily? I'll take you back.'

'No-one,' she said in a bored voice.

'Then you can come back to my cottage. Dan, you too.' She pushed Emily into the back seat of her car and nodded Dan to the front seat.

'We have a lot to talk about, Dr Walker.' She sped out of the carpark, wheels crunching on the snow as a horde of press rushed down the front steps and watched the back end of the car skid around a sharp bend.

Peter Day glanced at his phone. He had been at the front of the pack, with the presence of mind to take a picture of the departing car, catching the number plate. He would soon know who had whisked Emily Duggan away. Another name to add to his growing list.

Chapter 9

Belle now had a garage, five minutes' walk from the back gate of the cottage, which she used mainly for storage, but today she put the car inside and pulled down the shutter. She didn't want anyone knowing where it was. She had seen the reporters at the bottom of the hotel steps as she pulled away and guessed at least one of them might have had the presence of mind to photograph the car.

'Anyone need a drink?' she said once they were inside, nodding to the settees around the fire, which she piled up with logs.

'I could do with a gin and tonic,' Dan replied.

'Tea for me,' Emily said, staring into the flames that were starting to creep up from the logs. 'This is nice.'

As Belle sorted out drinks in the kitchen, she went through some questions she wanted to put to Emily, now she had her here, a captive audience.

'Emily, I hope you won't mind,' she said, putting the tray down on the table. 'I'd like to ask you a few questions. I'm not sure if you know who I am…'

'You're a friend of Aunty Bette and Uncle Bert. A good friend, I understand. What would you like to know?' She paused to take a sip of tea, then sat back, legs crossed.

Dan had also sat back with his drink, ready to listen.

'First of all, how are you? I was surprised to see you at the book event.'

'Thank you for asking. No-one else has. I'm OK, I suppose.'

'Where are you staying?'

'At my mother's old house. It's empty. I gather they can't sell it until I agree.'

'Are you planning to stay in St Foy?'

'No idea.'

Now to the big questions, Belle thought. 'What's the situation with the police?'

'My friend, Skinner – he's one of the people I've been living with – has been interviewed. I met him on the bus when I left town, not long after Aunty Bette dropped me off. We ended up in Scotland. That was the 19th of December, and they know now I was in someone else's company for the following couple of months. They have a statement from another of the students, I'm not sure which one, that Star Bright was alive on the 20th. So, that puts me in the clear. But, they want to re-check all the student statements. Once that's done, I'm good to go.'

'May I ask which student saw Star on the 20th?'

'Sure. It was Gabe. Gabriel Holmes, that is.'

'So as soon as the police find him and confirm his statement, you'll officially be removed from their list of suspects?'

Emily laughed, a short, bitter sound. 'Well, good luck to them with that. Gabe was a loser. Who knows where he is now? And, as I seem to have been the only person on the suspect list, I have no idea what they'll do next.'

'Why did you come back now?'

'I'd had enough of the Bohemian lifestyle. We did a lot of drugs and thieving. It had been great, a good place to get away from everything, including my shitty, crap family. But it was breaking down. Someone overdosed and died. So, I left. That was about six months ago. I've been living on the streets ever since. Then, I saw a couple of weeks ago that the Professor was going to launch a book, right here in St Foy. So I decided why not? My mother was dead. I thought the rest of them might have forgiven me by now. I contacted Skinner, told him I might need his help. He agreed. So, here I am. Clearly not forgiven in all quarters.' She shrugged and picked up the tea, cradling it in her hands. Her gaze hadn't moved from the fire.

'They had come to accept you were dead,' Dan said. 'Especially Bette and Bert, who spent months looking for you. You deceived Bette. Quite horribly.'

Emily didn't respond.

'Especially as you lied to her, Emily,' Belle added. 'You weren't pregnant. She found that out.'

Emily's head snapped around. 'It's none of your business.' She stood. 'I'll go now. Thanks for the tea.'

'I have more questions.'

'I bet you do. Well, tough.' She picked up her coat and headed for the door. As she reached for the handle and opened the door, she turned back and said, 'I expect you don't know this, but Star was totally infatuated with Professor Knight. She followed him around like a little puppy. Perhaps he got fed up with her.'

For a few moments, after Emily exited slamming the door, Belle and Dan stared at each other.

'That wasn't what I expected,' Belle said. 'I don't really know what I expected, but it wasn't that.'

'What, in your opinion, was *that*?'

'A performance,' Belle replied. 'Which suggests to me this is an iceberg, of which we've just seen the very top layer. God knows what's waiting beneath the surface.'

'For myself, I don't intend to be on the Titanic, and you shouldn't either,' Dan replied. 'My impression – that girl, or woman I should say – is back with an agenda.'

Chapter 10

At Bette and Bert's farm, an argument was in full, screaming-pitch flow.

'Don't tell me you're going to invite her to Christmas lunch,' Charlie shrieked in Bette's face.

'What do you suggest I do?' Bette snarled back. 'Leave her alone in that damp, smelly house. You know the state it's in.'

'That's exactly what I'm suggesting,' Charlie replied. 'If she's coming, I'm not.'

Bert offered up a silent prayer of thanks.

'Suit yourself,' Bette replied. 'So much for your Christian charity.'

Charlie blushed. 'We don't even know what the police have said. We could be harbouring a murderer,' she said, flinging out her arms.

'Don't be so melodramatic,' Bette replied. 'It won't be easy, but she's not being charged, there's a credible witness to her story and she's family.'

'Georgie won't be here,' Charlie responded, folding her arms.

'I'm going to see him now, to try to persuade him,' Bert answered. 'If he refuses, well, that's his choice.'

'I'm leaving,' Charlie replied. 'Trevor, let's go.' She swept up her coat, and marched, head up, to the door. 'I just don't know how you could do this to me.'

'Bloody drama queen,' Bette snapped when Charlie and the cowed Trevor had slammed the door behind them.

Bert understood that behind Bette's touchy exterior was a good heart and he knew it was breaking. Not just for the situation she now found herself in, but for having to keep secrets. He put his arms around her.

'Will you ask him?' she muttered into his shoulder. 'He's going to have to confess to what he did.'

'Yes,' Bert replied. 'But I'm going to suggest too that we somehow get through Christmas. All of the kids will be here. And don't think Charlie won't turn up. She won't be able to help herself.'

Bette smiled and pulled away. 'You'd better get off then. I'll go to the house to speak to Emily. Meet back here later.'

**

'Are you joking?' Emily laughed in Bette's face. 'Sit around a table with you lot, eating turkey and sprouts? I can just imagine how scintillating the conversation will be. *So, Emily, did you kill Star Bright. No, I didn't. Do pass me more of those delicious sprouts.*'

Bette stood up. 'It was a genuine invitation, Emily. But it's clear you want none of us.'

'Correct. I have plans,' Emily smirked.

'Really? Although, I suppose you could have, but who I am to judge? You're such a good liar, Emily.'

'Get out, Aunty Bette.'

'Gladly.'

Bette hadn't voiced all of her thoughts, even to Bert, but she had been praying that Emily would refuse the invitation. Although she was shaking, with both anger and distress at the encounter, she was mainly relieved as she drove home. She had done her best. Emily was on her own and good luck to her.

**

'A Doctor of cultural anthropology. I know, sort of, what anthropology is, but I didn't know there were sub-categories,' Belle said, sitting back with coffee, after Dan had accepted her invitation to stay for lunch.

'We explore how people live and understand the world around them, how they make their rules, what's important to them, how they treat each other and people from other cultures. Societies vary enormously, and we – I – want to understand as much as we can. I believe that understanding others, not judging them, but learning similarities as well as differences, can enrich our understanding of our species.'

'Sounds intriguing. It explains why you travel so much.'

He nodded. 'I spend my time in a wide variety of places and amongst very different peoples. I started as an archaeologist, examining the ways of ancient people, how they lived, how they used and adapted to their environments as they moved around. It was interesting, but I found I preferred the current world to the past. So, I moved on.'

'This is fascinating, Dan. Much more so than my job.'

'Human resources, I believe?'

'Yes. Specialising in working with very difficult people, who had no idea how to interact with anyone without conflict or bullying. I often had to move them out of the company.'

'You must have spent a lot of time in court. I guess you were sued by quite a few of them.'

'Yes. You get used to it, but it's never pleasant.'

'What made you take up the role?'

She thought for a moment. 'It came out of my life story, which I'm not going to tell you now. But bullying was one issue, an important one for me, that I wanted to deal with.'

'Maybe you'll trust me enough to tell me, at some point.'

'Maybe.' She like this man, but didn't feel ready to tell him about her mother, nor her school experiences and how they had entered her life again just over a year earlier, in such a devastating way. 'Now, to homework. What can you tell me?'

Before he could speak, Belle's phone pinged twice.

'WhatsApp messages,' she said. 'By the way, do you want to join the group?'

He shook his head vehemently. 'I have a phone, into which I speak to those who call me and to those I choose to call. That's it. No social media.' He spoke the latter with a frown of distaste.

'These are from Bette and Rose. Both asking if we can put off our meeting until tomorrow at eleven. Can you make that?'

'Of course,' he replied, standing. 'My information is about the Jones family and the Morrises, before Bette married the handsome Bert. It will give you some interesting reading.'

'Eleven it is,' she said, looking up. He was looking at her with an expression that was almost affectionate. 'What?'

'You like to organise.'

'I'm good at it,' she replied, briskly. 'I'll read what you've written, and I've asked the others to send theirs through tonight. We should have a comprehensive tranche of information to consider.'

'I'll see myself out. Thanks for lunch. Happy reading. Or not.'

**

Bette and Bert sat in silence, each with their elbows on their family kitchen table.

'That went well,' Bert said after a few minutes.

'At least he didn't attack you,' Bette replied. 'I thought Emily was going to physically move me to the door. What did he have to say about talking to the police about what he did?'

'That's when he threw me out of the house.'

'Emily apparently has plans.'

'Neither of them joining us, then. Honestly love, I can't say I mind. If Charlie doesn't turn up either, then it's you, me and the kids and grandchildren.'

Bette grinned. 'Much better. I'll tell Charlie we've invited Emily and Georgie and they're considering it. That should keep her away.'

'There'll be fifteen of us, including the brats,' Bert said.

'Then we'd better get going. You're cooking?'

He nodded.

'We'll need more food.'

'Leave that to me. What about your group meeting?'

'I'm going to cancel tonight. I'll suggest tomorrow morning, see if that's OK with everyone.'

She sent her message and received immediate replies. 'All agreed. Belle's cottage at eleven. You coming?'

'No, I'll get on with Christmas. Don't forget your "homework". Belle will be cross if you don't do it.'

'I'll write it up and send it through tonight.'

'Good girl. I'll get dinner going.' Bert moved to the stove, lit it and started taking food from cupboards and fridge.

Bette set up her laptop and began to type. She had a lot to share, far more than she'd given Belle so far.

After half an hour she was ready to send through her document, when her phone rang.

'It's the solicitor. Shall I answer it?'

Bert nodded. 'Put it on speaker.'

'I have some news for you, and it's not good,' the solicitor said.

'What is it?' Bert asked. 'What's happened.'

'The police went to re-interview Gabriel Holmes, you know, the student who said he'd seen Star alive the day after Emily went missing.'

'I remember. Has he changed his story?'

'No. He's dead, an accidental overdose. Seems he used a lot of cocaine.'

'That's going to change everything,' Bert said, putting down the knife he was using to chop vegetables. 'What will happen?'

'I've told Emily, of course. She's pretty upset. The original statement stands. But Gabriel died a couple of months before Emily re-appeared.'

'Was she anywhere near where he died?'

'We don't know, yet. She's being re-interviewed.'

'Thanks for letting us know, Simon.'

'I'll call you back after tomorrow's interview,' Simon Davies replied, ending the call.

Bert went back to his chopping board, hacking at vegetables with vehemence.

'I'll let the others know. Another death.' She shook her head. 'More complications. This nightmare isn't ending any time soon.
'

Chapter 11

At eleven the following morning the group, including Dan Walker and Harry Teague, sat around Belle's dining table, no-one speaking much.

'Thanks for sending through your homework,' Belle said. 'I must say, there was far more detail in it than I expected, so well done. I spent a couple of hours last night pulling it all together. What I've come up with is a list of all of the people who were around at the time, who were close to or personally knew both Emily and Star in some capacity. And thanks to those of you who added what you know of them now. I've included some personal opinions where I thought they were relevant. Here's the result. Take a few minutes to read.'

1.   Emily Duggan

Status and background: Former PhD student in 2nd year of study. Gained a first class degree in Economics, followed by a Master's Degree, again in Economics. Disappeared on 19th December 2016. Daughter of Rita and Ronald Morris. Ronald had abandoned family, then died. Rita idolised Emily in public, but not in private. Emily assumed dead by family until she re-appeared on 19th December.

2.   Star Bright

Status and background: Doing a Master's degree in Economics. Best friend of Emily Duggan, but had a major row the weekend before Emily disappeared. Very pretty, popular, outgoing in nature. Little known about her background. Not her real name. Claimed she made up the name 'Star Bright' but first name possibly Anastasia. Claimed she had grown up in the care system but never gave any details. Claimed she had no family alive. Maze Investigations currently investigating her background, as requested by Belle Harrington.

3. Gabriel Holmes

Status and background: Student of Management Studies. Died two months ago. drug overdose. Was a final year degree student at St Piran, sharing a house, known as Bedlam Heights, with other students mentioned here. Dropped out shortly after beginning of second term of final year. From a wealthy family. Known to have gone abroad after leaving University, for about one year. Known drug user at University.

4. Phil Singh

Status and Background: Kuldip Singh, known as Phil. Studying medicine, 3rd year degree student. Now a Junior Doctor, working in Paediatrics at Royal Cornwall hospital. Quiet, studious. No particular friend amongst the Heights group.

5. Billy Anderson

Status and Background: Final year student of Civic Studies. Now a policeman. Joined the local force after leaving University. Another of group sharing the Heights. Now married, no children. Working under Chief Inspector Susan Lewis on murder of Star Bright. At one time was Star's boyfriend and came under suspicion at the time of her death, but had already gone home when she was known to be alive, with alibi provided by family.

6. Jade Waters

Status and Background: Gained a 2.1 degree in English Literature. Lived at the Heights. Also a drug user and one time girlfriend of Gabriel Holmes. Had also left the area before Star Bright killed, but couldn't provide an alibi. Began to train as a teacher after University but dropped out. Current whereabouts not known.

7. Miriam Riley

Status and Background: Gained 1st class degree in Mathematics. Lived at the Heights. Quiet, conscientious. Not much liked, not a particular friend of other students. Thought to be the person who started rumours about who was sleeping with whom. Current whereabouts not known. Had left for Xmas holiday before Star Bright killed. Solid alibi, given by parents, Josie and Martin Riley (Chief Constable).

8. Professor Sir Joseph Knight

Status and Background: Personal tutor of Emily Duggan and Star Bright, also gave lectures attended by Gabriel Holmes and Billy Anderson. At time of Star Bright's death, married, no children. Now a widower, wife died of breast cancer earlier this year. Still lecturing part time, but has become economics expert and used by government. TV appearances from time to time have made him a familiar TV face. Popular. Pleasant manner. Recently published a book with launch in St Foy. Book has been internationally well received. Knighted two years after Emily disappeared.

9. George Morris

Status and Background: Elder child of Rita, father not known. Half-brother of Emily after Rita married Ronald Duggan. Married to Mandy, with one son. Left school at sixteen. Not academic. Works as a gardener and garden designer in and around St Foy. Known to have had a crush on Star Bright, to the point of infatuation. Distraught when she died. Believes his sister Emily killed Star.

10. <u>Edna Morris</u>

Status and Background: Mother to Rita, Lana and Bette Morris. Husband Max Morris known drunk who deserted the family. Social services called in on several occasions. Once, when drunk, Edna told Emily that she had killed Max. Now living in a retirement home in Castledore.

11. <u>Chief Inspector Susan Lewis</u>

At time of Emily's disappearance was an Inspector. Rapid rise to Chief Inspector. Known to be lazy, using juniors to do much of legwork. Not particularly intuitive. Likes a quick result.

12. <u>Kylie Nichols</u>

Status and Background: School friend of Emily, only one she remained in touch with when in University. Not spoken to by police when Emily disappeared, but known to have some information that might be useful. Works in a shop in Port Simon.

Belle watched as the group read the paper, seeing eyebrows raised, mouths forming an 'oh', scowls, questioning looks. After five minutes, they had finished reading and sat in silence with the papers on the table.

'Thoughts, reactions?' she said. 'Anyone like to start? I'm the only one here who wasn't around at the time, so I have nothing at the moment, other than the interaction with Emily and Joseph Knight yesterday, which we can come on to later.'

'Why has Edna been included?' Harry Teague asked. 'I can understand the others, they were all around or part of the group, but why Edna?'

'That was me,' Bette replied. 'My mother is not what she appears to be. You saw her at my birthday party. What you don't know is that she brought up Emily. Rita was often away working. She was a rep for a makeup company and travelled the country. That was after her husband left them, then died. Georgie was twelve and left to fend for himself. Emily needed caring for, so Rita handed her over to Edna. God knows what Edna put into that girl's head. She lived mostly with Edna from the age of seven, until Rita finally gave up travelling. Emily was doing brilliantly at school and Rita boasted about her whenever she got the chance. Georgie got nothing but criticism from her. He's a bit slow, as you all know. Rita hated that.'

'But he's immensely creative,' Belle said. 'Look what he's done with my garden. And, from what I hear, he's never out of work.'

'We know that,' Bette replied. 'He came to me, mostly, when Rita was travelling.'

'I'm wondering where some of this information came from,' Mavis said. 'I mean, it's not as if someone like this Kylie Nichols was close to anyone here, was it?'

'Unless anyone wants to say how they found out some of this information, I think we should keep it anonymous, sorry Mavis,' Belle replied.

'This is a huge amount of information to take in,' Rose murmured. 'This investigation will keep Susan Lewis occupied.'

'I don't think it will,' Bette said. All faces turned to her. 'I have more information about Georgie.'

She took in a deep breath, closed her eyes, sat up, and opened them again, staring straight ahead, but not at anyone.

'You already know the story of what Georgie did. You all know now that Georgie was infatuated with Star, and that he went to the Heights to invite her to have Christmas lunch with his family.' She shook her head briefly. 'When he arrived, he couldn't find her, so he looked in her room and it was clear she was still there.'

'I thought her stuff had been packed up,' Posy interrupted.

'Let her finish,' Belle said quietly.

Bette nodded. 'After finding her in the attic and sitting with her for about an hour, he made a decision. I have never been able to fathom out why he did what he did. It was something about honouring her.'

'He took her and put her on the tree, on the moor.' It was Harry who spoke. 'It was some kind of ancient custom. But he didn't get it right. No matter. He wanted her to be with nature; dignified, not hidden away in an attic until she became a desiccated, shrivelled corpse.'

'Bert went to see him yesterday, to beg him to go to the police and admit what he did. They're going to be furious,' Bette said. 'They'll probably arrest him, possibly try to get him to admit he murdered her, once the story of his infatuation with her comes out.'

'Are you quite sure he didn't? Mavis asked.

Bette glared at her. 'Georgie has never killed anything in his life, not an animal, not an insect even. Certainly not another human. So… yes, Mavis, I'm sure.'

Tears had started to run down her cheeks. 'Susan Lewis will arrest him. I know it.'

'How did he respond to Bert?' Belle asked.

'Asked him to leave. He insists Emily did it, because she was jealous. Bert has asked him to tell Mandy, then go to the police straight after Christmas.'

'Will he?' Mavis asked.

'I don't know. But somehow, it will come out. We're going to try again on Boxing Day, try to persuade him it's better coming from him.'

'It's just a thought,' Belle said. 'But would he speak to one of us? Me, perhaps? There might be something he could add to the story, something he saw, or heard, that might help his story. Then, when he does have to speak to them – and I agree that he will have to, like it or not – he can at least give them extra information to help the enquiry.'

'Bert can go ask him again, I suppose,' Bette replied. 'Nothing to lose by asking.'

Belle was about to speak again, when there was a knock at the door.

'Expecting anyone else, are we?' Dan asked.

'Definitely not. I hope it's not Margaret, snooping out gossip.' She stood and went to the front door, closing the door to the living room behind her. A man stood there, a microphone in one hand. A cameraman stood behind him and another man with a clipboard.

'Good morning, Mrs Harrington. Belle isn't it? Or should I say Virginia Arabella Somers? Would you like to tell your side of the story, about the boy you killed right here in St Foy, and the suspicious death of your mother? I'd love to come in to speak to your little group. May I?'

He went to step over the doorstep and for a few seconds, Belle was speechless. Then, she snapped back to reality and blocked his way.

'Don't you dare take one step onto my property, Mr Day. If you try, I will call the police.'

Her voice remained calm, her expression, she hoped, superior. She stared unblinkingly at him, until he retreated a step. He was far enough back, when the living room door behind Belle opened and Dan Walker took a few steps to stand at her side. He was grinning.

'I wondered how long it would be before you showed up, Peter. Slithering around as usual, I gather. Have you tried the dustbins yet? Richard sends greetings. I spoke to him this morning.'

If Belle had been surprised by Peter Day's appearance, she was now shocked at the change in him. His face had drained of colour. He opened his mouth, then turned to the cameraman. 'Turn it off. Now!'

'That's better,' Dan said. 'You can leave now.'

Peter Day thrust the microphone at the clipboard man, turned and marched off down the street, minions trotting to keep up.

Dan looked at Belle. 'Helps to know people who know people,' he said. 'You look like you need a stiff drink. Come on back inside.'

She followed him in without speaking. When she sat down, she took a few moments, then said to the waiting group. 'There's a story I need to tell you all, now. Two of you here know it already. It's about my history and why I came here. That was Peter Day and he has just flung a disgusting, horrible accusation at me.'

She proceeded to tell them – everything. From the day of the incident on the beach down at Cash Cove, after years of thinking she had killed a local boy, confirmed by her mother, but ultimately not true. She described the monster that her mother had been, how she had eventually escaped her, but had been forced to return when her mother was dying. How her mother had finally admitted on her death bed that she had made the story up, but how she, Belle, after over forty years of believing it, had then lost her husband and had come to St Foy, following a breakdown, to see if she could find the boy and discover the truth about what had happened to him.

'But suggesting that my mother's death was suspicious? There was no question but that my mother died of cancer. I can't believe he said that!' Her hands were shaking.

'It's the "when did you stop beating your wife?" kind of question that grubby reporters like Peter Day will ask,' Dan said. 'They know it's not true, but they want to put you on the back foot, make you defend yourself against an accusation that's made up.'

'I'd like to say something, Belle, if that's Ok with you?' Harry said.

She knew what he was about to say, and nodded. 'Belle told me her story at the beginning of this year, when she came back after the bullying crimes in Wales. What she told me then is what she has just told you all now. Peter Day is a disgusting creature. But it looks like he's going to go into the background of everyone here.'

'Maybe, maybe not,' Dan replied. 'His background is pretty dodgy, too. I must ask you all to leave him to me.'

'Well, you just saw him off good and proper,' Belle said. 'I agree. If you can deal with him, then please do so.' Her colour had returned, but she still felt shaky. 'Look, I wanted to talk about what to do next, but I'm not up to it. Could we meet again, later?'

They all stood, each giving her a quick hug, and were gone in minutes. Belle saw them all out and returned to the living room, about to throw herself into a chair and weep, when a sound from the kitchen made her spin around.

Dan came walking out, a glass of brandy in his hand. 'Thought you might need this,' he said, thrusting one at her. 'Sit.'

'For a moment I thought you were Peter Day, sneaking in at the back door.'

He laughed. 'No, I'll always be up front. And that's what I'm going to do now.' He sat next to her.

'This is going to come as something of a shock, probably more than that. Are you prone to fainting?'

She looked at him, puzzled. 'Never have before. Depends on what you're about to tell me.'

'Right. A local boy called Johnnie. Bit of a show off, yes?'

'Yes, do you know who he is?' Belle demanded.

'I do.'

'Then tell me, Dan. Please. I've been looking for this boy for years, I need, really need to know if he's alive and OK, that I didn't push him. I mean, I know I didn't, but if someone could confirm it, without any doubt, it would be – I don't know. I can't explain what it would mean to me.'

'I can assure you one hundred percent you didn't push him. He jumped.'

It took her a moment to take in what he was saying, and went to speak, but he hushed her.

'You want me to take you to meet him?' She nodded emphatically.

'Well, no need.'

She was puzzled, but a small pinprick of light started somewhere in her brain. Her expression turned to amazement.

'You mean…'

'Yes. I've always been known here as Dan, but my full name is John-Daniel Walker. You didn't push me. I jumped, and I have one almighty scar on my head from where I hit the rock. I was a bit concussed. But I just swam away. I saw you run up the beach.' He gazed at her with soft eyes. 'You didn't push me, Belle. I jumped. I was trying to impress you with my diving skills. Big fail, that was.'

Belle burst into tears.

Chapter 12

It was five minutes before she was able to speak again. Just when she thought the sobbing had stopped, it began again. Dan sat next to her on the settee, his arm around her shoulders, her head pressed into his chest.

'I'm going to have to change this shirt,' he said eventually, as her sobs changed to hiccups.

'Sorry. I need more tissues.'

'You certainly do. You'll have to go out to buy a new box. You've used up the one you had.'

Belle looked around and saw that the floor was covered. 'Yuk. I'll clear that up.'

'No, leave it to me,' Dan said, removing his arm with a wince and standing. 'My arm is dead and it's time for you to stop crying. You needed it, but now it's done and we need to talk about how to handle Peter Day.'

Belle jumped up to stand beside him. She put her arms around his shoulders and kissed his cheek. Then she started picking up the tissues. Dan sat down again.

'Thanks for the brandy. I needed that, but I'm going to make tea. You want some?'

'How very English,' he replied, with a grin. 'Yes, thanks.'

'I'm Welsh, but you're welcome.' She paused. 'Is that an anthropological thing?'

'Of course. Doesn't happen anywhere else in the world. It defines our culture. We associate the making of tea with people coming together for a chat, in a benign way. I could go on, but I won't.'

'Good.'

'Cheeky. Anyway; Peter Day. Are you up for having some fun with him?'

'Depends on what you mean,' Belle said warily.

'I mean, let him go on hinting about your killing a boy here in town, and coming back to make sure you did the job properly.'

Belle choked on her mouthful of brandy. 'What! Let him think I might actually have done it? Killed you, or rather, "the boy"?'

'Not for long, of course. Just long enough to embarrass him when we tell the truth, together. As for what he's saying about your mother, I presume you have her death certificate? Could you get more evidence of her natural death?'

'Yes, I can. I was just wondering where he got that story. I think he may have doorstepped the nurse who helped me out when Gillian was dying. She was a lovely lady, and she was the one who heard Gillian say that she made up the story that I pushed you, to get herself and me away from my father but keep his money.' She shook her head. 'I have the number somewhere. She came from an agency. I'm sure I can find her again.'

'Do so. Have her write a statement.'

Belle nodded. 'Thank you, Dan. This has shocked and shaken me more than I ever imagined possible.'

He put a hand on her arm. 'It would have come out at some point. You'd already started telling people. You said two. Harry Teague, obviously. I'm guessing the other one is Posy.'

She nodded.

'OK. Let's leave that for now and get back to the real business of who killed Star Bright, or whatever her real name is, or was.'

'Yes. I'm not sure there's much we can do before Christmas, though. I'm sorry you aren't coming to lunch with Harry and Rose. I've managed to buy a few presents.'

He shifted in his seat. 'I'm going to London, in the morning. I have a flat there, and a partner.'

'That's another surprise. This day is full of them. Wouldn't your partner like to come here?'

'I think it would be too much of a shock for some people,' he replied wryly.

'Why? Doesn't bother me that you're gay. I don't think the others will be shocked. Surely they all know already?'

'I expect so. I don't talk about my private life. Some people are not as perceptive as you. It's very traditional here. Some people haven't made it to the twentieth century yet, never mind the twenty first.'

'Your decision, of course. What's his name?'

'Richard. He's my husband.'

'Well, I'd like to meet him.' She paused. 'Is he the Richard that knows something dodgy about Peter Day?'

'Yes, he is. But I need to talk to him first. He'll have to be part of the plan. I'm leaving in the morning, and I shall spend the next couple of days in festive marital harmony. Then I'll come back to this festering situation, which I can only hope won't get any worse over the holiday.'

He stood, put on his coat and hat and walked with Belle to the door.

He kissed both cheeks and said, 'Don't let the likes of Peter Day get to you. We can take him down whenever we decide it's the right time. The important matter is to find out what really happened to Star. If it's OK with you, I'm going to discuss all of this with Richard.'

'Of course,' Belle replied. 'Thank you, Dan. You've changed my world.'

He waved a hand without looking back as he walked off down the lane. She watched him go until he turned the corner into the main square.

Belle went back and threw herself onto the settee, where she sat throughout the afternoon, unmoving, thinking, processing, until the afternoon turned to night, with no lights, just the shadows thrown out by the glowing fire.

At six o'clock she stood. Three days of Christmas, then, time to return to action mode. Who was Star Bright? Why did she die? Something terrible had happened up at that house. She was going to find out what had brought it about.

The first part of the answer came the following day.

Chapter 13

Belle was awake early, feeling a lightness that had not been there for many years. It would take some time to fully settle in. Receiving world changing, albeit good news was always a shock to the system and time would be needed to allow it to permeate and to become at peace with it.

She felt the cottage was less Christmassy than she would normally have made it, so she went up into the small attic space and brought down a box of the old decorations, the ones she and Jamie and Sam had used since Jamie was a baby. After an hour or so, she was satisfied. A long wreath across the mantle interspersed with candles, lit despite it being daylight, with the wood burner lit, gave the room a cosy feel. She would buy a small Christmas tree later on and decorate it with the baubles and figurines that the three of them had bought in different places over many years. Then, she would take photographs and send them to Jamie.

She had just accomplished the final act of Christmas, setting her phone ring tone to Jingle Bells, when the doorbell rang.

Dan Walker entered, armed with a bag of freshly baked croissants, a pitcher of orange juice and a wrapped parcel.

'I squeezed the oranges myself, not personally,' he added. 'A machine did it, but it's so much better and healthier than the supermarket offering.' He deposited everything on the dining table at the back of the room and looked around. 'This looks cheery. Where's your tree? This,' he indicated the wrapped parcel, 'must go under it and not be opened until Christmas morning.'

Belle, who had watched his progress through her cottage, laughed. 'Getting one is my next task. Would you like to join me for breakfast?'

'Thought you'd never ask. I have to be off after that. Richard's expecting me after lunch.' Again he paused. 'Seriously, I wanted to see how you were this morning.'

She took his hands in hers. His usual cheery round face with its slightly prominent chin had assumed a serious look. 'I am feeling well this morning. I don't know the right words. "Light" is one, "relieved" is another. But neither fully does justice to how I feel, thanks to you.'

'That makes me feel relieved too, and confident I can leave you alone for a couple of days. Now, let's eat.'

Belle made a pot of fresh coffee. 'Organic beans,' she said with a grin. She had just poured them a cup each when her phone rang. Jingle Bells. Dan rolled his eyes and gave her a "really?" look.

She blushed and answered, then her expression turned to concentration as she listened. It was her friend in Wales, Maggie Gilbert, the genealogy investigator.

'Don't tell me you've found something already?

'Possibly. Not one hundred percent sure yet, and for now it's just a name and a short story, but I thought I'd update you, so…'

'Just a moment, Maggie, I have a friend here for breakfast. His name is Dan and I'm going to put you on speaker.'

'Hello, Dan. This is Maggie. Belle and I went to school together.'

'Hello to you too. I presume this relates to Emily and Star?'

'It's about Star. Belle gave us some basics and my colleagues began a search. We found five girls with the name Anastasia, who would be around the right age. We've ruled out all but two, one of whom I think may be your girl. Her name is Louisa Anastasia Light. She was born in 1998, in Chelsea. Mother's name is also Light , no father listed on the birth cert, which I can get a copy of, for you. There were a few issues with Social Services, but she was never in care. She was a runaway. Left home at fourteen, and never got back in contact with her family.'

'Was there any police involvement?' Belle asked.

'Doesn't look like it, no.'

'Is there any family still alive?' Dan asked.

'I don't know. We haven't gone that far. I can't say for certain it's the right girl, but the name could translate from Louisa Anastasia Light to Star Bright, so I thought I'd let you know.'

'That's great, Maggie, thank you. We can take it from here, as soon as Christmas is over.'

'Do have a good one, my friend. Can you pick up the phone for a moment?'

Belle listened for a few seconds. 'I'm listening… no! It's not like that! What? About five ten, black hair, no I'm not sending a picture and I'll explain later.' She saw Dan grinning. 'I'll be back in touch after Christmas and tell you the whole story. Now, Merry Christmas and goodbye!'

'Our first lead,' he said, biting into a croissant and wiping dripping butter from his lips. 'Are you going to tell Susan Lewis?'

'Of course.' She stopped. 'Actually, I might tell that young policeman who was a student there at the time, Billy Anderson. Could be he'll tell me more about what's going on from the police side.'

'Good idea. Talk to Posy first. I think she knows him quite well. The information in your summaries came from her.'

'How do you know… oh, never mind.'

'Almost time for me to go. What are you doing today?'

'Christmas shopping. I will need some food of my own, although I'm going to have lunch with Harry and Rose, and Posy and Mavis. Should be fun, and I need a few more gifts. I thought I'd go into Truro, rather than the city. There are some nice shops there.'

'It's a lovely place.' He stood and put on his coat. 'Have a fun couple of days. I'll be back Monday or Tuesday, but if anything breaks in the meantime, please call me. You have my number.'

'I will. Have a good one too, you and Richard.'

He leaned in and kissed her cheek. 'Stay safe.'

**

On her way home, loaded with bags, both personal gifts and food and drink for Christmas, she stopped at the garden centre on the outskirts of St Foy and chose a tree, just tall enough to take the decorations and small enough to load into the back of her car. During the shopping she had deliberately put out of her mind both Dan's news about himself, and the information from Maggie about Star, if this was Star Bright. As she drove back into town, just after lunch, she decided she had to let the Curiosity Club know. Dan was Ok with them knowing he was the boy who had dived off the rocks. She pondered on whether or not to tell the others about Star, and decided that she should. The investigating could wait, but the news couldn't.

She spent the afternoon decorating the tree, wrapping gifts and planning.

At five thirty they were at their usual table in the café, lit by candlelight.

Belle began by giving them Dan's news.

'Well I'll be damned,' Bette said. 'I noticed he had stayed behind when the rest of us left. I never knew about his injury, though.'

'His mother had to take him to hospital to get his head x-rayed and stitched. But he was quite clear that he had dived as I was turning around,' Belle replied. 'His mum was cross with him.'

'Your mother was a dreadful woman,' Rose said. 'I wouldn't normally say that about anyone's mother. I mean, mine was a bit of an airhead, but she tried her best and never did anything like… like yours did to you.'

'What are you going to do about that reporter, Belle?' Mavis asked

'Nothing; for the time being. Dan wants to take him on and I'm happy to let him. But what he accused me of regarding my mother, that's different. Immediately after Christmas I can get in touch with the agency to ask if the nurse is still around and will give me a written statement. She was in the room with me when Gillian finally died.'

'That will be an end to that piece of nastiness,' Rose said. 'How are you feeling, Belle?'

'Honestly, a bit overwhelmed. You always think you'll be dancing around after good news, but that's not the case. It's taking time to sink in. I wish I could have told Sam.' For a second her voice trembled. Then she rallied. 'Right, now for the more important news. My friend Maggie may have traced Star Bright.'

She told them the story she had from Maggie Gilbert. 'I was going to get in touch with Chief Inspector Lewis, but I thought I'd ask you, Posy, to speak to Billy Anderson, instead. What do you think? Dan says you know Billy better than the rest of us.'

Posy nodded. 'That's true. His mother and I were friends, years ago, that's when I got to know Billy and I still chat to him when I see him out and about. Sure, I'll tell him. But can we leave it until after Christmas? It's all going to take off again, starting Monday. I'll call him then and give him the news.'

They all agreed. No need to spoil anyone's holiday unnecessarily, and there was nothing else of importance to discuss.

'Then, let's all get off. We'll meet again at the Christmas carol service tonight. I hope you'll all be there, at seven,' Rose said, evidently not expecting any of them to refuse.

'Wouldn't miss it,' Bette replied. 'Harry does a nice Christmas Eve service, even for those amongst us who don't believe.'

'That's aimed at me,' Belle replied with a smile, 'but I'll be there, of course, Rose.'

'Then we'll have a happy and joyful Christmas Day,' Rose replied, hugging each of them.

Chapter 14

Belle arrived at the Vicarage at ten on Christmas morning, following her earlier call to Jamie. The previous year Jamie had managed to get some time off and had joined her. This time they had a long call but she missed his presence and his company, and although she didn't say, she was worried about him. The country in which he was volunteering was volatile. Separate factions warred constantly, without respect for the safety of aid workers.

Rose let her into the lounge, where Mavis was already installed in an armchair, eating a mince pie. She had brought Dan's present with her, and placed it under the enormous Christmas tree.

'Posy will be here any minute,' Rose said, the bell on her Christmas elf hat jingling as she walked. 'Harry's in the kitchen, peeling spuds and sprouts.'

'Does he need help, with so many of us? Belle asked.

'No, he loves it. He cooks. I don't.'

'I can smell turkey and stuffing already. It's wonderful.'

Mavis nodded and wiped away crumbs. 'You should try these. Harry made them, too.'

Belle sat down with a mince pie and a glass of what Rose had called "punch".

'Wow. If I drink too many glasses of this I won't be able to find my way home,' she giggled.

The doorbell rang.

'Posy. I'll let her in,' Rose said, heading out to the front door as Harry came in, wearing an identical tinkling elf hat. Belle and Mavis laughed at Harry's questioning frown.

'What? It's Christmas. The Vicar is allowed to be silly.'

After what was one of the best Christmas lunches Belle had ever eaten, at the start of which crackers were pulled to reveal tiny racing penguins with which they had races across the table, and more silly hats, they opened presents. They had all bought something small for each other. Belle opened Dan's present, which was a beautiful long cashmere sweater, in her favourite light pink colour, with extra-long sleeves and a gap she could put her thumb through, so that the end of each sleeve covered her knuckles. It was exactly the kind of gift that Sam might have bought and it brought tears to her eyes, which she hid from the others. In the afternoon they played card games, then watched a traditional Christmas film.

By early evening she, Mavis and Posy, replete with food, fun and contentment were ready to go home. By mutual agreement no-one had discussed Emily and Star. Rose had made a quick call to Bette to see how she was coping. Bette had replied that she was so occupied with screaming grandchildren – and equally silly grown-up children who ought to know better – that she'd put it all out of her mind.

Belle was happy enough to spend Christmas evening alone, watching old films and retiring early.

On Boxing Day morning she woke early and went out for a walk. The snow had stopped, but the sky was grey and low, suggesting another snowfall was imminent. She walked along to the river bridge crossing and up into the woods on the other side, continuing upwards until she came to open ground. From here she could see the moor, but it soon disappeared under descending clouds.

She was still coming to terms with Dan Walker's revelation. Of course it was good news, which had brought back so many memories, both good and bad. Of the father she had loved so much and how she had been taken away from him because of the lies told by the mother she hated so much. Hate. Was that the right word? Professionally, she had prided herself on her ability to remain detached from the people, some of them vile, spiteful and hateful, who had sat in front of her. But her own family? Gillian? She stopped walking and closed her eyes. Yes, she hated Gillian, hard as it was to admit to such a powerful emotion. She would need to be careful in any further encounters with Peter Day that it didn't leak out.

At first the walking had been brisk and exhilarating, but after an hour, with feet and hands becoming progressively colder, she decided to head for home, just as the first snowflakes began to fall. She had deliberately put her phone on silent. There was no signal in the woods and fields, but she was surprised to find, as she reached the town and walked towards her cottage, that she had six texts and several missed WhatsApp messages.

With a sense of foreboding, she began to check.

The worst had happened. She called Bette immediately. Bert answered the call.

'Is it true, Bert?'

'Yes. The police were at the house at six this morning.'

'Has he been arrested? On what charge?

'Not sure. Been taken in for questioning in relation to the murder of Star Bright. Bette's gone to the station with the solicitor. She's going to insist he has an appropriate adult with him. Sorry, Belle, have to go. Mandy's just arrived. She's in bits.'

'But how…' Bert had cut the call off.

Georgie Morris was in police custody. She was about to ask how the police could have found out about Georgie moving the body. Someone must have told them. But who? Her phone rang.

'Belle, it's Posy. Have you heard?'

'I've just spoken to Bert. Do you know any more? How did they know?'

'Bette called me. It was her sister, she thinks. She and Bert were talking about Georgie going to the station himself, hoping they could speak to him again and persuade him. Charlie and Trevor were there. She thinks Charlie was listening, through the keyhole, so to speak. She must have called the police. They're saying it was an anonymous tip-off, but it wasn't one of us and no-one else knew.'

'Poor Georgie. Bert says Bette will insist he has an appropriate adult when he's interviewed. I hope that's allowed.'

'Me too. Susan Lewis will bludgeon him with questions and accusations until he can't tell night from day. Let me get hold of Rose and Mavis. We should keep going. I'll arrange to speak to Billy Anderson as soon as I can.'

'Good. Let me know where and when.'

**

The *where* turned out to be the vicarage. The *when*, early afternoon. Harry joined them. Belle had already called Dan. He had unbreakable family commitments later, but would set off for St Foy first thing in the morning.

'The circus will be back in town as soon as the news gets out about Georgie,' he warned. 'Try to keep out of Peter

Day's way. He never left, he stayed at the Grand over Christmas so he'll have a head start on the rest of the pack. And call me as soon as you hear anything more.'

Posy was late and simmering with anger when she arrived. They sat in Harry's small study; tense, worrying. Belle began with her discussion with Bert and their idea that it was Bette's sister who called the police.

'No,' Posy said. 'It was a man. Sorry I'm late, I've just been talking to Billy. He's on his way into work. He wasn't able to tell me more than that, but the caller was definitely a man. He also said you might want to know that Jade Waters was arrested recently, on a supplying charge. She told the arresting officers she knew something about a murder.'

'Could it have been Jade, disguising her voice?' Mavis asked. 'I've seen on TV how they can do that.'

'Could be, I suppose, but Billy seemed quite certain the voice was male. He's listened to the recording. The voice was disguised, you're right about that, Mavis. But it was a man's voice. It wasn't synthesized, but more muffled, apparently.'

'Which means that someone else knew. The only men we know of who knew about what Georgie did are Harry, Dan and Bert.'

'Definitely not me,' Harry said. 'Although I was planning to visit him, to try to persuade him. I was going to tell him I'd go with him.'

'It won't have been Dan, either,' Rose added.

'And definitely not Bert,' Belle said. 'We have to think of the wider circle of people who were around at the time. If you discount Billy, that just leaves Phil Singh, now that Gabriel Holmes is dead. Did Billy say what Susan Lewis is planning to do, Posy?'

'If she can, she'll charge him, with something to hold him. She'll try to wear him down until he admits to murder. She wants a quick result. Yet again, she isn't looking at anyone else.

Belle sat back. 'Who benefits from Georgie being charged with murder? Let's think it through.'

'Well, Emily, obviously. The other students, Billy, Phil, Jade Waters, Miriam Riley and possibly the school friend, Kylie,' Posy replied.

'Then there's Star's family, if any of them are still alive. Now that we know her real name, we should find out. Posy, did you tell Billy, like we agreed?'

'Yes. He was reluctant to claim credit. He knows Susan Lewis won't like it, but she'll have the news. He'll let me know if she follows up.'

'Is she doing anything about Gabriel Holmes' death?' Rose asked.

'Nothing yet. Billy doesn't know if she thinks it's relevant. They have a briefing later today. He's going to bring it up.' She turned to Belle. 'You're quiet.'

'I'm thinking, about something Bette said when she first told us about Georgie. When he was in the Heights looking for Star. Give me a minute.' She closed her eyes and sat back, recalling points in the conversation. Posy sent a text to Billy Anderson, to see if there were any further updates.

'Mavis, you haven't said anything. Do you have any thoughts?' Rose asked.

Mavis rubbed her hands together, then rolled her neck. 'There was something, once. But I want to speak to the people involved, before I commit myself. If that's alright with you?' She glanced around. Heads nodded.

'Got it!' Belle said. 'When Bette was describing what Georgie had told her about when he went to the Heights on Christmas Eve, he said there were some noises, rustling and shushing. I know it's an old house, but, and this is just a wild supposition, what if there was someone else in the house? Rustling I can understand, but what does "shushing" mean? Or am I going too far overboard here?'

'I would say everything's up for discussion,' Harry replied. 'The only way we're going to find out is for someone to speak to George directly, to ask him what he meant.'

Belle nodded, as Posy's phone pinged.

'It's Billy. Susan Lewis is interviewing Georgie now. He has an appropriate adult with him, as well as the solicitor. Bette is still there, waiting.'

'I think that's all we can do for now, just wait and see what comes of the interview, and what the police will do next, who they will be speaking to. We can't start talking to people if they are going to re-interview everyone there at the time.' She sighed. 'Let's go home and wait.'

Posy and Mavis nodded and stood up. 'I'll let you all know as soon as I hear anything more from Billy.'

As Belle was leaving, Rose helped her on with her coat. 'Mavis has something on her mind,' she whispered.

'I know, I could see,' Belle replied. 'But you know Mavis. She won't speak until she's absolutely certain.'

'What are you going to do now?'

'I'm going to draw up a list of who was there at the time, where we can find them, and what questions we might ask, as soon as we've heard from Billy.'

Rose nodded. 'Good plan. It's dark and more snow expected tonight. Take care. In every sense.

Chapter 15

'Bloody hell! Ouch!' Belle pulled herself up from the floor of the local supermarket, ready to speak sternly to the person who had crashed his trolley into hers, when she saw who it was, and paused. He held out a hand to help her stand.

'I am so sorry! I just wasn't looking. Are you hurt? What can I do?'

She shuddered, as a supervisor ran to her aid and took her other arm, watched by a curious group of onlookers, whose post-Christmas shop had been suddenly livened up.

'I'm fine,' she snapped at the supervisor. 'Injured pride. Bruised and embarrassed. Please, just leave it. I really am OK.' She was steadier on her feet now, but the fall had given her a shock. The man stood back.

'Sorry, again,' he said. 'Can I help you with anything?'

She grabbed the handlebar of her trolley to steady herself. 'No, Sir Joseph, you cannot. I'll just go and sit in the café for ten minutes with a cup of tea. That should do it.'

'Then allow me to buy it. I insist. And please, call me Joe. You're Belle Harrington, aren't you. You were at my book launch with Dr Walker.'

She scowled at him, but didn't object. They hadn't been formally introduced, so someone had told him her name. She moved towards the café, each step causing pain in her left calf.

'You're limping,' he said, as he took both trolleys and parked them. 'Should we get you looked at by a medical…'

'No. I lived with a medical consultant for thirty years. I know when it's serious and when it's not. Just get the tea.'

He blushed and walked to the counter. There being no blood or serious injury, the crowd had lost interest and dispersed. He returned with two mugs, putting one in front of each of them. 'Not the best, I fear,' he said, giving the contents of the cup a suspicious look. 'I was miles away as I turned the corner. And in a bit of a rush.'

'Am I keeping you from something more important?' She wasn't ready to forgive him too quickly and this was an opportunity. And her leg still hurt.

'I have a meeting. Just a moment.' He took out his phone and rattled off a text. 'Sorted. They can wait another half an hour.'

'Have you seen Emily since your book launch?'

He paused his cup at his lips. 'Yes. She's staying at her mother's old house. I went to see her the next day. She won't talk to me about where she's been or what she's been doing for the past three years. You know, she has a remarkable mind. I asked her if she'd like to work with me again.'

'Did she reply?'

'She said no, told me to go away and mind my own business.'

'Will you try again?'

He smiled. 'Probably. Emily is too clever to let that amazing brain just rot away. I'll give it some time, another week or so, then I'll try again.'

'What do you think about Georgie?'

Now he looked puzzled. 'What about him? I don't know him that well, but he did a wonderful job on our garden last year. We chatted a bit. He's remarkably knowledgeable about everything green, and passionate about nature, and I know he's Emily's older half-brother.'

'You haven't heard?'

He shook his head.

'He's been arrested. On Christmas Eve three years ago, he found Star Bright's body in the attic at the student house, wrapped in a carpet. He took it to the moor and put it on the tree branch, where it was found by the dog walker.'

Whatever Belle had expected his reaction to be, she wasn't prepared for what happened. He laughed, then shook his head. 'That makes perfect sense. I could never understand it, at the time. George and nature. He wasn't trying to hide her, though, was he? He was giving her what he thought was a natural funeral.' He put his cup down, shook his head again. 'They can't think he killed her, though, can they? Surely not. Not George. That's impossible.'

'We don't know, yet. He was interviewed yesterday.'

He leaned forward and took hold of one of her hands. 'Is there anything I can do, to help in any way? Please let me know.'

She wanted to pull her hand away, but there was something so urgent in his voice, that she left it. 'You could tell me what you remember about Star Bright, Professor… sorry, Joe. Emily told Dan and me that Star had a crush on you.'

He took his hand away, sat back and folded his arms. 'Male tutors have to be careful, when it happens. Yes, Star did, as you say, have a crush on me. Embarrassing, but there's a procedure. I reported it to the Vice Principal. He had a word.'

'Did it work?'

'If you mean, did she leave me alone, at first, yes. But then she came back.' He put his hand up to the back of his neck and rubbed it. 'She became something of a stalker. At the time, my wife was at the start of her treatment for cancer, and that girl was following me around. I did shout at her a couple of times.'

'Did you tell the police, when she died?'

He folded his arms again. 'No. Evie, my wife was ill. I had enough on my plate. I told them she had the "crush", and that I had reported it to the University, as per protocol. Nothing more ever came of it.'

'I didn't know your wife had cancer. I thought you were divorced.'

'No, not divorced. Evie died. She was a fighter, my Evie. But in the end it spread and overwhelmed her. She died six months ago. She never got to enjoy being Lady Knight.' He gave his head a quick shake and his eyes moistened. 'She'd have loved it.'

'Can I ask you, what you recall of the other students you tutored; those who lived at the Heights? I think they were Gabriel Holmes and Billy Anderson?'

'That's right.' He remained sitting back, arms folded, staring unblinkingly at her. 'You've done some homework.'

'Bette and Bert are my friends and they are in pieces. I'm interested in what happened, back then. Professional nosiness, I suppose. I used to work in Human Resources, specifically in Employee Relations.'

'Human Resources.' He said it with a moue of distaste. 'The branch that gets rid of people.'

She cocked her head to one side. 'I only recommended dismissing people who committed gross breaches of conduct. I believe in second chances. Had a problem?'

'Not personally. But I've observed some pretty bad stuff.'

'There's good and bad in every profession. I hope I was one of the good ones.'

'Ok, Gabriel and Billy. Gabriel was a waste of time. He didn't turn up for most of his lectures, which was a shame because he was a bright boy, not brilliant, but certainly more than good enough. He didn't take life seriously, though. Stuffed too much rubbish up his nose. Billy, on the other hand, was not as bright, but studious. He always tried hard and gave a hundred percent. I liked Billy. Still do.'

He sat up, glanced at his watch. 'Oh dear, more than half an hour. I must go. Are you sure you're going to be OK?'

'I'll be fine,' Belle said. 'But there's going to be a huge bruise.'

'Tell you what,' he said as he put his coat on, 'how about I buy you dinner, to make up for knocking you over. Least I can do.'

She took a deep breath. 'Yes, I'd be Ok with that.'

He took out his phone. 'Number?'

She rattled it off.

'I'll have to run now. I'll call you.'

Belle nodded and he left. She watched him as he grabbed his shopping and headed for the tills. So, Star Bright had been stalking him. Interesting development. She sat a little longer with her tea, wincing occasionally as pain shot up her calf. Something was nagging at her brain, some remark of his. She couldn't pin it down. It would come back. Her phone buzzed. A text from Dan. He was on his way back. She replied that she had something to discuss with him. He replied he would call her when he reached St Foy.

Belle stood tentatively, making sure she could put weight on her leg. It hurt, but took her weight. She took her shopping, paid and drove carefully back to St Foy, deep in thought.

Chapter 16

Back at her desk she wrote up a brief note to cover her conversation with Joseph Knight. There was no further arrangement for the club to meet until they heard from Bette, so she spent the afternoon with the romantic novel Rose had bought her for Christmas.

The text eventually arrived at five.

Georgie being held overnight on charge of Perverting the Course of Justice. Susan Lewis still trying for murder. Meet here tomorrow 9am.

Belle replied that she would be there. She was eager to find out more about Georgie, and any further news about the other students. She wondered for a moment if she was going to tell them about Joseph Knight's invitation to dinner. It wasn't a long think. Of course she was going to tell them. As she had been writing her notes, it had come to her that, in the past six months, a number of seemingly unrelated tragic events had occurred. She began a list, starting with the most distant to the most recent, June to December.

June: Sir Joseph Knight's wife Evie dies, breast cancer
August: Bette's sister Rita dies, breast cancer
October: Gabriel Holmes dies, of a drug overdose
November: Jade Waters arrested on a drugs charge, says she knows about someone being killed, but refuses to give details
December: Emily returns. Says she didn't kill anyone
December: Georgie Morris arrested: perverting the course of justice and potentially murder.

She had just finished when her phone rang again. This time it was Posy.

'Belle, have you heard from Mavis today? I was going to offer her a lift to the farm in the morning, but she's not answering her phone.'

'No, sorry Posy. I was out all morning, then at home all afternoon. Are you concerned?

'No, I suppose not. But she doesn't drive. And she's usually home by this time. She did say she was going to visit someone, a friend I think. Maybe she's just not back yet, or staying overnight.'

'Yes, you're probably right. It's freezing outside. Perhaps her friend didn't want to drive her back late in the dark. Bette's asked us to be there at nine, so if she's away she'll probably get a lift from whoever she's with, or a taxi, in the morning. We'll see her there.'

'Agreed. I have some news,' Belle added.

'Me too.'

But when they assembled the following morning, Mavis wasn't there. They waited half an hour, called her again, messaged her, without any response.

'I'm going back down to town,' Posy said. 'Do you all mind waiting? I'll go to her cottage, make sure she's OK.'

Dan arrived just as she was leaving. 'Sorry, I only arrived back at midnight, and I've overslept. Where's Posy going? What have I missed?'

Bette put a cup of coffee in front of him and explained they hadn't heard from Mavis. He frowned. 'I don't like the sound of that. I hope she hasn't had a fall anywhere. It was cold last night. As I drove back in, the roads were icy. Coming down the hill was a nightmare. My car slid and slipped a couple of times.'

'Aren't you just the prophet of doom and gloom?' Bette muttered as she made more coffee. It was twenty minutes before Bette's phone rang.

'Posy,' she said as she answered. They all turned to watch as she listened, then sat up stiff and anxious as Bette's face whitened and her mouth dropped open. She put the phone down on the table with shaking hands.

'Mavis's cottage was burgled last night. It's a complete mess. Posy let herself in and found Mavis unconscious on the hall floor, with a horrible head wound. Posy's called an ambulance. They're on their way now. She's going to ride to the hospital with them.'

'She must have lain there all night. Someone should be there with Posy,' Rose said, and stood up. 'Harry and I will go.' She grabbed her coat and marched out of the kitchen.

Belle, horrified though she was, hadn't moved. Mavis had said before Christmas that she had seen something once, when they were talking about the time of Star Bright's death. Posy had thought Mavis was going to visit someone yesterday.

'You're deep in thought.' Dan's voice pulled her back to the kitchen, where Bette was telling Bert what had happened, and he was offering to drive her immediately into Truro. 'We need to be in the magistrate's court at eleven. We can go to the hospital as soon as that's over and done.'

Bette nodded. 'We're going. You two, let yourselves out when you're done. The kids and grandkids have left, but Ben's still in bed.'

They were gone in minutes. Belle and Dan sat at the table.

'Back to your place?' Dan said after a few minutes.

**

At first, neither of them wanted to talk. They sat in front of the fire, phones on the coffee table, staring into space, waiting.

'I should have gone round to check, but it was cold and icy,' Belle said.

'You had a suspicion that someone might have fooled Mavis into opening the door, hit her on the head and left her dead?'

'No, of course not!'

'Then stop blaming yourself and feeling sorry for yourself. That's not you.'

She was about to reply when the first message arrived from Bette, following the hearing at the Magistrate's Court.

Georgie out on bail. Date will be set for trial. Lewis spitting tacks. Speak later.

'That's one blessing,' Dan said. 'The family will gather around him.'

'I want to speak to him, to ask him about the noises in the Heights, when he was looking for Star on Christmas Eve. He said there was a "shushing" sound, or sounds. I want to know what he meant, plus anything else he remembers about noises in the house at the time.'

'You think there may have been someone else there?'

She nodded. 'It may just have been his imagination, but it's worth asking. Dan, there's something else. This may seem like I'm putting two and two together and reaching a silly number, but I've been thinking about events that have happened in the past six months. Could you take a look at this?' She picked up the paper that had been lying face down on the table and handed it to him. He took it and read it through. When he had finished he put the paper back down on the table.

'What do you want me to say? Set out like this, they look like a story. But I can't see what the deaths of two women, who were already dying of cancer, have to do with anything else.'

Belle sighed. 'No more can I, for now. I just get this nagging in my gut. It's a bloody nuisance, but it tells me that I've hit on something. What, I have no idea, yet.'

'If there are links, you need to find them. Where will you start?'

She leaned across and hugged him. 'Thank you for not laughing at me.'

'I would never do that. Although, I think you'll find it hard to link some, or any, of these events. But a nagging gut must be obeyed. So, again, where will you start?'

'I want to speak to the students, to start with. Get their individual take on what was going on in that house in the weeks leading up to Star's death, before they all left for Christmas.'

'Unless it was just a senseless, random act borne out of anger, or frustration, or temper, and instantly regretted.'

'Possible, yes. Likely, no. They lived closely together. It was years ago, but I spent one year in a similar situation. Five girls sharing a house. It wasn't all fun and roses. There were arguments, petty squabbles, spiteful acts. Mainly borne out through relationships that went on during the year. We were all supposed to be friends and I suppose that's how it looked on the surface, but underneath, there was a current of discomfort that I've never forgotten. Perhaps it was the same there.'

'You were five young women. The dynamic at the Heights had the extra dimension of young men. Who was doing what with who, and who didn't like it. Yes, probably a good place to start. You'll start with Emily, or you'll try?'

'Yes. I think I might just go around to her mother's house, see if I can catch her in, and try to get myself invited in for a chat.'

'Good luck with that,' Dan said. 'I'll be surprised if you get beyond the doorstep.'

'Don't underestimate me, Dan Walker. Getting people to talk to me is something I do rather well.'

'That I don't doubt.'

Before she could reply, her phone rang. Posy. 'Before you start to tell me anything Posy, Dan's here with me, so I'm putting you on speaker.'

'OK. Mavis is in a bad way. She has a serious head injury. It'll be touch and go for the next twenty-four hours. If she makes it that far, no-one will say how she might be or what treatment she'll need. It's going to be a day-by-day decision.'

'Are you staying at the hospital?'

'Yes, for now. Rose and Harry have gone home, but they're coming back later. Bette and Bert are here, too.' She paused. 'Belle and Dan, how do you feel about carrying on with the Emily and Star case, just the two of you? Rose, Harry and I can give you any information we have, and help in any way; same for Bette and Bert. We want to make sure someone is always here, for when Mavis does recover. But the majority of it will be just the two of you.'

Belle looked at Dan. He nodded. 'Fine for both of us. Keep your phone handy, though, I'll need to call you. And to start, do you think you could ask Billy Anderson to speak to us? Strictly off the record?'

'I'll get hold of him. I don't know how much he's going to be involved with what's happened to Mavis. It's just a small police force. I'll do my best.'

'That's all we can ask of you,' Belle replied. 'You get back to Mavis now, and please let us know if there's any change. For the better, or worse.'

'Looks like it's just us,' Dan said. 'You can be Holmes. I shall be Watson, providing careful thought to your brilliant deductions.'

'And some common sense, when I get carried away,' Belle replied. 'Right, get your coat on, Watson. We're not sitting around here. We'll going to see if Emily Duggan is at home.'

'Now? What are we going to say to her? What questions?'

'No idea,' Belle replied. 'I haven't prepared anything, so we're going to wing it.'

'This is going to be fun,' he replied. 'I never imagined my quiet little retreat from the world would turn into a den of iniquity.'

'It's not that, yet.'

'But the possibility is to hand. Let's go, maestro.'

She gave him a sarcastic look and led him out of the back door, through the garden to her garage, so intent on what she would say to Emily, and discussing possibilities, that neither of them noticed they were being followed.

Chapter 17

Bette and Bert had taken Georgie back to the farm, despite his protests that he just wanted to go home. When they explained that Mandy wanted to stay with them for a couple of days, because she had had reporters constantly hammering on the door, and at the farm they wouldn't be able to reach him on private land, he gave in.

'Don't want to talk to nobody,' he muttered.

'You'll talk to Mandy and to me and Bert,' Bette said, in her "don't argue with me" voice. 'And to the lawyer.'

'I got nothing to say,' he muttered again from the back seat of the car.

'Oh yes you have,' Bette replied. 'We'll be helping you, whether you like it or not, to keep you out of prison.'

He didn't reply to that. One night in the local cells had terrified him. The drunks, both happy and hostile, the young man who had threatened to kill him – in fairness, he had threatened to kill everyone there – the woman who had tried to sell him drugs, was the stuff of nightmares for Georgie. The prospect of long term prison reduced him to horrified trembling.

Once they had installed him in the kitchen and after Mandy had both hugged and yelled at him, they sent him for a shower and a change of clothes. Mandy had brought a suitcase for each of them.

When he finally emerged from the bathroom his skin showed signs of attempts to rub it raw, which he had done to remove the smell of the prison cell.

'Look, Georgie, Bert and I aren't going to ask you any questions, but you know my group of special friends, including Belle Harrington. You like Belle, don't you?' He nodded. 'She wants to ask you a couple of questions. You are going to answer them, because, like I said, keeping you out of prison is our number one priority. We know you didn't kill Star, but what you did was…' she stopped as Bert pulled on her sleeve. They had agreed not to dump their anger onto Georgie's head. 'It won't make us feel any better,' Bert had said, 'and it's likely to make him mute, the fear of it all.'

Bette had seen the sense of that.

'Anyway, you and Mandy are staying with us for a few days at least, until the fuss dies down, or at least until we've found out what really happened to that poor girl. Your Will is with our grandkids. One of the lads is at the entrance down on the road, so the press lot can't get close. But remember, if you go outside, they do have those very long lenses.'

'Not going outside, then,' he said. 'Staying in here.'

'For the best,' Bert said gently, 'until this is all over, which it will be soon.'

'That policewoman says I killed Star,' Georgie raised his arms and hugged his head. 'I didn't kill her. I didn't kill her.' He began to sob.

'We know that, Georgie. Now, we have to prove it,' Bette replied. She turned to Bert. 'And the sooner we can get on with it, the better. I'm just going into the sitting room, to check in, see what's been happening, and see if there's any more news about Mavis.'

Bette left George to Mandy and Bert's gentle ministrations. She needed action. A message came back from Belle in immediate response to her contact.

Dan and I on our way to speak to Emily. Posy trying to set up a chat for me with Billy Anderson when he's off duty. Want to speak to all of the students. Everyone involved, asap.

This was more like it. She sent a message back.

Georgie here now. Told him you want to speak.

Not yet. Will let you know. come here when you're done with Emily?

Yes, we'll drive over.

**

Emily's mother's old house was at the top of the town, ten minutes' walk from the harbour, on Sugar Pit Lane. It was in the middle of a row of bland houses, built in the 1970s. Most of the row was well kept, with a few steps leading up to a path to the front door, with a small patch of garden. This house was the exception. It had been uninhabited for long enough to have become overgrown with weeds, which were also growing out through cracks in the path. They found a parking space on the road, which was the only one available. Planners in the 1970s had no vision of ordinary people being able to afford even one car, never mind several, so no provision had been made and the road was crammed full.

As they reached the broken gate at the bottom of the steps, Dan gave the pathway a dubious look. 'She hasn't made any attempt to make it safe. I can see ice.'

'She probably doesn't want people trying,' Belle replied. 'There'll be a back door she uses. Come on. We'll have to risk it.'

They made it to the front door, a couple of times hanging onto the branches of an overgrown hedge separating Emily's front garden from next door, and rang the bell. No answer.

Belle hammered on the wooden part of the door frame and peered through the frosted glass.

'I can't see any movement,' she said. 'I don't think she's here.'

Dan had stepped back to look up. 'Not so. The bedroom curtain just twitched. Knock again.'

Instead of knocking, Belle bent down and yelled through the letterbox. 'Emily! It's Belle Harrington, and Dan Walker is with me. We want to talk to you. Now!'

After a few moments' silence, there was still no sound and no obvious signs of occupancy. Belle shrugged and they were about to walk away when Belle caught sight of movement through the glass. The door opened a few inches.

'What do you want?' Emily looked as if she had just got out of bed.

Dan stepped forward. 'We want to talk to you, Emily. Your brother is out on bail, not yet charged with murder, but that's still on the cards. You said you didn't kill anyone. We don't believe you killed Star. However, someone did and we want to find out who that was. So, can we please come in because it's bloody cold out here.'

Emily hesitated a moment, then closed the door slightly, removed a heavy chain, and let them in. Ahead of them, on the immediate left, was a staircase. Belle could see a kitchen at the end of a corridor running beside the stairs. On the immediate right was a door, which led into a sitting room. It had a sitting area at one end and a dining area, with a door to the kitchen at the dining end. At the sitting end was an old fashioned gas fire, which Emily lit and warmth spread quickly through the room.

'Please sit,' she said. 'I'm going to get dressed.' She closed the door to the hall.

As they waited, they heard someone walking down the stairs. Whoever it was didn't enter the living room, but walked past in the direction of the kitchen. There was a faint sound of a door closing.

Emily appeared a few minutes later, in old jeans and a hooded sweatshirt, with bare feet. Her hair had been pulled back into an untidy ponytail. She settled into an armchair, sitting upright, the hint of a smile on her face as she watched Belle and Dan, both seated on the settee.

'Fire away, then. I'll tell you what I told the police.'

They had agreed to leave the questioning to Belle and the observation to Dan.

'Why weren't you in court this morning?' The question was meant to unsettle Emily, to rattle her, and the quick intake of breath told Belle it had done just that.

'Georgie and I don't get on. He wouldn't have appreciated me being there. He thinks I killed Star.'

'I was there when he went for you. Why does he think that?'

Emily shrugged. 'Because he was crazy about her and I was her best friend, until I wasn't. And he's a moronic idiot. Probably like his father, whoever that was. Mum never said.'

Belle bit her lips and ignored the provocation. 'You and Star fell out?'

Emily nodded. 'Big time.'

'Why?'

'Your questions are better than that policewoman's.'

'Humour me, please. Why did you and Star fall out, big time?'

'Because of Gabriel. She was nuts about him. He and I were sleeping together at the time.'

'At what time?'

'From about the middle of November.'

'Right up to the end of term?'

Emily nodded.

'At the book launch you said Star was obsessed with your tutor, Joseph Knight. You said she was stalking him.'

'Star wanted someone to love her. She moved from man to man, but none of them ever lived up to her expectations. At first, I sympathised. Then, it just became boring.'

'Did she have expectations of Georgie?'

Emily laughed. 'Hell, no, she could see he was a hopeless halfwit, but she felt sorry for him.'

'Did she encourage him?'

'Not really. But she didn't discourage him, either.'

'Does that mean she was kind to him?'

'Perhaps. I don't know.'

'Who else was involved with another person at the Heights?'

'Everyone. It was like Sodom and Gomorrah. Over the term, everyone had a go at everyone else. It was quite amusing.'

'What about you?'

'Not so much. I slept with Gabriel at the party…' she stopped abruptly.

'What party?'

'I can't remember much about it.'

'Try. What else happened at that party?'

Emily shrugged. 'I don't know, it was just a party, after term exams finished. You know, or maybe you don't. The usual, drink, drugs, shagging, fun. No-one talking about what they did and who with, the next day. Hangovers, the usual.'

'Was everyone there?'

'All except Miriam. She never joined in anything and mummy particularly disapproved of student parties. Phil didn't stay long. Gabe had invited lots of people.'

'How long had you and Star been best buddies?'

Emily shook her head. 'Not that long, I suppose. A couple of months.'

'Is that a long time for you to have a best friend?'

'That's really none of your business.'

'Where did you go after Bette dropped you in the city?'

'Scotland.'

'Why Scotland?'

Emily shrugged again. 'It just happened. I was pregnant. I had the termination, but not in the clinic Bette took me to, somewhere else. I'd had enough. I didn't want to go back to any of it. I got on a bus to London. When it arrived in Victoria, there was another bus going to Edinburgh. On that bus I met a girl. She lived in some kind of retreat, she told me. It sounded like somewhere I could go. So I went. I liked it. It was soothing.'

'Did it suddenly stop being soothing, last week?'

Emily smiled. 'I think you should go now.'

'Did you know your mother had died?'

'I said, you should go now.'

'I'll take that as a "yes". Who told you?'

Emily stood up. 'Please leave. You're upsetting me.'

'Of course. We don't want to upset you, but you've already upset a lot of people, people who tried to help you, like Bette and Bert?

Emily laughed. 'Those two, they couldn't help each other out of a paper bag. Uncle Bert still has his good looks, but Aunty Bette, typical farmer's wife. Huh. Short, fat, permed and stupid.'

Without speaking Belle and Dan stood and walked out of the room. Belle's fingers were itching to slap the smug grin off Emily's face. At the front door, Belle paused and took a deep breath. 'One more question, Emily. Same as before. Who do you think killed Star, if it wasn't you?'

'No idea,' she said, and slammed the door behind them.

After they had negotiated the steps, they sat in Belle's car. Dan spoke first.

'That was interesting,' he said. 'And you, amazing. I wanted to slap her. You didn't so much as twitch.'

'Don't think I didn't. What a bitch, after everything Bette and Bert did for her. We need to compare notes. I was concentrating on her. Did you notice anything in particular in the room, or the hallway?'

'Yes. She wasn't alone. Someone else was upstairs. A man.'

'I heard the footsteps. What makes you think it was a man?'

'There were two coats on the hall stand, and a couple of scarves and a hat.'

'The coats I get, but scarves and hats could have been there since her mother died.'

'True. However, one of the coats was a man's quilted parka, a cold weather coat and it looked new. The hat was a black beanie, also not three years old, which would have been covered with some accumulated dust.'

'A beanie, so a young man?' Belle mused. 'I wonder who that might be?'

Before she could say more, a car pulled up in a parking spot that had freed up in front of them. Joseph Knight emerged from the driver's seat. He was wearing a smart overcoat with a scarf and a pair of perfectly polished black leather shoes that looked to Belle like they wouldn't grip well on the pavement or the steps. As he closed and locked his car door he saw them, hesitated, then walked carefully towards Belle's car. She wound down the window.

'Hello to both of you. Are you just arriving or leaving?'

'Leaving,' Dan replied.

'Is Emily at home?'

Yes, we've just had a quick chat.'

'I'm hoping she'll speak to me. As you know, Belle, she wouldn't let me in last time I tried. I don't like doorstepping people, but I'm guessing it worked?' He rubbed his leather gloves together and blew on the fingers, as he spoke.

'She gave us ten minutes,' Belle replied. 'She's not in a polite mood.'

'I'll hope for the same amount of time, but a better mood,' he said with a grin. 'I'll give you a call later, about dinner. Those steps look daunting.' He turned and headed cautiously up to the door. They waited, as he knocked. This time, it was flung open, but as soon as Emily saw who it was, she went to slam it closed again. However, he seemed to have put a foot in the door. Words were exchanged, the accompanying gestures on both sides suggesting she didn't want to speak to him, despite his imploring. Then, she let him in and closed the door.

'This just gets more and more interesting,' Dan remarked, as Belle pulled the car out onto the road. 'Let's get to Bette's farm. You can tell me all about your dinner.'

**

The entrance to the farm was now guarded by two of the farmhands, their pitchforks keeping the rapidly diminishing crowd of cameras and press pinned to a narrow grass verge next to a deep ditch half filled with black snow melt. Bert and Bette had given them a list of people who could be allowed in. It was a short list. They drove past the half dozen shivering press, up the winding drive and parked outside the front door.

Bette let them in. 'Sorry about the armed guard. I don't know why they bother. Georgie isn't coming close to the door, never mind past it.'

'I expect they've been told they have to get something,' Belle replied, stripping off coat, scarf, hat, gloves and boots. 'It's lovely and warm in here.'

'It's the Aga,' Bette replied. 'Wood fired, so we can keep it on twenty-four seven.'

'How's Georgie doing?'

'Not well. He's in the living room with Mandy. Go on in, both of you. Don't expect to get much out of him.'

As soon as she saw Georgie, Belle understood what Bette meant. He was sitting in an armchair, his head down on his chest, his hands clasped behind his neck, elbows covering his ears, rocking back and forth. Mandy sat on the side arm of the chair, gently stroking his back. He didn't so much as glance up to see who had come into the room.

'Georgie,' Belle said, as quietly as possible. 'It's Belle Harrington and Dan is with me. You remember us, I think.'

No reaction or response.

'We aren't going to ask you any questions about what or why. You've been through a terrible ordeal. As far as we're concerned you did what you thought was right at the time, and that's good enough for us. We do have a couple of important questions about something we think may help you. Would it be OK to ask?'

Again, no response but the rocking stopped. Belle waited. He moved his elbows away from his head. 'What questions?'

'It's about what you heard that day, before you found Star. Bette told me you heard some noises as you walked around the house. I want to ask you about those noises, if you can manage that. Do you think you can?'

His head raised up a few inches. 'It was creepy,' he whispered. 'I didn't like that place.'

'Understandable,' Dan said. 'I don't think anyone liked it much. It wasn't just you.'

George's head nodded. 'It creaked. And it whispered.'

'I want to ask you about the whispering, George. Was it like voices?'

He shook his head. 'More like plants sometimes do, when the wind blows through them. They go...'

He took his hands off the back of his neck and made a sound of 'Shushhhh, shushhhh,' He was looking at her, now.

Belle nodded. 'I know what you mean.' She put a finger to her lips and made a noise. 'Shushhhhhhhhh... shushhhhhhhhh. Like that, Georgie?'

'Yes, that was it.'

'And can you remember where you were when you heard the noise?'

'I was just about to go up the staircase to the attic. I don't like the attic. The stairs creak. You think they're going to crack under your feet. There was a door, open, next to the stairs. Coming from in that room, it was.'

Mandy gave Belle a puzzled look, and went to speak, but Belle shook her head. 'Did you hear the same noise anywhere else in the house, Georgie?'

'No, just there, like the plants.'

'You've been back many times, since the house became unused and empty, right?'

'Might have done.' He shrank back in the chair.

'It's OK, Georgie. I just want to know, did you ever hear that same noise again?'

He sat up, frowning, thinking. 'No, I've heard the wind moaning there, deep and long, like it's crying almost, and the creaking. But, no, not the trees shushing to each other.'

Belle nodded. 'Thanks, Georgie. That's what I wanted to know. We'll leave you now. You take care. Bette and Bert will look after you. Dan and I have more things to do. Can we come to see you again, soon?'

'Yes, please, Mrs Harrington. We can talk about your garden.'

'A very good idea. I want to do a lot more when Spring comes and I'm going to need your help.'

She signalled to Dan and they both stood and went back to the kitchen, where Bette was waiting.

'Well?'

'My idea was right. I'm sure there was someone else in the house when Georgie took Star's body. Probably two people. I'm guessing now, but I think they didn't hear him come in, didn't hear him at all until he was walking towards the upper staircase, when one shushed the other. To him, it sounded just like trees sighing in the wind. But it wasn't. It was two people, who were also there to move the body. He beat them to it.'

'And now they, whoever they are, must be laughing their heads off, because unless someone can figure out who it was, Georgie is going to take the full blame.'

'Looks that way,' Belle replied.

'Will you stay for lunch?' Bert asked.

Dan began to nod, but Belle cut in. 'Thanks Bert but no. We have things to do.'

'Do we?'

'Yes, John Daniel, we do. We're going to Bedlam Heights.'

Bert grinned. 'I'll make you turkey sandwiches to go.'

Chapter 18

Dan had declined the turkey sandwiches, but was determined that, as soon as they had visited the Heights they were going to go somewhere of his choosing for lunch.

'We need to sit down, eat something pleasant and review the plan,' he said, as Belle drove along the A30, which had, mercifully, been cleared of the latest snowfall, and gritted.

It didn't take long to reach the turn-off that led down a series of lanes and find the entrance to the Heights. There had been no gritting here and Belle had to drive carefully to make sure she didn't slide into one of the ditches lining the road.

'Can I suggest we leave the car at the end of the driveway and walk up to the building?' Dan said, after a couple of near misses.

'Agreed,' Belle replied. 'Look, there's the entrance. At least there's a bit of a bank, not too steep and it doesn't look like there's been much traffic on this route today.'

They left the car, Dan praying that they would be able to get off the banked grass without either of them having to push, and began the short walk up the driveway.

The house stood not far from the edge of Bodmin Moor.

'You wouldn't think this was less than a mile or so from the main University and the town,' Dan said, as their boots crunched in the almost foot deep snow.

The driveway inclined up to the house. When they reached it, there was a view of the higher areas of the moor, bare and beautiful in the sunlit snowscape. It was surrounded by trees and leylandii that had grown untamed and were now almost as tall as the house itself. Not having been occupied for three years, there had been an attempt to board up the windows and the door, but some of the boards had either been ripped away or had just rotted off. A solitary piece of jagged edged wood covered the front door.

'Shouldn't be too difficult to find a way in,' Belle said.

'Before we try anything, or touch anything, put these on.' He handed her a pair of nitrile gloves and a mask. Best not to leave any evidence of our being here. He was looking around, puzzled, when Belle said, 'Are you able to climb through a window, if that's what we need to do?'

Dan gave her a scornful look, walked up to the door and turned the handle. The door creaked open. 'Or we could just walk in, your sense of adventure notwithstanding.'

She walked past him with a pout and into the main hall. Once, this had been a loved and cared for residence. Now, after years of student occupation and recent neglect, it was a dirty, smelly shambles, and freezing cold. Frost had penetrated to the bottom of the main wide staircase on their left. The remainder of the hall was square, with three doors leading off, all closed. Damp had also left its mark. Wallpaper hung in strips and the walls looked wet. Belle walked up to a door, stopped and pulled at a hanging strip of paper. It came away easily, taking crumbling plaster with it.

'Don't touch too much,' Dan warned, as she opened the door. 'You could take an entire wall down.'

The room she had accessed might once have been a sitting or study room. It was square in shape, with a substantial fireplace and had a bay window opposite the door, now covered by closed shutters. Dan tried a light switch. Nothing happened. He walked across to the window and tentatively lifted a latch that held the shutters together, then, with great care, moved one shutter back to let in light.

'There are no radiators,' Belle said, looking around. 'How did they heat this place in winter?'

'Maybe it's a room they didn't use,' Dan suggested. 'Let's take a look at the others on this floor.'

Two more rooms were of a similar size, again with shutters and a fireplace, but no radiators. A short corridor to their right led to a small cupboarded area, next to a narrow staircase and an open door into the kitchen and dining room, at the back of the house. The fixtures and fittings had been ripped away. The double size kitchen was bare. The cold floor, which had also been infiltrated by frost, was covered by an old-fashioned linoleum. There was a back door that led out onto a small patio. The view might once have been a panorama of the moor, but now was blocked by the wildly overgrown leylandii.

'Nothing more to see here,' Dan said. 'Let's go upstairs.'

Every step of the staircase creaked as they tiptoed up, turning on the halfway landing, then up to the top, where they found two bedrooms and a bathroom. A corridor wrapping around the corner had a further three doors. At the end of that corridor another turn led to a further landing, with two bedrooms and another bathroom off to the right, plus another narrower, steeper staircase leading down.

'That's the one down to the kitchen area,' Dan said. 'The original owners must have had servants. This is the "back stairs". The family wouldn't have used it.' They had walked slowly around as they passed each door, which they opened, finding only an empty room each time. Standing on the landing, there was another, narrower, wooden door. When they opened it, another staircase confronted them, this time leading upwards. After the first three steps it bent around, so that they couldn't see what was at the top. A skylight in the roof let some light in through its covering of snow. The attic took up the width and length of the house.

'Let's go, then,' Belle said, leading the way. The staircase was so narrow they had to go up single file. It was steep. After the bend there was a rail, which they each grabbed onto with both hands. At the top, they turned right and onto a short corridor, with a door at each end and one in the middle.

'Where shall we start?' Dan asked.

Belle opened the first door, to her immediate left. It led into the eaves at the gable end. There was no light at all. She took out her phone and activated its torch.

'Put your torch on, too,' she whispered to Dan.

'Why are you whispering?' he asked, as the second torchlight lit up the space.

'I don't know,' she replied. 'Because a dead body lay somewhere up here. I don't feel like I should make a lot of noise.'

'Well, it didn't lie here,' Dan replied. 'Look at the floor. Good job we didn't just step in.'

None of this area had been boarded. There were gaps between thick planks.

'We'd have gone through to one of the bedroom ceilings. It's empty. There's nothing to see here.' As he spoke something scurried past Belle's leg and she gasped and jumped back.

'Mice,' Dan said. 'Hopefully. There's probably bats in here too. Nice quiet habitat for them.'

Belle stepped further back and slammed the door shut.

'The other end is probably the same. Why don't you take a look in the middle section. I'll check out the other end. I like bats.'

Belle scowled at him, and took the few steps along the corridor to the middle door, as Dan passed her and opened up the opposite end.

'Nothing to see here either,' he shouted.

'There's plenty in here,' Belle shouted back. 'Come and see.'

The room was huge and filled with junk. Some of it was very old, she could see. A nineteenth century desk and chair, a few pieces of dark, heavy furniture that might have been moved up here when the original family moved out. And there were the remains of whatever the students didn't take: a couple of simple desks and chairs, a cheap plywood cupboard, and dozens of boxes full of discarded and unwanted junk.

'This is where he found her, wrapped in the carpet,' Belle said over her shoulder to Dan, who was standing in the doorway.

'Anything occur to you yet?' he asked.

'Such as?'

'We walked up the driveway through untouched snow. No-one else has been here since it began snowing.'

'So?'

'So, the police should have been all over this. When we decided to come here, I presumed they would have been all over it and gone already. I even thought we might have been barred from entering. But there's no evidence of any attempt to check it out. What the hell is that woman thinking? A murdered corpse was put here. Susan Lewis should have sent a team. I know it was years ago, but still…'

'Of course,' Belle said. 'You're right. I know she has a reputation for being lazy, but this is shocking. And unacceptable.'

'Trouble now is, if they do come here, they'll find they weren't the first.'

'If they come here, it creates a dilemma for us. Should we report that we've been here?' Belle said. 'If we do, she'll accuse us of tampering with evidence. If we don't, well, I don't know.'

'One more thing to do before we go,' Dan said. 'Come on, back down to that servant station.'

At the bottom of the staircase he stopped. 'Let's try out your theory. I'll stand here, you go into that bedroom,' he pointed to the one closest to the staircase, 'and make a shushing noise. Let's see if I can hear you. Leave the door ajar.'

She did so, making a short noise.

'I can hear you, but I don't think it's enough. Try a couple of shushes.'

He listened. 'That's better.'

When she came back out he was smiling.

'What?'

'There were two people in that room, one panicking, the other calmer, trying to keep the first one quiet. They probably crept down the backstairs once Georgie had gone up into the attic. They could have exited via the back door, then waited to see what he'd do. Must have been quite a shock when he came down with the body wrapped in the carpet.'

'Do you think they followed him?'

'Who knows? But they must have seen the 'get out of jail card' it gave them. They had put the body there, probably being careful to remove anything that would have led to them. Georgie just picked the body up and took it away. His DNA would have been all over it, a real gift to whoever it was.'

'We'd better go,' Belle said. 'Just in case Susan Lewis does decide to send someone in.'

**

They drove across to the north coast, to Padstow, where Dan knew a particular restaurant overlooking the pretty harbour. The town was busy, many of the holiday visitors either newly arrived for the New Year celebrations or not yet returned home after Christmas.

As they sat, Belle's phone pinged a text.

'It's from Rose at the hospital. Mavis is still very poorly. The doctors won't give a prognosis.' She shook her head. 'Whoever did this to her is a monster.'

Dan reached across the table and took her hand. 'Then it's up to us to find out what happened. Susan Lewis isn't going to do anything other than try to get Georgie to confess to killing Star. She may try to get him for the attack on Mavis, too. You're the brains and the planner. What do we do next?'

A waiter arrived and took their order, which gave Belle a few minutes to think. When she had gone, Belle said, 'Our original plan still stands. We have to find out more about what went on at that house in the week, or weeks leading up to Star's death. Next, we should speak to the remaining four students. And we do it today and tomorrow. Phil Singh works at the hospital in Truro. After lunch, let's go there.'

'Good plan, Sherlock.'

Belle's phone pinged a text. 'It's Posy,' she said. 'Oh, excellent, she says Billy is off duty at six this evening and willing to speak to us. He'll come to the cottage if that's ok with me. Can you do six?'

'Of course. Let her know. Ah, food. Tuck in. You'll like this.'

Following lunch and a quick walk around the harbour, they headed off to Truro. Before looking for Phil Singh they looked in on Rose in the Intensive Care area. They wouldn't be allowed in, they knew, due to Covid restrictions, but Rose was able to give them an update.

'It's just Harry and me with her. No-one else allowed. The protocols are very strict.'

'She's not too good, then?' Belle asked.

'No. Belle, she may not make it.'

Belle gave Rose a hug. 'She's tougher than she looks. I presume Harry has the whole town praying?'

'Rose smiled. 'Of course. How's the investigation going? Bette keeps me up to date about Georgie.'

'That's not a good situation either. Dan and I believe Susan Lewis is going to try to browbeat a confession out of him. We're doing our best, Rose, but there's still a lot more to uncover and that's why we're here. We're trying to find Phil Singh, hoping he's on duty and will speak to us.'

'Good luck,' Rose whispered. 'He's up in paediatrics.'

They made their way up two floors to the paediatrics department, rang the bell and asked for Dr Singh.

'Are you parents?' the harassed nurse said. 'I haven't seen you before.'

'No, we're here to have a word with Dr Singh.'

'He's very busy.'

'Please tell him we're here about Star.'

The nurse tutted and marched off, saying over her shoulder, 'I don't expect he'll have time for you.'

'Nice,' Dan muttered.

'They're overwhelmed, don't blame her. She's probably doing the job of at least three people, like everywhere else in the NHS.'

They waited outside the door for five minutes. No-one came.

'If he's not able to see us, that's OK, given we've doorstepped him at work. But he could have sent someone to tell us,' Dan said.

As he spoke, a tall man in a shirt with rolled up sleeves and waistcoat, with a stethoscope around his neck, appeared at the top of the corridor on the other side of the locked door. He paused for a few seconds, then marched down towards them, pushed a buzzer which opened the door, and stepped out in front of them.

'I'm Phil Singh. Who are you and what do you want? I'm very busy.' The voice was low and melodious, the kind to sooth anxious parents.

'I'm Belle Harrington, this is Dr Dan Walker. We're friends of Bette Jones. You know Emily Duggan is back?'

He nodded, swallowing.

'Have you heard the police have charged Georgie Morris for perverting the course of justice?'

'No! Georgie had nothing to do with what happened. That's madness.'

'We agree with you, Dr Singh. Look, would you be willing to speak to us, after you finish work?' Dan asked. 'We want to know more about what happened in that house in the days and weeks leading up to Star Bright's death.'

He thought for a minute. 'Yes, I'll talk to you. I'm here until ten tonight. Then, I'm on again at eight in the morning. I can see you either late or early. Up to you.'

'Where do you live?' Belle asked. 'We can come to you, if that makes it easier.'

'No, that's not convenient. How about here, tomorrow morning at seven? There's a small café at the entrance to the hospital grounds.'

Belle looked at Dan, who nodded.

'Thank you, Dr Singh. We'll see you in the morning.'

'That's a result,' Belle said as they walked back to her car.

'Yes and I'll drive this time. Pick you up at half six?'

'Works for me. Now we have to get back to get ready to speak to Billy Anderson.'

Chapter 19

Billy arrived exactly at six. He was a strapping six feet plus young man, with black hair. Belle imagined that in his police uniform he would appear a formidable force. Out of uniform he looked anxious and vulnerable, glancing around as he stood on the doorstep, relieved as he saw the curtains were drawn.

'Who are you worried about, Billy?' Belle asked as she guided him to a seat then went to get him a coffee.

'A few people; my boss, any of the reporters, most of the locals. You're coming to the attention of my boss, you know. She doesn't like it.'

'Let us worry about that, Billy,' Dan said. 'We're not interested in your current investigation, as such. We want to know about the past, before you joined the force.'

'University, you mean?'

The young man sat forward on the edge of the armchair, hands clasped on his knees. 'No-one asked as much as they should have done back then. I realise that now.'

'I suspect a certain no-one still isn't asking as much as she should. The past is as relevant to what you're facing now as it was back then,' Dan said.

Billy nodded, as Belle returned with a mug of coffee and put it in front of him.

'I was just saying to Billy, that the relevance of the events of the past are crucial to what's going on now. He told me his boss doesn't appear to agree,' Dan said.

'Absolutely. If we don't really know who did what, and when, around the time Star died, it will be impossible to understand the motivation to kill her. You were right in the middle of it, Billy. We're hoping you can share some of your memories with us.'

Before Billy arrived, Belle had decided on a gentle chat, rather than what might feel like a cross examination, more a teasing out of memory. Dan agreed that he would watch. He was an excellent observer of body language, even better than herself. He would only intervene if he felt there was a relevant fact that needed more probing. They were hoping for a revelation, as Billy relaxed and talked to them.

'How did you come to be one of the group at the Heights, Billy? Were you sent there or was it a choice on your part?' A simple non-threatening question to start, she hoped.

'A choice, definitely. I found the halls of residence too confining after a couple of years. I had a small car, so it was easy enough to get to and from lectures and study groups.'

'So it must have been a choice for all of you. Wouldn't that have been decided before term started?'

'Gabriel and I were the first two. There was a notice board for lodgings in the Student Union foyer. We'd already said we'd take the Heights and paid for the full term between us, but we needed more people to cover the rent, so we put up an ad. The other five were the quickest off the mark.'

'Did they come separately, or as a group?'

'Emily and Star came together. Phil was on his own. We needed two more, and Gabe knew Jade so he asked her and she said yes. She'd been in halls in the first year, but got thrown out. I don't know where she lived for her second year. She seemed really pleased to have been asked. Miriam was the last one to answer the ad. I was puzzled at that. She didn't seem the type. But, she had a car, a brand new one, so it would be easy enough for her to get to campus. Not that she ever offered anyone a lift.'

'Were you and Gabe in charge of the rent?'

'Yes, we asked for a term up front, to make sure no-one dropped out because they got into arrears. They all paid up.'

'What can you remember about that term, Billy, starting from the September when you all arrived at the Heights? How soon did the problems start?'

Clever question, Dan thought.

'The first couple of weeks were OK. We all got on well enough. Everyone stuck to the rules, you know, food, cupboards, no-one going into anyone else's room without permission. There weren't locks on the bedroom doors. We asked the Uni to install some, but they never got round to it. It began with small things. People's food disappearing out of the fridge, personal crockery and cutlery being used, then left unwashed in the sink. For me just usual student stuff, but Phil was crazy about it. After a month, sometime in October, I think, he installed a fridge in his room and a lock on his own door. Jade laughed at him. She was probably the main culprit.' He paused and took a long drink of coffee, staring into space. They waited. 'Emily and Star were joined at the hip to start, never out of each other's company. Star had a crush on Professor Knight, I don't know if you know that. She was always talking about him; how gorgeous he was, how he was especially kind when he spoke to her; how she thought they'd make a nice couple.'

'Did you know that Knight reported her to the University?' Dan asked.

'Yes. She went from loving him to hating him. She was called to a meeting with the Human Resources manager and the Vice Principal. She came back really angry, saying Knight was a piece of shit. We all guessed what had happened. What we didn't expect was Emily's reaction.'

'Which was?' Belle asked.

'We expected her to be sympathetic to her best friend. But she laughed, told Star she'd been an idiot, thinking a man like Knight could ever be interested in her. That he was not only married, but his wife was sick. After that, they barely spoke to each other.'

'Can you remember when that happened?' Belle asked.

'Not precisely, but it was after the half term break, so some time in November. That was when Star started to stalk him.'

'What was your impression of the character of each of your housemates, Billy?'

'Well, Star was lovely; beautiful, bright and funny, very outgoing and someone you just sort of gravitated towards, until after the Knight business. She started sleeping with Gabe around then, but she still followed Knight around. And I think she was stealing stuff from Emily.'

Dan raised an eyebrow. 'Do you have proof of that?'

'No, but I saw her coming out of Emily's room once, when she thought there was no-one else in the house. And later that day Emily said a trinket of hers was missing, some sentimental piece of jewellery. Emily had a lot of jewellery.'

Belle frowned. 'Expensive jewellery?'

'I think so. She said it was inherited from grandparents, etc. She was absolutely blazing when that piece went missing. She demanded to inspect all of our rooms. We all told her to shove off, of course. Gabe said she'd probably just lost it.'

'Do you think Star took it?'

He bit his lips together. Belle could see that he was struggling to give an answer.

'You don't have to say, Billy, if you don't want to.'

'Yes, I think Star took it. It was her expression, when Emily was raging about it. Sort of, smug.'

'Did Emily accuse her specifically?'

She accused each of us in turn. But, yes, I suppose she did home in on Star. They had a bigger argument than the rest of us had with her about it. At one point, Gabe had to hold her back when she raised her hand with her fist clenched.'

'Do you know what it was?' Belle asked.

'She called it a "lover's knot", something a man gave his sweetheart. She said it was over a hundred years old.'

'Not surprising she was upset it had gone.' Dan added.

'What about Emily? How did you find her, did you get on with her?'

'Yes, I did.'

'I detect a slight blush there,' Dan said.

'We had a bit of a fling, in November. It didn't last long. Finished mutually. No recriminations, on either side. I liked her, but I was wary of her. I'm not sure why. She didn't do anything to make me feel like that, it was just… I always felt there was something else going on. I don't know what, and she was always so busy. She was in her second year of her PhD, and I think it was quite a strain. Knight was known to be a harsh taskmaster, but he seemed to believe in her, so he pushed her. She resented the way he drove her sometimes, but she knew it was for her own good. She told me that one evening, when I found her crying in the kitchen.'

'Do you think she liked him?'

He grinned. 'I think she almost hated him, personally. But she knew she couldn't have a better person as her supervisor. She thought he was stressed too, because of keeping on teaching whilst his wife was ill.'

'What about Gabe?'

'Gabe was my mate and I loved him, despite his faults. I don't mean I was in love with him. For me, he was a reliable friend, even though he was sex mad, and he used far too many drugs. Gabe would try anything and everything.'

'Who was he sleeping with, amongst the girls at the Heights?' Belle asked.

He grinned again, wider this time. 'All of them, maybe not Miriam, but definitely the other three. He couldn't seem to help himself. You know, when people talk about Gabe he comes out as a nasty, uncaring, shit of a person. But he wasn't. He was charming, and funny. He had plenty of money and had been badly spoiled, particularly by his mother, in whose eyes he could do no wrong. But, if you were in trouble, he was the first person you'd turn to. He never let you down, ever.'

'And the others?'

'Phil kept himself to himself. I never really understood why he wasn't in halls. When he wasn't in lectures or sleeping, he was studying. He wasn't a bad bloke, joined in conversations, just didn't want to get involved in anything else. Jade was a bloody nuisance. She never stopped talking. She was always gossiping about something or someone.'

'Your housemates?' Belle asked.

'Not directly, but she was always trying to stir up trouble, dropping something into a conversation that would set them off, especially Emily and Star, after Emily's jewellery disappeared. I didn't realise what a junkie she was then. She still is now. If you want to talk to her, I can tell you where to find her.'

'That would be helpful, thank you. And what about the final girl, Miriam Riley?'

'Miriam was a ghost. We hardly ever saw her. She went out to lectures, or whatever, came back and shut herself in her room. Came out to eat, went back to her room. She never took part in anything. No-one liked her much. She spoke to Phil occasionally, but not to the rest of us. Odd girl. Her parents would visit occasionally. She was close to her mother, but I think she didn't like her father.' He paused, closed his eyes, thinking. 'There was something about her, like she was fine on the surface, cold but polite, but underneath, she was holding something in, and whatever it was, it wasn't pleasant. The way she looked at us sometimes.' He shuddered. 'I thought she might stick a knife in any one of us, you know, like someone who could just explode.'

'What was she studying?' Dan asked.

'Maths,' Billy replied.

'Do you know where she is now?'

'No idea. We were all moved to different accommodation after Star died and Emily disappeared. Then Gabe dropped out. That just left me, Jade, Phil and Miriam. I saw them occasionally on campus, but we never spoke to each other, apart from meeting up with Jade a couple of times. We discussed the murder, but honestly, neither of us had any idea who might have done it.'

'Or when?' Belle asked. 'Gabe told the police at the time he was the last person to see her alive, around the time, or just after, Emily disappeared, I believe it was?'

He didn't answer. Something was coming. Dan opened his mouth to speak, but Belle shook her head at him. If it was going to come out, it had to be on Billy's terms.

'It's time to get this off my chest,' he said. 'You'll have to decide if you want to tell my boss or not.'

This was why he'd agreed to talk to them.

'He lied,' Billy said, staring straight at Belle. 'He didn't see her that day. He hadn't seen her since the party.'

'Why did he lie, Billy?' One question at a time.

'He was paid, and I think, threatened.'

'Do you know who did that?'

He shook his head.

'He didn't need the money, you said he was spoiled. So, it must have been the threat that made him do it.' Belle said.

'I think so. It was to do with his drugs. He was selling, as well as using. He was in trouble with a supplier, too. He'd got himself into a corner and didn't know how to get out.'

'Do you have any idea who it was?'

'No,' he replied, but hesitantly.

'You have a suspicion?'

'Maybe. But that's not all. He got in touch with me a couple of months ago. He was being blackmailed. He'd made something of himself, at last. He wanted to tell the truth. But I think he made a huge mistake. He told the person who was blackmailing him what he was going to do.'

'How do you know this?'

'He came to see me. He told me.' Billy put his head down and his hands over his face. When he looked up again, he said, 'The following day he was run down, by a hit-and-run. I didn't think it was connected. He was three times over the legal alcohol limit and the result of his blood test showed cocaine and ketamine. And I found he'd been banned from driving, for being over the limit previously. He'd hit someone. The person he hit had to spend time in hospital and was suing him. I thought whoever ran him down was taking revenge for what Gabe had done. No-one was caught. There was no CCTV.'

'I thought he overdosed?' Belle said.

'No, I don't know why you'd think that.'

'That was the reason for his death on the official certificate,' Belle said.

'Well, it's wrong. He wasn't too badly injured and was able to leave hospital the following morning. He had taken drugs later that day, but not enough to kill him. He was suffocated. Whoever did it, suffocated him that night, less than twenty-four hours after they hit him with a car. Whoever did it, was quite determined he was going to die.'

'Who signed the death certificate?' Dan asked.

'The coroner, I think.' Billy replied.

'Where was Gabe when this happened?'

Billy shrugged. 'Somewhere in London. It was all so wrong. A mate told me, someone I'd been in police training college with. He said not to tell anyone I'd told him, to keep well away from it. He'd been warned off, all of the officers involved had.'

'Why didn't you report your meeting with him?' Dan asked.

'I didn't know what to do. When Emily came back last week, I told the Boss Gabe was being blackmailed, but she didn't think the cases were related. Whoever did it, in her opinion, was getting revenge for what Gabe had done, for the many things he'd done.'

He was breathing too quickly, anxious, angry. 'I told her Gabe was going to confess to lying about seeing Star, but she wasn't interested. She said to leave it to the team dealing with it.'

'When you say *she*, you're talking about Susan Lewis?'

'Of course,' he replied. 'I hate her. She's corrupt. Do you think maybe someone's paying her to ignore it?'

'She's sleeping with the Chief Constable,' Dan said.

They both gaped at him.

'You mean Martin Riley? Wow,' Billy said, a grin practically reaching from ear to ear.

'From what I saw of his wife at the book launch, Josie, I think you said her name was, she would not like that to come out. Definitely not. Terrible for her reputation amongst the County set,' Belle said.

'Josie Riley is known to have a bite that would put a piranha to shame,' Dan added. 'Bear in mind that Susan Lewis has support in high places. Don't mess with her, either of you. It will come out, eventually. Personally, I believe in Karma, and in this case, that's who should take care of it.'

'Just one more question, Billy,' Belle said. 'You told Posy that Jade was arrested recently, on a drugs charge. Why was that?'

'There was an anonymous tip-off that she was dealing, so the local boys picked her up. And this is another worrying thing; she told them she knew about a murder, but when she was being formally interviewed she said she'd made it up. It turned out there was no evidence of dealing, so they let her go.'

'No-one pushed her on the murder?'

He shook his head.

'Billy, you look completely done in. That's more than enough questions on our part, and thank you for being so honest with us. If you agree, Dan, we won't share this beyond our group. That's Posy, Rose and Bette.'

He nodded. 'I trust you.'

'Just one more question,' Dan said, 'And I think I know the answer, but I'd like you to confirm it. Who was the officer in charge of the investigation into Star's death?'

'It was Chief Inspector John Trevelyan. But it was overseen by the Chief Constable.'

'Would that have been our now Chief Constable Martin Riley?'

Billy nodded.

'Miriam's father.' Belle said.

Chapter 20

Belle let Billy out the back way and invited Dan to stay for dinner, but he refused, saying he wanted to walk home to digest what they'd heard. He had also promised to call Richard.

She wasn't sorry, not that she didn't enjoy his company, but she was pleased to have some time to herself, to write up as much as she could recall word-for-word of what Billy had told them, and to have some time to herself to consider the consequences of what they had learned.

They had made a sincere promise to Billy they would not reveal any of the details he had given them, apart from to the Curiosity Club members.

Miriam Riley being the daughter of the Chief Constable, went some way to explaining why the students hadn't been questioned too harshly at the original investigation. It would have been ascertained that Miriam had left the accommodation before Star died. But, did she? According to Gabriel Holmes' original statement, he and Star were the only two who remained after Emily left, but what about the others, now they knew that statement was a lie? It put Miriam, Phil, Jade and Billy himself back in the frame with Emily. The problem still remained that no-one knew exactly when Star had died.

There were three points from the conversation with Billy that she wanted to concentrate on. The first was Emily's ridiculing of Star's telling off by the University about Knight. She could ask him more about that when they had their promised dinner. The second was the theft, from Emily by Star. Billy said that Emily had been, what was the phrase, "raging about it". Why? She could understand if it was an heirloom, handed down by a family member. It could have been sentimental, but three years ago her mother was alive. It hadn't sounded like they had the kind of relationship that would include the random passing on of sentimental jewellery. The third was the story of Gabriel's death. That had been shocking. A murder, disguised as a drug overdose. The coroner must have known. This had been a high level cover up. She had an idea, but a real fear of asking questions.

She decided to call Bette, who might know about the jewellery.

'Sorry, Belle, no idea about that. I agree, it likely wouldn't have been Rita. I remember her jewellery was all costume. And our mother never had a piece like that, as I recall. If she had any jewellery at all, she would never have given anything away that was valuable. She'd more likely have pawned it.'

'Does anyone in your family like anyone else, Bette?'

'No,' Bette replied. 'Not amongst my sisters and our mother. Our grandmother was even worse. One day, I'll tell you more about it, but not now. Anyway, as I was saying, I don't remember any old, valuable piece of jewellery being in the family.'

'What about on her father's side?'

Bette barked a laugh. 'Ronald? The only way he'd have got his hands on that would have been if he'd stolen it. Rita's husband was a bastard.'

'Thanks, Bette. How's it going with Georgie?'

'He's still pretty morose. Do you and Dan have any more leads?'

'Not leads, as such, but we have interesting information, some of it a bit scary. Bette, do you think Georgie might be up to taking a trip out?'

'Where to?'

'Back to the Heights. Before you say definitely not, we must all get together again for an update. There's a lot more information now than we had earlier. We're going to speak to Phil Singh first thing in the morning, then Jade Waters, I hope, after him. How about we get together after that?'

'You can all come here,' Bette replied.

After the call ended, Belle sat back and thought about the piece of jewellery. If it hadn't come from Emily's family, how did she get it? Had someone else given it to her? And was it ever found? From what Billy had said, it seemed likely Star had taken it. Why? Was it just to upset Emily? But they were supposed to have been best buddies. Billy hadn't said if it was before or after the incident with Joseph Knight. She would check with him.

She turned her attention to Phil Singh, writing down a few questions she wanted to ask. Mainly, she wanted to know how his impression of the others compared to Billy's. Before he left, Billy had told them where to find Jade, in a café in Port Simon, across the bay. That just left Miriam. That was going to be a tricky one.

Always in the back of her mind was the question of Gabriel Holmes's death. She needed to speak to Dan.

She yawned. Dan would be around at six in the morning and if she could persuade him to drive over to Port Simon, then back to the farm, it was going to be a long day.

**

Just before seven the following morning they entered the café at the hospital entrance. Phil Singh was already there.

'We don't want to take up more of your time than is necessary, Dr Singh. You know that Emily is back and that George Morris has been arrested. For the time being it's for perverting the course of justice, but we believe something more is coming. What we want to ask you about is your impression of your fellow students in that first term at the Heights, and when, in your opinion, it all began to go wrong.'

He sat back in his chair, across the table from them, fingers steepled in front of his chest. *Power gesture*, Belle thought. She'd seen it too many times before when holding a "discussion" with a senior manager accused of bullying one of their staff.

'Please, call me Phil. What makes you think it went wrong, Mrs Harrington?'

'You installed your own fridge and put a lock on your door. That doesn't say happy atmosphere to me.'

He smiled. 'Jade Waters was a pain in the ass. She stole food, and it made me angry. I told her to stop, but she just laughed. It was the only way I could think of to stop her.'

'It used to annoy me too, when I was at Uni. It's how I met my husband. He nicked my yoghurt.'

Both Phil and Dan laughed.

'Seriously though, Phil, what about Emily and Star? And Gabe, of course.'

Now he frowned. 'Honestly, I didn't really like any of them. Gabe tried to sell me drugs. Emily and Star seemed to be good friends, but there was an incident of theft and they fell out. After that, they barely spoke to each other.'

'Yes, we know about that; a family heirloom, I believe?'

He frowned. 'Was it? I don't remember her saying that. She told me it was sentimental, and had been bought for her.'

Belle sat forward. 'Did she say who bought it?'

'No. I got the impression it was a family member.'

'Do you know if it was ever found?'

'I don't think so.'

'Do you remember when that incident happened?'

'It was a couple of weeks before the end of term.'

'So, Emily and Star only really fell out towards the end?'

He nodded.

'Did this come up during the police enquiry into Star's death?'

'They didn't ask me. I can't tell you about the others. You'll have to ask them.'

'We hope to do so. You said you didn't really like any of them. Were there any other incidents you can remember?'

'Nothing notable. I kept to myself most of the time. Studying to be a doctor is tough, Mrs Harrington.'

'I married one, so yes, I do know how hard it is.'

'Is there anything else you can tell us, that you think might be useful,' Dan asked.

'Not that I can think of. You should talk to the others. They'll have their own view on what it was like

back then.'

'We know where to find them all, except for Miriam. I don't suppose you know where she is, where we might find her now?'

He put his head to one side, giving Belle a quizzical look. 'Is this a joke?'

'No, Phil. Why would I joke about it?'

'Because Miriam is my wife.'

Belle and Dan gave each other a quick glance, then turned back to Phil.

'Were you together during that term?'

'No, but that's when we met. Afterwards, you know, we both went back into Halls of residence. Neither of us wanted to see or speak to Billy, or Gabe or Jade, ever again. But we found we did need to talk, and we spoke to each other. We became close. We've been married for two years.'

'Miriam was a student of mathematics. Does she work in that field?'

'She lectures at the University. I can give her a call, if you like. She's expecting you.'

Belle heard Dan's intake of breath.

'Yes, please. Whenever she has time. That would be very helpful.'

He looked at his watch. 'I have to go. My shift starts soon and I need to be at the handover.'

Belle and Dan stood. 'Thanks for your time Phil.'

'No problem. Give me a number. I'll text you when I've spoken to Miriam.'

**

'That was a shocker,' Dan said as they stood waiting for a lift to take them up to the Intensive Care Unit. 'Miriam could take anything and everything we say straight back to daddy.'

'And from there to Chief Inspector Lewis. I wonder if Miriam knows about them?'

'I think we'll just keep well away from the subject.'

'Maybe,' Belle replied, raising her eyebrows and smiling.

Dan shook his head. 'No, Belle.' She was surprised at the passion and vehemence in his voice. 'Martin Riley is a misogynistic racist, a loathsome, dangerous, despicable excuse for a human being. When you meet him, he's all bonhomie and jolliness, but it's superficial. Don't, whatever you do, get on the wrong side of him.'

'Which side of him are you on?'

'For now, the right side. But that could change in the blink of an eye.'

'I'll keep it in mind.' The lift arrived.

When they reached the Intensive Care Unit, they found Harry, coming out of the ward doors.

'She's doing ok,' he said. 'The Consultant has just been in. She's a little better this morning.'

A wave of relief passed through Belle.

'You OK?' Dan asked.

'I feel so guilty. Posy and I talked the night before Posy found her. We decided not to worry about her. If only…'

'Stop there,' Harry said, putting a hand on her arm. 'Posy's the same, blaming herself. The only person to blame is the one who hit her. The police will find him, or her. I call them at least twice a day to see if they have any leads yet.'

'That must make you popular,' Dan said.

'Perk of the job. You can't be too rude to a Vicar.'

'Stop laughing, Belle. We're going to meet at the farm this afternoon,' Dan said to Harry. 'Do you think Rose will make it?'

'I'll make sure she does. How's it going?'

'Interesting,' Belle replied. 'We're off to Port Simon next to see Jade Waters. We're trying to get a rounded view of what happened in the lead up to the murder and Emily's disappearance.'

'Excellent,' Harry replied. 'Off you go, then, and give my best wishes to Jade.'

'You know her?' Dan said.

'I haven't seen her for a while, but yes. She occasionally helps out with talks on the dangers of drugs. She's a very good advertisement for not getting hooked. And she's also an excellent public speaker.'

'We'll tell her,' Belle replied. 'Tell Rose we'll see her later.'

**

They found Jade Waters where Billy had said she would be; in a backstreet café called Smokey Nell, that smelled of stale fried food and body odour. Port Simon was one of the few coastal villages that didn't attract visitors at any time of the year. It had no harbour, being little more than a set of cottages set along a sea front with no beach, and alleyways that led off uphill.

Jade sat alone at a table near the kitchen, where the frying equipment gave out an obnoxious smell of burning fat, but had the advantage of allowing through a short draft of heat each time the door was flung open.

They knew she was around twenty-five years old, but the life she led had added years, in poor skin and greasy hair, and an emaciated, round shouldered body. Plus the skinniest legs Belle had ever seen.

'Harry Teague sends regards,' she said, as she and Dan trapped Jade on the four person bench, Dan next to her and Belle opposite. 'You don't seem surprised to see us.'

'Billy texted me, said you were coming.'

'And here you are,' Dan said. 'Does this mean you're willing to have a little chat?'

'If you're expecting me to wax lyrical about my former housemates, then prepare yourselves for disappointment. Before I say anything, you can buy me a fry up and a couple of coffees, for starters.'

'Order whatever you want,' Dan replied. 'I'm picking up the bill today.'

'We don't expect anything other than your impression of the people you lived with for that one term. I'd also like to know about Emily Duggan's missing necklace and what you knew about it.' Belle said.

A pot of tea arrived, with three mugs, each one with a small chip and crack. Dan pushed his away and Jade laughed. 'It's not the Ritz, Professor.'

'I've had enough tea already today,' he said. 'Over to you, Belle.'

'Right, let's start with a quick summary of each person. Off you go.'

Jade took a huge mouthful of tea, banged the mug down on the table and shouted across to the man behind the counter, 'Give me the full works plus, Carl. These mugs are paying.'

'Up front,' the proprietor said. 'I know how much you can eat.' Dan went to pay.

'Billy was OK. He didn't get involved in arguments. He was the one who tried to sort them out when they happened.'

'How often was that?'

'At least once a week, or more. And usually about stupid stuff.'

'Like someone taking food that wasn't theirs?'

'That would have been me. Yeh. Phil Singh got fed up in the end and brought in his own fridge. Stupid prig. And Miriam, I don't think she ever spoke to me. She used to peep out of her room to see who was around before she came out, then run down to her car.'

'Was she ever deliberately nasty to you, or to anyone else?'

'Nope. I never understood why she bothered to live with us. We weren't her kind of people. Gabe, well, I loved Gabe. He and I were together for a while, before he moved on to Emily, and to Star.'

'What did you think about Emily and Star?'

Jade snorted. 'Emily Duggan was a nasty piece of work. She and Star were supposed to be mates, but Emily knew how to push Star's buttons. Mind, we all did. I felt a bit sorry for her. She came out of the system, had never had anyone caring about her. She was just looking for someone to like her. She was beautiful to look at; tallish and precise, and she could be really good fun. She made me laugh a lot. She had a kind way about her. But there wasn't really that much to her. She was just a happy idiot, most of the time. Just once she mentioned family, when Gabe had given her some new stuff he was trying out.'

'What did she say?'

'Her mother used to chant a rhyme to her. "Twinkle, twinkle little Star. What an ugly kid you are". No wonder she cleared off.'

'That's very nasty. Did she ever say anything else about family or background?'

'No, and she got really arsy with me when I reminded her about the rhyme. She couldn't understand how I knew. I told her she had sung it to me when she had taken some of Gabe's really good stuff and was off her head. She asked me never to repeat it. She said no-one was ever allowed to know anything about her mother.'

'What do you know about the row about the necklace that went missing?'

'Emily threw a fit. She said Star had taken it. Funny thing was, though, after a week or so, she was wearing it again.'

'What? Are you sure it was the same one?' Belle asked.

'Positive. I know, because I saw Star sneak into Emily's room and put it back. She didn't know I'd seen her.'

The plate of food arrived and Jade began to eat, with such speed that Belle thought Jade might be sick. She didn't try to interrupt. This was clearly a rare treat. It took her five minutes to finish the heaped plate. She sat back, gave out a loud burp then picked up the coffee mug and drained it.

'Thanks for that. Billy said you'd pay me, too.'

Belle brought out two twenty pound notes and Jade tried to snatch at them, but Belle held them back. 'We haven't finished yet.'

Jade tutted, twitched and sat back, arms folded. 'I don't know any more.'

'What about your recent arrest for dealing? You told the police you knew something about a murder.'

Jade's eyes narrowed. 'I didn't say nothing like that. And I wasn't dealing.'

'The police report says you did say that, and that you were dealing.'

Jade shrugged. 'I was just messing with them, they knew that. They let me go.'

'There's something you're not telling us Jade.'

The girl sniffed.

'Is it about Billy?' No reaction. 'Gabe, Phil, Emily, Star?' she paused. 'Miriam?'

There was the reaction she'd been waiting form. A stiffening of the back, for a split second, a look of fear.

'Or would it be Miriam's father?'

With a lightening quick movement Jade's arm shot forward and she grabbed Belle's wrist, squeezing it so forcefully Belle's fingers began to turn white. Belle didn't move, didn't speak, despite the pain. She kept staring straight into Jade's eyes.

'If I tell you, I need your promise, your absolute promise, both of you, that it goes no further.'

'Only if you let go of my wrist.' Jade let go, but didn't lean back.

'I – we – can make that promise, with one proviso. We are a small group, just of friends. We call ourselves the Curiosity Club. We work together. We trust each other one hundred percent. I'm going to tell you who the others are. Then you can make up your mind whether or not to tell us about Miriam's father. They are Bette Jones, Rose Teague, that's Harry's wife, Posy Simmons, who runs a café, and Mavis Penhaligon. Mavis used to be Mavis Tregoss, but she divorced an abusive husband. She's lying in hospital, in the ICU, on life support, ostensibly because of a burglary gone wrong, but we know it was because she knew something. She went to tackle the person concerned. Later that evening, the "burglary" occurred and Mavis was hit on the head. Dan is also with us. Jade, please believe me, nothing you tell us will ever go outside the circle I've just told you about. Absolutely nothing.'

'I can confirm that,' Dan said. 'People think they're just chatty women. I can assure you, nothing is further from the truth. They're as sharp as razors.'

Jade bit her bottom lip and began twitching her head. She was thinking and Belle was content to wait. It took a few minutes, during which neither she or Dan spoke nor moved.

Then Jade leaned forward, speaking in a voice barely above a whisper. 'OK. I'll tell you. The bitch deserves it. Miriam hated her father, back then. That's why she came to live at the Heights, to spite him. But he wouldn't leave her alone. He came to visit. He wasn't ever allowed into her room. Sometimes she wouldn't even come out to meet him. Those times, he hung out in the kitchen. He liked to talk to the rest of us. Not me, particularly. He chatted to the guys, but he kept the deeper conversations for Emily and Star. The look on his face when he saw either or both of them come into the kitchen – Predator man.' She spat the words out. 'Star liked to chat to him. But Emily, she hung back, just smiling. She answered his questions, sometimes. But she looked at him like he looked at her.' She shuddered. 'I always got out of the way as fast as I could.'

'How often was he there?'

Jade shrugged. 'A couple of times a month, always when we were all there. He seemed to know.'

'How was Miriam with him?'

'Whenever he appeared, she paused in the corridor to take a deep breath and compose herself. I saw her do it a few times.'

'Did she speak to him?'

'She was polite. Mainly just "yes" or "no" when he asked if she was doing OK. Once he tried to give her a hug, but she pulled away.'

'Jade, do you know if Emily had something going with him?'

'No idea. If she did, she didn't give anything away. But...' she paused, bit her lip again. 'I had the feeling they knew each other, outside of Uni. She said something once, about an event, at a restaurant, I think. And he gave her one of those looks, like "*shut the fuck up*". Which she did.'

'Was he ever accompanied by Miriam's mother, Josie?'

'No, she came on her own a couple of times. She was snotty, like we were a bad smell under her nose. Miriam got on better with her. She used to talk to Star, though, seemed interested in her.'

'What about?'

'I don't know, just bits of gossip, the weather, people on TV, that kind of thing. That's it. I don't want to say any more.'

Belle didn't want to push the woman any further. She could see Jade's hands shaking.

'Thank you Jade. Here's the money. We'll keep everything you've told us to ourselves. You have my word.'

'And mine,' Dan added, standing up and slipping another twenty pounds into Jade's hand. 'Take care of yourself Jade. You're a clever woman. Don't waste it.'

She grinned at him. 'I've read your stuff. It's good. Interesting'

'See, I said you were clever,' he said, smiling back.

As they stood up to leave, Jade said, her head turning away from them, 'You should speak to that old schoolfriend of Emily's, Kylie something. She used to hang around us. She works at the Pounds for Pennies store in town. She's a useless pain in the bum. She's got a kid, no idea who the daddy is.'

'Why should we talk to her?' Belle asked.

'She was a nosy little cow. She sucked up to Emily, all the time. Emily used to make fun of her, but she never sent her away. I think she knew something, and once I saw Emily slip her a twenty. That's it, I'm done.'

Back in Dan's car, they both took a moment, before setting off.

Dan checked his watch. 'It's almost midday. Let's get a bite to eat before we head off to the farm. I don't know about you, but my head is spinning.'

'Mine too. I…' Belle paused as her phone pinged an incoming text. 'It's from an unknown number. It just says, "call me".'

'Do it now, then,' Dan said.

She dialled. The caller answered immediately.

'Hello, this is Belle Harrington. You just sent me a text…' was as far as she got.

'I know who you are. This is Miriam Singh. Just listen and don't interrupt. I am not going to meet with you, nor will I answer any questions. They were a bunch of losers, as time has proved. Emily Duggan was and probably still is, a sociopathic bitch. You know who my father is. My husband is too kind about them. Now, please leave me alone.'

Belle had just had time to put the call on speaker, so Dan could hear, but not enough time to record it.

'Isn't that just the icing on the cake,' Dan said. 'Let's go eat. And breathe. And if it's OK with you, I'd like to keep my thoughts to myself for a while.'

'Not a problem,' Belle replied. 'How about we buy some sandwiches and hot chocolate, back in St Foy, and sit on the harbour wall. It's a good place for contemplation.'

'Agreed. Port Simon is not one of my favoured places.' He started the engine and began the drive back around the bay, both too deep in thought to note that the car that had followed them out of St Foy was still behind them.

Chapter 21

They had an hour to discuss the implications of the information they'd received from the students about Emily and Star before heading up to the farm. Belle began.

'The first thing is, Dan, I don't know what to say about Billy's information about Gabriel Holmes's death. My feeling is that we shouldn't get involved, or ask any questions. If Billy has been told to leave it alone, I think it's likely Susan Lewis knows about it, and if she thinks we know, in my opinion that's a huge danger for all of us.'

'I agree. It's been hushed up at a high level. I suspect that Martin Riley has something to do with it, but we dare not ask any questions, or let it be known that we have any idea. I'd like to discuss the implications with Richard, though.' His face had paled. 'If we try to get involved, we'll be well out of our depth.'

'This is something we'll have to keep between the two or us, or three, including Richard. If – when – this is all over, we can tell the others. Ok with you?'

'Yes.'

'Let's carry on, then. The next issue that has stuck with me is that the relationship between Emily and Star was complicated. I began by thinking they were best friends. I don't believe that now. For whatever reason, Emily was using Star, I'm not sure for what, but Star turned the tables on her. Thinking back now to our discussion with Emily – was that only yesterday? – she never actually said that they were best friends. I was so upset by what she said about her family. I think we both thought that she's a nasty individual, and perhaps there might be something in Miriam's comment. Perhaps Emily has either sociopathic or psychopathic tendencies.'

Dan nodded. 'Star was just one in another line of people who might have been useful to her. That's part of the makeup of a sociopath or a psychopath. But why Star?'

'Because she was easily manipulated, I think, until she wasn't. When the time came for compassion, Emily laughed at her. That was followed by the incident of the necklace. Do you think there was something going on between Emily and Martin Riley? Could he have been the person who gave it to her?'

'That's too much of a stretch for me. A few looks observed between him and Emily, could have been just that. But, he's now revealed as a predator, in addition to his other vices, I'm not sure if Miriam was warning or threatening us, when she said, "you know who my father is". What did you think?'

'The same,' Belle replied. 'I couldn't say either way. However, what I am sure of is that we go nowhere near the man.'

'Agreed.'

They talked for a while longer about their impressions. They agreed that Star was a vulnerable young woman, looking for love and possibly protection. Phil Singh was a benign onlooker, Miriam a toxic observer. Belle thought the marriage might not be a long lasting one. Miriam's criticism of her husband, to strangers over the phone, didn't bode well.

It was now almost three thirty, darkening and cold. Belle stared out over the now black, choppy waters of the estuary.

There was still a great deal of snow on the ground, on both sides. The lights across the water in Porthdevan, which included a colourful Christmas tree on the harbour, made a pretty sight, and overhead, for the first time in days, the sky was clear. She was thinking back to a previous Christmas, long before, when Sam had been alive and they had gone out into the garden with a telescope on Christmas Eve, to examine the stars. Jamie had been six and had woken up. Sam told him they were looking out for Santa's sleigh. Jamie had been so excited he demanded to stay with them, but after ten minutes, had complained he was cold, so they tucked him back into bed and went downstairs, into the garden with cups of hot chocolate. A wave of immense sadness ran through her.

'Belle, we must go.'

'Sorry, I was thinking back to a Christmas years ago.' Her cup of hot chocolate was now empty. She stood, threw it in a nearby bin and started to walk off, watched by Dan. He understood sadness and didn't interrupt her.

At the farm, they were the last to arrive.

'Rose is going back down to the hospital as soon as we're done here,' Harry said, as Bette handed out tea and slices of cake. 'Mavis is stable, a big improvement.'

'That's fantastic news,' Belle replied. 'There's hope she'll wake up?'

'She's not out of the woods yet, but yes, the Consultant seemed more hopeful a couple of hours ago. If she continues to improve, they'll see if she can breathe alone, then they can think about slowly lessening the sedation, provided the brain swelling has gone down, which it seems to be doing. I think that's what he said, anyway.'

'What a relief,' Belle replied. 'You and Rose and Posy have helped, being with her, I'm sure.'

'They say talking to her, when we're allowed in, always helps,' Posy said. 'But we haven't said anything about what we're doing, or anything about Emily at all. We agreed it was best not. We've kept the chat very light. I've heard more from Billy, too, about the robbery. Whoever it was took her jewellery and some money she had in her purse, but didn't touch some valuable ornaments and of course, her mother's precious china. You know how desperate she was to keep that when she split from Andrew. It's worth thousands of pounds.'

'But would a smash and grab thief have any idea, or be able to carry it?' Belle asked. 'This says it was just one person. Posy, do the police know how the person was able to get in? Mavis was security conscious.'

'Yes. They think she let the person in. There have been some carol singers around, and someone collecting money for one of the Christmas charities. There's no sign of a forced entry.'

'Do we think Mavis might have answered the door to a carol singer?'

'Probably,' Posy replied. 'Although I think it's more likely it was someone she knew, and trusted. Or perhaps not trusted, but someone she didn't think of as violent. As soon as she opened the door, the person must have pushed their way in and attacked her. I found her on the hall floor, remember.'

For a few seconds, they all pondered the possibility Posy had described.

'You two have had a busy day,' Bette said, shaking them out of their reveries. 'Tell us what you've found out.'

'Belle will give you a summary of incidents and facts. I'll give you our thoughts on what it might mean,' Dan replied. 'Off you go, Holmes. I'm Watson, by the way.'

There were a few smiles and grins as Belle clown-scowled at him, then began her summary. When she had finished, Dan took over.

'My thoughts about them. To start with, that house share was a disaster waiting to happen. The atmosphere must have been toxic. What each of them has told us makes me think of an iceberg. A bit of trouble on the top, the part everyone could see, but beneath, lethal stuff brewing.' He turned to Bette. 'Bette, I'm sorry to say this, but your niece is probably a poisonous character. I'm not convinced about the story of some commune in Scotland, either, even though she's been alibied. But what I don't understand is the amount of time she stayed away. For me, there's just no accounting for that.'

'On that I agree,' Posy said. 'I've lived at one of those. I was bored after a couple of months.'

'I grew up on one,' Rose said. 'I got away when I was seventeen.' Harry reached out and took her hand. 'There are good and bad,' he said. 'Just like the rest of the world, but I agree that I can't see how it can have held Emily's attention for so long. She's too bright to sit and knit and sing "cum by yah"'.

Belle bit back a chuckle. 'Yes, Harry, she is. Joe is trying to persuade her to stay and work with him again, probably finish her PhD. We bumped into him at her mother's house. He was just arriving as we were leaving.'

'He's also invited Belle out to dinner,' Dan said, with a mischievous grin. 'As an apology for running her down with a supermarket trolley.'

'Will you accept?' Posy asked.

'Don't look so surprised. He probably just wants to find out what I know about Emily.'

'So why are you blushing?' Rose asked. 'He's very attractive, and a widower.'

'If he does call me, I will accept,' Belle replied, trying for dignified and ignoring the colour rising on her cheeks. 'I want to find out what he knows. It should be an interesting evening – if it happens.'

'Back to the subject matter, everyone. Let's leave Belle to her love life,' Bette said.

'It's not my… oh, never mind.'

'My question,' Bette continued, 'is what comes next?'

'There's one particular thing I'd like to do, Bette. I've already talked to Georgie about the shushing. Dan and I think the noise might have been one person "shushing" another, in a bedroom behind a door close by. I'd like to take him back there, to try it out, to see if he recognises the noise. What do you think are the chances of persuading him?'

Bette's mouth turned down and she shook her head. 'I can't believe he'll go anywhere near that place. Although, maybe if we can persuade him it's in his best interest to go… I don't know. Try. See how he reacts.'

Bette's guess at his reaction wasn't far off the mark. Georgie shook his head so violently Mandy had to take hold of his shoulders and demand that he look at her. Then, something surprising happened. Instead of telling him it was alright, that he didn't have to do anything he didn't want to do, she told him this might be good for him. If Belle could show that someone else might have been in the Heights, hiding, it could only be good in helping the police to look in another direction, look again at who else might have been there on Christmas Eve when they had all stated, in writing, that they were somewhere else.

Georgie sat and put his head down for a few moments, then he said, 'I'll do it. But only if you all come with me. Can't go without you all there.'

By "you all" he had swept his arm around to mean Mandy, plus Bert and Bette, Belle and Dan.

'We'll be there, Georgie, some of us.' Belle said. 'We'll go tomorrow, late afternoon. And we'll make sure no-one else knows you've done it. How does that sound?'

Georgie nodded.

'It's the right decision, and a good one,' Mandy said, hugging him. 'If there was someone else there, who lied about being there, then what were they doing, or planning to do?' She turned to Belle. 'Do you have any ideas?'

'Not about who it might have been, but why? Yes, I believe I do. They were planning to move her, probably bury her somewhere. Then, she'd only have ended up being a missing person. But because she was found, they must be worrying, right now, enough to call the police and tell them about what you did, Georgie. Another fact that's been on my mind. Bette, I think it was you said originally that when the police checked, it looked like she had packed up for Christmas.'

She was also thinking, *and it ties in with Emily's return. No doubt about that.* She wanted to ask Georgie why he was so convinced that Emily had killed her, but this wasn't the time. One stressful action for him to think about was enough. Once they'd been to the Heights, and if the experiment worked, then she would ask.

'Do you think you could manage it, Georgie? You've been bailed until after the New Year, and you don't have any restrictions on movement, do you?

He shook his head. 'But I don't want those newspaper people to see me.'

'Don't worry about that,' Dan replied. 'We'll work out a plan so no-one knows you've left. We'll be able to get you there and bring you back without them knowing.'

'Rose, let me know anything about Mavis. The time doesn't matter, wake me up if you need to. I do wonder what it was Mavis knew, or thought she knew. Dan, I think we should go now. I'm ready for home.'

Bert stood to show them out. At the door he said, 'You're doing a great job, both of you. I don't know how to thank you enough.'

'You don't have to thank us,' Dan replied. 'We're friends. This is for all of us.'

He drove back down into the town and stopped outside Belle's cottage, refusing her offer of dinner. They had agreed to meet in the morning. Posy had offered to meet her at the café at nine, to work out how they could get Georgie away from the farm with no-one seeing him.

Dan drove off and as Belle was searching in her bag for her keys, she noticed a black car drive past. It looked familiar. She couldn't see through the darkened windows, but she was sure it was someone she knew. She went to wave, but the car sped up the hill.

Chapter 22

Belle was at the café at nine the following morning, with a list. Dan had cried off, not for a bad reason, but he had called Belle early to say that when he reached his apartment he had called Richard and, after a long discussion, Richard had insisted on coming down to join him for the New Year. 'Just for a couple of days,' he said. 'He's worrying. He wants to be here for when Peter Day makes his move, plus he's worried about what we've learned about Gabriel's death. He's looking forward to meeting you,' he added.

'And I him,' Belle replied. 'When will he arrive?

'Should be sometime later this morning, but he's not sure what time. I've said I'll wait in. To be honest, I'll be pleased to have him here with me.'

Belle realised after the call ended that she knew nothing about Richard. Something in the way Dan had spoken about him gave her the impression that he wanted to keep the various parts of his life separate, and instinct told her not to ask. Now, she was curious, and wondering what the others might be able to tell her, before Richard arrived.

'No point asking me,' Posy said, as they sat with Belle's list in front of them. 'Dan's always been clear that his life is private, so we don't ask, either. But what I do know, is that we may all be in for a shock.'

'What do you mean?' Belle asked.

'Oh, just small things that have slipped out over the years. You know I haven't been here that long. Bette or Mavis are likely to know more.'

'Come on, what small things?'

'There's something very prestigious about Richard. He's a well-known person, in certain circles. That's it.'

'That's not much, is it? I guess we'll have to wait and see. But, if this is his first visit and he wants to meet us – and Dan has agreed – this sounds like it's a major step for Dan, too. Right, first things first. How are we going to move Georgie to and from the farm without anyone else knowing?'

'I've checked with Billy,' Posy replied, 'just to be sure there won't be any police activity at the Heights over the next couple of days.'

'We can go this afternoon, just as darkness sets in, maybe around four?'

'We'll need torches and a few other things. Let's get planning.'

For the next half an hour they discussed and finalised a meticulous plan, including who would need to be involved, what equipment they would need, who should be where, and when, and how to keep Georgie calm throughout the exercise. Finally, what they would do with the outcome, whatever it might be.

They had decided to involve as few people as possible, which Bette agreed with when Posy called her and went through the details. They would begin at three thirty, with Belle going to the farm. She thought she was now well-known enough to the diminishing band of press at the entrance for them to take little notice of her arriving. When she left, half an hour later, with Bette sitting next to her and Georgie and Mandy tucked down in the foot well of her back seat, covered by a blanket, no-one would take any notice again. They had anticipated that they would be back within an hour. Posy would already be at the Heights, having hidden herself away in the room leading off the small back landing from which Georgie believed he had heard the noise.

'It's a good strategy,' Posy said, ending the call to Bette. Bert was going to wait at the farm. 'What about the rest of this plan?'

'There's so much to check out,' Belle said. 'I want to find this other girl,' she pointed to Kylie Nichols on her list. Jade told Dan and me that she was a hanger on, that Emily often made fun of her, but never dropped her. Jade believes that Kylie knows something about Emily, so Emily kept her close.'

'Keep your friends close and your enemies closer,' Posy murmured. 'I agree, you should talk to her, find out which one she is, and why.'

'The Pennies for Pounds Store is open. I'm hoping there won't be many customers, and that she's working. I'll try to chat to her there, or arrange to meet her somewhere after work. That's if she'll talk to me.'

They were interrupted by a sharp knock on the door. Posy sighed. 'Ignore it. The sign is clear enough. The knock came again.

'I'll take a quick peek, just in case.'

'It can't be anyone we trust,' Belle said. 'They would have gone to the back.'

Posy went to the door and moved the blind a fraction, then turned back to Belle and rolled her eyes. 'It's Margaret.'

'Let her in,' Belle said. 'If she wants to tell us something, it might be useful. If she's just here to gossip, we'll get rid of her quickly enough.'

Posy unlocked the door and ushered Margaret quickly into the café.

'Oh, hello Belle,' she said, rushing towards the table. 'I didn't know you were here, too. How's Mavis, do you know?'

'She's improving, a little, but it's still very serious,' Belle replied, as Posy joined them.

Margaret saw the empty coffee cups and smiled hopefully at Posy, who smiled in return, but didn't offer. Belle had already hidden the papers, so it looked like two friends sharing a chat over a coffee.

Margaret's smile disappeared. 'I remembered something, and I wanted to tell someone,' she said, lowering her voice and leaning forward. 'Something that might be important; I wasn't sure, so I thought I'd see if I could find Posy.'

'Do tell,' Posy replied, thinking that, if it had been really important, most of the locals would already know whatever it was.

'I haven't said anything to anyone yet,' Margaret said. 'It didn't strike me at the time and now, I still don't know if I should speak to the police or not.'

Belle, who had sat back and folded her arms, sat forward and put her hands on the table. 'Posy, do you think your machine could manage a coffee for Margaret?'

Margaret gave her a smile of appreciation. Posy grunted and went behind the counter to set the machine going. In a few moments she returned with a flat white.

Margaret took a long, appreciative sip. 'I have missed this, Posy. You serve lovely coffee.'

Belle gave Posy, who was about to say something sarcastic, a quick *shut up* headshake. 'So, Margaret, what did you see?'

Margaret gave a quick, conspiratorial look around the café, then leaned forward. Posy almost laughed, but managed to hold it in.

'On the day that Mavis was, you know, injured, I think she was being followed by someone.' She paused, nodded solemnly, and took another mouthful of coffee.

'What makes you think that, Margaret?' Belle asked in an equally conspiratorial voice. Posy bit her bottom lip, hard.

'I was out taking a walk, early afternoon, around two, I believe it was, when Mavis came out of her cottage and walked down the steps towards the square. That's when I saw it. A black car, driving very slowly behind her. Turns out she was waiting for a taxi, which arrived, she got in and it drove off, and the black car followed them, down the High Street and out of sight.'

'Is that it?' Posy asked. 'It could have been a tourist.'

Margaret scowled at her. 'If it was, why was it back again, when the taxi returned with her an hour or so later? It came back down the High Street behind the taxi, waited until she got out, paid and walked back towards the steps to her cottage. The burglary happened later that night.'

She gave them both an excited look. 'Do you think it might have been the burglar, checking her out?'

'I'm not sure that's how burglars operate, Margaret,' Posy said. 'And how do you know it was the same car? Do you remember the make, or the number plate, or did you see who was driving?'

Margaret looked crestfallen. 'No, none of those things. I don't know anything about cars. Except this one was big and shiny. And it had blacked out windows. I only saw it from the side, so I couldn't see the driver.' She leaned in again. 'Do you think this is significant?'

Belle got in before Posy could say anything. 'It might be, Margaret. But I understand why you didn't go to the police. Not enough detail. Posy's right, it could have been a tourist and just co-incidence that another black car was behind Mavis's taxi. But thanks for telling us. Good to get these things off your chest.' She stood up. 'I have to go, now. Posy will see your out.'

She flicked her head at Posy, who took Margaret by the elbow and led her to the door. 'If you think of anything else you saw on one of your walks, Margaret, do come back and let us know. Something might be important.' She had spoken in a bored voice, but as she turned back to Belle, her expression was anything but bored.

'You recognised something in what she just said?'

'Yes,' Belle replied. 'When Dan dropped me off yesterday, a black car with darkened windows drove past the cottage. I almost waved. I don't know why, but I thought it was someone I might know. Then it sped off up the hill.' She sat back down again. 'As Margaret was speaking, I remembered why I thought it might be someone I knew. It wasn't. But it was sitting in the carpark over in Port Simon. Right across the other side of the carpark.'

'It must have followed you back,' Posy said.

'Probably. Right, I really must go. I need to find Kylie Nichols.'

'Whoever it was, is an amateur,' Posy said. 'If you're going to follow someone without them noticing, then you do it in an old Ford Fiesta, or something similar. Something that wouldn't catch anyone's attention. But,' she paused. 'If it was someone you might know if you could see them, that would explain the darkened windows, and they don't come with a tacky old car. Just an expensive, shiny black one. I don't suppose you saw the number plate, either?'

Belle shook her head. 'There are so many cars like that in St Foy in the summer. It's an upmarket resort and so many families have holiday homes here. It could have just been a co-incidence, I suppose.'

Posy shook her head. 'Keep a lookout for it. I hope I put Margaret off, but it does look like Mavis was being followed. I'm going to check with the taxi companies. There aren't many round here and I know a couple of the drivers. I'll find out where Mavis went.'

'Excellent notion. I will be careful. Right. We'll be at the Heights just after four. Fingers crossed I'm right about the noise Georgie heard.'

**

As she walked back home Belle's phone rang. She didn't recognise the number and was tempted to ignore it, but curiosity, as usual, got the better of her.

'Belle? Hello, this is Joe Knight.'

She stopped walking.

'I did say I'd call, and I apologise for it taking a couple of days. Are you free for dinner this evening?'

She was about to say no, but then thought, why not?

'Yes, Joe, I've nothing on this evening. Thanks, I accept. Just tell me, are we going somewhere posh?'

He laughed. 'No, well it's not fish and chips, if that's what you're thinking. It's a little restaurant I know over in Padstow. Very good food.'

'That's fine. What time?'

'I'll pick you up at seven fifteen.'

'I'll be ready. And thank you. I wasn't sure you actually meant it.'

'Of course I meant it. I'm looking forward to it.'

He ended the call. *I'm looking forward to it, too*, Belle thought as she resumed walking. *But not for the same reasons you are. Or maybe, our reasons are similar.*

**

She didn't enter the cottage, but went to her garage, got into her car and drove over to Port Simon. Its small shopping centre, with half of the shops closed down, was a forlorn place, with few shoppers. She had already checked that the "Pounds for Pennies" store was open. It had a couple of customers, wandering around, looking but not appearing to buy. At first she couldn't find any staff, apart from one bored looking lad, standing at the one open service till, picking at his nails. She thought about asking for Kylie, but changed her mind. She didn't want it to be obvious she was only here to speak to the girl, so she wandered around until she spotted her. Kylie was on her knees at the back of the shop, trying to tear open a hefty brown box, with broken fingernails.

'That doesn't look easy,' Belle said, smiling at her.

The young woman looked up and grimaced. 'You think they'd give us a pair of scissors, at least,' she retorted, then returned to her task.

So much for customer service, Belle thought. 'I'd like to talk to you, Kylie.'

'What are you looking for?' the woman replied without looking up.

'Information,' Belle said. Still no reaction.

'Aisles are all marked,' Kylie replied. She huffed and stood up. After all, this was a customer.

'Not that kind of information. I'd like to talk to you about Emily Duggan.'

Kylie took a step back. 'Don't know anyone called that.' She pulled at the elastic band holding back her greasy black ponytail.

'Yes, you do. You went to school with her. And you must know she's back. I've been talking to some of her old University friends. They all say you and she were close?'

'You police?'

'No. I'm a friend of Emily's family.'

'What's it got to do with them, or you?'

'You're very defensive, given you've just said you don't know her.'

'Leave me alone.'

'No. I'm willing to pay you.' Belle pulled from her pocket a wadge of twenty-pound notes. The woman's eyes widened. 'There's more, if you're honest with me.'

There was two hundred pounds in the handful of cash. And another two hundred waiting in Belle's bag. She could see Kylie weighing up her options, glancing around, but always returning to the money.

'I got a break in ten minutes. I go outside for a fag, at the back. Meet me there.'

She dropped back down onto her knees and returned to tearing the package.

Ten minutes later, Belle was outside the back service entrance to Pounds for Pennies, when Kylie emerged, furtively, looking around. She signalled to Belle to follow her towards the group of industrial size waste bins. For a moment Belle wondered if Kylie's plan was to mug her and take the money, but then gave herself a shake and followed.

Behind the bins, Kylie lit a cigarette with a shaking hand. 'How much was that you showed me?'

'Two hundred pounds,' Belle replied. 'And, like I said, there's more. Another hundred, if you answer my questions. All of them.'

'Another two hundred,' Kylie hissed. 'My information's good.'

'I'll think about it,' Belle replied. 'For four hundred, it would have to be very good indeed.'

'It is,' Kylie said, leering at her and blowing out smoke in her direction. 'Go on, then. I only got ten minutes.'

'Tell me about you and Emily in school.'

'First time I saw her do something to another kid, she stabbed herself with a pencil and blamed the other kid, because she wanted his chocolate bar.'

'Did he give it to her?'

'Well, 'course he did.'

'How old was she when that happened?'

'Five. There was lots more stuff like that.'

'Go on.'

'She was never the head of any gang, like, but the gangs kept away from her. She never wanted to be in any of their gangs. But if she wanted something from them, or wanted something done, they did it for her. No-one ever said "no" to Emily.'

'Did she ever physically hurt anyone?'

'Not that I ever saw. Didn't need to.'

'So why is your information so valuable?'

'Because I was the one who done it all for her.'

'What did you do, Kylie?'

'I stole stuff she wanted. I threatened anyone who'd cheeked her, you know the kind of thing.'

'Why did you do it all? It sounds more like you were the one they were scared of.'

Kylie put her head down, shuffled, then looked away from Belle and took another long puff on her cigarette.

'Because I threatened that she'd kill someone in their family, or their pet doggy, or whatever. They believed she'd do it.'

'Do you think she would have done it?'

Kylie shrugged. 'That's what she told me to tell them. There was something about the way she looked at them. Kind of blank.'

'What else, Kylie. I know you're holding something back.'

Kylie shuffled again. 'Give me the money.'

'No. Not until you tell me.'

Kylie threw the cigarette on the floor, stamped on it and kept twisting her foot.

'When she was fifteen, she got involved with men. Older men. She couldn't be bothered with boys our age. The men could give her lots of stuff. Her mother was an old bitch. Lovely to her when I was there, or anyone else who turned up. But Emily told me she used to call her all sorts of names other times. Bitch, whore, that kind of thing.'

'So, her mother knew about the men?'

'Yeh, 'course she did. Sometimes Emily gave her something from the stuff the men gave her. That shut her up.'

Belle could barely believe this was Bette's sister. She knew the sisters didn't get on, but this was something else. She wondered if Bette knew what her sister was really like.

'I'm thinking, Kylie, that you knew who some of these men were?'

Kylie nodded. 'Most of them didn't last long. She gave them the push, threatened to tell their wives. It was the way she said it, same as she did about schoolkids' families.'

'If you want the extra two hundred, give me a name.'

Kylie bit her lips together. Belle took another two hundred out of her bag. 'Here it all is. Four hundred pounds. Name.'

'A policeman. Can't remember his name.'

'Five hundred pounds.'

'Martin Riley.' She leaned in and Belle recoiled from the smell of tobacco on her breath. 'If she finds out I told you…'

'She won't. You've just confirmed what I already guessed. Did her leaving have anything to do with him.'

'No. She'd already given him the push, long time before. I think his wife found out. Now there's one evil slag you don't want to get on the wrong side of.' Another worker emerged from the fire door and waved at Kylie to get back inside.

'I got to go.'

'One more thing, Kylie, are you still in touch with Emily, and if so, why?'

'No. I've avoided her since I heard she was back. She wants me close because I know stuff. I know about him.'

Kylie walked away and Belle watched her go, at twenty-six already hunch shouldered, stick thin, looking years older, likely smoking since her early teens. She was the epitome of self-pitying failure. She had five hundred pounds in her pocket, probably more cash than she'd ever had in her life. Belle couldn't imagine what she was going to do with it. As she reached the door she turned back and gave Belle a grin before she slammed the fire door shut.

Inside Kylie took out her mobile phone and began to tap in a text.

She came to talk to me. I told her a couple of things, like we agreed. You owe me five hundred. I want the money today.

It was answered instantly.

I'll deliver it to your flat at six thirty. Be there ready.

Kylie was delighted. It had all worked out perfectly. She wouldn't have to pester Pete for support money for Noah, for now. And she could take Noah to Centre Parcs, like she'd promised.

**

Martin Riley. Belle had guessed there was something to it. She hadn't bargained on hearing more about how Emily had spent her youth. Basically prostituting herself to older, married men, for money. One of them – perhaps Riley – must have bought the necklace that Star stole from her. Had Emily continued to have these "affairs" throughout her time in University? Did Star find out and threaten to make it public? That might have provided a reason for Emily to kill her. But, having spoken to Emily, and seen her now on more than one occasion, although she could believe the shocking behaviour, she hadn't thought Emily a killer. Could she have been wrong? What Kylie had told her about Emily's behaviour from a young age had given her much to think about as she drove back from Port Simon.

However, there wasn't more time to think, because it had taken longer than expected and she would have to drive straight to the farm. She wasn't sure she wanted to share with Bette what she had found out. Not yet. First, they had to get Georgie to the Heights.

Chapter 23

'You seem distracted, Belle,' Bert remarked, as he pottered around the kitchen. 'Something happened?'

She took a deep breath. 'Yes, Bert. I've been told something about Emily and her mother. But I don't want to share it with Bette yet, not before we're done with Georgie. When we get back, Posy will be with us and I'll tell you all about it.'

'OK with me, as long as you do. I've never kept a secret from Bette. It makes me nervous, which she'll pick up.'

Belle laughed. 'I had a relationship like that, with Sam. We always knew when the other wanted to say something, but was keeping it back. We could never hold on for more than a couple of hours.'

'It's best to get it all out,' Bert said, as Bette arrived in the kitchen.

'Get what out?' she said with a piercing look at Belle.

'Information from Kylie Nichols. I'm going to tell you later, after we've done what we're about to do. It's nothing that can't wait. How's Georgie?'

'Nervous, as you'd expect. We should go through it with him, one more time.'

When they had talked to Georgie, who kept changing his mind about whether or not he should go, they eventually persuaded him it was the right thing to do. It was also just after three thirty and Belle was anxious they should keep to the timetable. Knowing there might be a long lens fixed on the front door, Belle had parked her car as close as possible, so Georgie could sneak out. They had made a small modification to the plan, in that Mandy was going to sit in the back seat. This way it wouldn't appear odd that the back door had opened for no reason, as there would only be two people in the car, both in the front.

Once they were all in the car, with Georgie on the floor covered by a pile of shopping bags, Mandy sat next to him and Bette in front with Belle, they made a rapid descent down the driveway and out of the gate. Bert had walked down to the gate, to check the road and when he signalled that it was clear, Belle drove the car without applying the brakes through the gateway, made a rapid right turn that had Mandy and Bette clutching at the door handles, and roared off up the road towards the main highway. No-one followed them and, although there had been some clicking of cameras, there couldn't have been enough time to spot anything out of order on the back seat.

They reached the Heights just before four. It was beginning to get dark. Much of the snow had cleared from the driveway and the moon was full in the sky, allowing Belle to drive right up to the old house.

As they all got out, the wind wrapped itself around them, tugging at scarves and coats. Georgie looked terrified as Belle pulled back the door. For a moment, she thought he was going to make a run for it, but Mandy took his hand, and he nodded and followed Belle inside, with Bette bringing up the rear. It was freezing inside the house.

'All we need to do, Georgie,' Belle said, as they stood at the bottom of the stairs, is to make our way up, then walk around to the small landing at the top of the back stairs. If you hear anything that sounds familiar from the night you found Star, just let us know.'

'OK, but I'm not going up into the attic,' he replied, his voice steadier now.

'None of us are going to do that,' Belle replied. 'Let's start.'

As they walked up the main staircase, each step creaked and groaned. Somewhere outside an owl hooted.

'Barn owl,' Georgie muttered.

At the top they paused for a moment. Belle ran her torch around, making sure everyone could see where they were. They turned left onto the short corridor and within a few steps were past the two bedrooms, whose doors were firmly shut, and onto the second, smaller landing.

Belle pointed out the thin, steep stairs to Bette. 'This was the servants' staircase, down to the kitchen. This door here,' she waved the torch at the narrow wooden door, 'goes up into the attic.' She moved forward and opened it so it was just ajar. She had seen that the only other door ajar was the closest one to where they were standing.

'On that night, Georgie would have opened this door and gone up the stairs. Right, Georgie?'

He nodded.

Opening the attic door had been the signal. Behind the open bedroom door, Posy immediately gave out a long, low "shushhhhhhhhh'. Georgie stiffened. Then another one, longer this time. "shushhhhhhhhh.'

'That's it,' he whispered. 'The wind in the trees. There must have been a window open in there. He stepped forward to open the door, but Mandy held his arm. 'Don't go in there, love.'

'Why not?' He had regained his courage. 'I want to see where that noise came from.'

'It came from me.' Posy opened the door and walked out onto the landing. 'What you heard, Georgie, wasn't the wind. It was someone behind that door, telling another person to be quiet. Whoever it was, knew you were here.'

'There it is, then,' Bette said. 'We can go now. I'm frozen and this place gives me the creeps.'

'Just a minute,' Belle said. 'Georgie, if we go to the police with this, they might say we made it up. You'll have to swear, on oath, that you didn't know Posy was there.'

'I didn't,' he protested. 'It sounded just like it did before. There are lots of noises in this house. Did you even notice the mice as we came up the stairs? They was skittering. 'Fraid of people, they are. Not like the rats.'

'There are rats?' Bette said.

''Course there are rats. Why wouldn't there be? Old place like this. Just leave them alone and they'll leave us alone.'

'I'm getting out of here now!' Bette said.

'Me too,' Mandy replied, grasping Georgie's arm.

Back outside, Georgie pushed himself into the well of the back seat and Mandy sat beside him, shivering.

'Where's your car, Posy?' Belle asked.

'Parked at the back. That worked out rather well, didn't it? But I don't think we can tell the police. They're bound to think it's a set up. Will you tell Georgie that?'

'I'll have to. How about you tell Billy, see what he thinks?'

'I will. He, um, he knows we've done this today.'

Belle gave her a quick hug. 'I expected no less. Let me know what he advises.'

'Will do, now let's all get out of this freezing cold.'

'Are you coming back to the farm?'

'No, Billy is coming to speak to me at the café. I'll call you later.'

**

Back at the farm, after they had warmed up with hot chocolate and Belle had explained to Georgie that they had to think about how to present this to the police, which he was cross about as he wanted to call them immediately, Georgie and Mandy left Bette, Bert and Belle in the kitchen.

'She wants to go home,' Bert said. 'But I told her, not yet. Not until he's cleared, which he will be soon, won't he?'

'He's due back in court in four days. That's the time we have left,' Belle said.

'We'll do it,' Bette said. 'Now, what was that you and Bert were talking about earlier?

Belle went through her conversation with Kylie Nichols, leaving nothing out.

Bette was speechless. She stood, walked around the kitchen, then out of the door onto the courtyard. Bert went to go after her, but Belle stopped him. 'Let her process this for a few minutes, Bert.'

He walked slowly around the table, until he couldn't bear it any longer. 'She'll be cold. I'm taking her a coat.'

As he reached the door, Bette walked back in. She had been crying. Bert held her in a tight embrace.

'I'm sorry, Bette. We don't have to tell anyone else…'

That was as far as she got.

'Of course we tell them,' Bette said, pulling away from Bert and wiping her eyes with her sleeve. 'Bert, get me a whisky. We're in this together. If we can't be honest and truthful with each other, then we'll fail, and this is important. You told us all about yourself.'

'It took me a while,' Belle said.

'Yes, but it didn't have someone's life and reputation hanging on it.'

'True. I don't think we should tell Georgie, though.'

'Ok, I agree with that. Would you like to stay for supper?'

Belle glanced at her watch, and jumped up. 'Thanks, but not tonight. I've been invited to dinner by Joe Knight. This might be important.'

'Might be something else, too,' Bette smirked. 'Very handsome. And single.'

'Isn't there a horribly clichéd saying, "handsome is as handsome does"?' Belle retorted.

'You just be careful of what he does on this date,' Bert joined in.

'I'm a woman in my fifties. I don't need advice, thank you both very much.'

**

Belle had planned something she hadn't yet told anyone about. She was becoming increasingly concerned about Emily, not about the woman herself, for her safety, but about the type of person that the conversations were revealing. She had decided to call a former school friend, who answered her call.

'Belle Harrington, you again. What is it this time?'

'Hello, Lennie. Are you at home or work?'

'Home. I have this week off, if that's what you can call it. I'm a taxi service. I am both looking forward to and terrified of the day any of them learn to drive. How can I help?'

'I need to speak to you, urgently. Can I come to see you? I know it's New Year's Eve tomorrow, but I won't take up much of your time, I hope.'

'As it happens all three are away this evening on sleepovers. But don't come too early. Charles and I are looking forward to a sleep in ourselves.'

'How about ten-ish.'

'Works for me. What are we going to discuss this time?'

'Sociopaths and Psychopaths, Lennie.'

'Righty-ho. See you in the morning.'

This meant Belle would have to be up and away by six the following morning. She couldn't afford to be too late this evening.

She didn't have much time to get ready for her "date", as Bert had called it. She chose a simple black dress, long and straight, with some discreet gold piping around the low neckline. As Joe Knight was around six foot, she thought about wearing a pair of high heeled shoes that she had kept in the cupboard for a few years, but then she thought of the snow still lying underfoot and chose a flat pair. At five foot six she was tall enough.

His car appeared outside at seven fifteen precisely. Belle was relieved to see that it wasn't black and didn't have darkened windows. The drive over to Padstow took around forty-five minutes, during which they chatted easily about their day, Joe having spent his indoors, researching for his next book, Belle lying about hers.

The restaurant sat on a corner of Padstow Harbour, with its own carpark. She paused for a moment at the entrance to look around. A substantial crowd milled around the harbour and all of the restaurants looked full and busy. The harbour itself was lit with fairy lights, as were many of the boats inside the enclosed harbour walls.

'It's very pretty here. And so busy,' she remarked to Joe.

'It does a thriving trade over Christmas and New Year. January and February are fairly quiet, but it's a place people like to come back to, often.'

They had been allocated a discreet table in a corner, lit with candles, in an elegantly decorated dining room. All of the tables were taken. The food was excellent. Belle chose locally caught fish, Joe ate steak. Over dinner they chatted about their lives and the similar experiences they shared with loved ones lost. They talked about grief and how they were both coping.

'I've been on my own for a few years now,' Belle said. 'Yours is more recent.'

'Evie spent her last weeks in a hospice,' he replied. 'I was with her at the end, which came quicker than expected. But, honestly Belle, it was a relief of sorts. She was in so much pain.'

She nodded, unable to speak, remembering her own feelings of despair.

He leaned across the table and took her hand. For a split second she wanted to pull hers away, but steeled herself and left it there.

'Thank you for agreeing to come out with me tonight, Belle. I haven't wanted to go out, much. I still don't like socializing, but I will be at the big charity bash at the Grand Hotel. Are you going?'

'No,' she replied. 'I like to be alone on New Year's Eve. Sam died a few days into January.'

'Perhaps, I could call on you, after all of the jollities are over? Just for a few minutes, on my way home?'

'Let me think about it, Joe.'

'Of course. I've enjoyed your company very much this evening.'

They now had coffee in front of them. Belle decided this was the time.

'How did you get on with Emily the other day, at her mother's house. She didn't look like she was warming to the idea of talking to you.'

He laughed and took his hand away. 'I don't know if you hung around long enough, but she agreed to let me in, when I pointed out it was freezing on her doorstep, and if she talked to you, why wouldn't she just let me have a few minutes. You warmed her up for me.'

'We saw you go in, just before we drove off. Did you get anywhere?'

'She's definitely defrosting. She's realised she can't stay in St Foy. Someone had spat at her on the street. She won't be accepted there for a long time. And anyway, what future is there for her in such a small-minded place? I've made her a proposal, that she come to London and work for me.'

'Did she accept?'

'Not yet. But I've suggested she continue her PhD. She's thinking about it. As I said before, she has a brilliant mind. It would be a terrible thing to let it go to waste.'

'What was she like as your student?'

'Bit of a nightmare, actually. On the subject of economics Emily is very, I mean very, opinionated. But that works for me.'

'Do you have any idea why she disappeared for three years?'

He shook his head. 'Not a clue, and she won't talk about it. I think she must have had a breakdown.' He frowned. 'Now she's back, I have been asking myself if I could have been in any way responsible for that. Did I contribute to it? Was I too hard on her?'

He looked distressed, and Belle took pity on him. 'No, Joe I don't think so. I've spoken to her a few times and she's never criticised you. Emily would have no issue with doing so, if she felt it was true.'

'Thank you for that.'

'You're welcome.'

'Poor Georgie is still in trouble, though, isn't he. That man wouldn't hurt a living thing. It was an incredibly stupid thing to do, to take Star from the attic; but covering her with his blanket, to me, that was an act of love.'

'I think it was more infatuation than love, but on the whole, I agree with you, though it still doesn't make him innocent in the eyes of the police. They might see it as a crime of passion, followed by terrible remorse, Joe.'

'True, true,' he said, with a sad expression. 'Are you OK, Belle?'

'Yes. I'm very sad about Georgie, and I'm rather tired. Would you mind if we went back to St Foy? I know it's still early, but…'

'No need to explain. I'll get the bill.'

'Please…'

'If you are even thinking of offering to pay half, don't. I ran you over with a supermarket trolley. This is me saying sorry. Remember?'

'Yes. Thank you. It has been a nice evening.'

He paused and gave her a deep smile. 'Then we should do it again.'

As they walked out of the restaurant a few heads turned to look at them, or rather, to look at him.

'You're a celebrity,' she whispered, taking his arm.

'Yuk,' he replied and they both giggled.

When they reached her cottage, he leaned over and kissed her on the cheek. 'Hope you don't mind. Thanks for a lovely evening.'

'I enjoyed it, too. We should do it again.'

She spent a moment fumbling for her keys in her bag, found them, turned and waved as he set off up the hill. He hadn't asked to come inside, for which she was grateful. She would have refused, which would have been awkward. She didn't want to get on the wrong side of this man.

The cottage was in darkness as Belle put her key in the lock. She closed the door behind her, then froze. She had left the kitchen light on. Now, it was off. And she had left the door to the kitchen open. It was shut. Very carefully, she took her shoes off, opened the porch door and listened. The very slightest sound of shuffling and a flash of light came from the kitchen. Someone was in the cottage, using a torch, searching.

Chapter 24

Her heart beat fast. Two choices. Fight or flight? Fight, definitely. If she could make her presence felt, they could escape via the kitchen door. She crept over to the fireplace, picked up a poker, then over to the light switch, and turned it on.

At the same time she shouted, 'Whoever you are, get out of my house! Now! I've already called the police.'

There was a crash from the kitchen and the sound of the back door being slammed open. Whoever it was, had already unlocked it. Belle took a deep breath, flung the kitchen door open and ran in, just in time to see a figure at the door. The figure froze for a moment, giving Belle enough time to reach them, but they were ready, and slammed a hand into her chest. She managed to reach forward with the poker, but couldn't be sure if she had connected, and fell backwards onto the floor, as the figure ran out of the kitchen, across the garden, up the steps to the lane. As she got to her feet and ran into the garden, she could hear the sound of heavy footsteps running away.

There was no chance of catching them, so she went back to the kitchen, where she found, when she put the kitchen light on, that as she fell her hand had caught a glass on the table, which had smashed and given her a deep cut across the palm. She pulled some kitchen towel from a roll, but couldn't staunch the bleeding. Damn! She would have to have this stitched. It was only ten. Should she call the police? Her immediate instinct was "no". This was no ordinary thief.

Holding a wadge of kitchen towel to her hand, she went into the living room. There was no damage, but her laptop was missing. Her instinct had been right. She smiled. Whoever had taken it was in for a big disappointment.

She picked up her phone and called Dan Walker. 'Sorry to spoil your evening with Richard, but someone has broken into my house and stolen my computer, and I've cut my hand rather badly. I was just wondering if you might take me to the hospital. It's in need of a couple of stitches.'

'Ten minutes,' he replied.

When he arrived he was out of breath and stood for a minute bent over and panting. When he could speak he said, 'Let me see. Yep, that's going to need a stitch or two.'

'I've not been drinking, but I can't drive with this until it's stitched up. Could you take me?'

'Of course. You can tell me what's happened. Belle? Belle, are you OK?'

The adrenalin had finally slowed down, and she stood still, feeling tears coming. 'Just shock. We need to go. I'll explain on the way.'

During the journey she told him everything she had learned during the day. Dan had run home and returned with a large, comfortable car. Belle gazed at the myriad controls on the dashboard.

'Are we driving or flying?' she said. 'This looks like it could do both.'

'Richard's car,' he replied. 'I thought you could do with something comfortable that glides over bumps in the road. It'll feel like you're flying.'

'Well, bless Richard, and thank him for me when you get back. I hope it won't be too long a night at the A&E department.'

They were lucky. Dan was allowed to go in with her, as she couldn't use her left hand, but only as far as the waiting area. Belle was triaged within fifteen minutes, her hand x-rayed and the cut pronounced not deep enough to have nicked bones or affected internal workings, therefore not requiring surgery, at which news Belle almost burst into tears again. A doctor stitched it for her and told her to return in five days, for a wound check. She was given strong painkillers and advised to rest it as much as possible. A nurse put her arm in a sling to emphasise the advice. She was back with Dan before midnight.

'Would you like me to stay with you tonight?' he asked. 'You shouldn't be alone after such a horrible experience. And this means you won't be able to come with us, which is a great shame.'

'Come where?' she asked.

'Richard has tickets for the New Year's Eve charity ball at the Grand hotel. It's a huge county event. Everyone who is anyone will be there. We thought it would be a good opportunity to see them all in the same place, together. Martin Riley will be there, and probably Joe Knight, plus a few other bigwigs. I don't normally like these events, avoid them if I can, but Richard is insisting. I think he may have decided to be just a little controversial.'

'Is he a controversial person?'

'Yes and no,' Dan replied

'Enigmatic. What does that mean? And don't tell me I'm not coming. Of course I'll come. It's just a cut hand. I'll be fine. A good sleep will help.'

'There's just no stopping you, is there? What about tonight?'

'I'll be OK, but perhaps you could come in and make me a cup of tea. A decent cup, not like that machine concoction at the hospital. The treatment may have been excellent and quick, but the refreshments were revolting.'

'At least it's my left hand,' she said. 'I have to be grateful for that.'

When they reached St Foy Dan made her sit in front of the fire whilst he made them a drink, then joined her.

'I called Richard. He's fine for me to stay.'

'Dan, I'll be OK. Whoever it was did this, was here for a specific purpose. They didn't get what they wanted, but I don't think they'll try again. They must have seen me leave earlier and thought they had more time. Lucky I cut the evening short. I have to be up in a few hours to get to South Wales.'

'I understand why you want to go, but there's no way you can drive. I'm driving you there, in that nice, comfortable car sitting outside. Don't argue with me.'

She leaned across and put her head on his shoulder. 'I was about to argue, but I don't have the strength. You know we have to leave at six?'

'Yes, that's why you need to drink your tea and get some sleep. You can sleep in the car, too.'

'Does the front passenger seat convert into a bed, like in business class flying?'

He laughed. 'Almost. Now, take your painkillers and get some sleep. I'll wake you at five thirty.'

Belle didn't expect to sleep, her mind being in such a whirl, but from the time she laid down to when she woke to find Dan shaking her, it felt like minutes. It took her a few moments to remember where she was and what had happened.

'Those painkillers are monsters,' he said. 'Knocked you out in minutes. Come on, up you get. Can you manage to get dressed?'

'I'll call if I need help,' she slurred. 'I should be able to manage.'

Every small movement of her hand was agony. Dan had already made her tea and put some in a flask to take with them.

'We're going to drive straight to Newport. Just give me the address for the satnav, then take some more painkillers and go back to sleep.'

She had no strength to so much as comment and was asleep before they reached the A30 main road through Cornwall. She woke up as they crossed the Severn Bridge into Wales.

'Welcome back to the land of the living,' Dan said. 'Satnav says we'll be there in fifteen minutes.'

They passed along the M4 until they reached the turn off for Caerleon. Lennie lived in the small hamlet of Kemys Commander. Belle explained its ancient origins connected with the Knights Templar and Hospitaller, its Welsh name being Cemais Comawndwr.

'Cemais means a bend or loop in a river. The Commandery was a district in medieval times and also the name given to the knight in charge of the district,' she explained.

The last part I knew,' Dan replied. 'Tell me about Lennie Maginnis.'

'She's a psychiatrist.' Belle had already told Dan about her school experiences, and how Lennie, a school friend, had aided her with information the previous year when she had come up against the former school bullies.

'She's a character,' Belle said.

'I'm looking forward to meeting her, if we can find where she lives.'

As they left the outskirts of the city and headed into the countryside there were few houses. They eventually found the hamlet. Lennie had texted that they should go past the church for about two hundred metres, then turn left along a single track lane. Her house was at the end of the lane and she would leave the gate open. They found it after a couple of wrong turns. Turning into the drive, they found themselves facing a substantial medieval former farmhouse, with outbuildings and stables. It was almost exactly ten and Lennie was waiting at the door.

'Heard you coming,' she said, 'not that that beast makes much noise. Electric, I presume?' she said admiringly.

'He's borrowed it from his husband,' Belle replied, leaning in to give Lennie a hug.

'I'd love a Porsche myself, just like that, big enough to fit the brats and all the gear they deem essential, but luxurious enough for me. But Charles says we can't afford one.' She pulled a face of disgust at the absent Charles.

'Work on him,' Belle said.

'Believe me, I do, in many ways,' Lennie replied, leading them through the house into a room at the back, an extension of kitchen plus seating area with glass on three sides that looked out over a beautifully manicured garden.

'Sit down. Tea or coffee, and Belle, please introduce me to this lovely looking man.'

Belle laughed. 'Lennie, this is Dr Daniel Walker.'

'*The* Dan Walker, the anthropologist? I've read your work. Fascinating.'

Dan nodded. 'But today, I am the chauffeur.'

'What happened to your hand?'

'I cut it on a glass, last night.'

'Really? Knowing you, there's more to it than that. I won't ask. Yet. Anyway, it's New Year's Eve and you haven't come here to talk social niceties. So, why psychopaths? You can talk whilst I make the coffee.'

'First, I'll tell you the story.'

Chapter 25

She began with the murder of Star Bright, three years earlier, Emily disappearing when she was expecting to have a termination and Georgie finding Star on Christmas Eve and placing her on the tree where she was found in mid-January. With nothing heard from Emily in the intervening time, no activity on bank accounts, and no sightings, the family had accepted that she too, was dead. Then, she went onto Emily's sudden re-appearance, her insistence that she hadn't killed Star, and the alibi provided by a member of the group she claimed she had lived with for the intervening three years. She also gave a quick precis of the students, the family and all of the other characters who seemed to have played a role in Emily's life at some point, trying to include every detail she could remember, up to the attempted burglary of her cottage the previous night.

'On the phone you said you wanted to talk about sociopathy and psychopathy. I take it you have a working theory about the murder?'

'I've heard many different accounts of Emily Duggan. She's a very horrible, nasty woman, but adamant it wasn't her who murdered Star. What I want to know is, does she have a personality capable of such a thing?'

'You know I can't give an opinion on an individual I've never met. Your account is interesting, but it has biases that I have to account for. However, from the stories you've told me, albeit also from people with bias, I would say sociopathic more likely than psychopathic. The term we use is anti-social personality disorder; a person who shows little or no regard for right or wrong, and who doesn't care about the feelings or concerns of others. Psychopath? We don't use that term, I leave it for television dramas. But sticking with your descriptives, I can only say a psychopath is a more extreme version; a person who has no conscience, nor moral compass. Usually they're more manipulative than violent. Could such a person kill without conscience? Yes, they could, but mostly not. Sociopath and psychopath, it's – how can I describe it – it's like the difference between hot and cold. A dangerous psychopath can be intelligent, charming, and good at mimicking emotions. They may pretend to be interested in you, but in reality, they don't care. They manipulate people for personal gain.

'Sociopaths don't pretend. They're not interested in anyone but themselves. They blame others and have excuses for their behaviour. Psychopaths are cold and calculating. They plot their moves. They'll take out anything that stands in their way, including people.

'This girl, Emily, sounds sociopathic. Your story about the whispering at the place you call the Heights, says that two people are involved. Given the circumstances, if she was one of them, that's a dangerous combination. Could it lead to murder? Depends on which one is leading, but I would say, yes, it could. Don't be the person in their way, Belle.'

'Thanks, Lennie. Is there anything in particular we should look out for?'

'The person leading this will be aware of the dangers posed by others, and will eliminate them if they sense danger. Has anyone else died or gone missing?'

'I believe – we all believe – Mavis is a victim of a deliberate attack because of something she knew. Something

I didn't mention; I think some of us are being followed. I don't know who it is, but I've seen the same car on a few occasions, and so has someone else, who was sufficiently concerned to come to tell Posy and me about it.'

'Have you talked to the police about this? Ah, no, you haven't. Martin Riley, I think you said the name is?'

'Exactly. He's having an affair with the Chief Inspector heading the investigation. She's determined to pin it on Georgie Morris, so any evidence we provide will be brushed off.'

They chatted for another hour, discussing the case and Lennie's interest in Dan's work. Belle sat back at this point, thinking about everything Lennie had told them. Much of it she had read, but hearing now from an expert, gave her much more to think about.

'Look at the time,' Dan said. 'We've been here two hours. We must start off back to St Foy. Lennie, lovely to meet you. We must arrange to speak again, given how our interests overlap.'

They exchanged phone numbers as Belle stood, thanked Lennie and she and Dan set off.

'That was both fascinating and informative,' Dan said as they made their way across country to the M4 motorway. Lovely woman. I like quirky characters.'

'She certainly is that,' Belle said. 'Do you mind if I sleep again? I took a couple more of those knockout pills.'

'Go ahead,' he replied. 'It will give me some thinking time.'

Belle closed her eyes, but didn't sleep. It was Lennie's warning about bias that occupied her thoughts for a while. What about Emily's family? Was Georgie telling the whole truth? And what about Bette? And the other sister, Charlie?

Did either of them know something they still weren't admitting to? Emily had said her grandmother, Edna, had boasted of killing her own husband, then pretended it was a joke; but was it?

She thought through each of the people who had been involved, both at the time of the murder and now that Emily had returned. The one thing she simply couldn't understand was why Emily had stayed away for so long, and off the grid. Harry Teague was right; now she had met Emily, she wasn't the type to stay so long on a commune. But if she hadn't been there, where had she been and how had she managed to live without any reference to or use of her former life? Someone had helped her. Had to be. Who? She was definitely going to the charity ball, even if it meant going without the medication, which made her too sleepy to think clearly. She was going to need a clear head.

They arrived back in St Foy just after four in the afternoon.

'Are you sure about tonight?' Dan asked. 'Those pills might make you face plant in the dinner.'

She laughed as he opened the door for her to exit the car. 'I'll be OK. See you at the hotel at eight fifteen. And no, I'm getting a taxi. You and Richard can bring me home.'

She had four hours before the start of the ball. She decided to try to sleep for three of them, and allow an hour to get ready. She would have to look the part to meet the great and good of the County.

First, sleep. She set an alarm for three hours and fell asleep almost immediately. The plan didn't work out quite as expected. After two hours she was woken by a buzzing which started, then stopped, then started again. Her phone. She grabbed it and peered at the screen. Maggie Gilbert.

'Maggie, hello.'

'You sound drugged.'

'I am, sort of. Cut my hand last night, needed stitches and the painkillers are turning me into a zombie.'

'I was going to give you some information about Star Bright, but you don't sound like you'll remember any of it five minutes after I've told you. It can wait. Go back to sleep.'

Belle glanced at the clock on her bedside table. 'No, tell me now. I'm going to a fancy New Year's Ball in a couple of hours, so I won't get back to sleep.' She sat up, squeezed her eyes and rolled her neck. 'Right, I'm ready.'

'My Maze colleague, Zelah, uses a PI sometimes and he got onto Star Bright. You already know that Star's name was Louisa Anastasia Light. And that she ran away from home when she was fourteen.'

'Yes, I remember that.'

'She said that she didn't have any family. As you know already, that wasn't true. She has a mother, whom we've found is still alive and living in London; Augusta Light. She's a Barrister.'

'That's unexpected, and not the sort of person you'd expect to not involve the police in the case of a missing fourteen-year-old.'

'No. Doesn't seem she looked too far or wide for her, either. She described her daughter to friends as a bloody nuisance that she was glad to be rid of. The kind of friends she had, the circles she moved in, still moves in, didn't encourage her to try.'

'That's shocking. Why not? What sort of people are they? What sort of person is she? Star's murder was widely reported, but she never came forward. This is something that's been bothering me a great deal, Maggie,' Belle said. 'Tell me more.'

'The mother, Augusta, works with and for criminals; the worst. Apparently she's very good at what she does. She had had an affair with a police inspector from the Met, and known to be as corrupt as hell. It produced a child.'

'Don't tell me – the police inspector was Martin Riley?'

'Possibly he's the father, but the PI didn't give a name, just a profile of a bent copper. She kept the baby. Or "it" as she referred to her daughter. Star was a wild child. Often in trouble, but the father got her out of some of it. When she disappeared, Augusta was relieved.'

'Poor little kid.'

'The PI has managed to find out something about Star's life between fifteen and seventeen, when she pitched up in Bristol. She'd been living in a squat in the city. No surprise there. She had some money, apparently. When it ran out, she decided to go to College, signed up for GCSEs, then A levels. Then she achieved a University place, in Bristol. She worked, to keep herself. Odd jobs, mainly off the books, before she pitched up in Cornwall at St Piran's, to do her Master's degree.'

'Do you know if she ever contacted her mother?'

'Not that we know, but she might have done. Just one thing more; there was some trouble at the University in Bristol. She took a fancy to one of the tutors, followed him around. He reported it, and the Uni threatened to expel her. She said she thought he was her father, and apologised, enough to keep her place. But there was talk of her often being in the company of older men.'

'She did something similar here,' Belle said. 'This Professor reported her, too.' She paused for a few seconds.

'Maggie, would I be right in thinking that Star Bright had no idea who her father was?'

'You would. She openly admitted it, in her days in Bristol. She said her mother wouldn't tell her. I wonder if she ever found out?'

'I'm not sure she did. But I think he did.'

'Are you going to tell me?'

'Not yet, Mags. I have an event to attend. I'll call you.'

Something told her this was going to be a night of revelation and, despite the pain in her hand, she was looking forward to it. There was a fireworks display planned immediately after midnight. That was outdoors. Belle thought there might be a few going off indoors, too.

Chapter 26

She arrived ten minutes late. Dan was waiting alone in the hotel foyer. He was surrounded by men in evening suits and women in dresses the cost of which could have fed the average family for a month. Belle had chosen one she hadn't worn for many years. It had been Sam's favourite and it took some mental courage on her part to put it on. She knew it suited her and Dan gave her an appreciative look as she walked up to him.

'I've said it before, but I'll say it again, you scrub up well. You looked beautiful, my dear. Gorgeous dress.'

Belle had been more than surprised, amazed that it still fitted. Long and straight, low enough at the front to reveal the top of her cleavage and even lower at the back, it was silk with a black background and dark, shimmering blue patterns. She had added a dark blue silk pashmina, which she handed off to an attendant. Her wild auburn curls were, as usual for a special event, caught up elegantly, this time at the back of her head, held in place with a shimmering blue clasp. She had put on gold jewellery. And makeup. This had taken the most time. Belle hadn't worn this amount of slap on her face for years and had had to watch a quick online tutorial on what to put where. The final result was good enough.

'You too,' she said, raising up to kiss his cheek. Dan was a little under six feet tall, slim and elegant. 'You've had a haircut,' she teased.

'And a professional shave. We must look the part. I feel like a tailor's dummy.'

'Well, you look fabulous. The best looking man in the room, I suspect.'

He smiled and shook his head. 'No, my love, I am about to be outshone.' He glanced over her shoulder and smiled. It wasn't the kind of smile she had seen before on his face. This was love. Richard must be about to join them. With a sense of anticipation she turned around. And froze. Walking towards them across the foyer, with the crowd parting to let him through, was a most gorgeous handsome, sexy man. He walked confidently, like a model on a catwalk. Taller than Dan, but with the physique of a body builder and, as he came closer, huge dark eyes.

'Close your mouth,' Dan whispered.

She hadn't realised it had dropped open.

Dan was holding in a grin as he introduced them. 'Belle, this is my husband Richard. Richard, this is Belle Harrington.'

Richard put his hand out to shake hers. 'I've heard so much about you,' he said. His voice was as attractive as his appearance, low and melodious. She wondered what he did for a living. Dan had never said. Probably an actor, she thought. Had to be with that voice and presence. Funny she had never seen him; or recognised him from some film or TV programme.

They exchanged pleasantries for a few minutes, before Dan said, 'Let's go find our table. It's just the three of us. This is bad enough without having to put up with some boring old farts.'

They were amongst the last to enter the room. They found their table, at the back of the room, which Dan had requested. There was a low murmur of noise, although Belle guessed there were well over a hundred men and women present. A number of people nodded at Dan as they crossed the room, many stared at Richard, some talking behind their hands. A few gave Richard a nod, which to Belle looked like deference and admiration. He smiled and nodded back. Then, as they passed the table on which Belle caught a glance of Joe Knight, came a loud, brash, slurring voice.

'Don't tell me to shut up, you stupid cow. Who's that jungle bunny?'

'Martin, for God's sake, shut up! You're embarrassing us all.'

Belle froze as she recognised Joe Knight's voice. She spun around. The comment had come from a table of seven, one of whom was Joe Knight, who all appeared to be squirming in degrees of mortification and anger. Martin Riley's wife was trying to talk to him, but he pushed her off. Joe Knight, on his other side leaned in to say something, but he too, was shoved away. Martin Riley continued to scowl at Richard, who, apart from briefly touching his top lip with the tip of his tongue, hadn't batted an eyelid or paused as he walked to their table. Dan appeared calm, but Belle could see red spots on his cheeks. Richard had just sat down, but now he stood again.

'Let's go meet them,' he said. 'Dan, you'll do the introductions.'

'Delighted, my dear,' he replied. 'Belle, you're coming too. This should be fun.'

Slowly, Richard approached the table. Ignoring Riley, he turned to the third man, who stood and took his hand, pumping it enthusiastically.

'I'm absolutely delighted to meet you again, Sir Richard. I'm a great admirer of your work. I watched you take Rawlings apart. One of the most important corruption cases in years in this country.' His expression was reverential and Richard looked appreciative.

'Sir Richard?' Belle whispered to Dan.

He replied with raised eyebrows. 'It gets better,' he whispered back.

'Everyone, I am delighted to welcome Sir Richard Henry-Williams, QC, one of this country's greatest Barristers, and tipped to become a senior judge.'

'No, no, Jolyon,' Richard replied. 'Let's not get carried away.'

Joe Knight had jumped to his feet and walked around the table to shake Richard's hand. He turned to Riley and snapped, 'Martin?'

Martin Riley got unsteadily to his feet. 'Pleased to meet you,' he slurred. 'Heard a lot about you.'

Richard's eyes drilled into him, and Martin Riley shuffled and looked down. 'Have you, Chief Constable? And I of you, particularly about your time in the Met.' Belle looked around the table. Two of the woman were gazing admiringly, but the third stared off into the distance across the room, a puzzled expression on her face, Belle noticed.

'Do have a lovely evening, all,' Richard said, turned and led Belle and Dan back to their table.

A whisper ran around the room, which they ignored as they re-seated themselves.

'I think that if Martin Riley could kill you, he wouldn't hesitate to do so,' Dan said conversationally as he lay a napkin on his lap and waiters began to appear with the first course. 'Belle, you're quiet. Are you upset with me? Perhaps I should have told you more about Richard…'

'No,' she interrupted. 'I'm calming down. So that's Martin Riley. What an obnoxious… I don't know what say.

He's totally drunk already. Let's hope they can keep him quiet.'

'He's just made himself a pariah. No-one will speak to him or go near him for the rest of the evening,' Dan said.

'Belle, are you OK?' Richard asked.

'I'm fine. You?'

'Yes. Martin Riley is a throwback to the Met of the nineties. He was corrupt, well in with criminal groups and families. He must have had a lot to drink, though, to let it come out; here of all places.'

'Richard, do you mind if I ask you a question?'

'Of course. Fire away.'

'Do you know Augusta Light?'

His smile turned into a frown. 'Indeed, yes. An unpleasant woman. I've been up against her a few times. Why?'

'Because just before I came here I had a call from my friend Maggie, in Wales. Augusta Light is, was, Star Bright's mother. And I now think I know who the father might be. At the time of conception, he was a corrupt Inspector in the Met.'

'You don't mean…' Dan stuttered.

'Martin Riley,' she said. 'It could explain why so little information came out about Star when she died. He deliberately supressed it.'

'Do you think he killed her?'

'It's a possibility,' Belle replied. 'That would depend on whether or not he knew who she was when he was visiting his daughter at the Heights.'

'Daughters,' Dan corrected.

'Martin Riley was indeed known to be a corrupt copper,' Richard said. 'But I didn't know about his relationship with Augusta.'

'He's moved up and moved on,' Belle replied. 'Now he's having an affair with the Chief Inspector leading the renewed enquiry into Star's murder, following Emily's return.'

'Dan told me. He must have known who she was. I can't think of another reason he would have supressed evidence, and it suggests a good reason why now he's trying to make sure the murder is pinned on George Morris,' Richard said, 'manipulating the enquiry from behind the scenes for a second time.'

'He's such an ugly git,' Belle said. 'Susan Lewis must be desperate for a promotion. Sorry, I shouldn't have said that.'

'Then she will face disappointment. He isn't going to be Chief Constable of South Cornwall for much longer. He's retiring at the end of January,' Richard said. 'It will be announced soon.'

'Isn't that rather short notice?' Belle asked.

'Yes,' Richard replied.

Belle and Dan stared at him. He picked up his glass and drank slowly.

'You know something you have no intention of sharing,' Belle said. 'I can understand that, and I won't ask. But I do hope it will be publicly shameful and humiliating.'

Richard nodded. 'There will be an interim appointment; health grounds, etc. But no matter the reason given, he's going to be disgraced and he knows it.'

'In the meantime, that puts on the pressure to have Georgie charged with the murder,' Dan reflected. 'And we aren't any closer to proof of his innocence, never mind knowing who actually did it.'

The courses of the dinner moved on. They chatted about many things; inconsequential, personal at times, each talking about the path of their lives and how they had reached this moment in time in the town of St Foy. Belle was surprised to hear that, far from a privileged background, Richard had grown up in Brixton, and at one time as a young boy had been in one of the notorious gangs. He talked about how, with help from his mother, he had removed himself – she had actually moved out of London, leaving her family behind, to get him away – and taken to education, which he had found came easily to him. Dan intervened, with Richard's permission, to tell her that when they weren't working, they had set up a foundation with officers from the Met, to help young men in London get out of the gangs.

'That's amazing, and a wonderful thing to do,' Belle said. 'She turned to Dan. 'I'm so glad I didn't kill you.'

He burst out laughing, as did Richard, and people on the tables around them turned to look at them.

'We're causing quite a stir,' she said. Then, more seriously to Richard, 'How do you put up with the likes of Martin Riley and what he said about you, before he knew who you were. I am not a violent person, but I wanted to punch him.'

'Water off a duck's back,' he replied. 'I can put the likes of Riley in his place very easily. But that's now. It hasn't always been easy.'

Dan put his hand over Richard's.

'I can see that you two have a wonderful relationship,' Belle said. 'I had the same with Sam. I still miss him, every day.'

'How did the dinner go with Joe Knight?' Dan asked, a gleam in his eye.

'Well enough,' she replied.

'Leave the woman alone,' Richard said to him. He turned to Belle with a mock frown. 'So, how did it go?'

She laughed. 'He's invited me again. I'll think about it, but I suspect he won't be spending much time in St Foy. His star is rising. He's bound for London and – I haven't got around to telling anyone this yet – he's trying to persuade Emily to work with him on his next book. I suppose that means she'll go, too, if she agrees, which she hasn't done, yet. As for another dinner, I don't know. It was only last night and with the burglary and the hospital visit, and the trip to Wales, I haven't had time to think about it.'

'What did you mean about whoever it was getting a shock?' Dan asked.

Before she could answer, the next course was served. As the waiters hovered around them, Belle took the opportunity to look over at Joe Knight's table. Martin Riley was well gone. His face was red and he waved his arms around in what she thought was an angry way, pushing a waiter who dropped a plate of food, then shouting at the girl for her clumsiness. The news of his imminent retirement had definitely not gone down well. As she watched she caught the eye of another man at the table, who stood up and began to walk in their direction. As he reached them, both Richard and Dan stood. He indicated to both of them to sit, but turned his attention to Belle.

'Mrs Harrington, I was wondering if you have any news about Mavis Penhaligon?'

'She's improving, I believe. Still in the Intensive Care Unit, but stable. We're more hopeful, but as yet no-one can say what direction her recovery might take.'

'I'm pleased to hear that, but still, worrying. When you are able, when the time comes, please give her my regards. I helped her out last year with an issue about her aunt's cottage, where I understand she now lives. She visited our archives.'

Belle jumped up, realising to whom she was speaking. 'I will, thank you, Lord…'

'Jolyon, please,' he said. 'I like Mavis. A local woman and very forthright. When she's sufficiently recovered, I'll invite her to tea. Perhaps you would like to accompany her?' He said this with a gleam in his eye.

'I'd love to,' she replied, grinning back at him. 'I already feel like I know your house.'

'Many people do,' he replied. 'I will pray for Mavis' safe and full recovery. Please, do let me know.' He turned to Richard. 'Sir Richard, I can only apologise for that… incident. If I could, I would have had him thrown out.'

Richard held up a hand. 'Please don't apologise, Jolyon. He'll be gone soon enough.'

Jolyon smiled, nodded and walked back to his table.

'Wow,' Belle said, flopping back down into her seat. 'If that actually happens, it'll be one off the bucket list.'

She turned to Dan. 'On that table, can you tell me more about the other people?'

'Sure. You know Joe Knight and Martin Riley, and now Jolyon. The woman sat between Martin and Joe is Martin Riley's wife, Josie. The woman sitting next to Jolyon is his daughter. His wife died about five years ago. The other couple are Jonathan and Maria Richardson, of Mabberley House. Why?'

'Why what?'

'You don't ask superfluous questions and you are neither a gossip nor interested in local bigwigs.'

'When we were at the table, being introduced, I noticed that Riley's wife wasn't paying attention. She was looking across the room. At first she seemed puzzled, then, angry. Look at her now, her face hasn't cracked a smile in two hours.'

Dan glanced over and back. 'I see what you mean. She looks like she's being forced to eat a bag of nails, although that's not an unusual look for Josie Riley. I wonder who she was looking at.' He watched the woman for several seconds, then strained his neck in the direction of the table in the opposite corner. 'Oh, good grief!'

'What?' Richard and Belle said simultaneously.

'That table in the corner. It's her daughter, Miriam, with her husband, Phil Singh.'

'Probably no love lost between Martin Riley and his son-in-law,' Belle replied. 'Given Riley's racism he can't be happy about his daughter being married to Phil Singh.'

'I haven't noticed that they've made any approach to each other, in either direction,' Belle said. 'Oh, the other couple with them, that's Billy Anderson, with his wife. I expect he's keeping well away from Riley. And, I can see there's someone else at the table with them, a woman, but I can only see the top of her head.' She stood up, then sat back down, quickly. 'I don't believe it. It's Emily.'

'Four of the housemates together,' Dan said. 'I thought they didn't speak to each other.'

'That's what they said. As soon as this course is done, I'll pay a social visit.'

As a waiter cleared the table Belle stood and made her way across the room. Richard and Dan watched her go.

'I hope this won't end in anything unpleasant,' Richard said.

'Trust her, it won't.'

'Good evening, guys,' Belle said as she reached the table. 'Are you enjoying yourselves? The polite smiles and small nods they all returned told her that this table wasn't having much fun. She glanced around at each of them. As she reached Emily, her eyes widened. 'That's a beautiful necklace, Emily,' she remarked casually, as the gold glinted in the subdued lighting in the corner of the room.

Emily's polite smile turned to a glare. Belle held her own smile, realising this must be the famous missing and re-appearing lover's knot. No-one else spoke.

'Well, Happy New Year to all of you,' she said, as she returned to her own table.

'That was interesting,' she said as she sat down. 'I didn't say anything controversial, just kept it to pleasantries. One thing stood out, though. Emily is wearing what I think is the infamous lover's knot. She scowled at my compliment, so I wished them a Happy New Year and left.'

'Jade's story was true, then. Star put it back.'

'So it seems. I'm still wondering what's upset Josie Riley.'

'Perhaps Martin won't let her go over to speak to her daughter.'

'Could be, but my impression is that she's staring at Emily, not at Miriam.'

The final course had come and gone and they were onto coffee, when the dancing began. Belle decided to hit the dance floor, the pain in her hand notwithstanding, dragging an enthusiastic Dan with her. It was energetic and at one point, her hair started to come loose, so she pulled off the slide that had been holding it in place and allowed her curls to flow.

Glancing over to their table, she saw that Richard was surrounded, smiling and answering questions. She pointed it out to Dan.

'Groupies,' he replied. 'Probably the local solicitors and lawyers.'

Twenty minutes later, the announcement came that it was a minute to midnight. The usual singing and glad-handing was to be followed by a fireworks display outside in the grounds, which guests were invited to watch.

'Might as well,' Dan said. 'Then we can clear off home. Belle, you will come with us for a quick drink, just the three of us?'

'Of course,' she replied as the countdown to midnight began and the bells of Big Ben were projected into the room. Everyone stood and counted down. As midnight was reached, the hugs and handshakes began. Many people approached Richard, Dan and Belle, but not Martin Riley or his wife, who were left sitting alone.

'Let's get our coats and get outside,' Richard whispered.

In the foyer Belle was intercepted by Joe Knight. 'May I join you?' he asked. 'You seem to be a happy party, unlike mine.' She couldn't refuse and when he had found his overcoat and scarf, he accompanied them into the carpark. Belle had only brought a pashmina and quickly began to shiver. Joe offered her his coat. She refused, but accepted the scarf. It didn't help much so he opened his coat and pulled her inside it with him. Out of the corner of her eye she could see Dan frowning.

The twenty minute display was spectacular, watched from beyond the hotel grounds by a large crowd of local people. When it was over, Dan announced that Richard had gone for the car.

'Quick getaway,' he whispered.

Next to them, another car was pulling up. Miriam Singh ran over to stand next to her mother, who was about to get into the chauffeured vehicle. They hugged and Miriam whispered: *Monday. Usual place.* Josie nodded and jumped into the back seat of the car, which sped off.

Joe Knight had also invited her for a drink back at his place, but she gracefully refused, to his obvious disappointment. 'Tomorrow, then. How about lunch? I'll cook. I'm quite good.'

She accepted, as Richard's car arrived. Back at Dan's flat they again toasted in the New Year with a glass of whisky, and non-alcoholic champagne for Richard.

Through the glass window, that tonight gave a spectacular view out over the estuary, they could see that many of the boats had strung coloured lights around their masts and rigging. Across the water the small town of Porthdevan was also lit up. Belle stood next to the window, looking out.

'It's lovely,' she said, 'I love my cottage. I bought it for its tranquillity, and I'm only a few minutes' walk from the harbour, but to have this view all of the time, must be so soothing.'

Dan and Richard went to stand next to her.

'It's a special place for me.' Dan said, 'When the rush and anonymity and unfriendliness of London becomes too much, I retreat here.'

'Except when he disappears for months at a time and I worry that he's been eaten by a snake in the rainforests of South America, or mangled by an unfriendly gorilla in Borneo.'

'The snakes rarely eat the people. It's usually the other way around. And the gorillas are friendly, if you approach them the right way. Belle, you never got round to answering my question about why the person who burgled your cottage would get a nasty surprise.'

'Oh, that. The computer on the workstation's a dummy. I learned a lesson years ago, when I left a real one on my desk at work. As you know, my work could be very confidential, and I worked at some prestigious firms. Now, I never leave my real computer on my desk. I lock it away, even for a five-minute break, and put a dummy one in its place. What the thief here has is a laptop that has no password protection and only one file. When they open it, they will find a collection of meaningless jumble. If they spend hours thinking it's some kind of code, all they will come up with is rubbish. The real one is in a safe under my desk, together with all of my notes and recordings.'

'Clever,' Richard said. 'I'm probably too careless with mine. Because everything's backed up on a server, I tend to worry more about losing the data than the computer. Perhaps I'll start to do that.'

'Dan, you're looking strangely enigmatic. What's on your mind?'

'Something is, but I can't grasp it. Something I saw tonight, that's clanging a warning bell. I can't figure out what it is, but I will.'

'I have a similar feeling,' Belle said, 'but now I'm too tired to think clearly, probably information overload and my hand is hurting. I need the knock out pills to kill the pain, and many hours of sleep. Richard, do you think you could drive me home? I know it's only a couple of minutes, but I'm too knackered to walk.'

I wouldn't dream of allowing you to walk. You could stay here, you know. We have a spare room.'

'That's kind, but tonight I need my own bed. I have no intention of rising early. And besides, I have a lunch date. Joe has invited me to lunch at his house and I shall keep the appointment. You both know that we've been invited to tea with Bette and Bert?'

'Absolutely. Wouldn't miss it,' Dan said. 'It's a good chance to catch up and Bert's cakes are to die for.'

Dan and Belle gave each other a hug, then she left for the short journey home. Richard insisted on going into the cottage with her, to check that there was no-one there.

'Quite safe,' he said. 'Enjoy your sleep and your lunch and I'll see you at Bette and Bert's farm at five.'

Belle thanked him, went inside, changed into comfortable night clothes and slippers, and sat in front of the fire, which she had left burning and now stoked up again with a couple of fresh logs. She made herself a hot chocolate with which to take her pills. They did the trick and she began to feel sleepy within ten minutes. Before she slept, she made one decision about a further visit. As soon as possible, she wanted to speak to Josie Riley, without her husband present. She needed to know why Josie had been so glum and angry throughout the evening. Her gut told her there was more to it than having to sit next to her obnoxious, drunken husband, and not being able to speak to her daughter. She had seen Josie and Miriam share a quick hug in the car park after the fireworks, so enforced separation wasn't the reason. There was something, or someone else that had deeply upset the woman. Her last thought before sleeping was that whatever it was, it was an important factor in the case of the murder of Star Bright.

Chapter 27

Belle awoke at seven, alert at once, despite having only a few hours' sleep. She had been dreaming about hospitals, having to be there with her mother, who was dying, but instead getting into a bed herself. And at the same time her car was being towed away in the hospital carpark. In the dream she was embarrassed. It unnerved her sufficiently to make her get out of bed, make herself a cup of tea and wander around the ground floor until the memory of the dream dissipated. She had no idea what it meant, but, whatever, she was awake, so she might as well do something useful with the time.

Her most important goal today was to speak to Josie Riley, if she could find a way. She couldn't just drive up to the house. Perhaps Joe Knight would know. Some roundabout questioning about the Rileys? That wouldn't be difficult after Martin Riley's performance at the Ball last night.

She knew too that Dan had something on his mind. Despite only having known him for a year or so, during which he had disappeared for several months, they had become good friends, good enough to read each other's moods and know when to not ignore them. Perhaps she could manage a quiet word with him when they met up later.

Walking round the sitting room wasn't enough. She poured her tea into a thermos cup, put on her coat and boots and walked down to the harbour. It was now almost eight and a few people were out and about. The sun was shining on the snowy landscape, but it was bitingly cold. Her usual spot being already occupied, she suddenly decided on a longer walk. Leaving the harbour, she walked back up towards the cottage, but turned left along the road that led to Cash Cove, and began a brisk walk. By the time she reached the cove ten minutes later she was glad to stop. Breathing in the freezing air had been exhilarating, but her lungs hurt.

She walked down onto the beach. The tide was full, but as usual, no more than a gentle lapping against the flat soft sands. She thought back to the summer, when she had come here to swim in the tranquil water almost every day. This place had occupied a prominent spot on the yes/no list when she had been thinking about buying the cottage from the couple from whom she had been renting it.

Her eyes closed, Belle thought back to the day, the last day, she had seen her father. They were playing on the beach here. It was a full tide that day, too. That was when she had climbed up on the rocks and the boy she had, until a week ago, known only as Johnnie, had swum up and joined her. When he jumped – as she now knew he had done – from the rocks, her life had changed in that moment. Her mother, Gillian had seen the opportunity, and told Belle she had pushed the boy, who was most likely dead and that she would be taken away by the police for murder. She had lived with that dreadful possibility for most of her life until Gillian admitted, when she was dying, that it wasn't true, that she had said it to remove Belle from her father but keep access to his money. She had come back to St Foy for one last time to try to find the boy. And it had turned out to be Dan. His revelation had changed her life, yet again. It had taken until now to sink in. But, standing here, on this beach, on New Year's Day, she at last knew that she was not only free of the spectre that had hung over her life through childhood to this late middle age, but that she had gained a very special friend. She began to laugh out loud. A family whose children were playing on the beach, gave her a worried look and called their children back close to them, away from the laughing mad lady. Life changing. She had heard the phrase so many times. Today, she understood it, felt it, embraced it. She took one last look at the cove. Each time she did this before leaving, she became filled with a warm sensation; her love for her father. Despite always preaching forgiveness, in this one matter, she had none. She would never, ever, forgive Gillian.

Back at the cottage she sat, calmer now, and thought through her list of things to do. *Belle's list* had become a joke amongst the Club members, one she knew was made in a spirit of comradeship. She began writing.

An hour later, her head clearer, the list had been re-formed into a list of priorities, a "top ten". Occupying the number one spot was speaking to Josie Riley, followed by another trip to Port Simon to ask a few more questions of Jade, then another visit to Emily in Sugar Pit Lane. For now, it would all have to wait. It was already past eleven and she was expected at Joe Knight's house at two.

She had decided on casual, jeans and a sweater, her hair left loose and just a touch of makeup. She didn't want him to think she had made a big effort.

As she was about to leave, her phone rang. Posy.

'Belle, some good news and some bad. Very bad.'

'Give me the good first.'

'Mavis is much better. She's breathing for herself. There's a possibility they may try lifting the sedation, to see how she reacts.'

Belle felt a sense of relief great enough to produce a few tears. 'That's wonderful news, Posy. Now, hit me with the rest.'

'The woman you went to see, Kylie Nichols? She's been beaten. She's in a bad way. Billy says she may lose an eye. And, Jade Waters is missing.'

For a moment, Belle couldn't speak.

'Belle, are you still there?'

'Did we do this, Posy? Was it our questioning that's brought this about? Someone knew. That car that was following us…'

'You just stop right there. None of us is to blame. This is down to whoever killed Star Bright, and why that happened. Don't you dare think for a nanosecond that we are in any way to blame. You've been injured, too. We're all in the line of fire of whomever is doing this. Would you like to come over here and have some lunch?'

'I'd love to, but I'm going to Joe Knight's for lunch. He invited me last night, at the Ball.'

It was Posy's turn to have a few seconds' silence. 'OK, but just be careful. He was there at the time of the murder; he supervised Emily and tutored Star. You are coming to the farm later, aren't you?'

'Of course. I'll be there, as will Dan and Richard and don't ask me now what he's like. You'll love him, that's all I can say. Have to go, Posy, or I'll be late.'

Joe had given her his postcode for her Satnav, but also told her a number of properties shared it, and described the location of his house. It was in the village of Trelowarren, about five miles from St Foy. She found the village easily enough, but had to drive slowly to locate the narrow lane that led up to the house on the clifftop, past a couple of farm entrances. She passed it once, reversed down the lane and turned in. The drive up was short.

It was a farmhouse, converted, as she could tell from the modern double glazed windows which had been made in dark wood in keeping with the uneven brick construction. For a farmhouse it was a good height, with two storeys and what looked like a loft space at the top. The front door opened.

Each time she saw him she felt the shock of appreciation of his good looks. He had also dressed casually today, in ripped jeans and an open-necked white shirt, with black loafers.

He walked forward as she closed the car door and gave her a quick hug and kiss on the cheek.

'As much as you looked gorgeous last night, I prefer the hair down. It's the more natural you.'

He led her through the house, which, although an old building, was furnished in a modern style. As they reached the kitchen, she paused and gasped. The fixtures and fittings were all simple, black and white, with a centre island. Beyond it was a new extension, with a glass panelled roof and folding glass doors, leading out onto a small, cottage style garden. At the end of the garden was a white picket fence. Beyond that the coastal path wound past, protected from the sea by another, ugly wire fence. And then, the sea.

'Can we go out there?' she asked turning to him with a smile that lit up her face.

'Of course,' he replied, leading her forward past the island. He opened the glass doors and they walked across a small patio to the fence. To her left was the great sweep of the bay leading round to Smugglers Point, with the seaside village of St Loos sitting just below the headland. Beyond and ahead, stretched an endless blue sea.

'I could just look at this all day.' Belle put her head back and breathed deeply.

'I often do,' he said. 'It was Evie's favourite place. You should see it when it's stormy, waves crashing on the rocks over on the headland. It's breath-taking.'

'Do you mind the walkers passing by?'

'Sometimes they can be too nosy. We could have put up a higher picket fence, but Evie wanted the view, so I put up with them. It's not too bad.'

They walked back into the kitchen, and he closed up the doors. A dining table had been laid ready for lunch.

'I thought we could eat here, if that's OK with you.'

'Fine with me,' she said, still looking out at the view.

'Take a seat. I'll just be a few minutes. We can talk as I cook. I'm not the greatest cook, I did tell a small lie last night, so please don't expect cordon bleu.'

She laughed. 'I'm here for the company. And I'm not a fussy eater. So long as it's not burned, I'll eat it.'

'That's a relief. How did you enjoy the Ball last night?'

'It was good fun, wasn't it? I enjoyed the dancing, brief though it was, for us. Haven't let my hair down like that in years. Literally.'

He laughed. 'As I said, I like your curls. The auburn colour is beautiful.'

'All my own hair and teeth,' she replied, keeping the tone light.

He came to the table with a dish of lasagne, and another of green vegetables.

'Looks good,' Belle said, as he poured her a glass of wine.

'And not burned. If I said it was my own recipe, I'd be lying. Don't ask.'

'Did you enjoy it last night? Belle asked, helping herself to the lasagne. 'Martin Riley was pretty drunk. That must have been embarrassing.'

'Not as much as for Sir Richard,' he replied. 'I must say, that was a surprise. I knew Dan was gay, but I didn't know he was married, let alone to one of our top barristers. Martin's a racist.'

'Did he make any kind of apology, after we went back to our table?'

'No, but Jolyon was furious with him.'

'What did you make of Emily being there?' Belle said. 'I was surprised, especially her being with Billy and his wife, and Phil and Miriam.'

He frowned. 'Yes, that was unexpected.'

'I noticed Martin Riley's wife, Josie, staring over in Emily's direction. She looked puzzled at first, then angry. Very angry. But not with Martin. I think, with Emily. I didn't see them at the fireworks. Did they leave?'

He stopped eating. 'Yes,' he replied. 'Martin has not been a faithful husband. There was a rumour that Emily had a fling with him.'

'Did she?'

'No.'

'You seem certain of that, Joe. How come?'

'You ask direct questions.'

'Yes, I do, when I find something that doesn't look right. I'm curious.'

'The Curiosity Club of St Foy. You're well named.' He paused. 'I know because I told Emily there was a rumour. This was three years ago, just before she vanished. Josie had heard and she was furious. She raged at me about it. That's why I spoke to Emily.'

'Why did Josie rage at you?'

He put down his cutlery and folded his arms. 'Because Josie Riley is my sister-in-law. She and Evie asked me to speak to Emily. Is that enough information for you?'

'Sorry, I'm being too nosy. I couldn't help seeing the way she looked at Emily.'

'She probably still believes it was true. She knows Martin better than anyone.'

They had both stopped eating. Belle suddenly felt nervous. 'Perhaps I should go. I can see I've upset you.'

'No, please stay a little longer. How is your friend Mavis doing?' They began eating again.

'Not too well. I'm meeting Bette and the others at the farm later. They'll have an update.' She had lied. She didn't know why, but something in her gut told her not to tell him the truth.

'That's very sad. I didn't know her, but Jolyon said she was a nice lady. I believe he helped her out last year.'

'When she split from her husband there was a problem over the inheritance of her aunt's cottage. He provided some papers.'

'Jolyon is a good man.'

'He's invited me to tea with Mavis, once she's out of hospital and more up to it. That's very exciting for me.'

'Would you like some coffee?'

'No, thank you. I'll go now, Joe. My hand is painful again, probably from driving. Thank you for lunch.'

She stood up and began to walk out of the kitchen, but he blocked her way. Quite suddenly, he pulled her into a tight grasp and kissed her, roughly. 'I like you very much, Belle Harrington.'

She let herself be kissed for a few seconds, then pulled away. 'I like you too, Joe, but this is too fast for me.'

He let her go and stood back, shaking his head. 'I'm sorry. I shouldn't have done that.'

'Don't apologise,' she said, smiling at him. 'Just small steps. OK?'

He nodded. 'I'll get your coat.'

In the hall, he took her arm, gently this time. 'Can I apologise again? I hope this hasn't put you off.'

'It hasn't. Call me tomorrow.'

'I will. I have to go to London in a few days. I was wondering, if you'd like to meet me there?'

'That's too much to think about. I want to see what happens here in St Foy over the next few days, when normal life begins again. I'm worried about Georgie Morris. He's due in court again at the start of next week.'

He walked with her to her car. This time he didn't attempt to touch her.

He watched her go until she was out of sight.

Back down in the village, Belle stopped the car and for a full minute took deep, slow breaths. How did she feel about what had just happened? She wasn't sure. She didn't want to reject him, but an idea was beginning that, somehow, Joe Knight was another piece of the puzzle, a critical piece, that would explain what had happened to Emily and Star. That he had loved his wife she didn't doubt. But the discovery of his relationship to Martin Riley meant that she couldn't trust him. She had thought as she had driven to his house that he might be a person worth trusting. Now, she wasn't sure. What she was sure of, was that she had to find a way to speak to Josie Riley, without either Martin Riley or Joe Knight knowing she'd done so, or that she had any intention of doing so.

When she felt calmer, she started the car again and drove straight to Bette and Bert's farmhouse. There were already cars when she arrived, although it was only half four, and, to her surprise and unease, the number of press at the gate had tripled. Her heart sank as she approached the farmhouse. Three of the cars parked in front of the farmhouse were police cars. She ran into the kitchen.

Two policeman held Georgie's arms. The third was issuing the standard caution. Georgie was being arrested in connection with the murder of Star Bright.

Bette and Bert held onto Mandy, who was sobbing, as Georgie, in a state of speechless shock was led out of the kitchen and driven away.

It had been a worthwhile wait for the photographers and reporters at the gate, at last.

Chapter 28

It was a moment before she noticed Dan and Posy.

'Bette's on the phone to Rose. She and Harry are on their way. We need to talk about what we can do.'

Belle turned to Dan. 'Where's Richard?'

'Gone to the station. He'll be there when Georgie arrives. We've contacted Simon, the solicitor, and Richard and he will talk whilst Georgie is formally charged. Richard will be able to give him advice, and it won't do any harm for DCI Lewis to see Richard there. He'll come back as soon as it's done.'

She sat down, as Bette burst in. 'Rose and Harry are on their way. I've been trying to call you,' she snapped at Belle.

'I've been at lunch, with Joe Knight.' She turned to Posy. 'Is Billy on duty today?'

'I don't know. Why?'

'Do you think he would join us? I saw the crowd at the gate again. Someone must have tipped them off. Peter Day is there at the head of them.'

'It'll be difficult for him,' Posy replied. 'But I can try. Maybe I can collect him, if he's willing and he can hide in the back of my car.'

'Please try,' Belle said. 'We need the insider information.'

Posy called. Billy was willing, but nervous. Belle could see from Posy's expression that he was telling her something. Whatever it was, it wasn't good.

'He's agreed. I'll take the Land Rover down to pick him up. He absolutely must not be seen. As you know, Jade

Waters has disappeared. He went to see her yesterday. She hasn't been seen by anyone since she spoke to you two in the café over in Port Simon.'

Belle closed her eyes. 'Not another one,' she said. 'Someone is following me – us – and I still have no idea who it is.'

'Let's wait until we're all here,' Bert said. 'I'm thinking that we all know bits of this story. It's time to put them all together. I mean, right back to when Emily disappeared and Star died.'

'That's going to be a long story,' Belle said.

'Then we should all get thinking about the parts we know,' Bette said, moving Mandy away from Bert. 'This includes you too, Mandy.'

Mandy sniffed and nodded. 'I can tell you what I remember, about that girl.' She spat out the last two words. Belle wasn't sure whether she meant Emily or Star.

Five minutes after Posy left, Harry and Rose arrived. Rose rushed into the kitchen.

'She's awake,' she said, beaming. 'I know this is a terrible time, for you and your family, Bette, but Mavis is conscious.'

'Does she remember anything about what happened to her?' Bette asked.

'I don't know, yet. If she's Ok overnight, they'll transfer her out of the intensive care unit, into a smaller room, much quieter for her, but she'll be monitored closely for a few days, still.'

'That's a great relief,' Belle said. 'I hope she can remember something, particularly whatever it was she wanted to tell us.'

They talked quietly for a further twenty minutes, when a knock came at the door. It was Richard.

'I didn't like to barge in,' he said. He walked up to Mandy. 'He's being charged with murder. He'll be in court in the morning. I've told his solicitor, who seems to be a competent man, that he can now ask for full disclosure of the evidence. I met DCI Lewis,' he added, turning to the others in the kitchen. 'It was my impression that she's nervous.'

'You have that effect on people,' Dan said.

'I don't think it was me. When I mentioned full disclosure, she began to twitch. They will have had to turn it over to the Crown Prosecution Service, to be sure there's enough to reach the threshold for a charge of murder. I'll be interested to hear what it is.' He turned again to Mandy. 'Try not to worry. We can't know what they're basing this charge on until we've seen the evidence.'

'Does that mean you're staying, Richard?' Belle asked.

'Yes, of course. I'll do whatever I can, but it will be limited to unofficial advice.'

'Posy is out collecting our insider,' Belle said. 'He's a constable. He was one of the students at the time of Star's death.'

'Billy Anderson,' Richard said. 'He was there at the Ball, last night. How was your lunch, by the way?'

'Interesting. I've found out something I didn't know. But I'll keep it until we've all here.'

Just before five, Posy's Land Rover roared back up the drive. She parked as close as she could to the kitchen door and Billy clambered out. He had on a heavy overcoat, sunglasses and a peaked cap.

'You look like someone out of an American cop drama,' Bette said.

'I can't stay long. If one of those press people saw anything...' He was pale and trembling, clenching and unclenching his fists.

'Relax. It's dark. Even if they did see someone climbing out of the Land Rover they wouldn't have a clue who it was. We've closed the curtains tight and the boys are back at the gate, and patrolling around the farmyard. They won't get anywhere close,' Bert said. 'You're safe here now.'

'Let's not waste any time,' Belle said. 'I've been thinking about how to do this, to put the whole story together. My idea – and anyone, stop me if you don't agree – is that we go right back as far as we can, and each of us chips in at a point on the timeline when they know something. How does that sound? I can start, because I know something about Star Bright, but then I'll keep notes, until it's my turn again. This should tell us how much we have, and what's missing, still.'

They all nodded.

'I'll start, then. I'll begin with Star Bright, whose real name is Louisa Anastasia Light. She was born in Chelsea in London, in 1998. Her mother is Augusta Light, a Barrister. Back then, she was a solicitor. She was in league with both criminals and corrupt policemen in the Met. The rumour was that the father of her child was a policeman, an Inspector. It might be Martin Riley.'

'Oh my goodness, the Chief Constable,' Rose said.

'Yes. I don't know if Augusta told him, but he most probably knew. He has never acknowledged Star as his child and I don't think she knew anything about him.'

'I was a junior barrister at the time,' Richard said. 'I knew about Augusta by reputation and I know her now. An unpleasant woman.'

'She never came forward when Star was murdered. Did she know it was her daughter?' Billy asked.

'Yes, I think she did,' Belle replied. 'Star had been a wild child and had run away at fifteen. Augusta didn't care, certainly not enough to identify her daughter's body. And the reason I think Martin Riley probably knew, and kept it quiet, was that he was behind the enquiry into Star's death. He didn't want his relationship to her to come out, because it might lead, via Augusta Light, to some very nasty criminals who were paying him. Billy told Dan and me that Riley used to visit the Heights, in the term Star died. Ostensibly, to visit Miriam. But perhaps he was keeping an eye on Star. He also had a gleam in his eye for Emily. His wife, Josie, knew and thought they were having an affair. Joe Knight told me today that he confronted Emily with the story, on behalf of Eve and also Josie, who is his sister-in-law. Emily denied it and he believed her.'

'I knew Josie Riley was Joe Knight's sister-in-law,' Bette said. 'His wife Eve and my sister Rita spent time in the hospice together. They knew each other. I met Eve when I went to visit Rita. They died within a couple of weeks of each other. They became close, both dying of the same disease.'

'Josie was watching Emily at the Ball last night,' Belle continued. 'At first she looked puzzled, then angry, then beyond angry. She and Martin left immediately after the fireworks. Anyway, let's fast forward to the term in which Emily died. Here's something crucial. The police have charged Georgie with murder, but no-one really knows when Star died. Gabriel Holmes said he saw Star after Emily disappeared, but recently told Billy he had lied. He was being blackmailed. We don't know who by. There's also the person who said they were on a bus with Emily the day she disappeared, which could be true. But as we don't know exactly when Star died, it could have been after, not before.'

She paused for a moment. 'Does anyone have anything to add about that part of the story? For those of you who don't know this part yet, Emily and Star started the term as buddies, but by the end were enemies, sort of. Emily claimed that Star stole a piece of jewellery from her, Emily called it a family heirloom, but Bette said it couldn't have been. Then Jade saw Star put it back.'

'Yes, she told me, about a week later. She was quite smug about it. After that, they were a nightmare to live with.' Billy sat forward. 'Something else I've remembered. It was at the party, just over a week before Christmas. Jade organised it, so there were drugs, as well as shedloads of alcohol. It was a crazy night. I was there, so was Jade, plus Emily and Star. Gabe was there, of course. Phil was there to start, but disappeared. Miriam had already gone. Jade had invited some tutors. A few turned up, including Joe Knight.'

'He was at a student party?' Belle exclaimed. 'Just days before Star died?'

'Yes. He didn't stay long, probably no more than half an hour. I'd always presumed Jade invited him, but looking back, that can't have been the case. Their dislike was mutual. It might have been Gabe. Emily certainly wouldn't have done so, nor Star. He was with another economics tutor, a woman, who did stay. Plus a few others. I remember Joe going out into the carpark. He looked furious. And, he was shouting over his shoulder at someone.'

'Can you remember who it was?' Belle asked.

'No. I didn't see. But it was a female.'

'Did you recognise the voice?'

'No, she only said two or three words. I didn't hear them properly. He pushed her off and left.'

'Where were you when this happened?' Richard asked.

Billy blushed bright red. 'I was in a bush next to the front door, throwing up. I didn't want to show myself. By the time I felt better, they'd both gone.'

'Did anything else happen at that party?' Belle asked. 'Anything you can remember, doesn't matter how insignificant it might have seemed.'

'Emily and Star had another row at the end of the evening. Emily was well off her head. She started calling Star a thief again. Star laughed at her, then said something like *it was never for you*. Or *never about you*. I think. Before you ask, I have no idea what she was talking about. The following morning, they just ignored each other. That was the last time I saw either of them. I went home later that day.'

'Thanks, Billy. What we know next, is that Emily asked Bette to take her into the city. She told the family she was going to do some last minute Christmas shopping. She was really going to have a termination. She was never seen again until she re-appeared last week. And there's a doubt whether she was pregnant. She's supposed to have spent the best part of three years on a commune, in Scotland until she suddenly decided to come back. Me, I don't believe it was that sudden a decision, or that she took it alone. But, let's park that for now.

'What happened next, apart from the search for Emily, is that Georgie knew that Star would be alone for Christmas, as she had no family, so he went to the Heights on Christmas Eve, to find her and take her to your house, Mandy. Is that how it happened?'

Mandy nodded. 'He'd been talking about it for days. I didn't want her anywhere near us. He was just, I don't know, infatuated with her. He went to the Heights whenever he could. He even went to that party, although he wasn't invited. He didn't go in, though. Georgie's much too shy. He told me he just hid, behind some trees, watching, until he was too cold and came home.'

'Mandy, has anyone ever asked him about that?' Richard asked.

'No. You know Georgie, he'll answer any question truthfully, he's that honest, but if the question isn't asked, he doesn't think to say.'

'Might he have seen the argument in the carpark, between Joe Knight and whoever was the woman or girl?' Belle asked.

'He never told me, but I suppose it's possible.'

'I'm going to call his solicitor. The question must be asked,' Richard said. He went into the hall to make the call. When he returned he had spoken to Simon Davies, who would see Georgie and ask him, before the court appearance.

'Is that it, for that time?' Belle asked. 'I have just a little more. I went to see Emily's old schoolfriend, Kylie Nichols, two days ago. Bette, I'm sorry but I have to tell the story.'

Bette nodded.

'She told me about Emily as a child, how she picked on and punished other children, using Kylie to do the actual threat of punishment. She also knew that Emily had a lot of affairs with older men. Martin Riley's name came up.'

Bette sat, stiff backed. 'Was he the father of the pregnancy?'

'Well, we don't think now that Emily was pregnant, but Kylie didn't say. However, she did say, *I knew about him.* Now, she's been very badly beaten.'

'That was her boyfriend,' Billy interjected. 'She had a thousand pounds on her. A neighbour called the police, he ran and we caught him later that night.'

'A thousand?' Belle said. 'I gave her five hundred. Where did the extra five hundred come from?'

'We assumed it was drug money, or something similar,' Billy said.

'From me, it was a payment for information. But the extra five hundred? Have you checked her phone?'

'It's missing.'

'Was there any evidence it was the boyfriend who beat her?'

'No. He claims he never touched her, that he found her when she was already in a bad way. But he's got form. It wasn't the first time he'd hit her, but this was the worst.'

'Then why didn't he take the money?' Posy asked.

'I don't know and how am I going to make something of it, given you gave her half the money?' Billy demanded.

'Good point. Awkward. We'll have to think about how to deal with that,' Belle said. 'I think that covers everything we know about the period around Star's death. Agreed?'

They all nodded. 'Now we come to the events of this past week, starting with Emily turning up here, at Bette's birthday party. She claimed that she hadn't killed anyone. Georgie rushed at her and said that she had killed Star. Mandy, do you know why he believed that?'

'No, he's barely mentioned Emily's name since she disappeared three years ago. But, I will tell you this. He wasn't unhappy she'd gone. He really, really disliked her. She made his life a misery when they were growing up. She used to get him blamed for stuff she'd done. She made Rita hate him. Not that Rita liked Emily much, not when they were alone together.'

'Kylie Nichols said the same. She says Emily told her that Rita used to call Emily bitch and whore. I'm sorry, Bette.'

Bette shrugged. 'Nothing to be done about it now.'

'After your birthday party, we all went back to my place. I could see, and I think Posy and Rose could see, that Mavis had something on her mind.'

They both nodded.

'But, as usual, Mave wasn't willing to say whatever it was,' Posy said. 'She went to see someone the next day, and that evening, her flat was burgled. Posy, did you find out where the taxi Margaret talked about took Mavis?

'Not yet. There hasn't been anyone there who would tell me. The driver I know is on holiday, but he's back in a couple of days.'

'Thank goodness Mavis is waking up,' Belle said. 'But she may not remember anything.'

'It was the day Bette told us the story about Georgie finding Star's body on Christmas Eve and moving it out onto the moor. From the experiment we did, we now believe that he wasn't alone in the Heights that day. There were two people there, behind a door.'

'I don't know how you're going to present that one, either,' Billy said. 'The Boss will say there's far too much bias to believe it's true.'

'That doesn't matter,' Richard said. 'It will cast doubt on the murder story. You should tell the DCI what you did.'

'If you think it's the right thing to do, and will help Georgie, then we will,' Belle replied. 'The past few days have been eventful. Mavis's burglary on Boxing Day; Georgie was arrested because of an anonymous tip; I was knocked down in the supermarket by a trolley driven by Joe Knight, with whom I have since had dinner and today's lunch. Dan and I went to see Emily. She didn't give much away, but someone was with her, who took the opportunity to creep down the stairs and out of the back door whilst we were waiting for Emily in the sitting room. We don't have a clue who it was. As we were leaving, Joe Knight pulled up in his car. He managed to get in to see Emily. He's trying to persuade her to re-start her PhD. We've spoken to each of the students in person, except Miriam Singh who phoned to tell us to leave her alone. Then, when I was at dinner over in Padstow with Joe, my cottage was searched. I think it might have been Peter Day.

' Anyway, that's when I cut my hand. One theme has emerged. Bette, sorry again. No-one we've spoken to liked Emily at all. Miriam called her a sociopath. A lot of what we've learned about her behaviour seems to confirm that.

'To find more information, Dan and I went over to South Wales yesterday morning, to speak to an old school friend of mine. Her name is Lennie Maginnis and she's a psychiatrist. She couldn't give an opinion on Emily, of course, not ever having met her, but from what we described, she agreed that Emily may have sociopathic predispositions.' She paused and looked around at the table, at the expressions staring back at her. Amazement, fear, anger, confusion.

'At the Ball last night I went over to speak to Billy and his friends. Billy, who organised that grouping? Who bought the tickets?'

'It was Emily,' he said. 'I couldn't have afforded it. She said it was about time we all met up again. I couldn't say no. It was just too tempting.' He was blushing again.

'But why did Miriam agree to go, after telling me she thought Emily was a sociopath?'

'Same reason. Curiosity. And Phil is a nice guy and couldn't say no.'

'Do you know if she gets on with her father, these days?'

'She still hates him. She manages to see her mother, though.'

'Do you have any idea why Josie Riley was sending hate waves to Emily?'

'No. I tried not to look at that table. Emily smirked a lot. I think it was at Martin.'

'Here we are, then. Dan, have I left anything out?'

'No,' he replied, and added 'for me personally, there's still something nagging at me. Something I saw, but I can't remember why it matters. Something about it jogged my memory last night, too.'

Richard, seeing Dan was upset, took his hand. 'You'll remember. When we're back home we'll talk it through. You'll get it.'

'That means he's going to cross examine me,' Dan said with a laugh, 'picking every tiny little detail out of my head.'

'If anything useful comes out, let us know,' Belle said.

'Anyone, anything else.'

'I have something to tell you,' Billy said. 'I shouldn't be telling you this, particularly not in front of a barrister. I'm terrified of telling you. No-one must ever know this came from me.'

'I'm here as a friend,' Richard said quietly. 'A friend with some special knowledge, but just a friend.'

'You know us all here, Billy,' Posy added. 'We're secret keepers.'

Billy nodded. 'The reason Georgie's been arrested for murder is because a witness has come forward. The person has made a statement. I haven't seen it myself but I heard DCI Lewis talking about it and why she was confident in arresting Georgie. The person says they were in the house on the night of Monday 17th December 2018. They have said in the statement that Georgie Morris was in the house, with Star, arguing with her. He was saying he would leave his wife for her. She told him not to be so stupid and go away. The witness says there was more shouting. It came from Star's bedroom. The witness says they didn't know they weren't alone. The witness crept up the stairs, and saw Georgie Morris hold Star down on the bed, put a pillow over her head and hold it there until she stopped moving.'

'And is this witness going to appear at the committal hearing?' Richard asked, after a few seconds of shocked silence.

'No. The police will refer to the statement, but not to the name of the person.'

'The solicitor can demand to know. You know, Billy, don't you. But I would caution you not to tell us. Please, don't say the name; it wouldn't be the right thing to do,' Richard pleaded.

Billy put his head in his hands and mumbled something that sounded like a "yes" accompanied by a sob.

'No. Tell us, Billy. I know you shouldn't but I'm asking you to.' Posy said. She moved around the table and put her arms around his shoulders. 'Whisper it to me.'

She put her head close to his. He whispered something. Posy's eyes widened. She looked up.

Richard was frowning. 'I don't want to hear this,' he said, standing and leaving the room.

'He can't,' Dan said. 'He knows on how many levels this is wrong.'

Do you want to leave, too? Belle asked.

'No,' Dan replied. 'He won't ask me and he knows I won't tell him.'

Posy stood up.

'The witness is Emily,' she said, in a hushed voice.

Chapter 29

Mandy had fainted, the shock too great. Posy, who had some basic first aid training, laid her out on the floor in a recovery position, checked she was breathing, then checked for any tight clothing. Bert had caught her as she fell, so there was no injury, but he asked that an ambulance be called. Posy said no, wait for a few minutes. If she didn't come around quickly, then they should send for the ambulance, but to give her a minute or so first. She gave Mandy a gentle shake, then called her name a few times. She was right. Mandy's eyes flickered open. For a few seconds she looked puzzled, then what she had heard flooded back and she began to cry, first sobbing, then howling. Bette dropped to her knees, hugging Mandy gently, trying to sooth her.

'Give her some space,' Posy said. 'No, Mandy, don't try to get up yet. Give yourself a minute. Your blood pressure took a sudden drop. Let's do this slowly.'

The others waited in agonised silence. It took five minutes before Mandy stopped crying and her breathing slowed down. Bert helped her to her feet and put her into a chair.

'Does a cup of hot sweet tea actually help in these situations?' Rose asked.

'It won't do any harm,' Posy replied. 'Make one for all of us.'

Richard had rushed back into the room.

'We should go,' he said. 'Too many people around won't help.' He knelt down by Mandy, who was now shivering.

'I'll be at the court on Monday,' he said to her, before he and Dan left.

'Is there anything more we can do?' Harry asked.

Posy shook her head. 'She'll need some peace and quiet. When she's ready, she can talk through the implications of what we've heard with Bert and Bette. It's probably best she doesn't have a crowd around her. Billy, I'll take you back home.'

Once they had smuggled Billy back into the Land Rover and Posy had driven off, Harry and Rose left, heading for the hospital for a quick visit to Mavis, before returning home.

Belle went to leave, but Mandy stopped her. 'I don't want to hear any more,' she said in a shaky voice, but please stay and talk to Bette and Bert. There's been so much information. I can't take it all in, but the three of you might be able to make something of it. I'm thinking about what to tell our Will about his dad.'

'Tell him nothing,' Bette said. 'He's forty miles away, with our grandchildren. 'He's fine for now. There's nothing he can do. How about, after the hearing we'll drive you over there and you can talk to him.'

Mandy nodded and stood up. Her legs buckled, and Bert helped her into the living room, sat her in a deep armchair with her tea, then returned to the kitchen.

'We shouldn't leave her alone for too long,' he said.

'Belle,' Bette began, 'what do you make of all of this we've heard?'

'I'm as shocked as everyone else,' Belle began. 'I don't believe what Emily has said in this statement. From what you've told me about what happened at the time, her behaviour in no way suggested she had witnessed a murder. From what Billy said, the murder took place on the Monday after the party. When did Emily arrange for you to take her into the city?'

'I… I can't remember, exactly. I think it was about a week or so before. I think I told you, we found a clinic – no, that's wrong, I remember now, she had found the clinic. I went with her to the first appointment. That's right, I didn't go in with her. I waited outside. She didn't want me in there. When she came out she said the termination was booked for the following week, on the Tuesday. That's when she told the family the story about more Christmas shopping and I took her there again.'

'But you didn't see her go in, the second time?'

'No. I drove away.' Bette paused, frowning. 'There wasn't any appointment, I know. She used me. But why?'

'She had been planning to disappear. She thought you would tell the family where she had gone and why, and everyone would have thought that she didn't come home because she couldn't face them. But you didn't tell anyone, except Bert. She must have known that's what you'd do. All she's said about where she went is that she got on a bus to London and there was another bus about to leave for Scotland. There's an inconsistency in her story. She said that her friend, Skinner, was on the bus to London. Isn't that what she told you?'

'Yes,' Bette replied. 'He gave her the alibi.'

'She told Dan and I it was a girl on the bus. Skinner is male. She said that in London there was a bus for Edinburgh. There was a girl on that bus who lived at some kind of retreat and took her there. That's what she told us. But she also said that Skinner lived at the retreat. Which was it? Both, or neither? Have the police even checked out the retreat in Scotland, to see if it actually exists? She told me she stayed because it was soothing, but when I asked her if it suddenly stopped being soothing the day before she came back, she threw us out.'

'What are you thinking?' Bette asked.

'What if she wasn't in Scotland?' Belle said.

'Where else could she have been?' Bette replied. 'Three years is a long time.'

'Bette, do you mind if I go now? I'd like some thinking time, on my own.'

'Of course. I need to get in to Mandy. Are you coming on Monday morning?'

'Of course. I'll see you there at ten.'

'Belle, is there anything you're not telling us?'

Belle bit her lips, hesitating. She hated lying. 'There is something, but at the moment it's not relevant and it's… dangerous. Bette, please, just this once trust me that I'm not keeping anything to myself for any reason other than everyone's safety.'

Bette stared at her for a few, tense moment. 'Ok, I trust you. But at some point—'

'Most definitely. Thank you for your trust. I think you're the only one who's picked up on it. Please, don't say anything to anyone.' She hugged Bette and left.

Belle drove rapidly down the drive, and out of the farm entrance. Peter Day was there, doing a piece to camera. It was just after six thirty. Was he live on the evening news? She could check as soon as she arrived home.

She ran into the house and turned on the television, restarted the local news programme and after ten minutes, there he was. She was right, it was a live piece from outside the farm. He began with news of an arrest, a charge of murder due to the appearance of an unexpected witness and the court appearance due the following morning. But he gave away a detail he should not have had. He kept referring to Star as "the girl in the tree". It was how she had been named before being identified when her body had been found. It was he who had given her the soubriquet, so not surprising he continued to use it. It upped the sensation level. But he said that she had been found to have been suffocated. How did he know that? The cause of death had not been determined at the time, although it was the most likely cause of death. But now he spoke of it as a fact. Was it someone in the police force? That wouldn't have surprised her, either. But again, he talked about Star having been held down and a pillow put over her face. Belle could hardly believe anyone in the police force would have given him that much detail. She thought DCI Lewis would be furious, to hear what should not be coming out until the hearing, delivered live to the nation by this reporter. There would be repercussions, she was sure. But then, he went on to say that it wasn't the only murder to have taken place in this quiet seaside town. Tomorrow, he would be revealing details of another shocking murder that had taken place in the past. The piece ended there. Belle felt sick. She knew he was referring to her. What was the vile man planning? Her phone rang.

'Belle, did you catch Peter Day's piece on the news?'

'I've just seen it. He has to be referring to you and me doesn't he?'

'I'm thinking yes,' Dan replied. 'Richard wants to go after him this evening. I've never seen him so angry. In fact, I've rarely seen him angry at all. He thinks Peter has done this now, because he's protected by his information about Georgie.'

'He's right. If he goes after Peter now, he could be compromised. Peter Day will have seen you both leaving the farm. He must have decided now is the time to pounce on me.'

'Then he's in for a nasty shock, isn't he. What are your plans?'

'I'm going to the hearing at ten. Then, I want to find a way to speak to Josie Riley. I have to find out where she and Miriam meet. I had planned to ask Billy if he or his wife knew, but after his revelation last night, I forgot. I'm hoping he'll be at the court in the morning. I'll try to have a quiet word with him.'

'How about this? Richard is going into the court in the morning. He's meeting with Georgie's solicitor. I'll go in my car and look for Billy. If he's not there I'll track him down whilst the hearing's in session.'

'Thanks, Dan. You're a good friend. The best.'

'I'll find out for you, Holmes. Don't you worry. I'll be back by the time the session ends. You and I are going to stay close.'

She put the phone down, feeling a little better. If her life was about to be exposed on television, at least she could, with Dan at her side, show what a charlatan Peter Day really was. And embarrass him. If she was to be exposed, so was he.

**

Now alone with her thoughts and the recording of the discussions and revelations at the farmhouse, Belle began to transcribe everything. It might be the modern age of electronics, but she needed paper, to see a picture emerge in written words. Once she had finished, she read through, made a few amendments, then printed the file. Then, she took a piece of A0 paper, put it on the floor and got down on her hands and knees with thick markers in different colours. She began a diagram, with Star Bright at the centre and lines leading out to all of the people involved in the girl's life. On each line she wrote their connection to Star, then cross connected the lines to show their connections to each other. After an hour or so, the paper was a mess, but it seemed to be leading in an unexpected direction, a line that went off the edge of the page. She tentatively wrote two names on the line. She couldn't be sure she was right, not yet. What she did know, was that the first part of the answer, and the confirmation that she was right, would come from Josie Riley.

Chapter 30

On Monday morning six grim faced people stood in silence in the waiting room of the courthouse in Truro. Mandy was white faced and shaky, hanging onto Bert's arm. Bette stared into space, standing apart, making it clear she didn't want to speak to anyone. Rose and Harry stood together in a corner. Belle had picked up Posy and they arrived together, just before ten.

Richard was not there, but Belle assumed he was with Georgie's solicitor. They had entered the courthouse through a barrage of cameras and photographers. Peter Day was there with his crew. He smirked at Belle as she went in. She smirked back. She probably should have ignored him, but she couldn't help it. There was no sign of Billy. She crossed her fingers and hoped that Dan would be able to find him.

At ten exactly the hearing was announced and they all entered the small courtroom. Georgie was brought in. He, too, was pale and shaking, but managed to give Mandy a small wave.

Richard joined them. 'This won't take long,' he whispered. 'It will be referred to the Crown Court. Georgie's solicitor will ask for him to be allowed release on bail, but it will be refused. He'll be held on remand. Brace yourselves.'

The three Magistrates entered. Everyone in the courtroom stood. Belle glanced up and saw that the gallery was full of press reporters.

As Richard had said, it was a short proceeding. The charge of murder was read out. The prosecution said that a witness had come forward and made a statement to the effect that George Morris had murdered Star Bright, on the night of Monday 17th December 2018 and had then removed her body on Sunday 24th December 2018, thereby perverting the course of justice, preventing the police in carrying out their duty to investigate her death and preventing a lawful burial. The solicitor for the prosecution described the events in great detail. It all sounded damning.

Georgie was asked how he pleaded. He whispered, 'Not guilty, sir.' As expected, the case was referred to Crown Court, date to be decided, and the application for bail was refused. Georgie burst into tears. It was agreed, however, that he should be allowed an appropriate adult to be present at all interviews. He was taken down to the cells, without looking at any of them.

Mandy was in floods of tears again, and Bert had to carry her from the court. They all moved as quickly as possible to their cars, fighting their way through the shouts and flashing cameras. Belle held her breath, praying Peter Day didn't choose this moment to pick on her, but she was lucky, his attention was all on Mandy.

There was no sign of Emily. Belle hadn't expected her to be there. She guessed Emily was now in hiding, somewhere, maybe not even in St Foy.

As she drove herself and Posy home, her phone rang. It was Richard.

'Sorry I had no chance to speak with you at the court. I waited until the press gang left. I have a message for you from Dan; he says to go straight home and he'll meet you there. I'm coming, too.'

'Should I be there with you?' Posy asked.

'We'll be OK,' Belle replied. 'This is about Peter Day.'

'I saw his piece on the local news last night, with him talking about revealing another murder mystery in St Foy.'

Belle grinned. 'If he tries it, he's in for a terrible shock. Serves him right.'

Dan was already waiting at the front door of the cottage.

'I should give you a key,' she said. 'It must be freezing standing out here.' He was dressed in a thick coat with a scarf around his neck and a flat cap pulled tight to his head.

'I've only been here a few minutes,' he replied, stamping his feet to keep the blood flowing. 'Richard's just left Truro. He'll be about a half hour. He says he has something interesting to tell us,' he said, as she let them both in and turned up the heating.

'I hope you have something to tell me,' she replied as she walked into the kitchen and put on the coffee percolator.

'Indeed I do. Miriam meets her mother at midday.' He looked at his watch. 'They go to a small café in Port Simon. Not the dive we were in when we met Jade, somewhere a little more upmarket, but not a place Martin could pass by accidentally. I was going to suggest that, as soon as Richard has delivered his information, we drive over. I can wait with you, and perhaps you can nab her on their way out. They usually have lunch, so they should be there until at least one thirty.'

'Sounds good to me,' she said. 'We don't know when Peter Day is going to pounce. Dan, why are you still wearing that cap?'

'Ah, this. Right. Well, I thought, if we're going to best Peter Day, he needs to be able to see the evidence.' He removed the cap and Belle gasped. He had not exactly shaved his hair off, but had given himself a serious buzz cut. He turned around and the scar across the back of his head stood out, angry and red.

'You didn't need to do that,' she said, through a burst of tears.

'Of course I did,' he replied. 'Richard thinks I look like a thug. I did wonder about getting a tattoo to go with it, make myself really look the part.'

She gurgled a laugh through the tears. 'He wouldn't stand for that.'

'Sadly not. But I might get to like this look.'

The doorbell rang. Belle went to answer, checking who it was. Richard stood there, shivering.

'The temperature today requires an additional coat,' he said, as Dan wandered into the living room and Richard shook his head.

'I told him he didn't need to do it,' she said. 'Warm up in front of the fire. Coffee's on.'

She brought in coffee, mugs, tea, and sugar. 'Dan says you have news.'

'Yes, I do. It was… unanticipated. Georgie's solicitor spoke to him about the night of the party and anything he might have seen. He saw Joe Knight leave. He also saw the girl who followed him, and who he shouted at.'

'Was it Emily?' Belle asked.

'No, it was Star. And something happened after that. Joe Knight drove his car off. She went back towards the door, but didn't go in. Then, someone came out of the bushes, took her by the arm and dragged her around the back of the house.'

'Who?'

'He said it was "the policeman".'

'What? Martin Riley? I didn't think he was there.'

'No, not Martin Riley. The one who's a policeman now. It was Billy.'

It took Belle a few seconds to take this news in. 'He lied. Billy lied. He said he went back into the party after he'd thrown up in the bushes outside the front door. Why would he do that?'

'We'll have to ask him,' Dan said. He went to add something, but the doorbell rang again.

Belle stood up. 'I don't know who that can be, other than Peter Day. I'm not expecting anyone else. Is this it?'

Dan jumped in front of her. 'Wait. Richard, can you take a quick look.'

Richard peered around the curtain, and nodded. 'It's Peter Day, with his film crew. Are you ready?'

Belle took a deep breath. 'As I'll ever be. You know the plan, John Daniel.'

He smiled at her, as she walked briskly to the front door and flung it open.

Chapter 31

Peter Day stepped forward, but Belle blocked his way. He tried to lean into the doorstep, but Belle leaned forward too, until she was in his face, forcing him to retreat. The cameraman and sound operator accompanying him had a barely noticeable smirk at each other.

'Belle Harrington,' he began. 'Another St Foy celebrity, for yet more sensational reasons. An interesting story has emerged, that you were responsible for the death of a boy, here in this town, back in the late 1970s. I'd like to hear your side of the story. I know what your late mother had to say, and the nurse who looked after her in her last days. The nurse has confirmed your mother's story, about you pushing a young lad off rocks down in Cash Cove. Now, we could make this a front page story, but I'd like to come in and hear what you have to say about it. Tell the story from your point of view.'

'No. And you're lying.'

'Pardon me?'

From her pocket she brought out the letter that had arrived by special delivery at nine that morning. She had taken a quick look at it whilst waiting at the courthouse.

'This is a letter from a solicitor in London, confirming that the nurse, whose name I won't give whilst we're being filmed, has given an official statement confirming that my mother admitted lying about what she saw. You try to say otherwise, Mr Day, and I will sue both you personally and your TV company.'

Day took a deep breath. 'Well, of course a dying woman would say…'

'Stop right there. Another word about my mother and you will leave my property. Now, ask your questions about the boy on the rocks.'

'Ah, yes, the boy you pushed to his death.'

The camera man focussed in on Belle's face.

'Mr Day, I didn't push the boy, whose name was Johnnie, by the way. No-one died. You will know this because it's easy enough to check official records to discover that fact. It would have been local news, but there was no news report, because it did not happen. But, if you want to ask me if there was a serious accident, the answer is yes. However, it was nothing to do with me. The boy in question was eleven years old. I was ten. He had been trying to impress me. He liked my hair. He tried to dive off the rocks, but flopped into the water. He hit his head, cut it, but swam off. I, however, did not see any of this. I was climbing down from the rocks at the time. My back was turned. When I reached the beach and looked back, he was gone. That's all I knew, or rather, all I knew then.'

'So you admit there was a serious accident.'

'Yes.'

'And that damage was done to a local boy.'

'Yes. He hit his head.'

'And he was seriously injured, by your recklessness.'

'No, by his own.'

'Then why did you run away?'

Here was Peter Day's moment. Now, she had to talk about her mother. It had become inevitable.

'My mother, who was not a nice woman, used the incident to remove me from my father. She lied for many years.'

The camera and sound men now looked serious.

'Belle Harrington, we only have your word for this, that it wasn't your fault, but can you prove it?'

'Of course I can.' Cue Dan.

The inner door opened fully and Dan walked out to stand beside her. Peter Day looked confused, and a little worried.

'Dr Daniel Walker, internationally famous anthropologist and former St Foy resident,' he said. 'Can you shed light on Mrs Harrington's claims?'

'Naturally, Peter, why else would I be here? And before you embarrass yourself further, let me explain something to you.'

The camera and sound operators focussed in on Dan.

'My mother was a proud Cornish woman. She gave me a traditional Cornish double first name. My actual name is John-Daniel Walker.'

Belle saw the shock on Day's face. He had seen what was coming, but couldn't stop it now.

'I'm the boy, I'm Johnnie. I was trying to impress this pretty girl,' he paused and put an arm around Belle's shoulders, 'as boys do, or at least, as I thought then a boy should do. But I flopped and failed spectacularly, crashed into the water and hit the back of my head on a rock. See?'

He turned around. The scar stood out, red across the back of his head. He turned back and spoke unblinking into Peter Day's camera.

'There's no story here, Peter. It was an accident of my own making. My mother rushed me to hospital, shouting at me all the time for being an idiot. I had a lot of stitches and spent a couple of nights as an in-patient, in case of concussion. I was fine. They let me out. The girl and her family had gone. End of story.'

Belle could see that Peter Day was thinking furiously about how to spin this. His great revelation had come to nothing. But there was more to come.

Richard emerged from the living room, stony faced, and stood behind Belle and Dan.

'Hello, Peter,' he said, unsmiling. 'You're still not past the doorstepping stage. I hope the explanation you have is sufficient for you to realise this is a non-story and that you will appear a great fool if you try to make something of it. Anything of it, in fact.' He turned to the camera and sound operators. 'I would strongly suggest you now turn that equipment off.'

But Peter Day was a survivor. He smiled. 'So, it turns out to be a happy ending all round. A story is a story, after all.'

'No, it isn't,' Richard replied. 'I saw Corky a few days ago, by the way. I told him I was coming down to St Foy and that you were here, covering a story. He said to say he's looking for you.'

Peter Day's face lost its colour and his mouth dropped open. He turned to his assistants. 'Turn it off,' he muttered. 'Now.'

They gave each other a quizzical look, but complied.

'That was quite a beating you gave him,' Richard said, his voice dripping with disgust. 'He won't involve the police. He'll deal with you himself. Have you moved on to another one, yet? Does the latest lad know your unsavoury history? Should I find him and warn him?'

The technicians were now open-mouthed, their equipment sitting on the ground.

'No story, Peter. Do whatever you will with the trial of George Morris. But there's no story here. Understood?'

Peter Day turned and walked away to a mobile TV van parked at the end of the lane. His technicians grabbed their equipment and followed him. Belle had no doubt that what Richard had said would be all over the local TV studios before the end of the day.

'Do you think that should do it?' Richard said, his arm around Dan's waist.

'I would say so. Did Corky really say that? I didn't see him as a thug.'

'Not exactly,' Richard replied. 'But the slapping he took from Peter has made him angry. His friends know. Peter needs to keep away from them. I'll get back in touch with Peter later on and make sure he understands that.'

They went back inside.

'You just blackmailed him,' Belle said.

'Yes. Couldn't have happened to a nicer person,' Dan replied. He looked at Richard. 'Are you OK?'

'Fine,' Richard replied, somewhat curtly. 'They weren't filming when I said what I did, so I'm confident my face won't appear on TV, threatening a reporter. But I do just hope it's enough for both of you.'

'It's enough for me,' Belle replied. She hugged Richard. 'I can't ever thank you enough. You put yourself out there, and I don't think that's your style.'

'Not generally,' he replied.

'Put my husband down, Belle. I'm not the jealous type, but…'

Belle poked her tongue out at him. She expected Dan to laugh but he didn't.

'There's still something puzzling me about Peter,' he said. 'I've wondered from the start how he came to be the first on the scene when Emily returned. I've found out he was actually at the Grand the day she came back. His team travelled through the night and were here first thing in the morning.'

'Someone tipped him off,' Belle said. She paced around the room for a few minutes, both men watching her.

'He knew,' she said. 'Which means that someone else knew.'

'Or she did it herself,' Richard said.

'Why would she do that?' Belle replied. She stopped pacing.

'That's another question for your list,' Dan said. 'But now, you and I have to get over to Port Simon. You don't want to miss Josie Riley.'

'Oh, damn. It's already past twelve. They'll be in the café. Come on Watson, let's go. Richard, what about you?'

I've had enough excitement for today,' he replied. 'I'll be at the apartment when you return. And don't forget, you still have to speak to Billy Anderson, to find out why he lied, in front of all of us, about Star on the night of the party.'

**

Belle and Dan didn't speak much as he drove them over to Port Simon. Despite the victory over Peter Day, Belle still didn't trust the man not to find some angle to pursue her. He was off her back for now, but it didn't feel permanent and she wondered if he would already be plotting revenge, for what Richard had said, in front of the technicians. Richard had spoken quietly, but they would have picked up some, if not all of it. She prayed it wouldn't end up doing Richard harm, in the longer term.

'Don't worry about us,' Dan said. 'Richard is much tougher than he looks.'

Belle laughed. 'So you can read my mind too?'

'I can read your face. Concentrate on how you'll approach Josie Riley, what you can say that will make her stop and listen to you.'

'Yes. I don't want to put her off, or have her run away from me. Not that she's the running away type, from what people have said about her.' She looked out of the window for a few minutes as they reached the houses on the outskirts of Port Simon. 'Dan, there's something I've been thinking about. An idea about what happened back in 2018, and before that. It's worrying me.'

'About Emily.'

'You did it again.'

'It's been worrying me, too, particularly since we met that psychiatrist friend of yours. I wonder if we're both reaching the same conclusion.'

They glanced quickly at each other, as they reached the carpark close to the café where Josie Riley and Miriam Singh were having lunch. It was now quarter past one.

'They should be coming out soon. Let's talk when we're done here. Can I come back to your apartment?'

'Of course. Something is telling me Richard has reached the same conclusion. The three of us can talk it out.'

They sat in silence for the next fifteen minutes.

'There they are,' Belle said. 'Miriam is putting on her coat, look, just inside the front door. Josie's paying the bill.'

Adrenaline began to run through her. This was it. The two women walked out of the café together. They hugged each other, then, to Belle's relief, walked off in different directions. She jumped out of the car and began to follow Josie Riley. The woman walked into a small jewellery shop. Belle looked behind. There was no sign of Miriam. Josie was having a conversation with an older man behind the counter. He was shaking his head. Josie's shoulders sagged. She appeared to thank him, then headed towards the door. Belle had been looking at the window display. Josie ignored her, and paused for a moment, her eyes closed. This was the moment.

'Mrs Riley?'

Josie's eyes snapped open. 'Yes. Who are… you? Don't answer that. You were at the Ball. You came to our table. What do you want?'

'My friend Mavis is lying in hospital with a serious head wound. She's recovering but it's been touch and go. Kylie Nichols has been beaten so badly she may lose an eye. Jade Waters is missing and now Georgie Morris has been charged with murder. I think your husband is somehow involved in all of this. I don't know how. Not yet. I have some information that you may not know. But why I'm here now is to ask you why you were so angry at the Ball? I saw you, staring over at Miriam's table. You were beyond angry. You looked like you were about to spontaneously combust. Please help me.'

Josie Riley looked as if she was about to assault Belle, but then, her shoulders sagged again. She had tears in her eyes.

'Mrs Riley? Are you all right? Do you need to sit down?'

'Call me Josie. No, I'll be fine. Are you seeing Joseph Knight?'

This was not what Belle expected. 'Not really. I know he's your brother-in-law. He knocked me down in the supermarket and invited me to dinner as an apology. I went out of curiosity. Then, he invited me to lunch, which didn't go particularly well. I have no plans to see him again. He wants to see me, though. Why are you asking?'

'I will speak to you. But not here, on the street. We'll need somewhere more private. Tomorrow?'

'Yes, if you'd prefer that. Where?'

'Can I come to where you live? Martin says you live in a cottage in St Foy.'

'I do, but if he knows that, then is it safe enough? I have another idea. My friend, Posy Simmons has a café in St Foy. It's closed at present. We meet there sometimes, and there's a back way in. It's down Cloth Alley. Do you know it?'

Josie nodded. 'I know Posy. She was a member of our circle, a while ago. I'll be there at ten. I'll tell Martin I'm going into St Foy to shop.'

'We'll be waiting for you. Would it be OK with you if my friend Dan Walker comes along, too? He's worried about me. I've been followed recently and I found an intruder in my cottage when I returned from dinner with Joe.'

Josie bit her lips together for a few moments. Then she nodded. 'I believe Dr Walker is a decent man. But no-one else.' She looked up and down the street. 'You'd better go. Miriam is fetching her car to take me into Truro. I pick up my car there, so he doesn't suspect.' She laughed, a bitter sound, without mirth or warmth.

Belle crossed the road and walked briskly back to the carpark. A few seconds later Miriam Singh's car appeared and Josie got in.

'Wow, that was close,' Dan said. 'What did you find out?'

'She's willing to talk to me, to us. I asked if you could be there and she agreed. We're meeting at Posy's.'

'Well done you,' Dan said, starting the car and heading out of the carpark. 'Let's get back and tell Richard what's going on.'

**

The snow was almost gone from the centre of St Foy, much to the relief of the adults, and disgust of the children, residents and visitors. Now it was the occasional heap of dirty slush. Richard had cleared away the remaining heaps that had been blocking Dan's two car parking spaces. He was still outside when they arrived back. Dan gave him a "thumbs up", parked the car and together they walked up the stairs to the apartment.

'You've had a successful encounter,' Richard said, divesting himself of overcoat, scarf and gloves. 'I have some hot chocolate waiting.'

'Yes,' Belle replied, relishing the thought of a home-made recipe that Dan had frequently boasted about. Richard brought them a mug each. It was as delicious as Dan had claimed. Belle sat back and stared out of the window, across the estuary to Porthdevan, where the snow still lay on the higher ground.

'It's been pretty,' she said. 'But I'll be glad to see the back of it now.'

'Be careful what you wish for,' Richard said. 'I watched the lunchtime forecast. It's predicting more, much more, later this evening and overnight. So, what was the outcome?'

'She's willing to talk and will meet us tomorrow, at ten, at the café.'

'Well done,' he said. 'Well done indeed. As the wife of the Chief Constable, she's taking a risk.' He turned to Dan. 'I'm sorry to say this, but I think I'll have to leave this afternoon. According to the forecast, St Foy may be snowed in for a day at least. I have to be in London, for a meeting with a client I can't afford to miss. I was planning to leave tomorrow anyway, but I must bring that forward, now.'

Dan's face fell. 'I understand. I want to stay here, to see this out. I know we have a theatre engagement.'

'It's OK. I understand. I'll take Corky.'

Dan jumped up out of his chair.

'Just joking,' Richard said. 'But, I really do need to head off soon. By the way, I've left a message via Georgie's solicitor, asking him to get in touch with Billy Anderson, and tell him you need to speak to him.'

'Thank you,' Belle said. 'I'm going to miss you. Very much. Permission to hug your husband again, John Daniel.'

'Help yourself,' Dan replied. 'Have you packed?'

'Yes, I'm about ready to go. He held Dan in a strong embrace and kissed him. You, be careful. Don't do anything reckless. Keep Belle safe. And grow your hair back.'

'Of course. All of that. I'll be back by the end of this week.'

'Fingers crossed,' Richard said. He went into the bedroom, came out with his suitcase and headed to the door. Dan went with him. When he came back, his face was red with cold.

'Snow's starting early,' he said. 'Are you going to stay for a while?'

'Yes. We both could do with the company.'

Chapter 32

It was dark by four o'clock but Belle didn't want to go home, yet. She and Dan had spent the afternoon reading and chatting, drinking the final mugs of Richard's hot chocolate, and watching as the snow intensified, accompanied by a howling wind, lashing against the window. She was warm and comfortable. They both needed this break. The past week had been intense and she'd been carried along by the tide of events, so much so that, now Belle was relaxed, she felt exhausted. It wasn't over, but here, in this beautiful apartment, warm and protected from the storm unleashing itself outside, it was a brief opportunity for peace. She knew it was just the eye of the storm and that events would ramp up again.

At seven, the snow seemed to be lessening.

'Time for me to go,' she said. Dan was snoozing on the settee, a book on his lap. She stood up and shook him gently. It took him a moment to come round, to realise where he was and who had shaken him.

'You don't have to, you can stay here tonight. Why don't you stay, then pop home in the morning before we meet Josie Riley? The guest room is comfortable.'

It was too tempting. She realised also how much he felt Richard's departure. She stayed.

She slept surprisingly well. At eight she woke, realised the time, dressed, and followed the smell of fresh baking into the kitchen where Dan was waiting.

'I was about to call you. It looks bad out there. You'll have to borrow a pair of boots to get down the street. In the meantime, breakfast.'

She sat with him, eating hot croissants and drinking fresh coffee.

'I have to try. I need to get home, shower and change. I wonder if Josie Riley is going to make it.'

'Don't be surprised if she can't. They live across the water, at the top of the hill. The bridge is probably blocked and clearing it won't be an immediate priority for the Council, plus I doubt the ferry is running.'

He was right on both counts. Belle borrowed the boots anyway and trudged home. It was still snowing, but the wind had lessened its intensity.

She managed to reach the café by ten. Posy let her in and Dan was already there. They waited half an hour. There was no sign of Josie Riley. Then, the café phone rang. Posy answered. She listened, said in a loud voice and an accent nothing like her own: *of course darling, quite understand. Dreadful conditions. Can we re-arrange?* More listening, then, *Wednesday would be perfect. Just a quick catch up. How about at three, same place? Yes? Wonderful. See you then, love to Martin.*

'She's snowed in. She called me Karen. Martin Riley must have been listening in the background. She said he's working from home today and probably tomorrow, until they can get out of the house.'

'No more than we expected,' Belle said. 'Bloody weather. It'll be the same here. I presume you can't get a car up the hills and out of here?'

'No, not at the moment, but the Council says it'll be clear by lunchtime.' Posy's phone rang again, this time her mobile. Again, she listened. *Actually, they're here. You can come over now, if you can make it… no problem. See you in ten minutes. Come to the back.* The call ended.

'That was Billy. He's on duty, but he has a car with snow chains. He's on his way, says he needs to speak to you urgently. What's going on?'

'Billy wasn't honest about some of the events of the night of the party,' Belle said. 'Richard managed to get a message to him before he left yesterday. He's coming here to tell us the truth, I hope.'

'Is it bad?' Posy asked.

'We'll know that when he arrives,' Dan replied. 'It could be.'

It took Billy fifteen minutes to reach them. 'That was scary,' he said, as he took his cap off and sat. Today he was in full uniform, including a stab vest under a police overcoat.

'You look intimidating in that get-up,' Dan said.

'Have to wear it all, these days,' Billy replied. 'Georgie's solicitor spoke to Richard. He said you needed to speak to me, urgently. So, here I am?'

'We'd like you to tell us why you lied,' Belle said.

He grabbed the edges of the table. 'What do you mean? Lied about what?'

'Georgie was at the party, outside, watching,' Belle said. 'He saw Joe Knight leave. He recognised the girl Joe shouted at. It was Star. He saw you grab her and pull her around to the back of the house. You told us you went inside after you stopped throwing up. You lied, Billy. Why?'

He stood up and took a deep breath.

'Did Georgie hear what she said to him?'

'No, he just saw what looked like an argument.'

'I heard it all. She was drunk and out of her mind on whatever drugs she'd been taking. She was trying to grab his arm, she was saying "*why not me, why not me*". Then she said something I'll never forget. She said: "*I know who my father is. He's a bastard, you know that.*" He stopped trying to get away from her then and just stared at her. He said: "I don't know what you're talking about. I have no idea who your father is." And she said, or rather, she slurred. "*It's that pig. He comes here, looking at us. He knows who I am, too. I can see it, the way he looks at me.*" Joe said again, "*I don't know who you're talking about.*' And then she said it.' He paused, took a deep breath. 'She said, "*Martin Riley's my father. My mother finally told me.*" I couldn't believe it. I thought she must be completely bonkers. Anyway, he got into his car and drove off. She was down on her knees, crying. So I came out from the bushes and grabbed her, took her around the back of the house and demanded to know if she was telling the truth. Hang on a minute. Why don't any of you look surprised?'

'Because we already know. Only just in the past few days, but we know. However, we didn't know that Star knew before she died,' Belle said. 'What happened next?'

'She told me it was true. Definitely. She wanted to get a DNA test to prove it. She had confronted him, but he had laughed her off. She was planning how to find a way to get his DNA without his knowledge.'

'But then she died,' Posy said.

'I'm still not convinced about which day she died,' Billy said. 'Gabe said he had seen her on the Wednesday, but that was a lie, too. There's been a lot of lies. And I don't believe Emily's statement about Georgie killing Star on the Monday.'

'Do you think Joe Knight went to tell Martin Riley what Star had said?'

Billy shrugged. 'He could have done. I have no idea. After she confirmed it to me, she went back into the house. I saw her briefly the next day, which was Sunday, before I left for Christmas. I never saw her again.'

'Did she tell anyone else in the house?' Belle asked. 'I'm thinking specifically about Jade.'

'She didn't tell Jade, but Jade overheard. She was in the garden at the back, smoking. She never said anything at the time, never has since, until a couple of days ago.'

'She's missing,' Posy said.

'Not really,' he replied. 'She's hiding. Stupid girl. As soon as she knew Emily was back she knew the whole issue of Star's death would come up again, so she went to confront Martin Riley, to see if she could get some hush money out of him. He threatened to cut her hands off, which she believed him capable of. She also told him you,' he pointed at Belle, 'knew some of what had happened and were getting closer to the truth. He tried to grab her, but she got free of him and ran. She came to me. I have her. She's at my house, hiding. God help me if Martin Riley ever finds out.' He puffed out a long sigh.

'There's no reason he should, and – you didn't hear this from me – his time as Chief Constable is coming to an end. He'll be gone by the end of the month.'

Billy's head, which he had dropped down onto his chest, shot up. 'No! Really?'

'Really.'

'That can't come quickly enough, for anyone I know. Except my boss.'

'No doubt she'll be devastated,' Belle replied. 'He's being allowed to retire on health grounds. Truth is, his past has caught up with him.'

He stood up. 'I have to go. My partner's in the car at the end of the lane. She'll be giving me the third degree on what's going on in here.'

'You can't say anything about Martin Riley,' Belle warned. 'The news will be out soon enough.'

He nodded, grinned and left them, with a lighter step than when he had arrived.

'That was interesting,' Dan said, when Billy had gone and Posy sat with them again. 'If Star knew that Martin Riley was her father, does that give him a motive to kill her?'

'Does in my book,' Posy said. 'Dan, you've been looking puzzled for a couple of days now. That crease between your eyes is going to be permanent soon. What's up?'

'I have seen something, Posy. It was the night of the Ball, I'm pretty sure. Something clanged like a broken bell. I just can't pin it down.'

'It will come back to you. These things always do, usually at an odd moment, so don't shout Eureka! if we're somewhere in public.' Belle said. 'How about going down to the pub, the three of us, for lunch, then a walk up on the cliffs. It's stopped snowing.'

They dressed up and waded through the snow down to the George and Dragon at the opposite end of the High Street. It was an old pub, with low ceilings and beams, popular with tourists in summer but today had only three other customers. At the end of the bar was a roaring fire, surrounded by armchairs. They ordered drinks and sat, staring at the flames.

'I do love a real fire,' Posy said. 'It's the colours, as well as the heat. The oranges and reds. They're my favourite.'

Dan picked up his pint of beer, then stopped with it half way to his lips. 'That's part of it – the colour. It's something to do with colour. Not reds and oranges. More like pale colours, blues and greens, with some lilac. I think.'

'You're frowning again,' Posy said. 'They sound like colours a woman would wear. Can you think of anyone at the ball wearing those colours?'

He and Belle both thought for a few moments, until Dan shook his head. 'It wasn't a dress. It was – I've got it! It was a scarf. Someone outside was wearing a scarf in those colours.' He turned to Belle. 'Can you remember who it might have been?'

'I certainly can,' she replied. 'It was Joe Knight. It was a beautiful wool and silk scarf. But why is it bothering you?'

'That I can't say. But it is. I must keep thinking on this.'

'No,' Posy said. 'You must stop thinking on it. Then, you'll get it.'

They ordered lunch. The landlord was glad to have some company and chatted to Dan at the bar for some time as he ordered the food.

'That was a long chat,' Belle said. 'Anything interesting.'

'Yes and no,' he replied. 'Mainly local gossip. Everyone knows about Georgie being arrested. And they all think it's ridiculous. Georgie has a good rep around here. He's a local lad, well know. Interesting was that Emily has no such good reputation. People don't seem to like her, they think she's smug and stuck up.' He looked at Belle. 'We never managed to speak to Richard about our thoughts regarding Emily. How about we share them now?'

Posy sat forward. 'I have some thoughts regarding Emily,' she said. 'I'd like to share, too.'

Their food arrived.

'Let's eat, then we can talk.'

The food was excellent, but no-one tasted much of it. They ate quickly. When they were done Dan took the crockery back to the bar.

'We can talk without interruption, now,' he said. 'Who'll go first.'

'I will,' Belle said. 'I have concluded that Emily Duggan did kill Star Bright, but not alone. She had an accomplice. And I think that person was Martin Riley. I believe this because of what I've learned about Emily from various people who've been in her life for a long time. They each have a varying version, but, especially following our meeting with Lennie Maginnis, I believe she is sociopathic. She came back to clear her name, because she's planning something with Riley, who's retiring at the end of this month. I also think she was in London, not Scotland for most of the past three years, somewhere organised by Riley, where she could live comfortably. Have you noticed her hands? They're smooth, manicured, not the hands of a person who's worked on the land for years. She has named her brother as the killer, which Riley has pounced on, via DCI Lewis. They're going to make Georgie take the blame.'

Dan nodded. 'I've had the same feeling for a while. Every time I see her I feel uncomfortable, and unsafe, which probably sounds ridiculous. I can't explain why, but that's how I feel. I agree about Riley. I think he's involved, but I don't know how or why. I can accept she could have had a relationship with him. What do you think, Posy?'

'I can't disagree with your conclusions. I haven't seen as much of her as you have. I agree that she definitely hasn't lived on a commune for three years. I've done something like that. You end up looking like a scarecrow, not a magazine front page model, with sleek hair and long painted nails. But here's where I have a problem. Why would they have killed Star Bright? OK, so she might have been going to announce to the world that Martin Riley was her father. So what? He could easily have laughed it off. She'd clung onto older men before, you told us she did it in Bristol and she tried it with Joe Knight. Would anyone really have believed her?'

'She had something else,' Belle said. 'She had a necklace that Star stole from her, then gave back. I thought that was very odd, not the stealing, but the returning. And Billy said that on the night of the party, she shouted something at Emily, like *it was never for you*. She was wearing that necklace on the night of the Ball. It could have been a provocation, to Martin Riley. His wife was absolutely furious. I think he might have had it made for her, but then given it to Emily. It's a lovers' knot. It has intertwined initials, but I could only make out the E.'

'It's a good story,' Posy said. 'But I just can't see Emily Duggan with Martin Riley.'

'Why not?' Dan asked. 'She has a history of sleeping with older men. He's rich and powerful.'

'I don't know,' Posy said.

'And there's the anonymous call about Georgie Morris and her statement that she saw him murder Star. It seems to me just the kind of thing that Riley could organise and follow up, to make sure it all goes through smoothly.'

'Richard has put a spanner in that works,' Dan said. 'The prosecution saw him talking to Georgie's solicitor and immediately called someone, might have been Riley. He told me he couldn't be sure, but the call sounded deferential.'

'What do we do?' Posy said. 'Confront her?'

'Not yet,' Belle replied. 'I need to speak to Josie Riley, and Dan needs to try to remember why he thinks the scarf Joe Knight was wearing the evening of the Ball is so important. That was an excellent lunch. Anyone fancy a walk? Don't worry if you don't but I think best when I'm walking.'

'I think about getting back somewhere warm,' Dan replied. 'If you're going up onto the cliff top, be very careful.'

'I will,' she replied. 'I'll head off now to get my snow boots. My thoughts will include a great deal of speculation and potential scenarios. I'll speak to you both later.'

As she stood up her phone pinged an incoming text. When she read it her face lit up.

'It's from Rose. She's at the hospital. Mavis has been moved into a side ward. She's quite confused, but wants to see us all. Rose says one at a time, two maximum. I'd like to go. What about you both?'

'I'll come with you,' Posy said. 'It'll be such a relief to see her again. How long will they give us?

'Rose says no more than fifteen minutes.'

'In that case, I'll see you in the morning.'

Chapter 33

Belle stopped at the cottage to put her boots on, reckoning she had an hour to walk, whilst there was still enough light. There was no sign of more snow on the horizon as she headed up to the cliff pathway. She had made a small flask of hot chocolate and intended to stop at one of the benches on the cliff top, to sit, drink and think.

She crossed the deserted beach at Cash Cove, up the steps and along the edge of the wood, past the castle and onto open ground. She was about to sit on the first bench when, to her amazement, she saw Emily Duggan walking towards her at a brisk pace, a scowl on her face. Belle glanced along the cliff. There were no other walkers. Perhaps, like herself, Emily had come up here to think. Judging from her expression, the thoughts had not been good ones. She was undecided about whether to call out to Emily. The woman was so concentrated on her own thoughts she didn't recognise Belle. Curiosity won out.

'Emily, hello,' she said as Emily drew alongside the bench. Emily looked across, surprised, then angry, then scared. She stopped walking. 'Would you like to sit with me for a few minutes?'

'No, I would not. Leave me alone.'

'I thought you might have left town, after what you've done to Georgie. Let's face it, we both know he didn't kill Star.'

'Oh, do we? I know what I know. You know nothing.'

'I know a great deal, probably more than you think or realise,' Belle replied. She knew she would have to choose her words carefully, not give too much away, but say enough to keep Emily's attention.

'Such as?'

'Nothing I'm going to tell you.'

'So why should I sit with you?'

'Because you have things to tell me. Why you've lied about Georgie, for instance. What your relationship is with Martin Riley. Where you got that beautiful gold necklace with the lovers' knot. Just for starters.'

Unexpectedly, Emily laughed. 'Like I said, you know nothing.' She walked off, picking up her pace until she was jogging.

I said something wrong, Belle thought. *But which part was it?* There was no doubt in Belle's mind that Emily had lied in her statement about Georgie. She definitely still had the necklace. She had worn it at the Ball. Was it Martin Riley? This was frustrating. For a moment she thought about going after the young woman, but decided there would be no point. Apart from any other consideration, Emily was younger and fitter and could easily outrun her. She wondered what Emily had been doing up on the cliffs. Had she met with someone? The speed and concentration with which she had been walking wasn't that of a person out for a bracing walk on a cold but sunny day. She had been deep in thought.

Belle poured out a small cup of hot chocolate and began to think through as much as she could remember about what people had said, where she might find clues, in between and behind the words. So often people gave themselves away without realising they had done so. The most innocuous remarks could lead to something of vital importance.

She picked her way through conversations with each of the former students, with Joe Knight, with each of her Curiosity Club friends, even with Peter Day.

Something came to her. Something to add to the list of questions to ask, something she had taken for granted, but shouldn't have done. A phone call was required. There was no signal up here on the cliff top. Time to go back home, and ask the question. The sky was darkening, the bright blue sky fading, low clouds appearing on the horizon. Soon, it would snow, again.

**

The person she needed wasn't available, so she left a message asking for an urgent call back. Nothing came that evening. In the end she decided to put aside her notes, settle down and binge a TV box set, something that she could really get into and would take her mind off the maelstrom going on around her. She chose The Blacklist, one of her favourites that she hadn't looked at for a while and had three seasons' worth to catch up on.

The following morning Belle was ready and waiting for Posy at nine thirty. On their way to the hospital they chatted about various aspects of the case. They were both worried about Georgie, how he was coping. Fortunately, he was on remand at a jail in Devon, so not too far to travel. Bette and Bert were taking Mandy to visit him later. On the way they would stop off at their son Albie's house on the Cornwall/Devon border. Mandy had decided it was time to tell Will about his dad being in jail. Belle was relieved to not have to play any part in that conversation. The shy, eleven year old boy, who had a close, loving relationship with his dad, would be devastated. On their return they would take Will back to the farm. Mandy was still undecided if he should go back to school the following Monday, when the new term would begin.

'She's worried about him being bullied, dad in jail and all that, and for murder,' Posy said as they arrived at the hospital. 'You know what kids are like.'

'Better than most, as you know,' Belle replied.

They found Mavis' room on the 5th floor of the hospital. She had been moved again, to a small ward, the nurse explaining that she was out of danger and didn't need to be near the ICU, but still needed a great deal of rest.

'You have fifteen minutes, and please keep it light. You can talk to her, but even a short period of trying to talk will wear her out. Which two are you?'

'We understand,' Posy replied. 'I'm Posy and this is Belle.'

'She'll be thrilled to see you. She says your names all the time.'

There were four patients on the ward, each separated by a curtain. They found Mavis in a bed next to the window. Her eyes were closed, but opened as they moved chairs next to each other and sat and as soon as she heard the noise and opened her eyes, a wide smile lit up her face.

Belle was shocked at how gaunt Mavis had become. Her hair, which had had some colour in it, had turned completely grey, her skin was sallow and her cheeks sunken in. But, she was still their Mavis, as she proved as soon as she saw them.

'At last. I've been desperate for people I know. The nurses are kind and lovely, but I wanted to see you all. Where are the others?'

'Rose will be here later,' Posy said, taking Mavis' hand. 'Bette is a bit busy at the moment, especially today, but she promises she'll be here as soon as she can.' She glanced around. 'They're only allowing us fifteen minutes, Mave.'

Mavis tutted. 'Seeing all of you is better medicine than sleeping.'

Belle noticed that Mavis was slurring as she spoke. 'You need the rest, Mave. My friend Maggie in Wales, told me last year about her colleague, Zelah Trevear, having a similar injury a few years ago. She's fully recovered, but it took a while. You must be patient.'

'I so wanted to help.'

'We want you back to your old self,' Posy said. 'Lots of patience. We'll keep you in the know, about what's going on.'

'Must have been a lot,' Mavis said. 'I can't remember anything. Did I miss Christmas? I know it's past New Year.'

'No,' Belle said. 'We had a lovely day, with Rose and Harry. It will all come back to you, in time. Don't try to push yourself to think about it.'

'I can't remember anything. But there's one – it's almost like a dream, that keeps coming back to me – about Emily Duggan. Was she here?'

'Definitely not,' Posy began, but Belle interrupted her.

'What happens in the dream, Mave?'

'I'm walking along the main street in Truro, then I'm standing, outside a café. I see Emily through the window. She leans across the table. She's holding hands with a man. An older man. They kiss. It's a long kiss. Then he strokes her face. Then I'm back in my car. You know what dreams are like. They jump about.'

Mavis had spoken slowly. When she finished she closed her eyes. Posy thought she might have fallen asleep. They waited a few minutes, until a nurse appeared around the curtain.

'Time's up,' she said.

They both stood. Posy bend down and kissed the sleeping Mavis' cheek. 'Get well soon, my dear friend,' she whispered.

'I intend to,' came a whisper from the bed.

Belle smiled. 'We'll be back, Mavis.'

The head tilted down enough for Belle to know that Mavis had heard her.

On their way back, Posy began the conversation.

'That was no dream.'

'I agree. Eventually, I hope soon, as she recovers, she'll remember the man.'

'If she knew who he was,' Belle replied. She was quiet for a few minutes. 'Posy, Margaret said she saw Mavis heading up the hill. Would that have been in the direction of Sugar Pit Lane?

'Possibly,' Posy replied. 'Do you want to ask her?'

'I'm loathe to do so, knowing Margaret. Goodness knows who she'll tell. The woman is a walking gossip pit.'

'Mavis was going in that direction, and we know that she went to see someone. Emily lives, for now, on Sugar Pit Lane, in her mother's old house. Are you thinking…?'

'Yes, I am. She went to see Emily Duggan, to tell her what she saw. That could mean she knew who the man was. Posy, when did Martin Riley become Chief Constable?'

'Seven years ago. So, yes, it could have been him with Emily.'

As she was about to drop Belle back at her flat, her phone pinged an incoming text. She parked in the lane at the back of Belle's cottage.

'Do you want to come in for a coffee and a chat?' Belle asked.

'No, thank you, not today. I'm using this period of being closed to organise some maintenance and decorating. I have the coffee machine man coming in an hour to give the beast an overhaul.'

'I wouldn't want to get in the way of that,' Belle joked. 'That machine is a masterpiece and it delivers the best coffee in Cornwall. When are you planning to open again?'

'Next week, probably just part time, something like Wednesday to Sunday.' She took her phone out of her pocket to check the text before driving off.

'It's from Josie Riley. I gave her my personal number. I thought it would be easier for her to get in touch without Martin hovering. She says they are still snowed in, but she's suggesting a meeting tomorrow. Three thirty, at the café. OK with you?'

'Definitely,' Belle replied. 'I'll let Dan know. Oh, now there's a text for me.'

She read it. 'It's from Bette. They're on their way to the prison now. Back around five. She's asked if we can meet up, as many of us as can get there.'

'I'll be done by five,' Posy said. 'I'll call Rose, let her know.'

'And I'll speak to Dan. I hope his memory will have delivered by now.'

**

Belle offered to drive up to the farm and Dan accepted her offer of a lift.

'No, it still hasn't come back to me, before you ask,' he said as they set off. 'How was Mavis?'

'I was shocked at how she looked, but I suppose I shouldn't have been. The medical staff say she's doing well. She's going to be in hospital for a couple of days yet. I was wondering about asking at this get together, if Mavis should come to stay with one of us when she gets out, or if one of us should stay with her.'

'The former, I think,' Dan mused. 'If she remembers who it was she saw with Emily in that café, she might still be in danger. Someone took the extreme measure of hitting her hard over the head with a blunt object. They may even have wanted to kill her. It may not be over yet, for Mavis. Will the police be questioning her, now she's awake?'

'She's already said she can't remember anything.'

'Then she should keep to that story. Even if she does remember whoever it was.'

They were the last two to arrive at the farm. Harry had accompanied Rose. Posy was there, grim faced.

'What's happened?' Belle asked, as they walked into the kitchen. 'What's the matter?'

'Georgie took a beating in prison yesterday,' Bert said. 'It's not life threatening, but he's a mess. Are we any closer to finding out who really killed that girl, because I'm beginning to fear for his life? I mean, that he won't be able to handle prison much longer and might harm himself.'

'Then we have to work faster. Dan, Posy and I have a working theory. That's all it is for now, and there are still parts missing. The main thing is, and Bette, I'm sorry to have to say this, but the three of us are agreed. Your niece is a sociopath and she most likely did kill Star Bright. But, she had an accomplice. Our main task for the past couple of days has been to try to find out who that was, still is. For now, we think it might be Martin Riley.'

She sat back, as Bette stared at her, open mouthed. Bert walked over to the kitchen door that led to the living room and closed it.

'I don't want Mandy and Will to hear this. Will's upset enough about his dad.'

'Definitely not,' Bette said. 'This is shocking, Belle. Can you please give me and Bert all of the detail you have so far. Every last little bit. Don't leave anything out.'

'For the next twenty minutes Belle took them through everything she knew, and what was still to come, the outstanding information, the unanswered questions.

Her phone rang. She was going to reject the call, until she saw who it was from.

'I have to take this. You should all listen. Billy, thanks for getting back to me.'

'No problem. It was a strange question and I had no idea, nor did Jade. I hope you don't mind, but I called Phil Singh and asked him. He didn't know, either. Then, five minutes ago, he called me back. He had asked Miriam and she, apparently, just laughed. She said, and I'll try to remember this word for word: *of course I remember. I've read it.* She won't say any more. He's asked her and she told him to leave it alone. Sorry, Belle, that's the best I can do.'

'That's fine, Billy. Thanks for trying.'

She ended the call.

'What was that about?' Bette asked.

'I asked Billy if he knew what was the subject of Emily's PhD. I didn't expect him to remember, but I'd been thinking about how I always took note of every little piece of information, when I was working. Sometimes the devil is in the detail. This was just one detail, but it was something I didn't know.'

'What do you think Miriam Singh meant? I can't imagine Emily would have allowed her to have anything to do with her notes or her script,' Dan said.

Belle bit her lip. 'She must have read something at the time, somehow. Or discussed some aspect of it with Emily. She was studying Maths. Maybe Emily needed to talk to her about some statistics?'

'Does it matter?' Posy asked.

'I don't know,' Belle said. 'Let's assume it's just another piece of incomplete information to be added to the puzzle.'

'I can find out, if you really want to know,' Dan said. 'The University should have a note of it, somewhere.'

'Yes, please, why not? Belle said. 'But it's not the most important thing right now. That will be the meeting with Josie Riley. Then, I think you and I, Dan, should talk to Emily again. I'm convinced she had been meeting someone up on the cliff top yesterday.'

'It couldn't have been Martin Riley,' Posy said. 'They're snowed in, remember?'

'Of course, you're right,' Belle said.

As Posy was about to comment again, the door opened and Will burst into the kitchen. 'Grandma, mum says can she help with dinner? I'm starving.'

'Of course, my darlin'. We're done here. Off you go and tell her five minutes.'

The boy ran out.

'How is he coping?' Harry asked. 'We have a youth club meeting at the church tomorrow evening. Do you think he might like to come along?'

'That's kind, Harry. I'll ask him, and let you know.'

As Belle and Dan drove back into St Foy, Dan had his eyes closed.

'What's occurring to you?' she asked. 'Something is.'

'Yes, but if I can put it all together, I'll call you later.'

'Call me any time,' she said.

A phone call came at seven, but not from Dan.

'Belle, it's Joe. I haven't seen you for a couple of days, but I've been totally snowed in here. My car even disappeared under a snow heap. How are you? Are we OK?'

'We're fine, Joe, thank you for asking.'

'Look, I want to apologise for what I did. I know it was much too fast. But I really do like you. And you were the first person I thought of when I had some news today, the person I wanted to share it with.'

'That sounds exciting.'

'It is. I've been offered a job in New York. At the UN, as an economics advisor. It's a wonderful opportunity. And my book has reached number one on the Best Seller list.'

'Congratulations Joe. I'm very happy for you, on both counts. When will you go?'

'I have to fly over in two days. So, I was wondering if we could meet again, before I leave. 'I'll be gone for a few weeks. I'll miss you.'

'What did you have in mind?'

'Lunch, at a restaurant, somewhere half way between St Foy and here?

'What about your car?'

'I dug it out this morning, and the lane has been cleared, so I can get out, at last.'

'Yes, I'll have lunch with you. Tell me where and what time.'

'Thank you. I'm happy you want to see me again. I know this is fast for you, too fast, but I do believe we have a special relationship, even though we haven't known each other long. I'll text you the place and time as soon as I've made a reservation.'

'I'll look forward to it,' she replied.

**

Belle made herself a meal and watched more TV, but turned it off, when she realised that half an hour had passed and she hadn't taken in any of the plot.

The call had been unexpected. Did she want to see him again? She was certainly attracted to him, and he had sounded genuinely sorry about his behaviour at lunch on New Year's Day. But she was not ready to commit to a relationship. He was good company, funny, interesting, the best looking man she had seen in a long time, apart from Richard, and she couldn't help being flattered that he was interested in her. He would be quite a catch. But, if he was going away, so be it. It sounded like he would be residing in New York for some of the year, and most probably travelling the world. Was he going to ask her to join him? The idea was attractive, yet she felt herself holding back. His text arrived. He had organised a pub lunch at a well-known gastropub. She would go to meet him, to see how it panned out.

Her mind went back to what was bothering her when she had turned off the TV, something Billy had related, but she couldn't think what it was, so she decided on an early night.

Which was just as well, because her phone rang at six the following morning.

'I've got it. All of it.'

Belle peered at her watch. 'Dan, you know it's six am? I was asleep!'

'You said any time.'

'I didn't mean… oh whatever.' She sat up. 'What it is that you've got? What's "all of it"?'

'Breakfast,' he said. 'I don't want to discuss this over the phone. What time can I come round?'

'Give me an hour.'

'Right. I'll be there at seven.' He ended the call.

He arrived promptly at seven. Belle, showered, dressed and alert, was waiting at the door to let him in. She had laid the table in the conservatory, turned on the heating and made fresh coffee.

'Your favourite,' he said, handing her a bag of fresh baked croissants. 'I walked over. Jolly's had his lights on and he let me in to buy these.'

'It's all about who you know,' Belle said, tipping the steaming hot pastries onto a plate in the centre of the table. 'Help yourself to a drink, and tell me what this is about.'

'I'm going to tell you and you can tell me if I'm crazy or not. I don't think I am. I've already called Richard and talked it through with him.'

'What time did you call him?' Belle asked.

'Four thirty,' he said, grinning. 'Your slightly annoyed response was nothing compared to his. But, when he heard what I had to say, he told me to get on the phone to you and tell you the same stuff. He's on his way down.'

'Then it must be serious.'

'It is.'

'Then tell me.'

'I believe I know who the accomplice is.'

'OK,' Belle said. 'Tell me everything.'

'There are three clues,' he began. 'The first is what Billy said was Miriam's response to the question about the PhD.

The second is the scarf that Joe Knight was wearing. The third is about who Emily had been meeting on the cliff top when she passed you on Tuesday.'

'Before you go on, as you've mentioned Joe Knight, I'm having lunch with him today. He called me last night. He's leaving St Foy. He has a new job, based in New York.'

'What!' Dan yelled. No, you can't go.'

'Tell me why not?'

'Because I think he's the accomplice.'

Chapter 34

Belle sat back and folded her arms. To her own surprise, his announcement didn't shock her. Somewhere, in the back of her mind, something had niggled at her to keep a distance between them, despite her attraction to him.

'Tell me,' she said quietly.

'I'll start with Miriam Singh's comment. According to Billy she said: '*I've read it.* Not: *I read it.* The latter is definitely in the past. The former suggested to me something more recent, which is…'

'Professor Sir Joseph Knight's book. The best seller.'

'Exactly. Miriam must have picked up at the time what was the full subject of Emily's thesis. The best seller is based on her work. For me, that explains what she's been doing and where she's been for the past three years. Somewhere, I don't know, London, perhaps New York, working with him to author the book.'

Belle nodded. 'That's feasible, but what about how they seemed to dislike each other? Billy and Jade both commented on it. And we've seen it since she returned.'

'Faked. That's where the scarf comes in. There's one more visit we need to make, and I suggest we do it as soon as we're done here. But, I'm digressing. Do you remember, when we visited Emily, we knew there was someone with her, up in the bedroom? We both heard the back door close.'

She nodded.

'As we left, Joe Knight pulled up in his car and went to the front door. They appeared to be arguing, then she let him in.'

'Yes. Where's this going?'

'He was wearing the scarf that day. But what I didn't recall until yesterday, was that, when she let us in, before he arrived, that scarf was hanging on a peg in the hallway. It was partly covered by one of the coats. But it was the same scarf.'

Belle sat forward. 'Are you sure of that? Quite sure?'

'Yes,' he said, emphatically. 'I wondered where he had bought it. It looked expensive. It's only sold at one outlet, in London. A very expensive and exclusive item of gentleman's outdoor wear.'

'And the third thing? Belle asked. 'Who Emily was meeting on the cliff top?'

'You said that when you mentioned Martin Riley's name, she laughed and said you know nothing. So, I thought, who else could it be? Billy was working, so was Phil Singh. Who does that leave?'

'Sorry, Dan, but you're wrong about that one. Joe told me last night he's been snowed in. He couldn't even find his car, never mind get it down the lane into the village.'

He smiled. 'You told me about his house, remember; how beautiful the view was from the garden?'

She looked puzzled, then it hit her. 'Of course,' she said, slapping her forehead. 'They met up on the coastal path. All he had to do was step over the fence, and walk. It can't be more than two miles.'

'It's much longer when you have to drive around, but you're right, along the coastal path, about two miles, less even. No more than thirty to forty minutes' brisk walking.'

'He and Emily were, and still are, a couple. And it's been going on for years. Oh Dan, he must have been seeing her when his wife was sick and dying.'

'Yes. Now comes the theorising part. Star Bright found out about them. She was going to expose them. So, they killed her. Emily went away. But why three years?'

'His wife only died back in the summer. Maybe they weren't expecting her to hang on for so long.'

'This is – I don't know what to say – horrible, disgusting. They've been fooling everyone. Dan, what can we do about it? Georgie Morris is suffering in prison for something he didn't do. If we can't prove any of this, they're going to get away with it. And I can't go to lunch with him today. No chance. The bastard!'

Her phone rang.

'Dan, it's him.'

'Answer it. Sound happy.'

'Ok, I'll try. Hello Joe, this is early. Is everything OK?... Oh, I'm sorry to hear that, still, it can't be helped. The weather has spoiled a lot of stuff, hasn't it... um, possibly. I can't remember what's in my diary. I'll need to check and call you back... Mavis? Yes, she's doing well, but no memory at all of what happened to her. She can't remember anything after Christmas Eve. The doctors think those memories may never come back.' She looked at Dan and grimaced. He nodded and mouthed, *'you're doing fine. Keep going.'*

'What, sorry I missed that... I thought you were flying out tomorrow?... Moved to Saturday? Then hang on, I've got my diary on my desk next to me. Yes, lunchtime is good. Will I be able to drive up to your house?... Good, then I'll see you at midday.'

She ended the call and breathed out. 'You heard that. Lunch today is cancelled because the pub can't get supplies in. He's asked me to go tomorrow, to his place.'

Dan shook his head. 'You definitely can't do that. Too dangerous.'

'But I have to, Dan. If I don't he'll get away with it. They both will. And it's puzzling me now. Why is he asking to see me? Surely Emily will be going with him?'

'He'll have his reasons. But you absolutely cannot go. No way.'

'Yes way. I have to. Don't argue with me. You said there was something you need us to check out, to confirm the scarf story.'

He scowled at her. 'If I'm remembering correctly, the back entrance to the house on Sugar Pit Lane has a set of garages. Joe Knight could have parked his car in one of them. When he left the house via the back door, he got into his car and drove around to the front, making us think he'd just arrived.'

'Then let's finish breakfast and go check,' she replied. 'I'll drive us up there. But, before we go, let's go over everything again.'

They left the cottage at nine. Belle was relieved the roads out of the town were clear of snow and ice, and had already been gritted. The main exit road was steep and she didn't like the thought of her tyres losing their grip and the car sliding back down the hill.

When they reached Emily's house, Belle parked directly outside.

'If she's up and about, she'll see us,' Dan said.

'Good. Hopefully, it will rattle her. Come on, let's walk around to the back.'

The lane at the back was narrow, barely more than a footpath, but with just enough room for a car to drive down. As Dan had suggested, at the end of the path was a set of five garages. They walked along the row. There was nothing to identify who owned or rented them.

'I was right about there being a garage,' Dan said, as they turned back. As they did so, a man came walking towards them.

'Excuse me,' Belle said. 'Do you own one of those garages? I live further down in town, with no parking and I'd like to hire one. Do you know who owns them?'

'That one's mine,' the man replied, pointing to the garage at the far right end. 'I know the next four along, but the one at the farthest end, that's been empty for years. Until recently, that is. I seen a big posh car coming in and out a few times lately.'

'Oh, that's no good for me. But if it was empty for a long time, do you know who owns it?'

He leaned in, breathing out misty breath at them. 'It's that woman,' he whispered. 'The one who's just come back, after she was supposed to have murdered that poor student.' He glanced furtively left and right. 'I think she's got herself a boyfriend. I saw him once, getting into the car.'

'Older chap, greyish hair?' Dan asked.

'Couldn't see the hair, nor much of the face. Wrapped up in a scarf, 'gainst the cold. Girly sort of scarf, I noticed.'

'Like, pale blues and greens with some orange,' Belle said.

'That's it. Girly.'

'Thanks for your help. I think we'll go visit her,' Belle said. 'See if she wants to hang on to it, or if she's interested in renting it out.'

'No point,' the man replied. 'She's gone. Left last night, with two big suitcases. Went off in a taxi, she did, in a hurry, it looked like.'

'We'll knock, anyway. Thanks for your help.'

The man tipped the brim of his hat and walked on to his garage.

'Done a runner?' Dan said.

'Sounds like it. Let's check.'

They walked back to the front, up the steps and knocked, several times. There was no reply. The curtains were drawn. They went around to the back again, worked out which was the right house and let themselves into the garden through the back gate. There were no footprints in the snow.

'No-one's been out here for several days,' Belle said.

A set of steps led up to the kitchen door.

'Frosted glass,' she added. 'We won't be able to see in. But, if I could find something to stand on, I might be able to get a look into the kitchen.'

'We can try the bin, if it will take your weight. Let's hope the neighbours don't call the police,'

He pulled the empty rubbish bin over to the base of the window. 'Up you go, Holmes,' he said, giving her a push until she was standing on top of the bin in front of the window. The bin shook worryingly each time Belle moved, and the lid began to sink in. 'There's nothing to see,' she said, jumping down just in time as the lid caved in. 'The lights are off, the kitchen's completely clear. She's gone. Come on, let's get out of here.'

Back in the car, Belle began a slow drive back down to St Foy.

'It proves your theory, he could easily have driven out of the garage and pulled around the corner to meet us. That was a lucky co-incidence, for him.'

Dan didn't answer.

'What's on your mind now, Watson?'

'You said that when you saw her on the cliff top, at first, before she saw you, she was walking fast, and scowling, looking deep in thought. Did she look like a woman who had just had a meeting with her lover and planned to go away with him?'

'No, but he didn't know on Tuesday about the job.'

'That's what he told you. Maybe he did.'

'Whatever, Emily is gone. If she really is gone, where does that leave her statement to the police about seeing Georgie kill Star?'

'Good point. We can ask Richard, as soon as he arrives.'

'What time will he be here?'

'By midday, I hope, weather and roads permitting. How about you come back to the apartment. It's already ten. We can talk to him together.'

'Sounds like a plan,' Belle said.

**

Richard listened without comment to Dan's tale of their latest findings.

'Is there anything so far that has a chance of him being arrested for murder?' Belle asked, thinking she probably knew the answer.

'Nothing at all. Just because he was having an affair with his student doesn't mean anything. Yes, we know he was conducting it behind his terminally ill wife's back. And it's likely he used Emily's work, with her knowledge and assistance. But there's nothing concrete. However, it's her witness statement that condemns Georgie. He was in the house, he moved the body. Unless she retracts, and confesses herself, there's nothing.'

'But what if she's done a runner?' Belle said. 'Surely the police can't then rely on her statement?'

'That's different. They may still try to claim he's guilty, but proving it would be far more difficult. If it came out that Martin Riley was Star's father, and he knew, that would muddy the waters sufficiently. You mentioned she was going to try to get a DNA sample from him. Do you know if she succeeded?'

'I don't know,' Belle replied. 'Just a minute. She was buried in the churchyard. Would it be possible – I know this sounds horrible – to dig her up?'

'Unlikely to be allowed. Not unless her mother supports it and knowing Augusta, I doubt she would consent. Given Martin's position, he's certainly not going to consent. And who's going to compel him? The next level above him is the Commissioner then the Home Secretary and they likely want Martin's past firmly hushed up, so no chance there.'

'Then what can we do?' Dan demanded.

'For now, very little. But keep digging. Belle, you're seeing the wife this afternoon. Tell her about Star, see if she already knew. And find out why she was so angry with Emily. If you push hard enough, something might give somewhere. But, I would caution you not to be alone with Joseph Knight. From everything you've told me, the man is a manipulative, dangerous criminal, a potential murderer.'

Let's see what comes out of the meeting with Josie,' Belle said. 'I can't see there's much further we can go, with anyone. This is so frustrating.'

'There is one thing we can do' Dan said. 'Emily's thesis for her doctorate was finished in draft, so my inside source at the University tells me. He's rooted out a copy, for a backhander. She saved it on the University server, but must have forgotten. We can have it this afternoon. Let's compare it to the best seller.

Chapter 35

Before they set off for the meeting at the café with Josie Riley, Rose called to say that Mavis had had a slight temperature overnight, but seemed better. So much so, that the hospital had agreed that she could come home the following day, provided she had someone to be with her. Bette and Bert had offered to have her stay for a few days, to which she had reluctantly agreed.

'That's good news, at least,' Belle replied.

'Is there bad news?' Rose asked. 'What's happened?'

'We should get together after the meeting with Josie Riley,' Belle replied. 'Do you think we can go back to the farmhouse?'

'Yes, I'm sure it will be fine with Bette and Bert. I know they're waiting for news of any kind. It's torture for them. They're trying to be brave, but it's hard.'

'Keep your fingers crossed some good will come out of this meeting. The problem I foresee is that, even if Josie tells us something useful, according to Richard, who's come back by the way, at present we have nothing that can help Georgie. We have to go. We'll see you at the farm, unless I hear otherwise from you.'

As they walked up to the café, they found Josie Riley, at the end of the lane, tentatively staring along its length, trying to spot the way in.

'Mrs Riley, hello. This is Dr Dan Walker. Please, come with us.'

'Of course I remember you,' Josie Riley said. 'This is all very odd.'

'It is, isn't it?' Dan replied smiling at her. 'Please don't worry, we're very discreet.'

Posy was waiting. She let them in and locked the door behind them.

'Can I make you a drink?' she asked. 'My machine is in good working order.'

Josie accepted and they moved to the Curiosity table.'

'Thanks for agreeing to speak to us. The café is closed to customers at present.'

Posy put the drinks in front of them.

'This is good,' Josie said. 'Ask your questions. I'll answer what I can, and what I want to. If I don't like the question, I'll say so.'

'Fair enough,' Belle replied. 'I'm going to be direct too, because some of what I have to say is raw and shocking. First of all, before we get onto the matter of Emily Duggan, I have something else you need to know, if you don't already. You remember the murder of the student three years ago, a girl called Star Bright?'

'Yes. I met her several times, at the Heights, when I went to visit Miriam. I liked her, she was a sweet little thing.'

'Did you know that your husband was her father?'

Josie's eyes opened wide, but she didn't shake her head as vehemently as Belle had expected. 'I always thought there was something odd there. However, I can assure you Martin wasn't her father. Martin isn't anyone's father, including Miriam. He can't have children. Doesn't have the fire power, if you know what I mean.' She picked up her cup and drank slowly from it. 'Miriam is adopted.'

'Star's mother is a barrister in London, name of Augusta Light. She apparently told Star that her father was Martin.'

'Then she lied. But knowing Augusta, which I do, I'm not surprised. He was probably sleeping with her. Then again, she was in bed in many ways with a lot of the people around him; police and villains. It could have been any one of them.'

'So Martin would have had no reason to kill Star?'

Josie spat out a laugh. 'No. He did interfere with the investigation, but that was to make sure his association with Augusta and her clients didn't come out. Anyway, we weren't here when she died.'

'Sorry, I thought Martin had been the Chief Constable here for seven years?' Dan said.

'Yes, I mean, we were on holiday for two weeks, right up until Christmas Eve. On a cruise to see the Northern Lights.'

'There's one theory to cross off the list,' Dan muttered.

'Do you have any others?' Josie asked.

'Yes, we do. At the Ball, you left early. You looked very angry. I thought you were looking in Miriam's direction, but you seemed to be focussing on Emily Duggan.'

'Is that a question?' Josie snapped.

'Sort of, yes. Were you focussing on Emily, or was it on Miriam?'

'I was surprised to see that group together at a table. Miriam and Phil rarely enter a room where Martin is present. He hates Phil. My husband, you see, is a racist, a racist misogynistic bigot. I'm divorcing him as soon as he steps down at the end of this month. For now, I have to be wary of him, but once he steps down he's going back to London.'

'My husband heard what he said. Unfortunately, he's heard worse,' Dan said.

Josie blushed. 'Yes, I'm sorry about that.'

'No need,' Dan replied. 'You aren't responsible for his views.'

'Can we get back to Emily Duggan,' Belle said.

'If we must.'

'What was it that upset you, Josie?'

'Josie paused, put down her cup and looked at each of them in turn.

'What I am about to tell you must never leave this room. I won't begin until I have a solemn promise from each of you.'

Belle thought quickly. She wasn't going to lie, but she had to persuade Josie to allow her to tell the others in their group.

'Our friend, Mavis Penhaligon, was almost killed just after Christmas. She's made a marvellous recovery. We are a special group of friends. Anything you say to us, she deserves to know. There are six of us in our group. Four you now know. The remaining two are Rose Teague, the vicar's wife, and Bette Jones. Emily is Bette's niece. That doesn't mean she will go to Emily with information. Quite the opposite. Do you know that Emily has given a statement to the effect that Georgie Morris killed Star Bright?'

'Yes, I know and I don't believe a word of it. I've known Georgie since we came here. He's helped me re-design our garden. He's a lamb. He wouldn't hurt anyone. And,' here she paused, 'Emily Duggan is a lying little bitch. She's a monster.'

'Can we tell Rose and Bette whatever it is you are about to tell us?'

'Providing you can guarantee this never came from me.'

'Absolutely.'

'My husband likes young girls. He was sleeping with Emily when she was around fifteen. I've discovered in the past few days, that he introduced her to my brother-in-law, Joseph Knight, when she was sixteen. They've been together ever since. Their relationship is one of evil and horror. When he married my sister he gave her a gold necklace,'

'The lovers' knot,' Belle said.

'Yes. It was so precious to Eve. She discovered, after she became ill, that it had disappeared. She was desperately upset. He said he'd buy her another, similar one, but she refused. She thought it was a special symbol of love, unreplaceable. And it was. Not just for its age and antiquity. And not for her. He'd taken it and given it to Emily Duggan. It's an incredibly old piece, around four hundred years old. She was wearing it the night of the Ball. I thought she'd gone for good when Star died. I thought she'd killed her, and run. My sister has been dead less than six months and that evil woman has come back, wearing my sister's precious necklace. I couldn't believe it. I never guessed, you see. He seemed so devoted to Eve.' She began to cry.

'How did you find out about them?' Dan asked.

'Martin told me. As soon as we got back home, I lost my temper completely. I demanded he tell me about Emily Duggan and Joe.'

'Have you challenged Joe Knight about it?'

'No, but I'm going to.' She wiped away the tears with the back of her hand.

'Please, don't do that,' Emily said. 'It isn't safe.'

'What do you mean?' Josie Riley asked. 'Why isn't it safe?'

'Because it may well be the reason Star was killed. Now I'm going to tell you something we believe. And I need your absolute confirmation that you will not tell anyone what I am about to say.'

Josie nodded, dry eyed now, her mouth open. 'You have my word.'

'I – we – believe Star was killed because she found out about Emily and Joe, and she knew about the necklace. We don't know how she knew, but she said something to Emily that made her very angry on the night of a party at the Heights, a few days before she was killed. She said: *it was never for you*. I think she meant the necklace.'

'I can hardly bear to ask this,' Josie whispered. 'but are you saying you think Emily Duggan and Joe Knight killed little Star?'

'Yes,'

'Can you prove any of it?'

'At the moment, no, not a thing. We are trying, but there's no actual proof.'

Josie sighed. 'I'd like to go now. This has all been too much.' She stood, but her legs gave way and Dan caught her.

Please, sit a few minutes longer, until you feel better.'

'Thank you, but no. I've heard enough. More than enough. Please, just give me my coat. I'll be fine. A short walk to my car will do me good. Thank you. I'm not sure what I'm thanking you for.'

'It's been brave of you to tell us all of this. If we do find any proof, we'll get back in touch with you,' Belle said as she accompanied Josie to the door.

When she came back, Dan and Posy were both caught up in thought.

'This story gets weirder each time we speak to someone new,' Dan said. 'Unfortunately, she didn't give us anything useable against Joe Knight or Emily.'

'No,' Belle said. 'Strange woman, though, didn't you think?'

'I didn't think she was strange,' Posy said. 'Why do you say that?'

'Not sure. Gut instinct. Nothing she said, at least I don't think so. More like she's holding something back. A couple of times, I noticed some flashes of contempt and anger. And when I told her we think it was Joe and Emily who killed Star, I thought I caught a glimpse of triumph.'

'I'm not surprised. She's had a lot to put up with.' Posy said.

'No, not about the people she was talking about. The contempt was directed at me, and you, Dan.'

'I didn't see that,' he replied. 'Are you sure?'

'Oh yes. I used to see those expressions so often, when I was working, in disciplinary hearings. When I had to bring up information or evidence that the person sitting opposite me didn't like. They're micro expressions. We all do it without knowing. They aren't easy to spot unless you know what to look for.'

'I think we should go up to the farm now, and share this with the others,' Posy said. 'It's more proof of what we believe about Joe Knight and Emily, but once again, nothing concrete we can use.'

**

They arrived at the farm, feeling gloomy and dispirited. As they drove up to the farmhouse building, they could see that there were several cars, including a police vehicle.

'Oh no. What's happened now?' Belle said, her stomach churning.

With a pounding in her chest she opened the kitchen door, expecting to find tragedy. Instead, the group gathered there was smiling, laughing and hugging each other, with a beaming Billy Anderson at one side, also smiling.

'Belle! Posy! Dan! Come in, come in. Billy's just come to tell us. Emily has withdrawn her statement. Not just that. She says she made it all up. She won't say why, just that it isn't true,' Bette said, coming over to hug each of them in turn.

'Will Georgie be released?' Belle asked Billy.

'Not immediately,' he replied. It will have to go back to the CPS, but given that there's now no witness and no other evidence, it's likely.'

She realised he was being cautious, and looked at Richard, who was smiling, but raised his eyebrows. He knew it wasn't over, but he wasn't about to tell them so.

'That's great news,' she said to Billy. 'What will happen to Emily now?'

'Not sure,' he replied. 'She wrote this in a letter to DCI Lewis, witnessed by a local solicitor. We'll have to check she made the statement of her own free will, not under duress. I've been to Emily's house, to bring her in, but she's not there.'

'She's gone,' Belle said. 'Dan and I were there this morning. She left last night, with two big suitcases. A neighbour saw her getting into a taxi. He said she seemed to be in a hurry.'

Billy took out his notebook. 'Which neighbour? Which house? Did he say which taxi company?'

'We didn't ask,' she replied.

'I have to go.' He slipped quietly out of the kitchen.

'Where does this leave us?' Dan whispered, smiling back and nodding at Mandy. 'Richard knows this isn't the end. I know that face.'

'Let's settle them down and tell Rose and Bette what we've learned from Josie Riley. I'm thinking the next move is that I have to take up Joe Knight's invitation to lunch. There's something else happening here, something we haven't seen yet, but whatever is coming down the line, is about to hit us like an incoming tidal wave.'

Chapter 36

'To the café?' Posy asked.

'Let's go to my place this time. Rose and Harry are about to leave. I'll let Bette know we've more news and ask her if she can get away.'

Belle took Bette aside and told her there was news from the meeting with Josie Riley that they couldn't speak openly about, and were heading back to her place to update Rose and Harry, and her, if she felt she could escape for an hour.

'I can, yes. You all head off, give me fifteen minutes and I'll be there. Is it good news?'

'It's nothing that will help Georgie, but it tells us so much more about Emily.'

At the mention of her niece's name Bette's face had darkened. 'I want to hear it,' she said. She turned to the rest of group.

'Time for you all to go,' she announced. 'Mandy and Will need a bit of peace and quiet now. Thank you all for coming. And Billy for bringing us the news… oh, he's gone.'

Bert gave her a rapid frown. She shook her head at him and he shrugged, knowing not to ask about whatever was going on.

Five minutes later the kitchen was silent again. Just Bette and Bert. Mandy had taken Will to watch TV with her. Ben had gone to his room to pack, as he was due back at University the following day.

'I have to go out, to Belle's. There's been a development,' Bette said, putting on her coat. 'I'll tell you about it as soon as I'm back.' She kissed him. 'Belle can't say it's good news, but it's about Emily, so I must go.'

'Indeed you must. Shall I wait dinner for you?'

'No, you all carry on. Save some for me.'

**

Back at Belle's, Harry had decided to leave when Belle had told him the promise she made to Josie Riley. If the woman had stipulated the Club members only, then he would leave them to it.

'If you've made a promise, then you must keep it,' he said. To Rose, 'I'll see you soon. Whatever you hear, you will decide if I need to know or not. You understand.'

'I do, Harry. I'll be home soon.'

'Richard, you're staying,' Belle said. 'Your advice is crucial, given what I'm about to say. Please.'

'I will. I'm not a vicar. If you need a legal opinion, I'm here for you.'

She hugged him. 'Thank you for coming back.'

'I have something to tell you, too. As soon as Bette arrives.'

Bette arrived five minutes later. 'Got here as quick as I could,' she puffed as she ran in and joined the crowd around the kitchen table. 'I've left the Land Rover in the lane, in front of your garage, Belle. So, what happened at your meeting with Josie Riley?'

'Dan and Posy, can you please go through everything she said. This time, I want to listen. I'll chip in, if I think I need to.'

Dan began, giving a clear, concise and accurate account of almost everything that had been said. He had asked that no-one interrupt. He had closed his eyes as he began speaking. Although they were all listening carefully, Richard, in particular had a frown of concentration. When Dan finished he opened his eyes and turned to Posy. 'Anything I missed?'

'No,' she replied. 'You had it almost word for word.'

'He has an exceptional memory,' Richard said.

'Belle, do you have anything?'

She shook her head. 'Nothing to add, yet. Richard, you have something to tell us?'

'I do. I'm about to poke a big stick into your theory and stir it up.'

Dan rolled his eyes, but stopped when Richard said, 'I've been to see Augusta Light. She's told me a very interesting story.'

'Go on, then,' Dan said. 'I just hope you aren't about to challenge everything we know.'

'Sorry, but I am about to do just that. In a nutshell, Star wasn't her child. She was paid to take her on and bring her up. The real mother would be allowed access to her on occasion, but only under supervision. The real mother's family was a well-known crime family. The child was registered as Augusta's child. The family paid Augusta well. Very well indeed. She was already on a good retainer for their defence work. Augusta employed nannies to do most of the work. The girl, Louisa, or Anastasia, as Star was known back then, received little love or attention from Augusta. Star went from school to school. She tried to burn one of them down. She had, from about the age of ten, demanded to know who her father was. She believed Augusta was her real mother and I don't think she ever learned the truth on that score. However, eventually, Augusta became sick of the continual questioning. She had had a run in with Martin Riley, so she told Star it was him and good luck in trying to get anything from him. As you now know, it wasn't true. But Star believed it.'

'When was that?' Belle asked. 'In Bristol she had said she didn't know who her father was.'

'According to Augusta, it was between Bristol and coming to study at St Piran. Augusta thinks that was probably why she chose to study here.'

'Is her real father in any way relevant to our situation?' Belle asked.

'No,' Richard replied. 'She wouldn't tell me who the real mother was, either. Even now, although she no longer collects from them, she's fearful of what they might do to her if she did reveal the truth. The only thing she told me was that the real mother was psychotic. One visit, she would be loving. Next time, hateful, spiteful and vicious, taunting the child, threatening her. Finally, she physically hurt the little girl, when she was about three years old. She cut her arm with a knife, made a wound deep enough to need stitches. The family stepped in and banned her from seeing her child again, and moved her out of London. Augusta told me that some years later, the mother married and returned to London, but by that time Star had gone.

'When Star died, the crime family knew it was her, but they warned Augusta not to admit Star's real identity. They also warned Martin Riley to make sure no-one ever knew the girl's identity. Augusta is unsettled, now it's all come back. But she won't say any more, nor name any names.'

He was finished. 'Any questions, anyone.'

'Two stories,' Belle said, breaking the silence that followed Richard's account. 'Which one is the truth?'

'At least Emily has withdrawn her statement,' Bette said. 'Georgie will be let out of prison.'

'Not yet,' Richard said. 'There are a number of people with a vested interest in keeping him in there. He was in the house and moved the body, and he impeded the police investigation. It will be up to the Crown Prosecution Service if that's still enough to keep him there. It will depend on what Emily says next, how she explains why she lied.'

'If they can find her,' Belle said. 'She left yesterday morning. I told Billy earlier. A neighbour saw her getting into a taxi, with two large suitcases. That's why he rushed off, to find out where she went, where she is now.'

Bette's smile had disappeared. 'Richard,' she pleaded. 'Is there anything we can do?'

'I'll speak to Georgie's solicitor first thing in the morning. He can try to force the issue. This must all be off the record. I'll tell him to ask for a copy of Emily's letter to the police. You know,' he said, taking Bette's hand, 'if DCI Lewis is determined to prosecute him, she might claim the letter is forged, especially if Emily is missing and can't be further interviewed.'

'The letter was sent via a solicitor,' Belle said. 'They'll find it's genuine. Billy said they had to determine there was no duress.'

'It would still be good to know if she said in this letter why she lied,' Posy said.

'I'm taking up Joe Knight's offer of lunch tomorrow,' Belle said. 'Don't anyone argue with me. My mind is made up. I also have another couple of issues to check on.'

'Belle, please, you can't,' Dan said. 'Richard agrees he's a danger to you. Given all that we know, why would you put yourself in harm's way?'

'Because I don't think that's what I'll be doing. My gut is telling me – something is there, in front of us, that we aren't seeing. I want to confront him.'

'The coastal path runs alongside his property. If you insist on going, Richard and I are going to be there, on the path. And don't you argue with me about that. We'll be frozen, but ready.'

'For what?' she smiled. 'He won't hurt me. But thank you.'

'How can you say that?' Bette demanded.

'I'll make sure I talk to him in the kitchen, in front of the windows that look out onto the path. If I think, at any point I'm in trouble, I'll signal to you to come to my rescue.'

'We can't stop you,' Richard said, quietly. 'But we will be there. If I get frostbite, you will be in even bigger trouble than any Joe Knight might cause you.' He winked at her and leaned in to kiss her cheek. 'You trust your gut, I trust you,' he whispered. Then he spoke to the group. 'I have a gut feeling too. Mine is telling me there is someone at the heart of this mystery, who has always been there. Not pulling the strings exactly, but with the ability to, shall we say, move events if they feel it becomes necessary. Before any of you ask, I don't know who it is, but you are moving towards finding out, and that could be very dangerous indeed.'

'You don't know who it is, or you won't say who you think it is?' Dan said.

Richard smiled, but didn't answer.

Five minutes later, they were all gone. As soon as the last one had left, Belle called Maggie Gilbert.

'Maggie, when we, or rather you, identified the girl known as Star Bright as Louisa Anastasia Light, you said you were sending for a copy of the birth certificate. Has it arrived yet?'

'Not yet, Belle. I ordered it on the priority service, but with the holidays, it will take an extra few days. It should be here in the morning.'

'Can you call me as soon as you have it?'

'Naturally. How's it going? Are you as snowed in as we are?'

'Yes, and now everyone hates it.'

'Same here. And we're expecting more overnight. Thank goodness we can work from home. Anyway I'll call you in the morning. Post usually arrives around nine.'

After the call ended, Belle made another.

'Billy, hi, it's Belle. Did you find Emily?'

'No. She's gone. We've alerted all ports, railway and bus stations, and the airports. Nothing yet.'

'I suspect you're too late. She's out of the country already. Tell me, is Jade still with you?'

'Yes. Why?'

'I want to talk to her again.'

'She won't go out. She's still terrified of Martin Riley and Lewis. So am I, to be honest. My wife is pretty fed up, too.'

'Can I come to your house? Please, Billy. It's important. More than important.'

'If you must, but you can't tell anyone, and I mean anyone, not any of your friends, that you're coming.'

'I promise,' she said. 'I'll make sure no-one follows me. Give me your address.'

Although she hadn't said anything, she knew that the information she would get from both Maggie and Jade would finally explain who had killed Star Bright, and why. She was almost a hundred percent sure she knew, now, especially after the hint from Richard. But what could she – would she – do with the information when she had it?

Chapter 37

Belle's phone rang at ten minutes past nine. It was Maggie Gilbert.

'I have it. Tell me what you want to know.'

'I know there's no father. The mother is Augusta Light. She was a single woman. She has an address and a profession. Plus a date of birth. I want to know who registered the birth.

'It was a family member, but not a Light. The person is a grandmother.'

'Give me the name, please Maggie.'

Maggie read it out.

'Yes! That's what I wanted to know.'

'It sounds important. Do you want to see this? I can scan and email it to you.'

'That would be fantastic. I'm going to need it. Thanks, Maggie.'

'No problem. Anything else I can do to help?'

'Yes please. Would you be able to work out a family tree for the grandmother?'

'No problem. It will probably take a couple of hours.'

'Excellent. If you could get something to me before lunchtime, I will be forever in your debt. How's family and work? All good with you?'

'I have enough to work on to last out the year. In fact sometimes I wish we weren't so busy. But, who knows what's coming? We're all comfortable and well and that's good enough for me.'

'Me too.'

Ten minutes later the email arrived with the attached birth certificate. Belle drained the remains of her coffee and headed out to Billy Anderson's house, via the local supermarket. This time, she left her car in the supermarket carpark, went in with a large shopping bag, spent fifteen minutes in the café, then went into the bathroom, changed her coat and shoes and pulled on a woolly hat, into which she tucked all of her easily recognisable hair. Then she put on a pair of glasses. When she came out with a different shopping bag, she got into a waiting taxi. No-one followed her. The black car that had discreetly parked at the back of the carpark hadn't moved as the taxi made its way to Billy's house.

Billy and his wife lived on a small development of houses five miles from St Foy. He welcomed her in and took her into the small living room. Its curtains were closed. Jade sat on the settee, on her hands, rocking back and forward.

'Who knows you're here?' She demanded, as Belle sat next to her.

'No-one. I left my car at the supermarket and came here by taxi. No-one followed. The taxi is waiting, as I don't expect to need more than ten minutes of your time. Billy will be sitting with us.'

Jade nodded.

My first question, describe Star to me, her physical details.

Jade looked puzzled, but said, 'She was about five feet six. Isn't that right, Billy?'

'More like five seven,' he said. 'She was an inch or so taller than Emily and they were both much taller than Miriam.'

'She had black hair, long, almost reaching her waist. Just like Emily, except Emily's was blonde. Her eyes were dark, brown I think. Billy?'

'Green and brown,' he said.

'You got closer than I did,' Jade smirked. Billy blushed and glanced up at the door to the kitchen.

'And she had a lovely figure. Like a model. Statuesque, like. Which Emily also had. But she was not as worldly as Emily. Much more naïve. She saw the good in people. Or she wanted to.'

'You told Dan and me, when we met in Port Simon, that she once, when Gabe had given her some drugs that made her less inhibited than usual, told you about her mother, how nasty and spiteful she was. She sang a rhyme to her. Can you sing it for me? Exactly as she did?'

'Are you crazy, or something?' Jade laughed. 'It was just a kid's rhyme, with personalised extras. You know, "twinkle, twinkle"'.

'I want to hear it all,' Belle said.

Jade shrugged. 'Ok, but this feels stupid. She called it "mummy's song" when she was off her head that night.' She sang the rhyme.

'Thanks. Did she say her mother physically hurt her?'

'No. But she did have a long scar on her left arm, on the inside. It looked old, but it must have been deep. I presumed she'd done it to herself.'

'One last question, did you see Miriam Riley at the party?'

'No, or at least, not at the party. She left before it started.'

'Thank you, Jade. That's all I needed.' She turned to Billy. 'I'll go now. I have to make my way back to the supermarket, then emerge as if I've just been shopping.'

'Good luck,' he said. He walked with her to the door and accompanied her to the taxi. 'I don't know what that was about. Was it helpful?'

'A part of a puzzle that's coming together,' she replied.

'Will it end soon?'

'A couple of days, I hope.'

'Thank God for that. It's a small house and Julie's fed up with Jade being here. She says if it goes on much longer she's going to go to stay with her mother.'

**

The trip back was straightforward. In the supermarket bathroom Belle changed her coat and shoes, took off her hat and glasses, bought a few quick items and re-emerged, driving her car away. She had been out of sight of the driver of the black car for just over forty minutes. It followed her back to St Foy. This time, she managed to photograph the number plate. She called it through to Billy, who said he would find out who the owner was as soon as he was back on duty, at six.

Back at the cottage, it was already eleven thirty. She was due at Joe Knight's house at midday. She changed into a smart casual outfit, slapped on some makeup and put on one of her more stylish coats. She wanted to look like she'd made an effort.

She arrived at twelve fifteen. Again, he was waiting on the doorstep.

'I wondered if you would come,' he said, as he ushered her in. 'I thought we'd sit in the lounge today.'

'Oh, no. I'd much prefer to be in your kitchen, with that wonderful view. I'm sorry for being late. I drove slowly. I'm always nervous when the weather's bad.'

'Up to you,' he said, taking her coat and opening a cupboard in the hall to hang it.

'I see your beautiful scarf, there. That's the one you were wearing on the night of the Ball. Can I see it again, close up?'

He gave her a baffled look but took the scarf out of the cupboard and gave it to her.

'My wife bought it for me, many years ago. She loved the colours. I wasn't sure, but she said they suited me.'

'They do,' she smiled. 'Where did she buy it, do you know? It's Dan's birthday coming up soon. I'd love to get him something similar.'

'It was from a gentlemen's outfitter in London, in an arcade in Knightsbridge. I can't remember the name now. Each one is individually made. Eve chose the colours. It's unique.'

'How interesting. If you remember, let me know,' she said, handing it back to him. 'Your Eve had good taste.'

'She did. Let's go through to the kitchen, then. Pity, I built up the wood burner.'

Belle smiled but said nothing. She sat in one of the armchairs close to the window, looking out across the garden and the coastal path to the sea. Joe stood at the counter.

'I haven't been able to pull much together for lunch,' he said. 'I hope you'll be all right with toasted sandwiches and fries. I've…'

'I'm not here for lunch, Joe,' she interrupted.

He put down the knife. 'I didn't think so. What are you here for?'

'The truth,' she replied. 'Just that, plain and simple.'

'There's no such thing,' he replied. 'Truth doesn't exist. Only opinions. History is defined by the winners.'

'That's a cliché,' she said.

'So is saying that you're here for the truth. Perhaps you can explain what you mean?'

'I've been information gathering, as you know. You know that, because it's why you keep inviting me to lunch or dinner or whatever, to find out how much I know, how much we've figured out. You and I aren't friends, Joe. I thought I liked you, at first. Now I know more, and I realise that I've been used, taken for a fool. Gloves off, now. To me, you're a murder suspect. To you, I'm a nuisance and a potential danger. Well, you can stop worrying on the murder front. I think you're a spineless coward who cheated on his wife with a sixteen year old, and is party to an attempt to implicate her brother in a murder. But do I think you actually carried out the murder? No, not anymore. I did, for a while, though.'

'Well, isn't this fascinating. You've come into the house of a man you suspect of murder, alone. Isn't that dangerous? Who knows what I could do with one of these knives?'

'If you so much as lift one of those above elbow level, Richard and Dan will come racing in here. They're out on the coastal path, watching. Could we perhaps invite them in? The minute they suspect anything off, they'll call the police. I wouldn't be surprised if Richard has them on speed dial already. It's freezing out there and they could do with hearing this. They still think you killed Star Bright. I think we should explain the whole story to them.'

He folded his arms and stared at her. She managed to keep her face emotionless, as she stared back. He began to walk slowly towards her and for a second she wondered if she was horribly wrong, but she sighed with relief as he walked past her, opened up one of the bi-fold doors and walked to the end of the garden. He was followed back in a minute later by Richard and Dan. They stopped as they reached the chair where Belle was sitting.

'He's a piece of walking human crap, but he didn't kill Star and legally, he probably hasn't done anything wrong. Morally, well, that's another issue. But, as we've just been discussing, that's an opinion, history being defined by the winners, as Sir Joseph has just told me.'

Joe Knight stood in front of Richard and Dan. 'I could just throw the three of you out of my house, or I could call the police, tell them you forced your way in.'

'Agreed,' Belle said. 'But don't you think they'd be just a little sceptical? I mean, Sir Richard Henry-Williams QC and Doctor Daniel Walker PhD forced their way into a house? I don't think so.'

He said nothing for a few moments, then stood back and nodded at them to sit.

'We're going to discuss history, dating back to 1969 – that's the year you were born, right, Joe?' Belle began.

He sat in the chair opposite Belle, crossed his legs and nodded.

'If I make a mistake with any of the dates and timelines, you will put me right, won't you?'

Again, he nodded. Richard and Dan had pulled up a couple of kitchen chairs, and stared uncertainly at Belle.

'The next date of significance is 1980. That's when Josie and Eve were born. They were twins. I discovered that this morning. Here's something important, Joe. They weren't identical twins, right?'

He nodded again. 'Nothing like each other. Josie is dark, Eve was fair.'

'What was their relationship like as they grew up?'

Joe Knight bit his bottom lip. 'They didn't get on. Mainly because Josie was obsessive and controlling. She wanted Eve to be exactly like her. She dominated, always. Eve didn't like that. She was her own person.'

'I thought so. Back to the dates. You and Eve married in 2005. She was twenty-five, you were older, thirty-six. You brought her from London to Cornwall, not just because you lived here, but to give her some distance from her sister. Josie was already married to Martin Riley. They married in 1998, when Josie was eighteen and Martin was thirty-eight. Another huge age difference. Miriam is not their biological child. She was adopted at the age of four. They arrived in Cornwall in 2014, when Martin was made Chief Constable.

'Martin Riley can't have children, according to his wife. No swimmers, or not enough to conceive a child. Augusta told Star that Martin was her father, to shut her up, because she kept asking and because she wanted to get back at Martin for something he had done. Whatever it was, doesn't matter. That's why Star was chasing him, trying to get a DNA sample from him. But there was an important fact that Augusta never told Star. She wasn't her natural mother. She was paid to take her in, by a client, whose business she looked after. Richard, you'll know

the name of this family. And I apologise for throwing all of this at you, but again, I only found out this morning. The family in question was, still is, called Abingdon.'

Joe Knight shot forward in his chair. 'You cannot be serious!'

'Oh, but I am. Richard, you know some of this. Augusta told you but wouldn't give the name of the family.'

'I'm not surprised,' he said. 'Their deeds are legendary. So much as a wrong look and they'll kill you.'

'One of their daughters had a child at the age of fifteen or sixteen. Augusta Light was paid to bring the child up as her own because they didn't trust the mother. Augusta didn't care about the child, but she did care about the money. They must have paid her well. Joe, I guess you've realised who I'm talking about?'

'Yes,' he said. He now sat very still, his face devoid of colour.

'Carrying on,' Belle said. 'The mother was allowed to see the child from time to time, but it had to be stopped when Star was three or so at the time. Now, going back to the timeline and Joe, here. He met Emily when she was sixteen. He was then forty. Personally, I find such a relationship repugnant. But, it's lasted eleven years and still going strong, so I suppose there must be some mutual attraction in it.'

She turned back to Joe. 'You coached her through school, and into University. You were her personal tutor. At some point Star found out. It was the necklace, I believe, that gave it away. Someone told her that you had originally bought it for Eve – we'll come to that – but when Eve was diagnosed with cancer, you took it away and gave it to Emily.'

'You don't know everything,' Joe Knight said. 'Our marriage was over. We were on the point of divorce when she was diagnosed. I couldn't leave her then. Emily understood.'

'But now Star had found out about you two and she was threatening to expose you. Like I said, Joe, you didn't do anything legally wrong, but it wouldn't have done your reputation any good if people found out you had been sleeping with a sixteen year old schoolgirl, would it? And whilst you had a wife with a terminal cancer diagnosis. It won't help your shiny new job in New York, either.'

'None of this explains why Star died,' Dan said. 'Why do you believe he didn't do it? He and Emily?'

'One of the reasons for the murder was to stop Star exposing them, but they didn't do it. The other was – psychosis. Their plan was for Emily to disappear. She was being threatened and blackmailed. She's been living in London, or New York, possibly, for the past three years. She's the co-author of Joe's best seller. They've been writing it together. After Eve died in the summer, they decided to leave it six months, then have Emily re-appear. They planned all along to blame it on Georgie. This is the part that makes me so sick and disgusted. Joe, would I be right in thinking that Emily conspired with Peter Day, to make sure he was here to cover the story?'

'Yes,' he replied in a tired voice. 'It was her idea. I thought it was too risky, but Emily thought she could control it. But there was someone else we didn't sufficiently consider and we should have taken account of the danger, or I should have. That's the person who killed Star, who put her body in the attic, and was determined that Emily should be blamed, and was blackmailing her because of her relationship with me. We thought we had got a step ahead, when Emily successfully disappeared. I went to the Heights on Christmas Eve, to retrieve a few of her things she needed in London. I parked at the end of the road. It was a shock when Georgie's van drove out, followed shortly after by another car. I honestly didn't know then what had actually happened. I walked up the drive, went to Emily's room, found what she wanted and left. She had gone up to London, you're right about that. Then on to New York. She only came back a few months ago.'

'To implicate Georgie, then leave again, which she has now done. Dan, you said she had an agenda and you were right on the nose. I presume she's in New York already, where you will be joining her?' Belle said.

He tipped his head.

'Do you have anything at all we can use against the person who murdered Star?'

'No, nothing at all. The threats had begun again. That's why she left so quickly yesterday.'

'Just as well I have something, then, isn't it?'

'What do you have?' Joe asked, his face gaining intensity.

'I have Star's birth certificate.' She opened the bag she had put at her feet, brought out the piece of paper and handed it over to him. He scanned it, mainly frowning. Then, suddenly, his expression turn from puzzled to amazement. 'Why would she,' he said, 'be the informant?'

'Exactly. I don't know if that woman is still alive. However, whether she is or not, this is what gave me the name of the family.' She turned to Richard. 'The person who was the informant on Star's birth certificate was her grandmother, Anastasia Abingdon.'

Joe Knight handed Richard the document. He scanned it, grimacing. 'If she was Star's grandmother, who was the mother? Was it your wife, Joe?'

'It wasn't my wife,' Joe Knight said, putting his head in his hands. 'Eve had problems from early youth. She had a hysterectomy when she was sixteen. I never wanted children,' Joe continued. 'It didn't bother me that she couldn't have them.'

'The only other Abingdon daughter was her sister, Josie Abingdon: Josie Riley. You saw it was her car leaving the Heights after Georgie, didn't you Joe?'

He nodded.

'She knew exactly who Star was. She killed her own daughter.' Belle said. 'Why? For her own reputation? To stop Star from exposing you and thereby exposing her sister as a deceived wife? Or just because she's a psychotic lunatic who cut a deep scar into her own daughter when she was little more than a baby, and hated her with a hatred that normal humans can't understand?'

'Is there proof, anything at all?' Dan said.

'Not enough for the law I suspect, but for us, yes. You remember what Jade told us about Star's mother, how she used to sing that horrible song to her. Jade told me she had called it "mummy's song"?'

'Yes. "Twinkle, twinkle little Star, what a horrible child you are". Very nasty. Star told Jade never to tell anyone what her mother was like, and never sing it, even as a joke.'

'I went to see Jade and Billy this morning. I asked Jade if there was more to the song. There was, and it was worse. But the "mother" in question wasn't Augusta. It was Josie Riley. She also threatened to kill the child, to "stick in a knife", which was a further part of the rhyme. I also asked Jade to confirm what Star looked like. She was quite tall, with long hair. The word Jade used was 'statuesque'. Billy agreed. Now, think back to our conversation with Josie Riley, the question she asked us.'

Dan was quiet for a moment, then his mouth fell open. 'She asked us if we thought Joe and Emily had killed little Star.'

'Exactly. Star wasn't little. She was tall and beautiful and Josie would have known that, from meeting her at the Heights. "Little Star" was Josie's rhyme. She gave herself away to us, without realising what she'd done.'

'It seems so base, so stupid,' Dan whispered. 'She killed her own daughter, to save reputations.'

'And the fact that she's psychotic. She was vitriolic in her hatred of her daughter, and I don't think that ever went away. Remember, she tortured her, mentally and physically, whenever she had the chance.'

'Murder usually is base and stupid,' Richard said. 'I've prosecuted enough of them. I've never come across a murderer with a motivation that made sense to a normal person. They think they're incredibly clever, that they'll be able to outsmart all around them.'

'Where is Emily now?' Dan asked Joe Knight.

'She's in New York. Belle is right, I'm joining her. I have a new job. I don't expect we'll be coming back. Josie actually threatened to kill her. She'll be enraged when she finds out Emily said it was Georgie and didn't confess herself, like Josie told her to do.'

'How much do you think Martin Riley knows?' Belle asked Joe Knight.

'He knows that Star was Josie's daughter. He knew that when he married her. Eve knew too. I think she may have told Emily's mother about me and Emily, when they were both at the hospice. Before she died, Eve wished me and Emily luck. I don't know if she meant it, or if she was being sarcastic, or if it was a warning about Josie.'

'Before you leave, you must tell your story to the police, or at least to Martin Riley. He can ensure that Georgie's charge of murder is dropped.'

'I'll think about it,' he said.

Belle jumped up out of her chair. 'No, you'll do it. Or I will. Or perhaps I'll speak to Peter Day. He's on the hunt for a good story, to make up for not being able to use my history for one of his stories.'

'OK, OK.'

'You disgust me,' she said, 'I'm leaving,' and walked out of the kitchen. Richard and Dan followed her.

'We'll need a lift back down to the village,' Dan said as they reached the front of the house. Joe Knight had not followed them, and Belle knew she would never see him again.

Richard was the first to speak. 'How about we go down to that nice little pub at the seafront, find a corner and decide what to do next?'

Chapter 38

The drive took just a few minutes. They were the only customers in the pub. The bar man tried to chat, but Dan ignored him, paid for their drinks and took them to a table under the window that looked out across the bay.

'My head is spinning,' he said as he sat down. 'Richard, you're good at summarizing. What, exactly, did we just hear?

'I'll have a go,' Richard said. 'Belle, interrupt me if I get something wrong. I'm pretty shaken too. The Abingdon twins, Josie and Eve were non-identical. Eve was fairly normal, as much as you can be in a family like the Abingdons. Josie was domineering, vicious and psychotic from an early age. She wanted to dominate her sister in all things, but Eve objected as much as she could. At the age of fifteen, Josie became pregnant. Henry and Rose Abingdon, a couple of people you never want to meet, arranged for the baby to be given to their then solicitor, Augusta Light, to bring up. They paid her well. She didn't do a good job and Louisa, or Star as we know her, grew up wild. Josie was allowed to visit the child for a while, but that stopped when the Abingdons discovered how Josie was abusing the child, mentally, and physically. She was married off to Martin Riley, who was in Henry Abingdon's pocket, and a rising, albeit corrupt, star in the Met.

'Eve met and married Joe Knight, also a rising star. He was a Professor at the newly appointed St Piran University. The marriage broke down after a couple of years. She had married him to get away from her sister and family, but chose the wrong man.

'Then, to what must have been Eve's horror, Martin was appointed Chief Constable and they moved to Cornwall, with Miriam, bringing Josie back into Eve's life. Louisa, who was now calling herself Star Bright, was in the wind.

'Then, it all changed when Star turned up at St Piran University to start her Master's degree. She and Emily became friends. Star kept her own secrets, but had been told by her mother that her father was Martin Riley, which we now know wasn't true. She also told Emily that her real name was Anastasia. From everything we've learned about Star, she was a beautiful girl in every sense, but naïve, and desperate for a decent, loving parent. She tried to latch on to Joe Knight but that didn't work. Belle, you said Josie went to visit Miriam at the Heights, I'm guessing that was when she saw Star and began to recognise the danger.'

'Yes, she did visit, and she would chat to Star.'

'To complete this story, the subject of those discussions will be an important piece of evidence. Here's my take on what happened. Josie befriended Star, and told her about Emily and Joe. She already knew from Eve that the relationship had been going on for years. Star told her about Emily's necklace. Star stole the necklace and showed it to Josie, then put it back. Josie would have been appalled, even more so, when Star told her she was going to publicly humiliate them to destroy his career and job. That would have been when Josie decided to kill her. She didn't want the publicity, which might lead back to the revelation that she was Star's real mother, and whatever else might come crawling out of the woodwork following that news.

'The rest, I think we know, except that it wasn't Joe and Emily who killed Star, although he knew Josie had done it. Josie had been planning to kill Star, for her own sick ends and needs, and convinced Emily that she could make sure the police thought it was her. That's when Emily and Joe made the plan for Emily to run. When Eve died earlier this year, they decided the time had come for Emily to re-appear.'

'Richard, is there enough to even begin an investigation into Josie Riley?'

'There might be something to get it started. But think about this, Belle. Who's going to start it? Martin? Susan Lewis? Martin will be gone at the end of the month, as will Josie, most likely. If they have their way – all of them – Georgie will go to prison for a crime he didn't commit, and they will all live happily ever after.'

'Then we have to do something now.'

'What did you have in mind?' Dan said. 'Challenging her to a duel?'

'The sarcasm is unnecessary. But actually, yes, challenging her. Face to face. How about we doorstep her?'

'You're mad.'

'I'm desperate and if that's the same thing, so be it,' she said. 'I'm going to drive to their house, face her and put it all out there. Hopefully, Martin will be there, too. If he thinks we have more than we do, he may not be willing to defend her. I'll say that Joe Knight has confessed that he saw Josie at the Heights on the night Star's body was moved.'

'Couple of problems there,' Richard said, in his quiet, calm voice, 'before you carry out this plan. One. You need direct confirmation from Miriam that her mother visited the Heights, never mind that others saw her there. Two. You said that Josie told you she was on a cruise with Martin to see the Northern Lights and therefore wasn't even in the country when Star was killed. Three. Emily has recanted, but she's in America. Will she be prepared to come back to admit what the real plan was? I think not. And four. On the night Georgie turned up and found Star, there were two people behind that door, not just Josie. If Martin Riley was the second one, you've even less chance of getting a confession.'

Belle's shoulders sagged. 'I got carried away. Sorry. Not like me. I just don't know what to do, how to help get Georgie out of jail.'

'Verify some facts,' Richard said. 'If you're planning to doorstep someone, make it Miriam Singh. She may slam the door in your face, but if you tell her you think her mother committed murder, there's an outside chance she might listen to you, even if it's only on the doorstep. Don't despair, either. With that birth certificate we can throw a lot of mud onto DCI Lewis's story.'

Belle nodded. 'I'll give it a go. Can I take you two back to St Foy now? If I'm to try facing Miriam, I want to get it done now, today.'

'Certainly,' Dan replied. 'Who do you want to come with you? You should have a witness.'

'Probably me,' Richard said. 'Josie knows who I am. With me beside you, there's a better chance she won't slam the door in your face.'

**

After leaving an anxious Dan at his apartment, Belle and Richard drove to Phil and Miriam Singh's house. It wasn't too far away, just at the top of the town, an old house, in its own grounds. As they drove in, Belle's stomach began to churn. She knew Miriam had never wanted to be involved.

Richard looked calm, as always, as they parked the car and approached the front door. Belle knocked three times with the old fashioned knocker on the tall, wide black front door. No-one answered.

'Maybe they aren't in. We should go,' she said, turning around.

'Patience,' Richard replied. 'And bravery. We've come this far. Don't run away now.'

A few seconds later they heard footsteps approaching. Miriam Singh opened the door and for a few seconds, scowled and stared at them.

'We'd like to talk to you, Miriam. It's important,' Belle said.

'I don't care. I've already said I don't want to speak to you.' She went to close the door, when Phil appeared behind her.

'Sir Richard. This is unexpected.'

'We're sorry to approach you in this way, but it really is important, as Mrs Harrington has said, to speak to Miriam. It's about her mother.'

Miriam took a step back, but bumped into Phil. He put his hands on her shoulders. 'Maybe we should listen to what they have to say, love?' he said.

Miriam shook her head and pushed Phil's hands away. Belle decided this was the time to apply shock tactics. 'Miriam, did you know that your mother was also Star Bright's mother?'

It took Miriam a couple of seconds to react. 'That's not possible. My mother couldn't have children. That's why I'm adopted.'

'She could, and did. If you will let us explain, I can tell you the whole story.'

For an agonising few seconds, Miriam weighed up her options.

'You'd better come in.'

They had decided that Richard should tell the story. His skill of precision and clarity was outstanding. Both Phil and Miriam listened without interrupting, until the story reached the point of Star's death, and the trip to the Northern Lights.

'She didn't go,' Miriam whispered. 'She pulled out at the last minute. I took her place.' She turned to Phil, who was frowning, and began to cry.

'How do you get on with your mother, in truth?' Richard asked.

It was Phil who answered. 'Miriam's mother is… unpredictable. She insists on their weekly meetings. Sometimes, she's in a good mood, sometimes not. When it's the latter, she can be threatening. There have been occasions when Miriam's been quite frightened of her mother.'

'She taunted Star when she was a baby, so much so that her family refused to let her see Star, or Louisa, which was her real name.'

'I've never met most of them,' Miriam snivelled. 'Because I'm adopted, I'm "not one of them". Not part of the family.'

'Count yourself fortunate in that,' Richard said. 'You've had a lucky escape.'

'I did once meet Anastasia Abingdon, the one you say registered Star's birth. Horrible old woman,' Miriam said.

'As I said, you're well out of that family,' Richard said. 'Thank you Miriam.'

'Miriam, I believe your mother visited you at the Heights, during that term you were there?'

Miriam nodded. 'Yes, she used to talk to Star. Did Star know that my mother was her mother too?'

'No, we don't believe Josie ever told her,' Belle said. 'She used her to get information.'

'But why did she kill her?' Phil asked. 'If she was her mother, that's shocking beyond belief.'

'She had hated Star from the day she was born. Your mother is psychotic, Miriam. She would have felt no compunction in killing her. She was more concerned about protecting her own name and her family's reputation, and maintaining Martin's position.'

'Her sister was my Aunt Evie, Joe Knight's wife. He was sleeping with Emily, I knew that.' Miriam said.

'You knew that? But you didn't tell the police at the time?'

'Mummy said it was best not. She said Emily had killed Star and that if it came out about Emily and him, she and her sister would suffer, as would my father. Not that I cared about him.'

'I'm going to confront her,' Belle said. 'I may exaggerate, but hopefully, say enough for her to confess to what she did. Can I rely on you not to forewarn her.'

'Definitely. And good luck with that,' Miriam said, returning to her usual acerbic self. 'Will you go, now, please.'

Belle and Richard stood.

'Thanks for letting us in,' Richard said. 'We weren't sure you'd be prepared to speak to us.'

'If it had just been her,' Miriam said, tipping her head at Belle, 'I'd probably have slammed the door in her face.'

Outside and back in the car, they paused for a moment. The snow had begun again, and the wind.

'She has more in common with her mother than she knows, adopted or not,' Belle said. 'I don't mean she's a nutcase, but, really, "her"? I was in the room.'

'Lucky you had me with you.' He paused. 'There was something wrong there. Let's get back to St Foy, before we can't drive down the road.'

They stopped at the apartment for half an hour, bringing Dan up to date and calling each of the others. After the initial shock, opinions were divided on whether Belle should confront Josie Riley.

'Richard, you said you thought there was something wrong? Was it something Miriam said?'

'Josie has exposed Miriam to the Abingdons. She said that she'd met Anastasia Abingdon. That's Henry's mother. I wonder if she knows them better than she's admitting.'

'Let's all sleep on it,' she said after the calls. 'I think I can drive home. I want to be back before that becomes impossible.'

'I was supposed to go back in the morning but it's looking like I'll be snowed in again. Belle, think with your head, not your heart.'

She kissed them both, then drove, gingerly, down the High Street and up the small incline to the lane at the back of her cottage, slipping a few times, but making it, with a sigh of relief as she garaged the car and went into her cottage.

She sat for a long time in the kitchen, staring out at the falling snow. Richard had sensed something wasn't right. So had she, but not about the Abingdons. There was a phone call to make, to Billy Anderson, to ask him to check something out in an official capacity. She told him it was important and could he let her have the answer as soon as possible.

He called back an hour later.

'I have the information you want, Belle. There was just the one person on the cruise. The company confirmed it.'

'Thanks, Billy.'

'Is it really important?'

'More than important. It's the final piece of the puzzle.'

She sat for a long time. Eventually, she made up her mind. Provided she could get out of St Foy in the morning, she was going to the Riley house. The pieces had all fallen into place. What would be, would be.

Chapter 39

Belle hadn't eaten or slept for almost twenty-four hours when she set off the following morning. However, she had given into the urge to tell someone her plan.

Posy was furious with her.

'Don't you dare go alone. Anyway, the bridge is shut, so you'll have to go the long way round, if you can even get out of St Foy.'

'The Hill is clear,' Belle said. 'I don't want to put anyone else in danger.'

Exactly. Danger. We don't want either Martin or Josie Riley cutting you up into small bits and throwing you into the outgoing tide. Wait. I'll be there in ten minutes.'

She could have set off, but Richard's instruction the previous day to think with her head, not her heart, had struck home. Posy was right. She waited. Posy turned up twenty minutes later, accompanied by Rose.

'I would have brought others, if I could. I didn't want to involve Bette and she'd have been too angry anyway, and Mavis absolutely can't know what we're about to do.'

'They won't hurt me,' Rose said. 'I'm too well known in the town. And three of us versus two of them. We can take them.'

'Take them? You've been watching too much TV crime. Rose, does Harry know you're coming with me?'

'Of course he does, and I'm going to tell them. He insisted on that. They may want to try to pour scorn on three middle aged women, but the local vicar? I don't think so.'

Belle had to laugh, despite her heart hammering and her blood pressure probably rising. 'Come on then, let's get it done.'

**

'I saw a curtain twitching,' Posy said as they reached the front door. It had taken over an hour to reach the other side of the estuary.

Martin Riley opened the door. Belle took a step back as he stood in the doorway He was a daunting character close up, over six feet tall, balding, with steely blue eyes, a small mouth and prominent chin, which was dark and unshaven. Casually dressed in jeans, cable knit sweater covering the protruding gut, and loafers, he stood as if about to repel attackers.

'What do you lot want?'

Belle stepped forward. 'We'd like to speak to Josie,' she said, as confidently as she could manage, staring unblinking at him.

'Why?'

'It doesn't concern you, Chief Constable.'

'It probably does.'

'Well then, perhaps we can speak to you both together. It's about the murder of Star Bright, who thought she was your daughter but wasn't. Shall I go on?'

He hesitated a moment, then stood back and held the door open. He led them into a sitting room.

'I'll let Josie know you're here,' he said, smiling, as they sat down on the luxurious deep settees.

When he had left the room, Rose said, 'I don't like that he's smiling. Belle, you're in charge. Do you know where you're going to start?'

'Yes, I do. But it won't be where you expect. Just don't react to anything, OK?'

They both nodded.

It was almost ten minutes before Martin Riley returned. 'Josie will be with us in five minutes,' he said. 'Can I offer you coffee, or tea?'

They all shook their heads and he sat down.

'I hear you were on a cruise to see the Northern Lights when Star Bright was killed. Did you enjoy the holiday?' Belle asked.

'Very much, thank you.'

'Pity you had to go alone.'

He shrugged. 'I like my own company. What does this have to do with the death of Star Bright?'

Before Belle could respond, Josie entered the room. She too, was casually dressed in sweatpants and top. She went to sit next to her husband, but far enough away to be sure they didn't touch each other.

Before she could say anything, Belle went on, 'I was just asking the Chief Constable about the cruise he went on, to the Arctic Circle. I've always wanted to do that. Sounds amazing. I'd have liked a companion, though, unlike Martin here. He says he enjoyed his own company.'

Josie gave Martin a glare. No-one responded. 'Tell me, did you plan it between the three of you, before you went?'

'What are you talking about?' Josie demanded. 'Plan what?'

'You told Posy, Dan and me that you were away on a cruise Josie, but you didn't go. Yesterday Miriam told us she took your place at the last minute, but that wasn't true either. Jade Waters told me that Miriam was at the Heights – she caught a glimpse of her before the party started – on the Saturday night. I checked. That cruise left from Liverpool on the Thursday before. So, did you plan it between the three of you?'

Martin Riley began to shuffle, but Josie didn't move, as Belle spoke again.

'We know that Star thought Martin was her father, because that was what Augusta Light told her. But it wasn't true. However, what she didn't know was that you, Josie, are her mother. Nor did she know that Miriam was her sister, sort of. I wonder how that actually works? Never mind. Miriam knew, although she claimed yesterday that it came as a complete surprise. Miriam hated Star, didn't she, Josie? Almost as much as you did.'

Josie continued to sit motionless. Martin's face had lost all of its colour.

'Shall I go on? I will. You've all been lying for years. Martin, you deliberately sabotaged the investigation into Star's murder. No-one, not even her mother, and the woman who was made responsible for her upbringing, claimed her. She was buried as Star Bright. How utterly despicable. But, not as despicable as her own mother and sister killing her.'

'You can't prove a thing?' Martin Riley snarled. 'Josie and Miriam were at a spa resort. We have receipts.'

'Somewhere not too far away, though. Somewhere from which they could easily have popped back, done the deed and returned as if they'd just been out to lunch. Which I expect they did, eh Josie?'

'As Martin has just said, you can't prove a thing,' Josie said in a lazy voice.

'When did you actually kill Star, Josie?'

'Keep your mouth shut,' Martin hissed at Josie, but her eyes had taken on a glazed look. Then she snapped back to life and turned to Belle, with a look of such venom that Belle could barely breathe.

'You're right, I hated that thing. I was working my way up to killing it once before, but my family stopped me.

'I used to chat to her, in that rat's nest of a building. Miriam always made sure it was there when I visited.'

'That's why Miriam signed up to live at the Heights, to keep tabs on Star, for you,' Belle said.

Josie nodded. 'My luck finally came on the Monday, after the others had gone. I went with Miriam, around lunchtime. It was still there; it had no-where else to go. I told it Miriam needed to collect more of her things for our spa trip. Miriam went up to the bedroom and little Star – twinkle, twinkle – and I had a cup of tea together. I put something in to make it sleepy. It felt unwell after five minutes or so, then Miriam and I helped it upstairs, put it on its bed and I put a pillow over its face. We carried it up to the attic and wrapped it in a carpet. We planned to leave it there for a couple of days, just in case anyone came back unexpectedly, then go back on Christmas Eve, to move it and bury it somewhere no-one would find it, but, you know the rest.'

'Georgie Morris foiled that plan,' Rose said. Belle could see that Rose was holding back tears, and Posy had moved to sit on the edge of her seat, gripping the edges.

'Indeed. What a useless fuck that man is. Still, it's turned out well enough.'

'Carrying on,' Belle said, trying to hide her shaking hands. 'You thought you could pin it on Emily Duggan. She'd been having an affair with Joe Knight for years, right under your sister's nose. Star was going to expose it, Star trusted you with that secret, Josie. Was that when you decided to kill her as soon as possible? It would never have gone anywhere. She'd already been reprimanded by the University for stalking Joe. But I don't suppose that really mattered to you. I expect you were salivating at the thought of being able to kill Star, at last.'

Josie jumped up, her face contorted with fury, but Martin pulled her back down.

'I will say again, you have no proof,' he said.

'Not directly, no. But what I do have is Star's birth certificate. The interesting item is the informant: Anastasia Abingdon, grandmother. Now, that's interesting, isn't it. It's not proof, but it's the starting point of a very interesting story, one that will eventually lead to murder, as the pins fall and people start to talk, to tell the truth.'

Martin Riley glared at her. 'What do you want?'

'Georgie Morris cleared, for a start. Was Emily in on all of this with you? And Joe Knight?' Posy asked.

'No,' Martin said. He looked defeated now his bluster deflated. 'But it was awkward when she came back. Susan let me know straight away she had Emily in custody. I managed to persuade her, when we took her in for an interview that first day, that she was still the main suspect. She already had a plan, with Knight. She knew who to persuade to make the anonymous call.'

'Peter Day,' Rose intervened.

'He wouldn't have been my first choice, but it worked well enough for us to arrest the idiot. His moving the body was a bonus. He never realised Josie and Miriam were there when he did it.'

'We know,' Belle said. 'At least we didn't know it was Josie and Miriam. We thought it was Joe and Emily. Joe turned up to collect something for Emily, but he was at the end of the drive. He saw Georgie, then Josie, drive out. Thank you for confirming it was Josie and Miriam.'

He glared at her.

'So, can Georgie be freed?'

'If that's all you want.'

'Like you say, we can't prove anything else. Emily is gone, she's in America by now. She's retracted her statement, so it shouldn't be too difficult for you. Georgie's reputation will suffer, so he'll need an apology, publicly, from you. That should help. Joe Knight is also going to America, later today. Good riddance to both of them. Neither will be missed.'

'I thought you and he had something going?' Josie smirked.

'You thought wrong,' Belle replied. 'I was flattered by the attention, but I had a bad feeling in my gut about him. And my gut rarely misleads me. It didn't mislead me about you, Josie. You rang huge alarm bells.'

'None of this has been recorded,' Josie said, in case you were thinking you could use a secret tape of this discussion.'

'Not possible, in this room,' Martin Riley added. 'You'll find your phones are dead, too. Ordinary phones don't work in here. Perk of the Chief Constable.'

'If that's the case, then perhaps you can confirm, Josie, that you were the person who blackmailed and killed Gabriel Holmes.'

'I thought he died of an overdose?' Rose intervened.

'No,' Belle said. 'He was suffocated but it was covered up, made to look like an overdose. I'm guessing you pulled some favours there, Chief Constable.'

'He was a cocky little sod,' Josie said. 'He had to go. It wasn't difficult.'

'He had a family,' Belle spat at her. 'Parents, friends.'

'And you gave Kylie Nichols the money?'

'Yes,' Josie replied, in a bored voice. 'Silly little cow.'

'Then had her beaten? She's lost the sight of one eye.'

Josie shrugged. Martin put his head in his hands.

'You really don't care, do you? Richard said there was some monster at the centre of this maelstrom, pulling strings. It was always you, following us around, almost killing Mavis Penhaligon.'

'Actually, that wasn't me. Try Emily Duggan on that one,' Josie replied, flicking a strand of hair out of her eyes.

'But you did arrange the break-in at my cottage. You can keep the computer, by the way. You already know it's a dummy.'

'You're a psychopath,' Posy snarled.

'Tut, tut. Labels, you people just love them,' Josie replied with a condescending smile.

Belle shook her head and turned to Posy and Rose. 'I'm ready to go. I don't want to be in their company one second longer than I have to. There are no words to describe what a malignant serpent you are, Josie.' She turned to Martin Riley as the three women stood. 'Jade Waters will come out of hiding, without any consequences or retaliation. You will pay even more recompense to Kylie Nichols, Josie. And you, Martin, will guarantee that every member of our Curiosity Club will be left alone. No police harassment. Ever. Keep in mind that Sir Richard Henry-Williams also knows this entire story. He helped us work it out. And you'll need to keep that "thing",' she nodded at Josie, 'under control.'

He nodded. 'All done, then?'

'We'll see ourselves out. I expect to hear by the end of the day that Georgie Morris is to be freed.'

They walked in silence to the door and got back into Belle's car. She started it, then drove away, out of the short driveway and onto the main road. They were half way around the long, circuitous route back to St Foy, before she suddenly stopped, got out of the car, bent over a ditch on the side of the road, and took three long breaths, before retching for five minutes.

Posy turned off the engine and she and Rose went to stand beside her. Rose patted her back.

'You were brilliant,' she said. 'How you kept your cool with those monsters, I'll never know.'

Belle stood up. Posy handed her a handkerchief. 'Keep it,' she said. 'Where are we going now?'

'To the farm,' Belle replied. 'Rose, would you mind driving?'

**

As they reached the pathway up to the farm and began the upward incline, an ambulance was coming down. Rose pulled over to get out of its way.

'What's happened now?' Posy said, anxiously.

'It wasn't an emergency ambulance,' Belle replied. 'It was transport. I wonder…'

As they reached the door, Bette was waiting for them. 'Come in, come in and warm up. Big surprise!'

Sitting at the kitchen table surrounded by cushions and knees covered with a blanket, was Mavis. She looked exhausted and a shadow of her former self, but on seeing them a huge smile lit up her face.

'Mave!' Posy shouted, running up and hugging her. 'You're back!'

'Well obviously,' Mavis replied. 'I'm going to be here with Bette and Bert for about a week, before I can go back to my house.'

'And very welcome she is, too.'

'We have news, too,' Rose said. 'You know we've been to see Martin Riley and his vile wife…'

'How did they know?' Belle asked.

'I told them, of course,' Rose replied. 'Georgie is going to be released. The announcement should be later today.'

Bette burst into tears. 'I haven't cried this much for years,' she said, as Bert handed her a tissue.

'Someone else arriving,' Bert said, as another car pulled up outside.

Dan burst in, followed by Richard.

Dan gave Belle a crushing hug. 'You're OK, in one piece,' he said. 'What happened?'

'Why don't we all sit down,' Bert said. 'I'll make us all a cup of hot chocolate and I've just finished a chocolate cake. It was going to go to Posy, for her opening, but this seems like an occasion for a good slice of something satisfying. You can tell us all about it. Belle, judging by the colour of your face, you look like you need it.'

She told the story, fielding the questions that constantly interrupted.

'So they're going to get away with murder?' Bert said.

'Probably,' Belle replied. 'Martin Riley has made sure of that. Every possibility covered. I can't find a weak spot in any of his machinations. The only thing we have is the birth certificate, and it's a long road from there to murder.'

'You're right,' Richard said. 'I'm sorry to have to confirm it, but from a legal point of view, there's nothing on which to base the possibility of a conviction, particularly not for a Chief Constable.'

'At least he won't be, for much longer,' Rose said.

'I think he and Josie will go away. They really are a match made in hell, even though someone else made the match,' Belle said. 'I suspect Phil Singh and Miriam will also be leaving in a hurry. She must know by now that we've found out she lied. And that she helped her mother kill Star.'

'So, we can get back to normal,' Bette said.

'Not for Star Bright. She was killed by her own mother, who hated and manipulated her. This is no justice for her,' Belle said.

'Sadly not,' Richard said. 'Who knows, one day, one of them will slip up. But not today.'

Rose began to cry. 'When she described how they did it, she kept referring to Star as "it". Like she wasn't a person. I don't think I'll ever hear anything that evil again, no matter how long I live.'

'There are no words to describe what Josie Riley is,' Belle said, 'so let's not try.'

'I remembered, by the way,' Mavis said in the ensuing silence. 'What I saw in that café. It was Emily and the man was Sir Joseph Knight. He was kissing her and it was a passionate smacker.'

'Did you go to see her, to speak to her?' Belle asked.

'I can't remember,' Mavis said. 'I've tried, but it just gives me a headache.'

'Then stop trying,' Posy said. 'One day it may come back to you, but for now, let it be, Mave. More important you get well. Eat lots of Bert's cake; you need fattening up. You've turned into a wraith. I think it was Emily who hit you. You were going up towards her mother's house, where she was staying. You were probably going to ask her about Sir Joseph Knight.'

'You think she would go that far?' Mavis said.

'I do,' Posy replied. 'She may not have murdered Star Bright, but she had good reason to stop you talking about her relationship with Joe Knight. What do you think, Belle?'

'I suspect you're right, Posy. But Mave, if you don't remember, don't push it. Posy's right. It will come back to you. Now, if you'll all excuse me, I'm going home,' Belle said. 'I didn't sleep last night. Sorry about the cake, Bert. After what we did this morning, I was fuelled by adrenalin, but that's gone now. I have to sleep.'

'I'll drive you,' Dan said. 'Richard, wait for me at the apartment. Don't go without seeing me first. I won't be long.'

On the drive home, he said, 'I have just one more question, Belle. How did you know Miriam was part of the conspiracy, plot, whatever you want to call it? Yesterday, she told you she was with her father on the cruise ship.'

She yawned. 'Billy. I called him last night. Asked him in his official police capacity to check the passenger manifest. The only Riley was Martin and there was no Miriam Singh. Has there been any sign of Peter Day lately?'

'No. Nor his crew. Now that Emily's gone, he has no more insider information. But, he's probably still around somewhere, lurking.'

'He can find someone else to lurk near. If I see him, I'm likely to attack him. Now, sing to me or something, before I fall asleep in this car and you have to carry me up to my bed.'

'Not a pleasant prospect, nor is my voice, but I'll give it my best shot.'

'I'll have to find a way to make it up to Billy. He's been a real star throughout this.'

'From what you said, getting Jade out of his house should do it. It'll save his marriage at least.'

She laughed. 'And what about you, and Richard? How can I thank you?'

'No need,' he said. 'I am an honorary member of the Curiosity Club of St Foy. That's good enough for me. And my marriage can survive anything you lot come up with.'

'Excellent. Now, sing!'

**

Back at the vicarage, Harry had been waiting anxiously for Rose to return. When she pulled up in Belle's car he rushed out to her. For a few moments she sat, not attempting to get out of the car, gripping the steering wheel. Harry opened the door and gently prised her hands away. Without a word she stepped out and fell, trembling into his arms.

He took her into their small sitting room and sat her down.

'Tell me, ' he said. 'Don't leave anything out.'

She gave him as close as she could to a word-by-word account of what had happened with Martin and Josie Riley, as he stroked her hand.

When she had finished, he stood and paced around the room. Rose watched him, barely breathing. He turned to her.

'So you all think they're going to get away with it?'

'Yes, Harry. That's Richard's opinion, too.'

'Well, it's not mine.'

Rose jumped up. 'Harry, can you please leave it to fate?'

'Those monsters sat in my church, week in, week out, smiling and courteous. Sorry, Rose I can't leave it.'

He marched out of the room and she ran after him. He had reached his car.

'Harry, what are you going to do?' she shouted.

'Something very un-vicarish.'

Chapter 40

No-one could explain how it had happened. There was no brake failure, although the car hadn't slowed down. They should never have been on the road that day, nor trying to cross the bridge over to St Foy. The snow hadn't been cleared. The 'Road Closed' sign had been in place. The car had swerved, observed by horrified onlookers. The driver was unable to control the spin, and, given the speed, the car had crashed through the safety barrier and into the water.

People on the embankment had called the police immediately, but by the time they arrived, the car had disappeared and the driver and passenger with it.

The car was recovered later that day, the body of the passenger, the following day. That of the driver, however, wasn't found for several weeks.

The funeral was full of pomp and ceremony, as deemed fitting for that of a Chief Constable, despite the fact he was retiring soon due to ill health. Full honours. None of the Curiosity Club attended.

There were a few minutes devoted to Martin Riley on the local news that evening, including a somewhat muted tribute from his daughter.

When Josie Riley's body eventually surfaced, the funeral was private and small. Friends and family only. A very small group. The body had been identified by Miriam, but only because of the remaining clothes and a gold and sapphire ring, still attached to one of the remaining fingers.

There were rumours of course, of sabotage, but these were discounted when the constabulary confirmed there was nothing wrong with the car. It had been in good working order, although why Josie Riley had chosen to risk driving over the bridge that day remained an unsolved mystery. One particular rumour circulated that she was trying to get to her daughter's house and thought she was a good enough driver to risk the bridge. An examination of the Chief Constable's mobile phone had shown a long conversation earlier that morning, between him and his son-in-law, Phil Singh. One onlooker thought the couple had been arguing, furiously.

Belle Harrington thought they were probably right. The "accident" had happened the morning after their visit. That same evening, Martin had made a statement, exonerating George Morris. Peter Day had been at the forefront of the press pack. Then, he had disappeared from St Foy.

Georgie was released a few days later, to the joy of Mandy, Will, Bette and Bert. His reunion with his family was private, the Club members electing to not be present, although Bette did invite them.

'They have a lot of healing to do. Georgie will be traumatised for a long time to come,' Belle said to Posy, Rose and Mavis. They held their celebration of his release in the café, after Posy had opened for business again.

Rose had told the group what Harry had done.

'He's assured me he only went to see them; he told them he knew what they'd done and he'd see to it that they were held to account. They laughed at him, and he left. He made a statement to the Chief Inspector but nothing's happened.'

'They're hushing it up,' Mavis said. 'No point in taking it further when both Rileys are dead.'

'I heard Miriam has left Phil Singh,' Mavis said. 'Margaret told me when she came to visit.'

'I said that marriage wouldn't last,' Posy said. 'It was based on lies. Phil's a nice guy. I wonder if he knows Miriam was involved in Star's murder?'

'I think he must have done,' Belle replied. 'He knew Miriam wasn't on that cruise. He's chosen not to talk, although I suspect it was he who left her. He's now left with a terrible burden of knowledge that he'll carry with him for the rest of his life.'

'If he can bear it,' Rose said. 'If the burden becomes too heavy, one day he may decide to confess what he knows.'

'I wonder if Miriam realises that?' Belle replied. 'Maybe she thinks he's too nice a guy to confess. Time will tell. I still have a concern about her confirmation of the body being her mother.' She also had a concern about whatever Harry might have said, or done, but she wasn't going to say anything, particularly not to Rose.

'Do you really believe they could have risked it?' Posy asked.

Belle sighed. 'It was a terrible risk. But the witness who said the couple were arguing was able to provide some detail of what the argument was about, and that could only have happened if the window was down. Why would Josie have the window open on such a freezing cold day?'

Posy shook her head. 'Sorry, Belle, I have to disagree with you on that one.'

'It makes me furious still that no-one will be punished for Star's death,' Rose said. 'I've suggested Harry hold a memorial service for her, so she isn't forgotten. Maybe in the Spring, when Dan's back again. He says that's the least he can do for the poor girl. He feels quite helpless.'

'That's a nice idea,' Belle said, taking Rose's hand. 'We'll all attend. I heard from Dan yesterday. He's taking off again soon, to Brazil this time. Richard's going out with him for the first week. Dan'll be there about four months. He promises to come to St Foy as soon as he's back.'

'Let's hope things quieten down around here, for some considerable time,' Posy said. 'In the meantime, I need to find the owner of that dratted dog that keeps turning up at my front door every morning.'

Why is it coming to you, Posy? You don't like dogs. You won't have them in the café.'

'I allow guide dogs and therapy dogs. But this is just a scruffy mutt. I have no idea why me. It's been on my doorstep every day for the last five days.'

'I expect you'll find out,' Belle said. 'Let us know if you need help.'

'Finding the owner of a stray dog doesn't sound like anything interesting,' Rose said.

Belle grinned at her. 'You never know, Rose. You just never know.'

**

The End

The Curiosity Club of St Foy will return in 2024 with
'The 9am Dog'

Thanks and Acknowledgements

My grateful thanks and acknowledgements go to my first readers, Rose and Cheryl, who have again given me encouragement, feedback and advice on how to get out of plotholes!

I must also thank Dr Emma Alofs for her advice on psychology and Dr Pauline Cutting, for checking medical matters.

My development Editor, Jo, worked with my manuscript to make excellent suggestions on how to improve my writing. And once again, Ellen Morrow has done a superb job of proof reading.

My family, as always, give me support and encouragement, technical advice and plenty of tea.

The cover, as for all of my books is designed by Alison Morgan at AliCat Design of Monmouth.

Thank you for reading this book!

If you have enjoyed it, it would be great if you could leave your feedback on Amazon and/or Goodreads. If you have any questions about anything featured within it, please contact me via my website:

www.mkjonesauthor.com

As well as the website, there's also a Facebook page (currently Maze Investigations) and an Instagram page @mkjonesauthor.

I also write a newsletter, about my research and writing. You can sign up on the website and as a thanks for signing up, you'll receive two Maze Investigations case file stories:

"The Missing Air Raid Warden 1941"

And

"Murder in the Family 1840"

Following these there will be a new story with each newsletter.

Happy reading!

Have You Tried My Genealogy Series?

Maze Investigations now has seven books in the series, all available on Amazon. They begin with:

Printed in Great Britain
by Amazon